THE LITTLE GOBLIN GIRL

by Illy Hymen

Book One of the Goblin Girl Series

This book is a work of fiction. Any references to historical events, real people, or real places are used fictitiously.

First Digital Edition January 2019

All sex acts depicted in this book are explicitly consensual. If you are in a sexual situation and are unsure if consent has been given, stop immediately and ask your partner(s) for consent.

A PRIMER ON GOBLINS

by Maro Stanwick

Aside from a few wealthy entrepreneurs, the majority of the current goblin population migrated to the city-state of Trinity during The Green Passage, referred to as the "GP" in the goblin community, and often called The Goblin Passage interchangeably. The GP was caused by the awakening of the long buried demon Ka Tuk (K'-tk'). His awakening sent waves of hellsfire rolling across the goblin homeland of Greenlan which killed tens of thousands and displaced tenfold more. Trinity, with its massive build up of military force, intervened to prevent countless more lives from being lost but has since been unable to defeat the demon Ka Tuk. Trinity's efforts in the region have been mixed, but the latest reports suggest the demon's influence has been contained for the time being.

A massive portion of the goblin population in Trinity, numbering anywhere from 8,000-12,000, has settled in the rolling ghettos known as The Steps: named after the tendency of goblins to stack their domiciles one on top of the other in escalating towers. The Steps are a maze of densely packed neighborhoods resembling an insect burrow and have little or no access to Trinity's services or utilities. Disease, crime, gaming, prostitution, and breeding are all left completely unchecked in The Steps as the Trinity government fails to manage the area.

Reactions to the massive influx of goblins have been mixed at best. Merchants and entrepreneurs have seen unprecedented levels of wealth and expansion due to the goblin community's taste for gaming supplies, candy, scrap metal, gambling, and jewelry. Unfortunately, common laborers and rousters have seen their wages and work opportunities evaporate with the influx of cheap goblin labor. A common anecdote is you can trade a hume worker for three goblins and still have copper leftover for an ale. The labor situation has seen a marked rise in anti-goblin sentiment as well as an increase in hate crimes against the goblin population.

Many rumors and conspiracies have surfaced since the arrival of the goblin population. One of the most insidious rumors is of a sterilization campaign by the Trinity government against female goblins in order to combat their alarmingly high fertility rate. While there is no evidence a female goblin has ever been sterilized by the Trinity government, this conspiracy still persists. Another rumor purports female goblins are constantly “in heat”, they have extremely high sex drives, or they are extremely fertile, and their desire to breed can override their higher faculties. While it is true female goblins have nearly four times the fertility rate of humes, there is no reliable information they are prone to bouts of “heat”.

Another common anecdote (one I can attest is completely true through my firsthand observations of goblin culture) is the pervasiveness and detriment of gaming and gambling in the goblin community. I should preface this report by saying adult goblins (males only, strangely enough) do not have any interest in childhood games such as tag, hide and seek, or slay the dragon, but are obsessed with games suitable for adults such as settlers, cercesern (ker-keh-sern), bones, leave! and virtually any game involving the use of dice. You would struggle to find a goblin who is not willing to stop whatever it is he is doing and play any conceivable game of strategy or chance. Their vast knowledge of rules and tactics is awe inspiring. While this eagerness to play games may seem endearing at first glance, it is a scourge on their community. Goblins do not consume alcohol, and they do not participate in opioid use or the abuse of potions or poultices. In my studies, I have been unable to find a single case of goblins ever consuming alcohol. Instead of finding vice in consumables, goblins will often spend a majority of their lives playing games with other goblins. Neglecting their responsibilities, families, and even their own health, goblins may game days at a time before stopping to continue their daily lives. One such session I recorded lasted almost six days! The worst cases of goblin gaming involve placing stakes on the outcomes, leading to violence and financial hardships.

The goblin diet consists exclusively of candy. Goblin candy is much sweeter than candy manufactured by humes and comes in an endless variety of colors and flavors, often infused with fruits or bitters. Even through their excessive consumption of sweets, their teeth are not prone to damage, nor are they prone to excessive weight gain.

Female goblins are a peculiar bunch as they are simultaneously the heads of their households as well as the lowest members of their households. It is considered improper in the goblin community for a female goblin to play any games or perform any kind of work outside the home. Goblins also hold mixed opinions on the consumption of candy by females, but generally agree chocolate is women's candy and "real" candy is reserved for the men. I can confirm goblin women breed frequently, often having eight or more children in their lifetimes.

The incubation period for goblins is only ninety days, so it is fully possible the original Steps population was only around 5,000 when the goblins first arrived fifteen years before this report was published.

Goblins as young as eight years of age often have several piercings in their ears and at least one facial piercing. The reasons for their metal based jewelry vary from family traditions, self expression, affordable art, and commerce. The metal jewelry market in Trinity has exploded since the Green Passage and was also a massive enterprise in Greenlan before the GP. The demand for metal jewelry also explains the abundance and demand for scrap metal which is often fashioned into jewelry or game pieces. I emphasize metal jewelry because most goblins are unable to afford the gems which are commonly fastened in high-end hume jewelry.

Whether the influx of goblins is a positive or negative event remains to be seen, but we can all agree it marks a new era in our history.

CHAPTER 1

Maja stared out over the rolling ghetto from the edge of her home situated high up in The Steps. The wall of her home had fallen off over a year ago and was quickly scrapped by locals before she could retrieve it. Losing the wall had left her and her mama exposed to the elements and the occasional birds but provided an incomparable view of the city. Locals buzzed through the narrow lanes of The Steps a hundred feet below. Almost every goblin in The Steps had immigrated during the Green Passage and settled in Trinity, but an increasing number were native born. As the sun slid behind the massive stone rotunda which protected the city, it gave their city a strange atmosphere as if it was some divine doll house for the Devs. Several hundred, metal shacks gave way to proper homes built in the hume-style with large frames, glass windows, and slanted roofs.

Maja's stomach fluttered and her tiny calves tensed. She desperately wanted to go out into the hume part of town that night to see what their culture was like firsthand. The desire to explore their strange world had existed in her for years, but this day in particular felt special. She wanted to try their food, especially their candy, and maybe even have sex with a hume! The idea made Maja blush and hug herself as she imagined a massive hume man taking her to bed, putting his giant hands on her tiny body, and making a little toy out of her. She covered her mouth with both hands and squealed into them. In the pocket of her ragged dress, she found her last sour chomper and tossed it in her mouth. The chomper broke with a satisfying crunch, and the sour, fruity flavor cascading over her taste buds made her face tense up.

"I, I just need to calm down. I'm getting way too excited." Maja took a deep breath and looked longingly out at the city. So many possibilities, humes...guys. She tensed her lips to prevent another squeal from escaping. Patting her other pocket, she heard the satisfying jingle of spare coppers. Tonight was definitely the night as soon as her mama came home from work. Too many lonely years lay behind her. Too much isolation from a community which did not approve of a single mother and her daughter even if her father was killed during the GP. Her mama would need to be reasonable.

As if summoned, she heard the familiar sound of her mama climbing up the metal hallways to their shack. Maja darted to the couch and tried to pretend she was a normal wholesome girl who did not entertain lewd thoughts about hume men. The rusty metal sheet which served as their door slid open and revealed her mama sweaty and gasping. Her mama entered, turned to shut and latch the door, then collapsed on the hunk of metal and pile of rags that served as their couch. She rested her head in her daughter's lap. Her face glistened with stray hairs plastered against it, but she was still gorgeous in a mature way, the spitting image of Maja. Her mama's hair was a darker shade of blue than Maja's, and her melon-green skin still carried radiance.

"Rough day, Mama?" Maja asked as she moved the stray hairs out of her face and rubbed her arm.

"Same as every day, baby green. Just...that climb is rough, I'm getting too old for it..."

"Mama! You're still young."

"You're as young as you feel. And right now I feel a million years old."

"Yeah..." Maja stared out the side of their home and imagined all the years she had waited for permission to leave The Steps. She was already eighteen and just about everyone her age had started families. The fact she was stranded at home at such an advanced age with no man or child only reinforced her family's pariah status in the community. But she forced those thoughts from her mind and tried to focus on her goals that night.

"Something wrong, sweetie?"

"I was just, I really REALLY want to go into Trinity tonight and uh, buy some hume candy, maybe try some hume food. I'm getting shack fever staying in The Steps every day and night."

"Maja..." Her mother sighed and looked away.

"Mama, come on! Nothing's going to happen. I'm just going into town to buy some candy."

"Hume town..." her mother muttered.

"Yeah, the hume part of town, right on the edge of The Steps, not even three steps out."

"It's dangerous out there, baby green. You remember what happened the first time I had to cross into hume town?"

"That was the one time, when humes weren't used to goblin yet. That was over ten years ago!"

"And Ro-Rok at work told me Trinity is sterilizing young goblin women like you. I'd hate for you to be one of them. If a man knows you can't provide children...you'll be alone forever! You're the only child I have left!" Her mother sobbed.

"Mama, come on!" Maja pleaded and cradled her mama's head. "Nothing's going to happen to me. Ya' know, The Steps aren't exactly safe either. Last time I went to buy candy, a prostitute bit me."

Her mama snorted a laugh through tears

and looked up at her daughter, reaching to cup her face.

"I'm a big girl now. I'm not your baby green anymore."

"You'll always be my baby green."

"And you'll always be my mama."

"I should have never taught you to read," her mother sighed to herself, "getting too many ideas in that little head."

Maja lowered her brow and scowled.

"You have no idea how much those books mean to me..." She stuck out her bottom lip and sulked in hopes of yielding some sympathy. Her mama embraced her after she sat up and walked to the pantry across the room. The metal floor thumped with each step. She did not react when she discovered they were out of candy but simply leaned against the counter a moment to compose herself.

"Lords and demons, I don't feel like cooking tonight." Her mama sighed and held herself up against their makeshift counter.

"Well, it's settled! I have to go into town and buy us candy." Maja darted for the door and unlatched it.

"Do you need some copper?" said her mother as Maja was halfway out the door. She spun back inside, snatched the pieces of extra copper from her mama, and shouted "I love you!" from the hallway as she barreled down the corridor. The hallway was dark and shifted side to side with every step as she ran. No one from Trinity had built the tower of homes they lived in. Families simply stacked their houses on top of one another. As she ran for the exit, she was forced to drop to her chubby butt and lower herself each time the hallway declined to a new level. She stumbled in the dark as she reached the last hallway on the ground floor. At the exit, she caught herself before running out into the roadway.

This was the night. This was going to be the most exciting night of her young life. Candy, food, humes, and hopefully some kinky hume sex, Lords and demons willing. She walked as slowly as she could, which wasn't very slow at all, passing the countless rusty shacks and piles of garbage. The streets were coated in grime that stuck to her bare feet and left her soles perpetually black. Groups of goblin men sat outside homes and stores, most playing settlers or cercesern. She tried not to resent them even as they gave her disapproving looks. She tried not to think about her culture and how blatant it was about taking joy from women, but seeing the men gathered outside, laughing, arguing, eating candy, she could not help but be agitated. Her thoughts turned to her mama, and how much happier she could be if they had a game to play together. She had learned to cherish her books in place of games. Though only few in number, it was likely a few more than any woman in The

Steps. Her books were an escape from the filthy cramped Steps and were closer friends than anyone in real life. She loved to shut her eyes and daydream for hours about running free through The Great Northern Forest, or sprinting across the Infinite Plains. In nature there was no poverty, no filth, no crime, no culture to hold her and her mama down. The resentment swirled in her mind until she passed the last of the goblin shacks and crossed into the hume neighborhoods on the fringe of The Steps.

And there they were--two humes casually walking down the road. They didn't look tremendously different from goblins, just gigantic with rounded ears and sand-colored skin. She hadn't see humes up close in years, possibly since she and her mama migrated to Trinity when she was only three. Ever since her mama was almost snatched on her first day of work all those years ago, she had promised her to avoid humes. But that only made them seem more dangerous and exciting. They were so incredibly tall with big tan hands and five fingers. The muscles under their shirts, the hair on their faces, all of it was exotic to her.

"I wonder what a hume penis looks like," she thought and burst into a big orange blush. She cupped her face with both hands and turned away from the men in embarrassment. The passing humes didn't seem notice her as they continued to talk as they walked.

"Okay, seriously, I need some candy or I'm not going to make it," she thought out loud before she wandered down the roadway to find a candy man. She found a clean cobblestone road past the massive hume houses made of wood and decided to follow it. The further she got away from her neighborhood, the nicer the homes seemed to be with fresh paint and glass windows. The road was the pleasant grey-ivory of clean stone instead of the brown-black of the roadways in The Steps.

"How could anyone need that much space?" she thought as she tilted her head all the way back to see the tops of the houses.

"Move, stupid!" a voice came out of nowhere, followed by a knee which knocked her off balance to the ground.

"Gahh!" she cried out and picked herself up off the reasonably clean road. "Where is the candy store!"

"Yoo-hoo!" called a voice. She turned to see a hume with a wrinkled face and silver-white hair sticking his head out the door of one of the houses.

"Are you looking for candy, little goblet?" The man beckoned Maja to him. She wasted no time darting across the street and up his steps which cut back and force parallel to the road and allowed her to walk up them with ease. Inside the house was the greatest sight she had ever seen in her entire life. Candy, so much, fucking, candy. Jar after jar after jar filled with endless varieties. It was the Ur Tra of candy. This was not like goblin candy stores which often carried just one or two varieties the owner made personally. This store had sour chompers, baby greens, dragon eggs, gold bars, witch's noses, womp womps, evil smiles, smackers, kickers, bee stings, fruit fire, falling stars, gummy goblins, crispy Ka Tuks, angel hair, mouth busters and tooth chippers, giggles, frizzies, chocolate queens, chocolate gems, chocolate fruit fire, and a dozen other selections which Maja had never even seen before. She felt the powerful urge to dump all of it on the floor and roll around naked in it, and if there weren't a half dozen other goblins in the store filling linen sacks with candy, she very well might have.

"Is there anything I can help you find?" asked the hume as he stepped around a goblin customer and squatted down to her level. His old smile was disarming.

"I uhhhhh, I wanted to buy some cand...y?" were the only words she could manage, overwhelmed by the entire experience. The owner belted out a huge hume laugh and nearly fell backwards before catching his balance. He tousled Maja's blue hair and smiled bigger.

"You are the cutest little goblet ever," he said. The goblin shopping behind him flinched at the inappropriate word choice. She found his ignorance amusing.

"I uh, I actually wanted to try some hume candy. I've never had it before," said Maja.

"Really now? Well, I do have some. It's not very popular though. Most goblins complain it's too mild, and humes refuse to shop here anymore, so I have quite a bit left if you're interested." The man led her to the corner of the store where jars sat holding unfamiliar offerings.

"I'll, I'll take all of it!" Maja declared then rummaged in her dress to grab all the copper she had for the hume man.

"Whoa now, little one, why don't you try a piece before you buy out the store?" he said with a chuckle. He opened one of the jars and fished out a small piece of chocolate before handing it to her.

"Are you fucking serious?" She stared at the large white hand extended towards her, becoming suspicious at this point.

"Heh, hehhhh!" The owner laughed again. "I take it goblins aren't used to free samples? It's okay, sweetheart. The candy has been here awhile, and I'm not sure it's going to be to your taste."

She hesitated only a split second before snatching the candy from his hand and stuffing it in her mouth. Two bites in and she knew the hume was right.

"Bleh! What's in this?" she cried then swallowed it down hard.

"Well, we're actually very fond of putting

peanuts and raisins in our food, and that includes our chocolate."

Maja took a long hard wince at the man to make sure this wasn't some cruel joke he had played on her. He seemed sincere.

"Why would you do that to chocolate?" she said to no one in particular. "Well, instead of the hume candy, how about I get a quarter sour chompers, quarter baby greens, quarter chocolate queens, and a quarter of whatever you think I would like."

"Sure thing, sweetheart." The hum took a burlap sack off the wall then walked around the store to fill her order. She followed him to the counter at the front as he weighed the bag using a brass scale suspended from the ceiling.

"I can't see. It says one pound?" She stood on the balls of her feet to try and see the gauge of the scale. The owner stepped around the counter and lifted Maja under her arms so she could see the gauge. His hands on her body made her feel small and feminine. The needle on the gauge hovered on one pound.

"Okay."

The man set her down and returned to his spot across the counter. He pushed down some brass levers making his register pop open with a ring.

"Let's call it three coppers and you bring that sack in anytime you want for a free sample."

Maja fished three copper pieces from her

dress pocket and held them up to the man who leaned over the counter to take them. A little expensive, but she had a good feeling about him and expected to be back within a day.

CHAPTER 2

"Go with the Lords," called the candy shop owner as Maja walked out into The Steps. Dusk settled on Trinity, and the street lamps were lit one at a time by a tall hume who flicked fireballs from the tips of his fingers into each one. He was tall, even by hume standards, and wore a black coat that went down to his heels and a tall dark hat. Maja sat on the steps of the candy shop as she inhaled several sour chompers and munched them open mouth. She watched as the flame porter walked lamp to lamp with his wooden ladder, climbed it each time, lifted the top of the lamp off its post, and flicked a fireball into the stem from his gloved hands before he replaced the glass.

"Humes are so fascinating," she thought as she devoured more candy. Maja wandered aimlessly through the hume-dominated area until she discovered one long building where humes endlessly shuffled in and out. Several lamps hung in a row above filthy windows which glowed from the inside. Large hume shadows shifted across the orange vista, and a din of hume voices could be heard inside. She tied her candy bag ever so carefully to the belt of her dress, checked it twice for security, and climbed up the steps of the building which were not intended for goblins. She dodged around plodding hume legs that did not seem to see her or just ignored her. After passing down a crowded hallway, she found a large, brightly lit room with dozens of humes talking, shouting, arguing, laughing, and drinking from mugs. She stepped into the room and off to the side of the entrance to avoid the humes who came and went.

Never before had Maja seen so many humes in one place. It was a veritable hive of humes gathered in random clusters, many at tables, all of them drinking something from tin mugs. Some were very tall and some were even closer to her height. Many had hair on their faces, and some had face hair that went down to their stomachs. Almost all the humes were male which excited Maja to the point of trembling. She could not begin to imagine what a hume penis looked like, but assumed they were massive and exotic like an animal's. The candy rush she was riding did nothing to slow her racing thoughts about hume penises.

"You there, little goblet! You going to buy something?" shouted an unseen voice. Maja turned to see a wide hume with no hair on top his head leaning over a long, high table. His face was pink, shiny, and mildly unpleasant. A man carrying several mugs stepped away from the bar and revealed an empty stool as tall as her. She walked to the throne sized chair and used all of her dexterity and daring to scale it. Standing at the summit, she was eye to eye with the pink faced man.

"Hi," said Maja with a smile. The man eyeballed the little goblin in front of him.

"You have coppers?" the man asked, "If you're not here to drink, I suggest you leave."

She reached in her pocket and placed a copper on the long, high table, wondering what would happen next. The man's face lightened as he slid the copper piece to his pocket. He reached under the bar and produced a mug full of liquid just like all the humes held, then he slid it across the table and turned to leave.

"What's that?" Maja eyed the mug suspiciously then sniffed it. The mug smelled like bitter flowers and the sickly sour yeast candies she didn't enjoy. The man turned back to her and shook his head.

"It's ale. Drink up," said the barkeep as he walked away. She stared at the mug for several seconds before daring to sip it.

"Gahhh!" Maja flinched away from the bitter, nasty beverage. Surely, this was a hume trick. She looked around the long table to see several hume men drinking deeply from their mugs. She bit her bottom lip in contemplation.

"Excuse me, hume sir, excuse me?" Maja

tapped the hume man sitting next to her. He turned and flinched slightly when he saw her. He had a wide shiny face framed by long hair on top and bottom.

"I, uhhh, something I can help you with, little goblet?" he said with a condescending grin. His words spilled out of his mouth like an overfilled barrel.

"I'm sorry to bother you, but can you tell me if this ale?" she said and nodded towards her mug. The man grabbed her mug and took a deep chug before setting it back down.

"Sure is, little lass," said the man followed by a deep breath of satisfaction.

"Is it supposed to taste like that?"

The man helped himself to another swig.

"Eyyupp, that's some smooth ale."

Maja pursed her lips and stared at the table in front of her. Was there anything humes made that didn't taste awful?

"Well, you can have it. I need to find some cola or something," she declared and carefully climbed down off the hume throne.

"Ah, yeah? Should check the end of the hallway, might find yourself some cola there!" The man erupted into a giant laugh and elbowed the guy next to him who was not in on the joke.

"Thanks, I'll go look," she said and left the room. The hallway wasn't well lit, and there were no humes towards the back. At the end, the hallway was intersected by an even darker hall.

Off to her right was a room with an oily lamp hung on the wall. She walked over to the room and was taken aback to see a strange feature hanging off the wall. It certainly was not a beverage. It almost looked like a long mushroom, and it was twitching. She reached up to touch it and a moan came from the wall which made the mushroom shift and move. Then it dawned on her. It was a hume penis! Maja's heart raced. She carefully clenched the penis with her four fingers and rubbed it. It was so massive and smooth to the touch, completely different from the size and shape of a goblin penis. It hardened in her grip and rose at an angle, too high to put her mouth on.

"I'll be right back, please don't leave," she said to the hume penis and ran back to the receiving hallway to find something to stand on. Against the wall near the entrance was a small wooden box. Inside the box she found a few onions and dumped them on the floor. With all the speed her tiny, chubby body could muster, Maja hurried back to the room. She planted the box on the floor and lifted herself on it. Standing on the box, she was face to face with the penis.

There was a plump, spongy red bulb on the end followed by a shaft of white flesh which was as big and as thick as her arm. It was so bizarre and animal like. She carefully rubbed it underhand and heard feet shuffle behind the wall.

"This is so fucking hot," she thought as

she massaged it, rubbing the tiny slit in the bulb with her thumb. She took the spongy head into her mouth, and at that moment, her brains left her. The hume cock was massive and barely fit in her tiny goblin mouth. It was firm and spongy at the same time with a salty, sour flavor. The cock was not the pleasant sour of candy but the sickly sour of ale. She swirled her little tongue around the bulbous tip and bobbed her head. Every inch of the cock made itself known as she tried to fit more in her mouth. She wasn't halfway down the shaft when it pushed into the back of her throat and stopped its progress.

Maja reached in under the hem of her dress and her underwear to touch herself. She pushed one thick finger inside herself as she bobbed her head on the cock. Drops of drool hit the box as she tasted and licked every inch. It was better than any candy. Not the taste, just how alive and animalistic it made her feel. She aggressively tapped her clit and massaged it in circles as she kissed the cock and pressed her face into it. There was a pounding on the wall, and thick tendrils of goo spurted onto her face from the tip. She sat down on the box in shock as the cock withdrew. She furiously played with her tiny green clit and thought about being a little goblin whore that hume men passed around like a toy and viciously penetrated. She thought about being spitroasted on two hume cocks, suspended in air, and violently fucked. She thought about how lowly hume men would think of a goblin girl. She thought about what her mama would think of her.

Maja threw her head back, knocking the box over with herself. She crashed onto the floor as juices sprayed into her hand and underclothes. The smell of her drippy pussy filled the room as she lay on the floor and composed herself. She looked up and saw another hume penis sticking through the wall, this one even thicker than the last!

"What fucking magic is this!" Maja thought to herself as she set the box up again and climbed it. She threw herself into her perversion, sucking the thick, hume dick with all the love and eagerness of a goblin girl in heat. It was big and strange and made her feel like she was doing something taboo. She loved the way sucking a hume dick made her feel. She loved the way her tiny green clit ached as she played with it. She wished there were more dicks to play with. She wished they would penetrate her. She wanted to throw her clothes away and go into that first room naked to offer her body up to each and every man. As her brains drifted away, the second hume cock squirted cum in her face with a strange mild smell. She kissed the cock before it left and sat on the box, rubbing her clit like she was starting a fire until she reached another squealing orgasm. She lay on the box for several minutes, but sadly, another cock did not appear. After her brains came back, she pulled up her panties and found a rag on the floor to wipe the cum from her face and neck. After she cleaned herself up the best she could, she quietly stumbled out of the dream room.

She half walked, half staggered down the dim hallway, her brains not as intact as she thought they were. Once she was outside, the cold night air caressed her face and brought most of her agency back with it. She reached in her candy bag and grabbed a fistful of sour chompers. Her hand would not stop shaking as she brought them to her mouth.

"Okay, maybe just a few," she said to herself as she let a single candy fall back into the bag before stuffing the rest in her face and chomping down. The sour sweet shards of sugar surged over her pälette. She had to sit. The walk home seemed like an epic quest, and her knees were still loose and unreliable. She wished she could ride a hume home like an archon.

"Well, isn't this a sight?" said a hume voice. She turned to the voice and saw a tall man who was handsome in a hume sort of way with soft features and dark shaggy hair that stuck out at angles from his head. His smile was mischievous. Maja was already imagining his hume penis and felt her clit twinge with need. She had no words.

"I didn't know goblins drank alcohol."

"We still don't." Thinking about that bitter beverage made her face bunch up in disgust.

"Ha! Well if you don't drink, may I ask what you're doing in front of a bar then?"

Maja met his eyes suspiciously. This hume was a little too interested in a goblin girl.

"I was just going home." She clumsily got to her feet and cinched her candy bag.

"Oh, that's too bad. I went shopping today, and I'm afraid I bought a little too much candy. Was hoping to find someone to share it with." The man opened his long dark coat to reveal a candy bag at least three times the size of Maja's. Her heart raced, and she inhaled through her nose.

"Well if it's that nasty hume candy, you can forget it," she said, finding an ounce of will-power.

"Heh, ever since I tried goblin candy, I can't go back to the old stuff. You people certainly have a way with sugar." The man reached into the candy bag and removed a sour chomper. He placed it in his mouth and tucked it in his cheek.

"That's now how you eat it," she said and took one from her own bag. She held the candy up to show him, flicked it in her mouth, and bit down hard. The man smiled.

"How about you come up to my room, and show me how to eat these the right way." He nodded towards the doorway. Maja thought about this proposition, but only for a single second.

"Yeah, okay," she said and followed the hume into the bar. He led her down the same dim hallway from earlier. At the end, instead of turning right to the magic dick room, the hume turned left and then up a dark stairway. Maja tackled each one individually, lifting herself up on her chubby butt, standing, then ascending the next stair. Seeing her struggle, the hume lifted Maja into his arms and carried her the rest of the way. She found this intensely erotic. At the top of the stairs was another dim hallway much like the receiving hall, except this one had several doors on each wall. The man turned into one of the rooms and cradled her in one arm as he latched the door. Without putting her down, he lit a lamp on the table near the door with a flick of his fingers.

"Are you going to put me down?" Maja giggled and looked at the floor. The man stared deeply into her big, copper-colored eyes. She stared back and felt herself moisten.

"Can I touch you?"

Maja's heart raced. She reached out for the hume's free hand, brought two of his fingers to her mouth, and eagerly sucked them together as she imagined his dick. The man pushed his fingers in and out of her small greedy mouth as she drooled.

"Lords and demons, I want to fuck you so bad," whispered the hume as she fellated his fingers. He laid Maja on his bed and pulled her underwear all the way off to reveal a bright blue bush between her chubby thighs. He lifted her dress off, and her tiny, chubby breasts bounced free, hanging to the sides. She had little orange nipples that blended into her soft, minty green skin. Maja sprawled out as her little slit dripped into his bed sheets. She didn't want her brains anymore.

The hume pressed his face into her soft, helpless body and kissed her chubby tummy that had a fuzzy candy trail riding up to her belly button. He held her thick breasts together and alternated nursing each teat. Maja held onto his head as he nursed. She yipped as two fingers suddenly found their way inside her welcoming slit. The hume lifted his head to kiss her mouth, and she kissed back lovingly, holding his head as he masturbated her. His tongue was so big it overpowered her much smaller tongue, taking up her whole mouth.

"Are you a bad girl?" asked the hume, face to face with her. She bit her lip and nodded. He grabbed her by her ankles, lifted her body back, and spanked her fat green butt. She cooed with each slap as her butt jiggled, half her body up in the air. He spanked her several times, causing her juices to splash on the bed. Then he hooked his middle and index finger and worked them into her asshole. She gripped the bed sheets and squealed as his fingers explored inside her. Her tiny asshole clenched at his fingers, but she was helpless to his inquiries. He kissed her face and told her she was a good girl.

The hume finally took off his long coat and dropped his pants, revealing an excited, pink cock which sprung up at attention. He grabbed her by her hair, pulled her to her feet with ease, and pressed her face into his dick. He rubbed it up and down her face then slapped her with it, never letting go of her hair. Her whole body couldn't fight against the strength in his arm.

"I want you to suck my cock, okay?" he said, getting permission before he used her body like a toy. She nodded, knowing nothing could happen which would stop her from desiring his cock.

Pressing his hume cock into her mouth, he forced it in as deep as it would go, making her gag on it. His two massive hands gripped her little head and fucked her brains away. She was just a toy, an object. She stopped existing as he used her throat to masturbate. Viciously, he fucked her cute little face and made her ugly. He grunted and seemed about to scream when cum shot down her throat. He held his hume dick in as deep as it would go, painfully gripping her head. Spurt after spurt of cum dripped down her throat and directly into her stomach. After several seconds, he let go of her head and allowed her to collapse onto the bed. She coughed and turned on her side, but the stickiness remained in her throat. He sat next to her and rested his giant's hand on her back.

"Did I hurt you?" he asked with genuine concern in his voice.

"Yes..." said Maja with a hoarse voice.

"I'm sorry, it's just, you're so sensual. Your fat little butt. Your breasts. That tiny little mouth. I just wanted to empty myself in you. You're like a drug...or a candy," he said with a halfhearted laugh to himself.

"No...it's okay, I like when men use me..." She looked away after her whorish admission. He turned her face back and kissed her tiny mouth.

"I think that's beautiful," he said, no lie in his voice, "I want to fuck you so bad right now."

"I want you to fuck me too." She stared into his hungry eyes. He lifted her tiny body up and gently guided her onto his massive hume cock. He was still hard from earlier but had to be forceful to spread her tiny slit. He gripped her chubby thighs and pushed her warm, wet pussy down on his dick until he could fit himself inside her. In one sudden motion, her body relaxed and the hume cock was inside her. It was too big. She was stretched too far. He was taking up her insides. She panicked and flailed, gasping for air. It was too much dick. It was like eating way too much candy only much worse. She was uncomfortably full.

"Whoa, whoa, baby girl," he said, gently grabbing her arms and kissing her neck, "You're okay, you're okay. You're not the first slutty little goblet I've fucked."

He grabbed her soft waist with his big hume hands and used her body to masturbate. Up and down she went as her body relaxed, and her tiny pussy stretched. He stood up, and she found herself impaled on his hume cock. Her feet were high off the floor, and she had no control of her body. She was helpless, just a toy for this hume to fuck. A little green trash can for hume cum.

He picked up his pace as he fucked her tiny body. He was no longer gentle as he quickened his strokes. Her chubby breasts bounced wildly as the massive hume cock stuffed her and retreated countless times. Her brains were long gone. She was deep in the swamp of utter whorishness. She wished there was a group of humes to watch her be used. She wished he would ruin her asshole. She wished her mama would see what a stupid whore she was.

"Tell me I'm stupid. Say something nasty to me," cried Maja as her pussy drooled on the mighty hume dick. The self deprecating words incensed him as he relentlessly rammed his dick into her tiny body.

"You're the third goblet I've fucked this week. You're all fucking whores. All you do is breed. You're worse than animals. I knew I was going to fuck you the moment I saw you. You're all the same. Goblet trash, all you're good for is collecting cum."

Maja cried and orgasmed on the giant hume dick, the spasms amplified by the limits to which she was stretched. The hume was not long behind her. He pinned her to the bed and held her in place. He forced her tiny body down on his dick as deep as it would go and unleashed a torrent of cum inside her. Short angry cries escaped him as spasms rippled through his dick. He fell to the bed and wrapped his arms around his tiny prize. He curled around her, his softened dick slipping free of her painfully tight cunt. Maja sobbed uncontrollably.

"Shhh, it's okay," he said as he hugged her and kissed the top of her head, "I didn't mean those things. I was just doing what you asked."

"I, I know." Maja sniffed up a bunch of snot and wiped the tears from her face. "I know. I just, I'm feeling a lot of things right now. I like being told I'm trash. I don't know why."

The hume hugged his tiny goblin tighter and kissed her again. Maja felt very safe and cared for. They lay together several minutes in silence, completely awash in afterglow.

"I really need to get home." Maja realized as she thought about her mama who had gone all this time without candy, poor thing. She quickly gathered up her cum-stained clothes and made for the door as she dressed.

"Take care, little one," called the hume. Maja bounced down the steps on her ass and ran down the hall which had few humes in it so late at night. Once she was outside, she made her way in the direction of the highest homes of the Steps, not knowing exactly how to get there, but having a great landmark which was visible in the moonlight. She sprinted down dark and deserted streets. The night's events had made her nervous and excitable. The Steps took on a dream like quality as she meandered down empty roads, leaving half her brain in that hume's bedroom. She realized then that they never exchanged names, and she had fucked a total stranger. The whorishness only made her more excited.

After turning another corner and seeing the familiar goblin shacks of her neighborhood, there was sudden darkness. She could not see anything, then she couldn't move. Something was restraining her. She screamed, but there were no reply. She was up in the air, someone, a hume most likely, had grabbed her. She was carried through the air and then heard a door open. She fought and struggled, but the hume easily kept her restrained. Her body descended with the clap of feet on stairs. She was slammed onto a hard metal surface with a metallic clang. Her clothing was removed. After her bottoms were removed, she felt an agonizing streak of heat and pain slide across the inside of her thigh which forced a squeal from her. She tried to escape the pain and the horrible situation she was in. Her mind snapped closed like a powerful weariness followed by rest.

"Stop!" screamed a strangely familiar voice followed by the sounds of a scuffle. The shout snapped Maja back to reality. There was a crash, shuffling of feet, hard packing sounds, and then the room lit up. Maja realized she was covered with a hoodwink. Her hands were now free, and she removed the hood to see two hume men in fisticuffs battling on the other side of the room with a third hume figure unmoving on the floor. A fireball appeared, scorching one of the men's faces off with a nightmarish shriek. In the light, she could see that the other man was her lover from earlier.

"Are you alright?" Her hume ran over to the table she was bound to and singed off the rope ties binding her feet. His tears glimmered in the dark, and he was breathing heavily. A fireball appeared in the air, balanced on the tips of his two fingers. He placed his hand on her head and peered intently in each of her eyes.

"I think I'm okay..." said Maja, planting her hand to leave the table. As she moved to climb off, her hand slipped.

"Oh my Lords..." her hume whispered. Beneath Maja, atop the table, was a pool of blood almost black in the light of the basement.

"We have to get you out of here!" said her

hume as he snatched her up and fled the basement. She felt cold and dizzy, and her vision became dark and unfocused. As he ran, her hume would occasionally look down with wide horrified eyes then back to the route in front of him.

"What happened..?" said Maja, her voice weak and far away like in a dream.

"Those fucks back there, they just tried to sterilize you. You're bleeding badly. I need to get you to my chirurgeon."

"What's a churr-jun..?" said Maja whose world went black before she could get an answer.

CHAPTER 3

Alexander bolted through the streets of Trinity, clutching his precious green package to his chest. Her dark red blood slowly dripped down the front of his tunic, sticky and matted against his skin. The blood was warm and sickeningly comforting in the cold night. The morbid thought brought bile up in his throat. He darted past an alleyway then doubled back. Barreling down the dark corridor, he cursed himself for the precious seconds he wasted. He launched himself in the air and came down boots first on a cellar door, shattering it into pieces. Sliding down the basement stairs on a flow of debris, he shielded his precious green friend. At the bottom of the stairs was his guild chirurgeon, Mort, hunched over in a filthy lab coat. Mort lit a lamp on the nearby table.

"You have to help her!" cried Alexander, stuffing the little person into Mort's arms.

"She's blee--they tried to sterilize her! I don't know what to do." Alexander slammed his palm against his drenched brow and tried to catch his breath. The blood vessels in his ears thrummed like tribal drums.

The chirurgeon calmly laid the chubby goblin girl on the table. She was naked with a disturbing amount of blood coating the inside of her plump thighs. Mort slowly crossed to the side of the table, spread her thighs open, and examined them with the tips of his fingers.

"Give me some light," he said in an even tone. Alexander lit a brilliant fireball atop the tips of his two fingers and held it near the chirurgeon who mumbled something.

"WHAT!" screeched Alexander, gasping for air.

"Her femoral artery has been severed. That's the only thing that explains this much blood from one so little. I'm afraid she doesn't have much time left." The evenness of Mort's voice brought more bile up Alexander's throat, threatening to escape. Alexander clutched his chest and took rapid breaths.

"No! No! Lords and demons no! This is all my fault!" He paced back and forth, unaware his fireball was still lit.

"Only a Healer could save her now," said Mort. Alexander went cold and stopped. He gathered up his precious bundle and fled the basement, slipping on the stairs as he went. As he sprinted through the streets and back alleyways of Trinity, the city air was heavy and cold like a graveyard. The roads were dark, save the street lamps, and bereft of life. Buildings seemed to lean in and draw his breath away. There was no one to help him here. A whisper came from his bundle. Alexander looked down to see those big copper eyes looking up at him. Her small delicate mouth made silent words.

"Am I going to die?" asked his little goblin, her unfocused eyes slowly blinking. His chest tensed up, and the tears could not be stopped. He shook his head stupidly.

"If I die, tell my mama, Kaja, I love her."

Alexander lowered his head and sprinted as fast as he could into the upper class neighborhoods of Trinity where the streets were much brighter. In Gold Town, the houses were painted in bright happy colors which rose to pointed roofs. A few well-dressed people strolled down the even cobblestone road in a neighborhood that did not know the threat of crime. The contrast between his situation and surroundings felt like a living nightmare. He kept looking down to make sure his little goblin girl was really there. *Was this his punishment for what had happened to Finn?*

After minutes that felt like hours, he found what he was looking for off the main road: a big yellow home that could be called a mansion by Steps standards. He had no time to knock, so he threw himself shoulder first through the decorative front door and toppled onto the floor inside. Rapid footsteps approached him, a spell zipped through the air whining like a large insect, and then his eyesight was gone.

"Oh my Lords! What are YOU doing here!" came a delicate but mature voice in the darkness.

"Help her!" he cried as held out the goblin girl towards the voice. The weight of his package was lifted into the air and took him off balance to the floor. Using his fire magic, he scalded his eyelids with his fingertips to remove the debuff on him. The home he found himself in was gorgeously appointed with paintings, flowers, and professionally made furniture. He stumbled room to room until he found Mei in the kitchen scrutinizing the tiny goblin girl on her marble counter.

"What happened to her?" she asked, not looking in his direction.

"Some--someone tried to sterilize her...it was my fault," said Alexander.

"Of course it was." Her short, dark hair hung in a face of pure concentration as her hands glowed brilliantly, assessing the little green person in her kitchen.

"I didn't mean to bring this on you. I went to Mort, but he said it was beyond his skill. I never meant for you to see me again."

"Funny how that happens." She pressed her pale white face into the goblin's washed out face as her hands caressed the goblin's body. "You realize I'll have to use Back From The Brink to save her, yes?"

Alexander swallowed hard.

"You're the only one that can save her now," was the only thing he could say.

"You better fix my fucking door by the time I get back, Alexander Song." She cast her hateful green eyes at him before returning to the goblin girl. "And here we go. BACK FROM THE BRINK!"

Mei's words shook the entire house, knocking decorations off the mantle and walls. Her voice was much louder and more powerful than her small frame could have accomplished. The incantation seemed to linger in the air like it was caught in an echoing cave. She collapsed, and Alexander caught her. He lifted her in his arms and carried her petite body into the receiving room where he laid her on an ornate sofa. He rested his hand on her face a moment as his pulsed with sickly sweet nostalgia. He returned to the kitchen to check on the goblin girl. She stirred on the counter and gripped the edge to stop herself from rolling off. Her bright copper eyes flashed with vitality, and she smiled upon seeing him in the doorway. She reached out her stubby arms for him as he held back tears.

"I'm sorry...about all of this. You didn't deserve this. I put your life in danger." He wanted to hug her but didn't feel justified. She was too precious, too authentic, too full of love and life. He sat at the kitchen table and stared at the floor. His past regrets screamed in the back of his mind. The little person let herself down off the counter as if climbing down a cliff side. She stood in front of him naked and covered in blood before hugging his leg.

"You saved me," she said, looking up into his face. He couldn't meet her beautiful eyes.

"I'm the reason they targeted you. I knew...I pretty much knew that if you had sex with me, they were going to target you."

The goblin girl lowered her brow in confusion.

"My guild--we've suspected there are people out there sterilizing young goblin women like you. We didn't know how they chose their victims. It was still guess work at this point. But you, out and about in the hume part of town, I had a feeling they were going to target you. Wanted them to get an idea you were sexually active. After you left, I followed you from afar. I, I couldn't keep you safe. I'm so sorry." Alexander hung his head low. The goblin girl stared at the floor for some time as if figuring things out. A high pitched yawn escaped her mouth like a wolf pup's howl.

"I need to go home. Mama must be so worried about me," she said, looking for an exit.

"I can't let you walk home alone, and I can't just leave her house like this. I'll take you home in the morning. I promise." He felt stupid making promises to her.

"Well can you, I mean, can you hold me while I sleep?" she asked, apparently still naive to the entire situation. He looked at her with a mixture of disappointment and disbelief then scooped up her chubby little body and held her against his chest. She clung to him. Her tiny heart beating against his chest brought on quiet tears. He set her down in a large plush chair then dragged a table to the foyer. There he flipped the table up on its side to block the doorway.

"Not exactly a bad part of town," he said to himself, "should do for the night."

He moved around the receiving room to replace decorations which had fallen to the floor from Mei's spell. After fixing the decorations, he scooped up the goblin girl and sat in the chair, placing her in his lap. She squirmed and shifted creating an erection that pressed into her chubby butt. She giggled when she felt it poke her.

"Night," She clung to his arm and was fast asleep in seconds. His thoughts raged and stormed inside his head. There was so much to consider.

What was the next step in stopping these people?

Go back to that basement and look for clues.

Should he tell The Guard?

No, not yet.

Was this little person safe?

He didn't know.

The thoughts whirled endlessly and caused Alexander to flinch awake twice before he was actually able to sleep. The little person in his lap was a great comfort. Her tiny heart beating against his wrist soothed his guilty soul.

Maja awoke to find herself in an unfamiliar setting. She was in a giant hume building. Hume paintings and polished hume furniture were everywhere. Across the room in the foyer, her hume lover stood in the doorway and talked to someone outside. She crawled off the big comfy chair and walked over to him, her thighs sticky with dried blood. Her hume was taken aback when he saw her approach. She smiled up at him. He only returned her gaze.

"Good morning," she said as she fidgeted in place, so happy to see him and feeling bashful about the night they shared. He narrowed his eyes in confusion or apprehension. The person outside heaved a new door onto its hinges. Maja stared at her hume and kept smiling to herself.

"I guess you're feeling better," he said dismissively as he walked away from the construction project and into the kitchen. Maja followed after him. She started to believe he was not happy to see her. In the kitchen, he laid a folded towel on the counter and soaked a rag in the sink. He bent down and lifted her up, placing her in a sink filled with warm water. As he bathed her, his expression led Maja to believe this caused him great pain, but she felt feminine and cared for to be bathed by her big hume lover. She kissed his mouth as he leaned in, making him flinch.

"Don't do that," he said as he wiped the dirt from her grinning face. This wasn't foreplay to him; this was work.

"Why not?" she asked as she batted her eyelashes. He rinsed the rag in the water and wiped the sweat from her breasts, lifting each one up to wash underneath. She scratched the inside of her thighs as he fondled her. She thought about his thick, pink, hume dick and wanted to drool on it again.

"Listen little girl...do you even understand what happened last night?"

Maja burst into a giant grin and held her face from the intense sensation of smiling. Her hume scowled.

"Not that," he snapped, "after we...did that. Do you even remember anything after that?"

Maja thought about her previous night and hugged herself before covering her mouth to muffle her squeal. She had been a very bad girl. The magical dick room, her hume lover, how rough and degrading he was with her, and how closely he held her afterwards. She was definitely smitten with him, even if he was mad at her for some reason. She remembered walking home and then…

"Oh my Lords and demons!" Maja shouted, looking around the kitchen. "Where is my candy bag?"

Her hume punched the water, splashing Maja. She playfully splashed him back, smiling even bigger and grabbing at his hand. He whipped his hand away from her.

"No, you lordsdam idiot! You were almost killed!"

"Are you YELLING at her?" said a female hume in the kitchen doorway. She was a beautiful, sugar-white hume with short dark hair. She was petite by hume standards and wore a plush white robe which looked very expensive. Her face was pink with anger which Maja found both frightening and adorable.

"What is your malfunction, Alexander?" The woman snatched the rag from his hand and turned towards Maja. "Are you okay, sweetie?"

Maja blushed as she realized she was still naked.

"I'm fine. My lover was just giving me a bath," said Maja, holding her face in another sensitive grin. The hume woman's face softened. She dipped the rag in the water and wiped the rest of the blood from Maja's thighs then scooped her out of the sink. She placed Maja on the nearby towel and patted her dry.

"Her lover, huh?" The woman smirked and turned to Alexander whose face froze in panic.

She held Maja's head as she lifted her eyelids and stared deeply into each eye.

"Now, you went through a lot last night, and I'm pretty confident you are fully healed, but I would like to be certain that everything is okay down there." The hume woman's eyes fell then returned to meet her stare. Maja giggled which made the hume woman smile more.

"Buy a girl some candy first," said Maja as she tapped the hume woman on the arm, making her giggle too. The woman removed the towel to expose Maja's soft tiny frame. Her small chubby breasts hung on her plump tummy which sat on her meaty green thighs. She gently opened Maja's thighs, guiding her to lean back and exposing her furry blue pussy. Maja covered her mouth to muffle any squealing, but the moment was as erotic as anything that had happened the night before. The woman traced her slender fingers over Maja's thigh which made Maja tremble with erotic excitement.

"Everything seems okay," she said, resting her hand on Maja's knee. "We really need to get you some clothes though, huh?"

The woman left the kitchen and returned with a leather coin purse. She pulled out a pair of gold coins and looked at Alexander who leaned against the wall.

"I want you to take her to a tailor and buy her a nice dress she can wear."

"And candy," Maja chimed in.

"And candy. I want this little person to know that not all humes are evil." The woman turned to Maja and kissed the top of her head. Maja reached up to pull her head down and kissed the top too as was apparently the hume custom. The woman smiled at her.

"You don't deserve the bad things that happen to you." The woman looked at Maja lovingly who wished the woman would pin her down. Maja stood up on the counter, eye to eye with her hume host. The woman stepped in for a hug.

"My name's Maja," she said into the hume's ear as they embraced, "thank you for helping me."

"My name is Mei. If you're ever in trouble, don't be afraid to ask me for help. I know humes do awful things to your people, and I should be doing more to change that, but...just don't be afraid to come here, okay? You're a friend in this house. Now I think someone has a day of shopping ahead of her."

Mei gave Maja a kiss on the cheek and stepped back, making Maja blush and hug herself. Mei turned to Alexander and held out the twin pieces of gold for him. He stepped forward and snatched the money from her small hand.

"Why aren't YOU doing this?" said Alexander, not breaking eye contact.

"Because I have to work, you archon's asshole," snapped Mei, "not all of us can run around ruining everyone's lives like you."

Maja did not know what to make of this exchange, so she only watched. Alexander stepped away, snatched Maja up in her towel, and carried her out of the home.

CHAPTER 4

Outside, the carpenter had finished installing the door and had taken the broken one with him. The sun was still low and cast the empty roads in dim shadows. Maja hid her face in her hume's chest.

"What is your deal?" said Alexander, looking down at her. She looked up at him with a smirk.

"What?" she asked as she nuzzled her face into his broad chest.

"I almost killed you last night. You almost died. Why are you acting this way?" He walked as he talked, ignoring the stares from the few passing humes awake so early. Maja looked up into the pink blue sky and contemplated an answer.

"Well, like, I don't remember most of what happened last night. I know you and Mei saved me. And there was candy. And you made me lose my brains," said Maja with a grin. Alexander rolled his eyes.

"I guess I try not to think about the bad stuff. I mean everything is bad. But I have Mama, and candy, and now a big, sexy, hume lover, and we need to go see Mama as soon as possible."

"I'm not your lover and that's fine."

"Well, we made love and it was beautiful, and you made me lose my brains. You make me feel safe and cared for. I'm actually happier now than I've been in a very long time, maybe since ever. I guess when you have nothing, anything seems nice."

"That's actually a very sweet sentiment, but you need to take life more seriously. Not all humes are as kind as Mei."

Maja giggled.

"What's so funny?"

"Mei hates you, but you said she's kind."

"She is kind. She's the sweetest, most caring person I've ever known."

"But then why does she hate you?"

"Because I killed the only person she's ever loved." Alexander broke eye contact.

"What?"

"Not now, we're here." He walked up the steps to the tailor's salon.

"No, wait, what happened?" Maja squirmed in his arms.

"I'll tell you some other time. Now is not that time." He carried her through the threshold into a building filled with endless rolls of fabrics. Stands, mounts, and walls were coated with every conceivable pattern and color with only a few examples of actual clothing on small mannequins. The room was a waterfall of fabric cascading into every hue, shade, and tone.

"Is this place open?" Alexander called out to the storm of fabric.

"Is the door open?" A woman called from somewhere in the ocean of material. From seemingly nowhere, a hume woman with brown skin stepped out of the sea of fabric wearing an extravagant corset of leather and lace with matching leather pants. Her dark wiry hair was in a giant bun, tied with fabric which complemented her outfit.

"What's going on here?' said the woman with amusement as she looked at Maja in Alexander's arms.

"It's a very long story," he answered.

"He rescued me from a castle," Maja chimed in and covered her smile with her hands. The woman smiled back.

"Well aren't you the cutest thing ever," said the hume woman as she rubbed the top of Maja's head.

"Can you make clothes for a goblin?" said Alexander.

"Of course I can. All I need are measurements. Now the real question is, can you pay for clothes for a little goblet?"

Alexander held Maja in one arm as he reached in his pocket to flash two gold pieces at the woman whose eyes lit up at the sight.

"That's all I needed to know. Now, if you

just hold one moment." The woman stepped around Alexander to close the door and lower the shades on the front facing windows.

"I have nothing against goblins personally, but my clients most certainly do. I'll make her an outfit, but if anyone comes in and sees her, I'm going to lose customers."

"That's pathetic," said Alexander. She didn't seem interested in his criticism as she continued preparations.

"It is pathetic. It's fucking pathetic, but this is my livelihood, and if I could live off of mix customers I would. But goblins don't have money, and I can't afford to sacrifice my livelihood just to make a statement. Now if you don't like that, please leave."

Alexander seemed to seriously consider the idea until Maja leapt from his arms and landed on the floor. She felt so slutty as yet another hume saw her naked.

"Can I just get a new outfit, please? I've never had new clothes in my entire life and I'm really excited," said Maja as she stood naked in the middle of the floor without an ounce of self-consciousness.

"Fine," said Alexander. The tailor disappeared into the sea of colors and returned with an ornate silver box the size of a book. She removed a cloth tape from it and measured every part of Maja's tiny curvy body. Maja giggled as the tailor's quick hands inadvertently tickled her. The tailor stopped a moment to properly tickle her as she fell over laughing hysterically.

"Can we finish sometime this era?" Alexander moaned and crossed his arms.

"What do you see in him?" said the tailor as she helped Maja to her feet.

"He makes me feel like a lady," said Maja, blushing and looking at the floor.

"I completely understand." The tailor finished her measurements and removed a pair of shears from her box before disappearing into the forest of fabric. She returned several moments later with a random assortment of fabrics and a child sized mannequin. In a flurry of shears, needle, thread, and sweat, she transformed the scraps of fabric into a proper outfit.

"You didn't even ask us what we wanted," said Alexander.

"Trust me to make your girlfriend beautiful," said the tailor with three pins clenched in her teeth as she knelt beside the tiny mannequin.

"She's not my girlfriend."

Maja stared in fascination as the strips of cloth slowly took form into a beautiful outfit. The tailor had created an elegant corset with black, lace striations and copper-colored inlay which matched Maja's eyes. Along the hem was a ring of tiny black bows which hung over a simple, pleated black skirt. On the floor was a pair of black legging next to the tiniest pair of black panties. The tailor finished sewing garter straps to the leggings and beckoned Maja over. She scampered over to the tailor who helped her into the outfit. They started with her panties, then the legging that accentuated her shape, and finally the skirt. After the garter straps were secured, the tailor helped Maja into her gorgeous corset and cinched it for her, pushing her chubby breasts up and out with each cinch. The tailor lifted a large black bow off the floor and secured it to the back of the corset. Maja bounced up and down with excitement and femininity.

"She looks like the world's tiniest prostitute."

"Oh shoosh, you, she's beautiful. She's a young sensual woman, and she wants to look as beautiful and sexy as she feels." The tailor stood up, disappeared into the fields of fabric, and returned to her cash register with a small bundle of fabric under one arm. "Now she certainly needs a good pair of boots to complete the outfit. I'm writing down the name of a place that does children's shoes. He'll be able to help you. All of this is going to come to four silver."

"Lords and demons, are you serious!" said Alexander.

"It's two silver for a custom outfit and I'm charging you for the clients I missed closing the shop. Stop being a child and pay me."

Alexander reluctantly handed over a piece of gold and received six silver pieces in return along with a simple tunic. Alexander gave her a quizzical look, and she nodded towards his blood stained shirt. He gave her an awkward smile and quickly redressed himself before leading Maja from the salon. The tailor smiled at them one last time before they left the store.

CHAPTER 5

"Stay beautiful, darling," called the tailor as Alexander and Maja left the shop together. Outside the salon, more humes were in the streets and the sun was up.

"They're still staring at us," said Maja as she reached up to hold Alexander's hand.

"They've probably never seen a goblin up close before," he said as he stepped into the road.

"I must frighten them horribly." Maja giggled and wondered what one of the well dressed humes would do if she roared at them.

"You're a frightening one alright. Come on, I think the place is this way."

The trip to the cobbler was uneventful. Maja left with a tiny pair of black boots which were the first pair she had ever owned. She happily skipped out of the store and twirled for her lover. He looked at the coins leftover in his hand and gave them an approving smile.

"Candy, candy, candy, caaaannn-day!" shouted Maja, bouncing around the sidewalk.

"Lords and demons, you need to settle down. There's more to life than candy."

"No. There's. Not...maybe sex." Maja nuzzled her grinning face into Alexander's hand who whipped it away. She hugged his leg instead.

"Would you please settle down. You're embarrassing me. You can't behave like this in public. This isn't The Steps."

"Then you better hurry up and find me some candy, or I'm going to pull my bottoms down in front of everyone."

He sighed and held his face in his palm. "You said you don't eat hume candy. We'll have to walk back to The Steps to get you candy...that's fine. Can drop you off wherever it is you live and finally be done with you."

Maja latched onto his hand as they walked.

"Do goblins even eat meat, or bread, or anything besides candy?"

"Uh, not really. I think I heard little-big-ones do."

"And what is a little big'un?"

"It's one of those wealthy trade goblins who tries to pretend to be hume. Buys a hume house and eats hume food. Thinks he can stop being a goblin."

The couple departed the upper class neighborhood of Gold Town, strode through the working class hume neighborhoods that crowded the cobblestone circuit, and entered the hume part of The Steps where many of the houses were unpainted and in need of repair.

"Can we have sex after we get candy?'

"Absolutely not. I'm not going to do anything to put your life in danger again. As far as anyone knows you're a simple, virgin, goblin girl."

Maja stopped and laughed, doubled over, and forced to hold her sides to keep them from splitting.

"You are too funny, Mr. Alexander."

"I'm dead serious. If I caused you to get hurt again, I could never forgive myself."

"I think I should have some say in this."

"No. You shouldn't. You're young, dumb, and full of cum. I've watched you lose your brains. You're not capable of rational thinking."

"Well, I love you, and I want you inside me, every day."

He was forced to lean forward as he walked to hide his erection.

"You don't love me, you stupid goblin girl. You're just obsessed with sex. You don't know what love is."

"Well I know you care about me, and you spend time with me, and you make me feel beautiful. You were kind to me up until this point and in bed I'm your little fuck doll."

Alexander was forced to stop and find a bench.

"You can't just SAY things like that. You have no sense of modesty. Look at your lordsdam outfit. You could be the world's tiniest street walker."

"I've thought about it," said Maja.

"What? No. If you want to be attacked again, that's where it starts. If you start selling your body, they're going to find you and hurt you."

"Hey! Listen! Goblin girls don't get a lot of choices in life. Goblin men get every opportunity, and we're supposed to stay at home and be baby fountains. Maybe like, maybe I want to be more than that. I don't know."

"And you're going to accomplish that being a little callback girl?"

"It's something! I don't know my life. I know Mama suffers because we've lost so much, and I'm all the family she has left, and no one will marry her, even though she's the sweetest, most caring person in the entire world. I don't want that for myself. I want to suck dicks, and eat candy, and have control over my own lordsdam life!"

A pair of goblin girls across the street cheered and hooted upon hearing Maja's little speech. Alexander hurried her along before they drew more attention to themselves.

"Here, stop. This is the place." Maja found her way back to the candy shop from yesterday and hurried inside to hug her favorite person in the world. The owner bellowed with laughter as she launched herself into him for an extended hug.

"Here," said Alexander, handing a silver piece to Maja as he followed her into the store. "That's all you're allowed to spend."

Maja took her favorite person by the hand and led him around the store, picking out candies for her and her mama. She left the store with two sacks of candy which Alexander easily carried over his shoulder with one hand.

"This will feed me and Mama for weeks!" shouted Maja as she stuffed a fistful of sour chompers in her mouth and savagely crunched them. Alexander stared in grim fascination as she devoured the candy.

"I need to make a stop," he said, turning off the main cobblestone road. He led her through narrow twisting alleys until they stopped at a weirdly familiar cellar. He stepped through the open cellar doorway and down into a basement.

"Mort, you down here?" Alexander called into the darkness. Maja stuffed a few more sour chompers into her face and watched her lover from the stairs.

"Damn right I am," came a sickly voice from the darkness. A lamp sparked to life, and an old hunched over man with long hair that was balding on top appeared in the darkness near a table.

"I see your little goblet has persevered," said the eerie man.

"No thanks to you," said Alexander, "Has Tan-tan been around since yesterday? I wanted to go with her to a crime scene and collect some clues. That place has to stink to high hells by now."

"Knowing Tantra, she's down here right now, eavesdropping to make sure we're not talking about her. She always seems to have a way of appearing when she's not wanted," said the man.

"Oh, before I forget, for the door." Alexander flicked a silver piece towards the table, but it vanished in mid-air.

"Yoink," said a disembodied voice. A tall green woman who wasn't quite hume appeared in the middle of the room out of the air itself. She was at least a head taller than Alexander with a long slender neck and broad shoulders. Her body was wiry with a tiny pair of breasts and a small round butt. She had several piercings in the cartilage of her ear and one in her lip. Her ears were pointy like a goblin's, and her hair was cropped on both sides with a long row of purple locks on top cascading off to the side. She pocketed the silver piece as she stepped past Alexander to stand face to knee with Maja.

"Well, if you aren't the cutest goblin woman ever, then my name isn't Tantra Charbelcher."

"Your name ISN'T Tantra Charbelcher. Stop comparing yourself to a guild hero, Tantan."

"Someday."

"Well, if you want to be a guild hero,

maybe you can help me with a quest. Some scumbags tried to sterilize this poor creature last night, and I wanted you to help me investigate."

Upon hearing the word "sterilize", Tan-tan's fist trembled and her teeth dug into her plump purple lip.

"I will kill every last one of them for hurting this perfect person." Her severe expression turned to a smile as she looked at Maja who was in awe of her incredible height and beautiful slender body.

"I appreciate the passion, I really do, but I already killed everyone involved when I saved her. I just need another set of eyes to help me gather clues, find out who these fuckers were, and if there are more of them."

"Of course I'll help. Lead the way."

"We need to get this little girl home first."

Maja fidgeted as she looked at Tan-tan then Alexander. "Uhhhh, can I help? I mean, I know I can't fight, but I want to help. I want to have some control in my life. And if there's other people out there hurting goblins, it's my responsibility to stop it."

"I don't--"

"Of course, beautiful," said Tan-tan with a grin. "Nothing wrong with having a third set of eyes at a crime scene."

The three exited the cellar together with Mort grumbling as they left. Alexander led them through a series of twisting alleys created by the unplanned and impromptu housing of The Steps.

"Asuna's not around?" said Alexander as they navigated through the maze-like neighborhoods.

"Nah, you know how she likes to sleep in," said Tan-tan.

"Tan-tan, can I ask you something?" said Maja as she stared up at the giant person.

"You can ask me anything, baby green." Tan-tan smiled down at her.

"Um, what are you?"

Alexander flinched and halted their progress. He turned to glare at Maja who ignored his reproach.

"What is wrong with you? We were just talking about this earlier!. No--"

"I'm a halfbreed. My mom was a hume and my dad was a goblin."

"Ohhhhh! I didn't know goblins and humes could do that. Ok, second question, why are you so big?"

Alexander palmed his own face and continued everyone walking.

"No one really knows. I mean, Trinity says a goblin and hume can't breed, but I know that's a lie. Not everything has a reason. Some things just are, because they are."

"Wow. I'm learning so much today. You know my mama calls me baby green too?"

Tan-tan smiled and touched her chest. “My father used to call me baby green.”

“Andddd, we’re here.” Alexander stopped at a new cellar where a horrible stench emanated.

CHAPTER 6

"Lords and demons, Alex, when did you kill them?" Tan-tan growled through her slender green hand as she covered her mouth.

"Last night."

"Gahhh, let's fucking do this." Tan-tan blurred into the air like a summer haze and disappeared. "Never know if more of those fuckers showed up since last night"

She led them down into the dark cellar which contained no windows or light save the entrance. Alexander set the sacks of candy on the stairs and sparked a large fireball on his two fingertips. He reached behind him to touch Maja's face who tried to nuzzle him.

"Stay behind me at all times," he said as he scanned the room. Near the stairs, a corpse was slumped on the floor below a splatter of blood on the wall. The room stank of shit, blood, and barbecued meat. As they encroached further into the cellar, the other corpse, and the horrible metal table from the night before, came into view.

"Lords damn you, Alex. You fucked these

guy up. Good job," said Tan-tan's voice from the dim basement. The body near the table shifted which made Alexander and Maja flinch.

"I'll check this fucker. You check the sorry sack against the wall," said Tan-tan as she examined the body, making it appear to get up and peel its jacket off. Alexander walked over to the other body, squatted down, and extinguished his fireball to search the pockets.

"Can't see, stupid!" said Tan-tan. Alexander stood up and swirled his hands, conjuring a ball of blue flame. It grew and grew until it was nearly the size of Maja. Alexander passed the flame to her as if it was in a jar. Maja hesitated to touch it.

"It's safe, don't worry. Just reach out your hands," he said.

She reached for the flickering, sky-blue fireball and was pleasantly surprised to find it cool instead of hot. It weighed nothing, but she was able to guide it with her hands.

"Ha, you mastered coldfire?" said Tan-tan.

"Not mastered, but I'm getting better at it."

"You going to train to be a Lavamancer? How much more mastery do you think you need?"

Maja slowly walked over to the other dead body, afraid she might drop the swirling blue flame if that was even possible. The body on the floor turned and undressed with ghastly movements by Tan-tan's unseen hands.

"I was actually thinking, maybe Pyre Shaman?" said Alexander as he turned the corpse's pockets inside out to look for clues. He found a few pieces of silver which he had no shame in keeping for himself.

"Whaaa! You want to be a Healer like Mei? You know Pyre Shaman's have to throw themselves onto a Pyre as part of their test."

"I didn't know tha--TAN INCOMING!" screamed Alexander as he burst up the stairs after a shadow. He took the basement stairs two at a time after the man who had taken one step into the cellar and bolted after seeing Alexander. The man was fast, so Alexander whispered an incantation which sent sparks flying from his leather boots. The spark boots spell would have allowed him to gain in the chase, but the twisting alleys of The Steps did not allow him to reach full speed. His prey dodged through the convoluted roadways, either extremely familiar with the layout, or extremely lucky. Alexander was not completely familiar with the maze of filthy corridors even after a lifetime in Trinity. The alleys bent and turned so randomly behind the homes, there wasn't a moment Alexander had a clean shot at him with a fireball, and he didn't want to accidentally destroy any homes in the process.

"You better hope I don't catch you, fucker!" shouted Alexander in frustration, "I gutted your fucking friends, and you're next."

The man fumbled in his pocket and let some caltrops fall from his hand which Alexander blasted with a torrent of fire to clear away. His target stopped and pivoted on his heels, catching Alexander underarm around his torso. He used Alexander's momentum to throw him into one of the brick walls of the alleyway before fleeing again.

"FUCK! Fuck fuck fuck! Lordsdamit, fuck!" Alexander screamed then wheezed, the breath knocked out of him. He managed to his feet on shaky legs, using the wall for balance. His body ached from the toss, especially his shoulder. He walked back the way he came and collected the caltrops which were the only evidence as to who was behind the attack on Maja.

"Alex!" shouted Tan-tan from somewhere in the distance.

"I'm here," he shouted back as he caught his breath with his hands on his knees.

"Where?"

"Here, lordsdamit!."

"Did you catch him?" Her voice was closer now.

"No!"

Around the corner came Maja floating in the air with two sacks of candy. Tan-tan materialized with her long sinewy arms wrapped around Maja like she was a doll.

"Well, what in the hells happened?" said

Tan-tan.

"He got me close, got me off balance, then tossed me into a fucking wall."

"That's rough...well, it might be better you didn't catch him."

"What!" Alexander winced in disbelief. Tan-tan set Maja on the ground, reached in the satchel on her waist, and pulled out a small white octahedron a few inches in length. The gem was snowy but translucent and had a golden rune barely visible inside it.

"What's that?" said Maja as she looked up at Tan-tan.

"It's a guardian rune. Fucker is with The Guard." Alexander's face bunched up in disgust.

"Like The Guard, The Guard? Like the people that enforce the law?" Maja looked to Alexander then back at Tan-tan.

"Yes." He stared at the ground in frustration.

"Just because one of them's in The Guard, doesn't mean they all are," said Tan-tan as she pocketed the gem.

"If they are, how could we ever stop this?"

"Well, it won't be by kicking heads in. We'll have to expose them somehow...we should go talk to the people at The Starlight. They always print stories about corruption in Trinity. Let's see if they're interested in exposing this."

"And what if they're not? What if we're the only people that care about goblins? What then?"

Tan-tan did not reply immediately. The idea was heavy, and the weight of the nihilism showed on her face. Maja reached over and touched her leg. Tan-tan smiled down at her.

"In this whole time, has anyone that met Maja not grown to love her?" Tan-tan bent down to pinch Maja's cheek.

"Well, uh, Mort doesn't seem to like her..."

"Who cares what an enpaycee thinks? Rather have Mei back."

"Mei isn't coming back. I saw her today. I, I had to take Maja there. Was the only way to save her."

"And Mei didn't tell you to go fuck yourself? There's something special about this little person if she can make Mei tolerate you." Tan-tan scooped up Maja and nuzzled their faces together, making Maja giggle and nuzzle back. Alexander's face lightened. He gently placed his hand on Maja's head.

"If that guy was in The Guard too, they know what I look like now. I'm not going to be safe in town. After we go to the Starlight, I'm going to have to leave Trinity. It's not safe for me to be here anymore, and if they want to print this story, it's not going to get any safer."

"I'm sorry, Alex. I really am. You're one of the good ones," said Tan-tan as she stroked Maja's head. "Maybe I should keep an eye on her then?"

"Yeah, I guess you'll have to."

"You're leaving?" Maja was already in tears as she leapt from Tan-tan's arms and clung to Alexander's neck. Her face was a smear of tears and snot, and her lower lip trembled.

"I have to. That fucker is probably with The Guard. If they're involved, I won't be safe. They'll probably have me arrested for murder then executed. You're safe with Tan."

"But I want YOU!" wept Maja as she kissed his face and hugged him around the neck. "You're my lover. I love you. I want to be yours. I-I-I'll leave with you. I'll stay by your side. I'm yours."

Alexander pried her off and shoved her into Tan-tan's arms, his face twisted in anger "Don't you get it, you stupid little whore? They're going to kill me, and if they find you with me, they're going to kill you too. This isn't a fucking tale, this is real life. We need you alive. Lords damn both of you!"

He stormed off, marching several paces ahead of them to hide his tears. The three of them traveled through the residential parts of Trinity, out of The Steps, and into the Administrative District at the heart of the city. Tan-tan carried Maja the entire way, occasionally pressing her face into Maja's hair. The beat up homes of the hume Steps gave way to middle class homes with bright paint and glass windows. The cobblestone road lead them over the canal, and they entered the Administrative District of Trinity.

The buildings there were tall, multiple stories, and made from dark stone. None of them gave any indication of their purpose, but they were obviously intended for serious business. After passing a block of such buildings, they stepped into The Square. The central square of Trinity was a large open space, covered in pink and white bricks which created elaborate and interesting patterns on the ground. The Square was surrounded on every side by the largest and most imposing administrative buildings. The Central Palace, where the Lords and Vanguards administered to the city, dominated the northern quadrant, rising like a small mountain in the city. The architecture appeared to be from another world compared to the simple yet functional buildings of the rest of the city. Pointy spires punctured the sky mixed in with polished cobalt domes. Hundreds of Trinity banners with their three point crests wafted from every window hole and pole which gave the impression of a stationary ship ready to sail.

"I have the strangest feeling I've been here before," said Maja.

"You probably have. You probably came through here when your family immigrated here. How old were you during the Goblin Passage?" said Tan-tan.

"I was three when me and Mama came here. I don't remember much about it. I don't remember Greenlan. I barely remember my Daddy or my brothers..."

"What happened to them?" said Tan-tan as she squeezed Maja even tighter. "You don't have to say if it's too painful."

"Mama says Daddy died in the GP when it first started. When Trinity forced us out of Greenlan, we were separated from my brothers, and we have no idea what happened to them. I like to think they're out there somewhere, maybe helping take Greenlan back."

"That would be nice, huh? I'm sure you'll get to see Greenlan again someday. I never got to see it. I was born on Patriam. My father was a trader and moved here long before the Goblin Passage. He met my mom here too. He must have been very charming to marry a hume woman, right?"

Tan-tan and Maja shared a giggle and nuzzled faces.

"This is the place," said Alexander as he gestured towards a tall building with a large dome over the entrance. Atop the golden dome was a single, five-pointed star shimmering in the sunlight. Under it were two rows of stone columns guarding an open air entrance. Alexander looked around before entering and saw a pair of Guards in the city square watching them.

"You two draw way too much attention. I don't even think goblins are supposed to be in this part of town."

"It's not our fault we're drop dead sexy,"

said Tan-tan, making Maja giggle.

"So, what are we going to tell them?" Alexander huddled with Tan-tan and Maja to converse quietly.

"Well, just say there's a sterilization campaign against the goblin community, and we have a bunch of proof. Let them talk to Maja and fall in love with her cuteness, and if they're not convinced, we bring up The Guard," said Tan-tan.

"You think they'll be put off if we say The Guard is involved immediately?" said Alexander.

"No, I...I know The Starlight isn't afraid of Trinity. I read their pamphlets. They're really critical of the government. I don't know, I feel like if we go in saying The Guard is doing this, this, and this, then they might think we have some agenda."

"Right. Okay, yeah. Let's go tell our story. Her story." Alexander nodded towards Maja, and the three companions entered the Starlight headquarters. Once inside, they were immediately stopped by a pair of uniformed women. Their faces were stoic and their white uniforms were pristine. The uniforms were halfway between a mage's robe and a military uniform with golden thread epaulets. Alexander was not familiar with their class.

"Can we help you?" one of them asked as she stared through the group.

"Uh, yeah, we wanted to talk to an investigator about a...crime campaign taking place in The Steps." Alexander looked past them to see if anyone could help.

"Preferably a female investigator," Tan-tan chimed in. He shot her a glare then turned back to the twin female guards.

"We are interested in hearing from you," said the other guard who also did not make eye contact, "but we can't let all three of you in here. Especially not a Stalker and a Fire Mage. Our investigators have many enemies."

Alexander turned to Tan-tan and Maja. All of them seemed frustrated with the situation.

"Well, I'm not sending you in there alone. You'll probably end up blowing the investigator," said Alexander, looking at Maja who giggled at the insult.

"How about this." Tan-tan stepped forward which made the guards plant their feet, ready to repel an attack. "I'll surrender my weapons and poisons, then me and this little princess will come in and tell our story--"

"That plan is suitable," one of the guards answered faster than it could have been considered. Tan-Tan set Maja down and started to unload daggers and tiny vials from her belt and satchel which she handed over to the guards.

"Guess this is where we part ways, boss man." Tan-tan turned to Alexander and placed her hand on his shoulder before stepping in for a quick hug. After she let go, Maja reached up for a hug, whimpering and shuffling her feet as she started to cry. Alexander scooped the little person up, and she threw her stubby arms around his neck.

"I'm going to MISS YOU!" she howled through tears, her butt resting on his forearms. "I love you!"

"I'll miss you, too." Alexander pulled his arms around the sobbing girl and felt her tiny heart beating against his chest. He let out the heaviest sigh of his life, pried Maja off, and held her out for Tan-tan. Maja hid her face in Tan-tan's chest as he left the entry way.

CHAPTER 7

"Good luck, stay strong, Alex," Tan-tan called after him. Alexander clenched his jaw as he left, so the girls wouldn't hear him cry. He trusted Tan-tan to complete his quest, and he trusted the Starlight investigator to be charmed by Maja. As he walked down the receiving hall, he thought about that chubby little goblin sitting outside the bar. He thought about how his stomach dropped when he saw her strapped to that table. He thought about her big coppery eyes staring at him with hope and affection. The beautiful curves of her tiny body, how she made him feel like a man, and how she made him want to be stronger for her. Her warmth, and light, and touch.

Once he exited The Starlight headquarters, he ducked into the nearest alley and caught himself on the wall to cry. The tears flowed freely and his breath caught in his throat over and over. It felt like drowning. Taking several minutes to compose himself, he half walked, half ran to Mort's cellar. As he walked, he felt strangely nostalgic for the city he always resented. It was his home as much as anything could be called a home. He had friends here, good loyal friends. He had become a leader here. He helped people here. He gave back to his community. This sacrifice was worth it though. He was doing the right thing, and that thought gave his legs the strength to move and stay steady. Alexander dodged through the twisting alleys of The Steps to avoid any chance encounters with The Guard and finally entered Mort's cellar.

"Morty, you here?" he said as he stepped into the dim basement.

"You know I am," croaked Mort from the darkness as he lit the lamp on his operating table.

"Well, uhh....I gotta' get the fuck out of here. Asuna's in charge now. Tell Serana I didn't have time to tell her goodbye. Tell Lila, Lou, everyone else, good luck and stay strong." Alexander started up the stairs.

"Serana was looking for you," said Mort which made Alex stop.

"Tell her not to follow me. It's dangerous. I don't want her following me." Alexander left the cellar without any confirmation and hurried to his room at the bar. He used the back alleyways as much as he could, until he was forced to cross the cobblestones to enter the bar. The bar was nearly empty after midday. He hurried down the hall and up the stairs to his room without anyone noticing him. Inside his room he grabbed his ratty but reliable rucksack and started packing.

Few elixirs, never know when you might need them.

The guild fund, which he hesitated to take, but didn't want to make a second trip to Mort.

Some spare clothing.

Rations.

"Alex! So glad I finally caught you." Serana burst into his room with a huge smile and the fright of his life. He seriously considered knocking her down to flee, but resisted the urge.

"Hey, I heard the news. You're stepping down from the guild?" Serana stepped in for a hug which was not returned. Her considerable breasts pressed against his body.

"How could you possibly know that? I just told Mort ten minutes ago!"

She pulled a glowing blue octahedron from her pocket and showed it to him. Inside the gem was the guild symbol he had come up with years ago. Alexander palmed his face.

"I don't even own one of those! Why do YOU?" he nearly shouted. Serana smiled.

"I just want to, ya' know, participate fully in the guild. It's such a good group of people. I don't understand why you're leaving. Why are you leaving, Alex?" Serana kept her arms around him as she spoke. She had real concern in her delicate, olive-colored face.

"I can't tell you...all I can say is, you're not

safe with me. I really have to get going. I'm sorry to leave like this." He made to move past her, but she clung to him.

"Let me come with you! I'll stay in the guild, and then you can still keep tabs on everything. I can send Mort messages with this, ya' know?"

Alexander sighed.

"No, Serana, just no. You need to learn to take no for an answer. You're a good guildie and a loyal friend, but you can't come. That's the end of it." He lifted her arms off of him and made for the stairs.

"I'm coming whether you want me to or not." She ducked into her room and emerged with her large purse slung over her back. "Can't get rid of me that easy."

Serana grabbed his hand and grinned. He grumbled to himself as he led the way down the stairs.

"We're leaving Trinity. I can't stay in this city. It's not safe anymore."

"Well then, you're lucky you have me to protect you."

"I don't need protection," he said as they stepped out of the bar hand in hand and hurried for the closest alley.

"The Guard is after me. I have to leave Trinity until this all blows over."

"Oh my Lords, Alex! What did you do?" Serana gasped and squeezed his hand tighter.

He guided them through twisting alleys as they spoke.

"Found out The Guard was up to some shitty business. They very well might have seen my face, and they're probably already looking for me at this point. Tan-tan is talking to The Starlight about what I saw."

"Oh my! What did you see?"

"Some fuckers in The Guard were sterilizing a goblin girl. I stopped them, but they know I know now."

"Lords, that's awful! Are you okay?"

"Yeah," Alexander said somberly. The trek to the gates of Trinity passed through many different neighborhoods all of which were segregated by wealth. Different levels of cleanliness and architecture steadily flowed into each other until Alexander and Serana reached one of the great gates of Trinity. The portcullis hung high in the sky and left the gargantuan entryway free for traffic. The entryway was as wide as a city block and over a dozen stories high. He stopped to admire the masterwork as much as in awe of the engineering feat as in caution of the Guards who protected it. Two enormous weights hung off twin pulleys secured to the outer wall of Trinity to balance the weight of the gate.

"I never really believed in the Devs, but it's hard to believe any hume built that," said Serana as she squeezed Alexander's hand. "So what's the plan? Do we just make a run for it?"

"No...no, we'll wait until they call last wagon and calmly make for the gate. Just travelers from out of town heading home. We're not going to do anything that makes us look suspicious."

"What are we going to do once we're out of Trinity?"

"There's no we. I'm going to the Scoured Sands and onto the Blasted Mountains. I seriously doubt you want to go to such a lordsforsaken place. The only reason I'm going is to class change."

"I have plenty of summons to aid and protect me, and I have a Fey I captured a few years ago. I'll be fine."

Alexander seriously questioned this claim of Serana's like he questioned every claim she had ever made. Fey were impossibly rare and only ever seen, let alone captured, by the most accomplished Summoners. Still, with Serana, it was best to just play along instead of trying to constantly confront her on her endless lies.

"Regardless, this is too dangerous. Where I'm going is no place for you."

Serana pulled on Alexander's arm until he faced her. Her eyes were dark and serious with tears forming on the edges.

"I will follow you anywhere. I love you, Alexander Song."

Alexander took a deep breath through his nose. "Serana, I've told you countless times. I.

DO NOT. LOVE YOU. You're a sweet girl, but for Lords and demons sake, you need help. You need someone worth your time, that cherishes you the way you cherish me. This is sad, and I don't think it's fair you keep putting me in this position. If you insist on saying these things to me, I have no choice but to leave you in Trinity."

Her face was unreadable. She looked as if she had just sat through an inscrutable magic college lecture. Her lip started to tremble, and her body started to convulse. Her spine stretched and bent, making her hunch over. She planted her hands on the ground.

"Lordsfuck, not here! If you transform here, you're going to get me killed. Fuck's sake, stop!" said Alexander in his loudest whisper. Her Mage's gown tore apart at the seams, and she threw her head back in an earsplitting howl, forcing Alexander to cover his ears. Serana towered over him now. Her face protruded in a long lupine snout. Her hair was a wild mane of dark fur. She was not ugly, but she was not pretty. Her considerable breasts, now covered in fine fur, hung out over her torn gown, revealing purple-pink nipples.

"I'm sorry, Alex," she said in her sweet hume voice as she bounded into the street. "I'll always love you!"

A nearby woman shrieked at the mere sight of her. The remaining populace fled in every direction and knocked each other over in the process. Even a Guard fled with the civilians. The more hardy Guards near the gate lowered their spears and pointed them at Serana as they moved to surround her. Not one to waste a sacrifice, Alexander sprinted for the gate while their attention was squarely on the beast before them. Seeing him clear the gates, Serana slashed at the air around her a few times and ran for the gates too. A Guard flinched as she bounded towards him, allowing her to escape. It took her only moments to catch Alexander who was sprinting past the horse stables and wineries gathered around the road to Trinity.

"That was hilarious!" she shouted and let out a satisfying howl. "I was good, right?"

Alexander did not reply but instead ran into the woods beyond the winery. He caught his balance on an old twisting willow to catch his breath. His heart pumped furiously and not just from the mad dash.

"What in the hells is your malfunction!" he screamed at her. He wanted to shake some sense into her but hesitated when she was in her lycan form. Once again, she did not register his reproach and only looked at him hopefully.

"Could say thank you..." Serana looked at the ground and shuffled her paw in the dirt.

"For what? You could have been killed! I told you what my plan was, and you just completely ignored me! This is one of MANY reasons I don't quest with you anymore. You don't listen to orders. It's like there's something wrong with your brain." He had to catch his breath from all the shouting. He looked up and rolled his eyes when he saw his words were once again bouncing off of her.

"But I got you out of Trinity, right? That's all that matters? And now you can be a Pyre Shaman."

"Serana, just, lordsdam...I just...Lords! Is what I'm saying even registering with you? Do you understand why I'm upset? Do you even understand?"

"I mean, I know it was dangerous, but I'm a lot more capable than you think I am. And I love you and will protect you. Should let me be there for you. I want to be there for you."

Alexander punched the tree and immediately regretted it as pain shot through his hand and arm.

"How can I trust you? How? You don't listen. You're reckless. Did you even think about the effect you'd have on the lycan population?"

"Humes are going to hate lycans no matter what I do. I think you're just afraid to let me love you. You're afraid to let someone help you."

"Serana! Lords--just today me and Tan--no, forget it. I'm leaving. Goodbye, Serana." Alexander entered the road and marched north towards his destination. Serana scampered through the woods alongside the road, his silent guardian for the journey ahead.

CHAPTER 8

Tan-tan entered the Starlight with Maja in her arms, brimming with hopeful anticipation. She had read many of the succinct pamphlets about the events of Trinity, several of which regarded the mistakes and corruption in the city-state. This is where the magic happened.

The twin guards led them down a long stone hallway and into a large room with vaulted ceilings. The room contained several stone desks, almost all of which were empty. Bronze sconces hung from the ceiling held cold-fire which gave the space a comforting light. There were only narrow slats for windows like in an Archer's parapet. The guards, who Tan-tan began to suspect were also enpaycees, pointed her to a woman furiously writing and shuffling through papers at one of the desks. Her dark hair was up in a sloppy bun, and her glasses balanced precariously on the tip of her nose. Tan-tan stepped up to her to make her presence known.

"I don't have time for this shit," said the woman without looking up. "Tell Rosewater to stop sending me assignments, and get me another energy draught while you're up...now, please!"

Tan-tan was oddly pleased to see a woman condescend to someone, even if it that person was herself.

"I actually came to talk to you about a very serious problem in The Steps," said Tan-tan, squeezing Maja for reassurance.

"Well, write it down, give me your address, and I'll follow up with you in a few days. Buh-bye now!" The woman did not look up for even a moment. Tan-tan plopped Maja on the desk which made the investigator flinch. Tan-tan then dragged over a nearby chair to sit face to face with the woman.

"Yeah, we're not going to do that," she said as she lifted Maja into her lap.

"What...is it that you want?" said the woman who was flustered but resumed the work on her desk.

"Miss..?"

"Miss nothing. I'm not my father's name. My name is Amy. What is it that you want?" Amy looked up and was taken aback when she realized the person she was talking to was not exactly hume. Tan-tan smiled, having seen that look many times.

"Amy, my name is Tantra. This beautiful person in my lap is Maja. Last night some fuckers tried to sterilize her. My associate burned their faces off, and we want the people of Trinity to know what's happening in The Steps."

Maja waved and smiled at Amy who seemed to relax.

"Most people in Trinity would rather pretend The Steps don't exist," said Amy as she took a break from her work.

"Well it does exist, and there's a group going around torturing and mutilating goblin women. And I think The Starlight is the only thing that can make the government care." Tan-tan clenched her fist and squeezed Maja tighter. Amy chewed on her pencil as she studied the two women at her desk.

"Is there any way you can substantiate this story? I can't just take you at your word. I'm sorry."

Tan-tan was ready to drive her fist through Amy's face. Goblins were being tortured, and this bitch was acting like she was talking about a dog that had run away. A different guard in a similar white uniform approached them.

"Is everything alright here?" he asked in a monotone voice.

"Yes Peter, thank you. She's a just a bit... passionate. Some awful business down in The Steps."

The guard stepped away but not out of striking distance. Maja squirmed in Tan-tan's lap to get some air.

"You were the one sterilized?" Amy leaned

over to be face to face with Maja.

"No I...I was attacked last night, but Alexander saved me! He said I almost died, but Mei healed me! And now Tan-tan takes care of me."

Amy couldn't help but smile at Maja's innocent nature. She pulled up some papers and began taking what Tan-tan hoped were notes.

"Well, I think this story has hooves. I want to ride it. I'll need to speak with this Alexander person and Mei. Where can I find them?"

Tan-tan looked away across the room and lowered her brow in frustration.

"Well?" Amy looked at Maja for some indication.

"Alexander had to leave Trinity."

Amy stopped taking notes and set her pencil down.

"That's no good to me. I need this story fully corroborated, or I simply can't bring this to my boss. It's just the way we work. We're all about integrity at The Starlight."

"He's not here because of this." Tan-tan rummaged in her satchel, took out the guardian rune, and placed it on Amy's desk. "One of the guys he killed while saving Maja had this on him."

Amy stared at the gem like Tan-tan had just placed a severed head on her desk.

"You cannot be serious. Are you saying The Guard is behind this attack?" Amy snatched up her pencil and immediately started taking notes again.

"We don't know. This is all the hard evidence we have. Alexander has left Trinity in fear for his life. I'm staying behind to make sure this perfect little person gets justice." Tan-tan laid her cheek on Maja's head, and Maja reached up to touch it.

"Please tell me I can talk to this Mei person, the--" Amy checked her notes,"Healer? Please tell me I can talk to her."

"Mei? Yeah, yeah! She lives in Gold Town with all the rich humes. She's a very kind person. I'm sure she'll want to see justice for Maja."

"A female Healer in Gold Town? Can't imagine she'll be hard to find. Okay, great, perfect! Just let me get your stories, and I'll visit Mei tonight for an interview."

Maja calmly described her tale to Amy who scribbled furiously in her papers as sweat beaded on her forehead. She described, in brief, that she and Alexander had spent the night together, the kidnaping and the blood, ending up at Mei's home, returning to the cellar, and Alexander chasing the third man. Tan-tan felt her blood roil in her veins as Maja got to the bloody part of her story. The little person in her lap was a great comfort.

"There was a third man involved? Was he in the Guard?" said Amy, still scribbling notes.

"We don't know. Alexander said he couldn't prove it, but he knew hand-to-hand and had caltrops. It's not proof, but it sure is suspicious. You have to be an Acolyte to learn stuff like that. And you have to be an Acolyte to become a Guard..." said Tan-tan.

"Well this is great. Sorry, I mean, this is going to be a big story. I mean, if your Healer checks out, this could be huge. You girls are doing the right thing, especially you Maja. Thank you for coming to see me. Peter, come on, we're going to Gold Town."

Amy stood and shook Tan-tan's large powerful hand then Maja's tiny chubby hand. She gathered up the papers on her desk in a messy bundle against her chest and left the starlight with her guard.

CHAPTER 9

"You were so brave, little one." Tan-tan kissed Maja on the head.

"We have to get back to Mama now. She must be worried to death."

"Sure, baby green." Tan-tan carried Maja back to the hall where she regained her supplies then exited The Starlight. Their trip home was long and full of silence like most trips home. After a half hour of walking, they arrived at the goblin part of The Steps where Tan-tan set Maja down to walk and lead the way. She felt self-conscious as she towered over many of the goblin shacks until the neighborhoods gave way to the stacked housing.

"You could never fit in a goblin shack." Maja laughed as she stuffed candy in her face and offered Tan-tan some.

"No thank you. I don't eat candy."

Maja stopped and stared up at her. Her face was frozen in horror as if Tan-tan had just revealed some awful truth about humanity.

"That's the saddest thing I've ever heard," said Maja with a shudder before continuing the trek home. Tan-tan giggled and bent down to pat Maja on the head as they walked. Her stature drew stares from all the goblins they passed, especially the men who gazed at her but avoided eye contact. Finally, they stood outside the towering shacks that contained Maja's home.

"I guess this is goodbye," said Tan-tan with genuine sadness in her voice.

"It doesn't have to be. I just want to see Mama and drop off this candy for her. We can do something after--MAMA!" screamed Maja, darting past Tan-tan as she spied her mother coming around the corner. Her mother's slow sullen trod became a sprint when she heard her daughter's voice. They crashed into each other and fell into a deep embrace.

"Where have you been, baby green? I was so worried about you! Lords and demons, I didn't sleep a wink last night. I thought something happened to you!" Her mother sobbed with a smile. She refused to relinquish her daughter and bit her pointy ear with affection. Tan-tan's heart felt close to shattering as she watched the mother and daughter embrace so lovingly. What she would have given to hold her mother like that one more time...

"Mama, it's okay. I made some friends, and I met a guy. And I ate a bunch of candy and brought some home for you." Maja finally pulled away and led her mother to Tan-tan who hefted the sacks of candy on the ground.

"Oh! Oh my! How did you afford all this candy?" said her mother as she held onto Maja's hand. "What are these clothes? What did you do, Maja?"

"Mei bought them for me!" Maja reached in one of the sacks and handed her mother a tiny chocolate hume. Her mother took it but hesitated to eat it.

"I don't understand. Are you...are you Mei?" Her mother looked up at Tan-tan who smiled.

"No, ma'am. My name is Tantra. I'm a friend of your daughter."

"Then who is...why did Mei buy you all these things?"

Maja hesitated with the truth.

"Maja?" Her mother's tone reminded Tan-tan of her own mother when she had gotten in trouble as a child. Maja's mother bit into the chocolate as she awaited an answer.

"Well I, I met a guy last night, and he took me to Mei's house, and she thought I was adorable and gave us some money to spend because she felt bad about how mean humes are to goblins."

"Hume guilt..." said her mother, already digging in the sack for another piece of chocolate.

"Yeah, and then I met Tan-tan, and she's the nicest sweetest person I ever met. We're going to go into town later."

Tan-tan turned away to hide her blushing. Maja's mother eyed the two women in front of her.

"Well, as long as you're safe, baby green, that's all that matters to me. Are you sure two women will be safe going into Trinity after dark?" said her mother, already starting on her third piece of chocolate. Tan-tan laughed with satisfaction before she flipped a hidden dagger from her belt, slashed the air twice in a split second, and concealed the dagger once again.

"Your daughter is very safe with me. I would never let anything happen to her." Tan-tan squatted down face to face with Maja's mother to show how serious she was about protecting Maja. "I know Trinity is a dangerous place, but Maja is completely safe with me. I promise you."

Maja's mother smiled and reached up to touch Tan-tan's face who flinched away at the touch.

"Alright then. I'm just so glad my daughter is safe and has friends that care about her. Come help us take this candy home, would you?" Maja's mother reached in the sack for a fourth piece of chocolate and led them to the deepest reaches of the Steps to a towering stack of homes which almost reached the lip of the rotunda.

"I'll be right back." Maja touched Tan-tan's leg before she helped her mother carry the candy upstairs. Tan-tan stood outside the towering obelisk of rust and tried to determine how high it went. She examined her surroundings and glared at some goblin men who took too much interest in her. They quickly found a new place for their board game. Several minutes passed before she heard the metallic patter of Maja scampering down the rusty tower.

"Ready to go?" Maja looked up at Tan-Tan with a big grin.

"Yeah, I just need to stop at my room really quick."

The two women left the goblin part of The Steps and made their way into the hume neighborhoods. Tan-tan guided them to the cobblestone circuit and then back to a familiar bar.

"I've been here," said Maja.

"I know. I could hear you and Alex fucking across the hall last night. I stay here too."

Maja blushed at her words. Tan-tan scooped her up like a babe and walked into the bar. She carried her down that familiar dark hallway and made a right turn at the end.

"Before we go to my room, I want to watch you suck some hume dick," Tan-tan whispered in Maja's ear as she set her down in the treasure room. Maja waddled into the room and set up a little box to access the large hume dick hanging off the wall. Tan-tan rubbed her crotch in a slow circle and grabbed herself through her pants as Maja took the hume cock in her tiny green hand and kissed the head.

"Lords fuck..." whispered Tan-tan as she rubbed and pulled her nipples through her top. She carefully stepped into the room, using every ounce of her willpower to not devour Maja sexually as Maja rubbed and suckled the erect cock. Tan-tan knelt behind her and flipped her pleated skirt up along her waist, grabbing her chubby thighs. She kissed Maja's chubby butt then bit down on it, making Maja whimper and shuffle her feet on the crate. She carefully removed Maja's tiny black panties and watched a tendril of her juice drip into them. Tan-tan stuffed the tiny wet panties in her satchel and whispered in Maja's ear. "You don't get to wear panties anymore, you little slut."

Tan-tan's considerable hands enveloped Maja's small body as she pulled down the front of her dress-corset and kneaded Maja's chubby little breasts between her fingers. Her long powerful fingers pulled and massaged Maja's chubby teats, making her drip directly onto the crate. Tan-tan lowered her head and spread Maja's plump butt with her thumbs to reveal the tiniest asshole. She lapped at Maja's asshole, kissing it, licking it, and pressing her tongue into the tiny muscle. Maja's squirmed and let out a squeal which was muffled by the hume dick she drooled on. Tan-tan reached around Maja's thick thighs and played with her tiny green clit, massaging it with one calloused finger until Maja's legs trembled in orgasm.

Tan-tan sucked her middle finger and gently pressed it into Maja's vulnerable little asshole, exploring her insides. As her long powerful finger sunk deeper into Maja, her free hand pushed on the back of Maja's head, forcing the dick as deep as it would go down her throat. Tan-tan finger-fucked Maja's asshole and used her head to roughly masturbate the hume dick hanging off the wall. With the familiar knock from the wall, Tan-tan knew Maja was being force-fed cum. She held Maja's head in place for several seconds until the dick disappeared. Tan-tan spun Maja around and forced her tongue in her mouth, stealing the hume sperm Maja was given. She kissed Maja lovingly yet whorishly, letting some of the cum fall from her mouth and back into Maja's.

Maja's eyes were unfocused, and she couldn't form words. Her brains were thoroughly gone. She could still feel the sensation of Tan-tan's long powerful finger inside her even though it wasn't. She knew there was cum in her mouth, but Tan-tan had stolen most of it. She knew she had orgasmed. Tan-tan was biting and sucking her breasts now. She pet Tan-tan's head as she nursed, loving the velvety sensation of Tan-tan's short cropped hair under her fingers.

Tan-tan sat on her butt with her legs around the crate. She laid Maja on the crate and buried her face in Maja's tender thighs, kissing the insides of each one and sucking them. Then she devoured Maja's pussy, sucking the juices from her. Furiously, she kissed and sucked her tiny green clit, focusing all her attention on it. One of her hands was on Maja's face, and Maja sucked her finger with whorish need. Tan-tan inhaled the soft, musky smell of Maja's blue pubic hair. Maja's whole body flinched and bucked. Her juices sprayed out in a cascade, covering Tan-tan's face. The two goblin women lay there overcome with emotions, brains soft and mushy like wet bread.

Tan-tan clumsily removed her leather pants and tossed them against the wall along with her vest and tunic. She sat against the wall completely naked, heart beating furiously, on the verge of tears. Maja sat up, her brains still partially gone. Her heart jumped seeing Tan-tan naked against the wall. Her powerful, slender body was gorgeous. Her thighs were narrow but powerful with muscular contours. She had well defined abs, and even her vulva was rigid and toned. Two, tiny, perky breasts hung under her broad shoulders. She looked incredibly sad.

"Please beat me up," cried Tan-tan, "I want you to hurt me. Please hurt me, Maja."

Maja understood that need on a fundamental level. She helped herself down off the crate and walked over to Tan-tan, slapping her in the face. Tan-tan cried silently but didn't flinch or try to stop it. Maja slapped her again, as hard as she could. Tan-tan played with her hairless toned pussy.

"You can punch me. It's okay."

Maja hesitated for a moment and punched Tan-tan in the eye with her tiny fist. Tan-tan sniffled but continued masturbating.

"Tell me I'm shit. Tell me how weak I am."

Maja had never said a mean word in her life and had some difficulty getting started.

"Shut up." Maja kicked Tan-tan in her drippy pussy. Tan-tan flinched in pain but kept masturbating. Maja kicked her between the legs again and knocked her head against the wall. Then she lifted up Tan-tan's tiny firm breasts which barely moved and were exceptionally firm.

"Look how little your breasts are." Maja attempted to sound cold. Tan-tan was crying, but her fingers still worked her clit.

"I'm barely a woman," said Tan-tan through tears, covering her breasts with her arm. Maja pulled Tan-tan up and gestured for her to get on all fours. Then she spanked Tan-tan's tiny, firm butt. Each spank drew a coo from Tan-tan's lips. Her tiny breasts hung off her chest and Maja reached around to fondle them.

"They're so small. No one could want you." Maja fed Tan-tan her own insecurities about her appearance. Tan-tan reached between her legs and massaged her clit again, whimpering and sniveling. Maja climbed on top to ride her like an animal.

"Your room is upstairs?" said Maja as she planted her hands on Tan-tan's shoulders.

"Yes," whispered Tan-tan.

"Then crawl there with me on your back."

"What if someone sees me?" Tan-tan's heart was racing.

"Then you better go fast," whispered Maja. Tan-tan took a deep breath and crawled out the doorway as fast as she could. The first hallway was as dark and as empty as usual. Her mind was somewhere else, but her fears were right there in the hall. The experience was all so surreal, like everything was happening at quarter time while also racing past her. She crawled to the next hallway, and at the end, near the entrance, were two hume men talking. Tan-tan crawled as fast as she could for the stairs, keeping her eyes on the men. She was acutely aware of her nakedness as she left a trail of juices from the treasure room. Just as she reached the stairwell, the men casually glanced down the hallway and saw her. Two hume men saw a naked half breed being ridden by a half naked goblin woman. Tan-tan bolted up the dark stairway as fast as she could on all fours, scraping her shins as she went. At the top of the stairs, she dove for her bedroom, slammed the door behind her, and latched it. The whole thing was a blur. Her powerful heart pounded against her rib cage and threatened to explode. She was dripping profusely down the inside of her thighs.

"Good girl," said Maja, lifting herself up off the floor. Tan-tan knelt for her like a paramour.

"Please abuse me," said Tan-tan, her voice cracked and trembling. She would do anything for Maja at this point. Maja held her head and kissed it, petting her. She gently nibbled on Tan-tan's ear as she held her head. Her sweaty breasts hung in Tan-tan's face.

"You're a slut, and no one will ever love you." Once again, Maja tested out her own insecurities on Tan-tan. Tan-tan cried and played with her nipples.

"Can I touch myself?" Tan-tan asked through tears. Maja nodded. Tan-tan sat on the ground and furiously played with her hard clit, crying quietly as she massaged it in circles at a lightning pace. Maja watched in fascination as another female masturbated in front of her.

"You're a disappointment to your parents. Imagine what they would think if they knew you were doing this. Their daughter, a slut," said Maja, helping Tan-tan get there. Tan-tan slammed the back of her head against the door, and her long beautiful legs kicked out as she reached orgasm. A low guttural sound escaped her mouth as if she was suffering a muscle cramp. After she finished, Tan-tan crawled into her bed, wrapped herself in the blanket, and cried hysterically. Maja lifted herself onto the hume-sized bed and dug into the blankets to be face to face with Tan-tan.

"I'm sorry I'm such a disappointment!" said Tan-tan, crying into Maja's hair as she wrapped her arms around her.

"No, no you're fine. I like you. This was very kinky."

Tan-tan attempted to compose herself as she sniffled and looked into Maja's big copper eyes. Maja kissed her on the nose and smiled. Tan-tan smiled back.

"I didn't mean to put this on you, just watching you suck that hume off, I lost myself. I get to this point where I can't think rationally, and I'm just this dumb, needy whore that wants the shit kicked out of her."

"I understand. It happens to me too. I lose my brains, and I'll just do anything."

"It happens to you too?"

Maja nodded, kissing Tan-tan's nose again.

"Thought it was just something wrong with me..."

"I think it's a goblin thing. I swear, one time Mama came home, and she's usually so wise and reasonable, but she was so goofy. I think she was with a man."

"But I'm not a goblin...not really."

"You are to me. You have the ears and the skin."

"Why are you so fucking sweet?" Tan-tan nuzzled her face into Maja's.

"I guess it's all the candy."

Tan-tan smiled.

"What are we going to do now?" said Maja. Tan-tan took a long soulful look at her.

"I want you in my life, Maja. You're sweet and beautiful and sensual. Even if we can't be like Lorena and Tantra Charbelcher, I still want you as a friend."

"I want you as a friend too, Tan-tan."

Tan-tan melted hearing Maja say her name.

"So we stick together," said Tan-tan, resting her face against Maja's. "Tomorrow we'll go down to The Starlight and see if Mei cooperated. I hope she did."

"Mei is a good person."

"Yeah she is."

"Tan-tan?"

"What is it, baby green?"

"I-I uh, wanted to ask, well I wanted to know, how can I be powerful like you and Alexander? I mean, he can make fire and you can use a dagger. I don't want to be a burden forever. I want to be able to fight. Can you show me how?"

"You want to learn a class?" Tan-tan shifted so she was spooning Maja's tiny chubby body.

"A class?"

"Yeah like Fighter, Archer, Acolyte, like every guildie ever."

"I-I guess so. What class are you?"

"I'm a Stalker."

"Well then I want to be that."

Tan-tan smiled again, squeezing Maja against her strong naked body.

"We should see a class interpreter. Find out what class suits you."

"Did you go to an interp-uh-ter?"

"Yes, baby green. We did a lot of work before we found out what suited me."

Tan-tan rested her head on Maja's and dozed off. Maja felt very safe and feminine with Tan-tan's powerful arms wrapped around her.

CHAPTER 10

Alexander was not a quarter mile down the road from Trinity when he dove back into the woods to avoid a mounted Guard coming up the road. He trekked as deep into the wilderness as he could while still keeping sight of the road to make sure the Trinity Guard had not pursued him. The Guard road a shaggy brown archon and continued his route down the road, not even bothering a glance in Alexander's direction.

"What are you runnin' from, hun?" came a woman's voice from behind him.

"Serana, I told you I--lordsdamit! What are you!" shrieked Alexander as he spun away from the female form and conjured a fireball in his palm.

"Whoa! Hey now. I don't like fire," said the woman, putting her hands up. She appeared similar to a hume woman but not completely. Her hair was a cascade of emerald green moss. Two eyes sparkled like clear ponds in the sun but had no irises or pupils. Her breasts were like two swollen gourds hanging off her bare chest. She had a soft stomach which gave way to a mossy pubis. Her hips were thick, and she did not appear to be ashamed of Alexander's eyes on her.

"You're a dryad, aren't you?" said Alexander, extinguishing his fireball.

"That's what humes call me."

"Whatever it is you need, I can't help you. I have a long ways to go." Alexander turned and started for the road again.

"If you're trying to get away from here, I can help you with that. The Forest holds many secrets, many hidden paths." The dryad approached and placed her arms on Alexander's shoulders.

"I'm going to the Blasted Mountains. How close can your 'paths' take me?"

"I can put the Scoured Sands on your horizon," said the dryad as she pressed her naked body against him. In the back of his mind, he could hear the calls of birds, the trickle of flowing streams, and the sighing wind. He became aroused against his control.

"I'm assuming you want something in exchange." Alexander wanted to pull away from her but couldn't will his legs to move.

"All I want is your seed. I could take it from you if I wanted, but that would ruin the air of your primal masculinity. I'd rather you put it in me," cooed the dryad as she bit her lower lip and covered her hanging breasts. She knelt on the ground and kissed Alexander's erection through the material of his pants. He placed his hand on her mossy head and tried to imagine Maja and the way she had gagged on his dick. Her tears and drool had made her soft face gorgeous.

The dryad tugged Alexander's pants down and pressed her green lips to his swollen, pink cockhead. She tilted her head back and took his full length into her mouth. Her tongue was like a flower petal caressing his cock. She easily swallowed his entire length which allowed him to push into the back of her throat. His hips moved back and forth, gently fucking her mouth. The sparkling pools of her eyes stared up at him as he made love to her mouth. Her tongue flicked back and forth through the opening of his urethra, making him shiver. She pulled back to nuzzle her face into his crotch, kissed his hanging balls, and nuzzled her nose into them. She kissed each of his balls individually, sucked one into her mouth, and then his whole sack. She drooled and sucked on it with lust, his swollen cock hanging over her face. She went deeper, her flower petal tongue trying to find his asshole. She knelt lower, under him, and kissed his asshole and tongued at it. Alexander gripped his cock to stop himself from cumming on the forest floor.

"I want you inside me." The dryad lay on the ground and opened her thick thighs to reveal tiny flowers growing in her pubic moss. She spread her moss to reveal the green-pink folds of her labia which dripped copious amounts of nectar. Alexander knelt on the ground and turned her shockingly light body over. He positioned her so her fat butt hung in the air, and her face pressed against the ground. His thoughts returned to Maja and her fat green butt. He guided his aching cock into the dryad's drooling slit and gripped her hips which were firm like melon rind. He fucked her quickly and with anger, wanting to finish his task. His frustrations boiled in his mind, and he took it out on the dripping dryad who cooed and whimpered with every thrust. He slapped her plump ass making it jiggle, and she pushed her fat butt back into him. Her nails dug into the ground, and flowers sprouted from the soil around them. Long tendrils of grass and tiny wildflowers filled the bare forest floor. He smacked her ass again.

"Destroy me, hume. Destroy me," she cried as he fucked her.

Serana knelt behind a large fallen tree to watch the dryad suck Alex's cock. Her heart raced faster than it ever had before as she watched another woman fellate her boyfriend She removed her tattered panties and massaged her furry sheath until her red-pink cock poked out. She laid her chest against the fallen timber, so she could simultaneously watch Alex and touch her cock. She was outraged another woman would even touch her boyfriend but was overcome with sexual lust to see his dick in her mouth. She imagined it was actually herself who was loving his dick as she carefully massaged her canine cock through her sheath. She took great care not to touch her glistening pink cock directly which was extremely sensitive, instead using her furry sheath to masturbate. She continually sprayed watery lycan cum against the side of the fallen tree as Alex fucked the dryad's mouth.

"Why can't you love me like that, Alex?" she said to herself. More watery sperm splashed against the dead tree as Serana's cock pushed further out of her sheath. Now Alexander had the dryad face down in the dirt as he fucked and smacked her. All Serana ever wanted was for Alex to love her and take her like that. She would have given anything in the world to switch places with that dryad. A puddle of cum formed on the forest floor as she continued to play with her canine dick. She pinched her nipple hard and cupped her breast, imagining Alex's hands on her. She imagined his fleshy hume cock in her, pounding her, making a proper woman of her with his genitals. Tears soaked into the fur on her face and more cum soaked into the earth. Small pleasant orgasms rolled through her cock and hips over and over.

Alex lurched over the dryad and stopped thrusting. His hips spasmed and his face twitched hilariously. He came inside her! Serana pumped out the last of her cum and sat on the ground, facing away from the action. Her mind was a maelstrom of emotions and desires. She would make him love her. She knew what he needed now. He could fuck anyone he wanted as long as she was the most important person in his life.

Alexander gasped and fell backwards after filling the dryad with his sperm. She lay on her side in a crumpled heap with a mischievous smile.

"I love the feel of thick hume seed coating my insides," she said, touching above her mossy mound. "Humes have the thickest seed of any animal. It's an exquisite feeling."

"I gave you what you wanted...show me the secret path to the Scoured Sands." Alexander tucked his wet and sensitive dick away and stood up as he straightened his clothing.

"Sure, hun. Follow me." The dryad stood with one graceful motion and strolled deeper into the Great Northern Forest as afternoon turned to dusk. Alexander took care to step around the flowers which had sprung up during their exchange and followed the dryad. As they walked deeper and deeper into the woods, the atmosphere changed in intangible ways. The dryad took turns around trees and stony outcrops seemingly at random. At each random turn the world seemed to pass over and through Alexander like an invisible fog. A massive sense of distance between him and the city grew in his subconscious. He felt the passage of many years and lifetimes as he walked. He began to suspect they were no longer in the same world as before. His sperm slowly trickled out of the dryad as she walked, making the inside of her thighs stick together.

"We're very close now." The dryad looked over her shoulder and smiled at him. Alexander remained stoic. They came upon a moss-coated, half-buried cave: a natural structure older than all time, like the eye socket of a great beast protruding out of the ground.

"Sleep here tonight." The dryad gestured towards the cave.

"What trick is this?" said Alexander, lowering his brow in anger.

"You have given me more than I could have possibly imagined. Trust me to uphold my end of our bargain." She nodded towards the cave then approached him. Her hand grabbed his dick which instantly rose to attention. Her lips on his tasted like honey and flowers and fresh water.

"Thank you, love. I'll never forget what you did for me." She released his dick and wandered back the way they came. Alexander sighed and crawled into the cave which wasn't even high enough for him to stand in. He lit some coldfire which didn't do much to disperse the invading darkness of the night. He thought about

Maja and Tan-tan. He missed them a lot and had to convince himself he would see them again someday. The city and his friends seemed like an unnaturally distant memory after following the path of the dryad. He had seen them just earlier that same day, but it now seemed like years since he had spoken to them or looked upon their faces. At least there was Serana...

"I know you're out there," Alexander shouted to the darkness, guessing there was a fifty percent chance Serana would still stalk him after his encounter with the dryad. He heard the soft crunching of dead leaves and saw her black silhouette appear in the darkness.

"I know you saw what happened," said Alexander.

"I still love you," she said as she sat by the coldfire.

"I don't love you, Serana. I worry about you, but I don't love you."

"Just let me have this," she said as she crawled behind him and wrapped her arms around him. They fell asleep that way and woke the next morning as Alexander felt himself dripping with sweat. His head rushed with pain as he opened his eyes to a blinding desert landscape. They were now in an identical cave but in a small stand of palm trees. Beside them was a crystal clear pond, and they were on the outskirts of a desert. In the distance was the edge of a forest. Alexander squeezed his eyes and opened them to make sure he wasn't dreaming. He gently shook Serana awake who licked at his hand with her long, coarse, canine tongue and smiled at him.

"Serana, we're not in Trinity anymore."

CHAPTER 11

Tan-tan awoke to the wonderful sensation of Maja stirring in her arms. She kissed the back of her head and cupped her furry pussy as she pressed Maja's naked body against her tight, powerful frame. She gently masturbated Maja awake, letting her tiny clit slip over and through her long calloused fingers. Maja gently bit down on her arm and squirmed in the bed, dripping into her hand.

"Morning, beautiful," said Tan-tan as she kissed Maja's head again and slipped a finger inside her. Maja's chubby tummy pressed into her palm as Tan-tan fingered her. Her juices dripped down the back of her hand as Maja grabbed at the bed sheets, whining through clenched teeth.

"Come for me, baby green. Come for mama."

Upon hearing those words, Maja spasmed and let out a long squeak. Tan-tan threw off the bed sheets to gaze upon Maja's tiny body sprawled out before her. She looked like a wounded animal, gasping and unable to flee. Her soft tummy rose and fell, and her juices dripped down the inside of her thighs and into the sheets. Tan-tan felt that visceral roil inside her hips that said this was the hottest thing she had seen up until this point in her life. That roil said she was going to devour Maja's body and brains. She clenched her fist and took a deep breath to regain her composure.

Tan-tan hunched over Maja like a carnivore and kissed her tiny mouth then her chest. She kissed her little tummy then the trail of pubic hair leading from her perfect belly button to her pussy. She buried her nose in the fur and the maddening smell. She smelled like a woman, an animal, sex, mothers, and insane desire all rolled into one. Tan-tan sucked Maja's miniature clit which made her squirm and push against her head. Tan-tan easily pinned her short chubby arms and had her way with Maja, devouring her defenseless slit that tasted of candy and animal musk. She was voracious as she accidentally inhaled Maja's juices up her nose, tasting her prey in the back of her throat. Maja sounded like a dying animal as she cried out. Tan-tan rolled her own erect nipples between her fingers and pulled on them. She stumbled backwards against the wall and sat on the floor, reaching down to touch her clit which pulsed with ache.

"Come here, baby green," said Tan-tan as she played with her nipples. Maja composed herself then managed to climb off the bed and onto the floor. Tan-tan was as needy as she had ever been in her life.

"Tell me something filthy. Anything. Like really depraved. Please..." Tan-tan was nearly in tears. She rubbed her clit in quick circles and took in the reality of Maja's copper-colored eyes on her.

"Oh, uhhm, Alexander came inside me."

Normally Tan-tan didn't care to hear about her guild leader's sexual exploits, but her brains had left her which allowed her sexual need to devour the secret. She stopped to play with her nipples again, twisting and pulling them harder.

"Keep going, you're doing great. Filthier."

"I uh, sometimes when I lose my brains, I want my mama to watch me have sex and judge me..." Maja reached down to touch her clit too, not seeming to realize she was doing so. She plopped on the floor and masturbated with Tan-tan.

"I've never told anyone that..."

Tan-tan clenched her teeth and worked her clit with urgency. She was riding the wave now, her depravity wave. It had to be darker and filthier until she crashed and orgasmed.

"You're a bad girl, Maja," was all Tan-tan could think to say. Her critical thinking had flown away faster than a cannonball. Maja looked away as her chubby fingers did their job.

"I-I-I-I want a hume to make me have sex with my mama!" Maja blurted out, reaching another chirping orgasm. Tan-tan's orgasm hit her faster than her brain could register the words. She spurted on the wood floor, throwing her head back against the wall.

"Tantra, you up, babe?" Asuna called from the hallway.

In the half second between climax and her girlfriend's voice, Tan-tan grabbed Maja and stuffed her into the blankets on the bed before a new realization made her freeze. Her clothes were gone! They were still in that lordsdam treasure hole downstairs.

"Uh, yeah, babe. I just woke up!" Tan-tan unlatched the door without thinking; apparently her brains weren't completely back yet. In the doorway stood Asuna. She was slender with subtle curves covered by a crimson body suit that encompassed everything but her ashen grey arms and face. Her charcoal hair sat behind her shoulders revealing a warm smile that grew upon seeing Tan-tan.

"Hee! Oh my Lords, Tantra! Guess you weren't expecting me? Can I get a hug though?" Asuna playfully shuffled her feet.

"Uh, yeah, sure." Tan-tan stepped in to hug her girlfriend with one arm. Asuna threw her arms around Tan-tan and squeezed her tight. Her tiny firm breasts hung in Asuna's face due to their height difference. Asuna inhaled her scent.

"Smells like sex in here, babe," Asuna said half playfully as she looked past Tan-tan.

"Heh, yeah...I was...I was masturbating before I got dressed..." Tan-tan tried to sound embarrassed. Asuna giggled and kissed her cheek.

"Were ya' thinking about me, babe?"

"Mmm, you know it," Tan-tan lied as she squeezed her girlfriend's soft butt with both hands.

"Unhand me!" Asuna said with a laugh and slapped her hand away. "I'm going to order breakfast downstairs, babe. Want anything?"

"I'm sure whatever you order me will be fine, babe," said Tan-tan with a grin, making Asuna blush.

"Love ya, babe." Asuna blew a kiss and left for the downstairs bar.

"Love you too..." Tan-tan said to herself as she closed and latched the door. She sat on the bed and thought about the stupid situation she had gotten herself into.

"You can come out now," said Tan-tan as she pulled some of the blankets off the bed. Maja emerged from the bedding and sat beside Tan-tan.

"Who was that?" said Maja with no accusation in her voice.

"That was my girlfriend...I should have told you..."

"Why do you want to have sex with me if you have a girlfriend?" Once again there was only curiosity in her voice, nothing judgmental.

Tan-tan sighed and looked at the perfect tiny person sitting next to her.

"I want both of you. You're a beautiful, young, goblin woman. You make me want to do crazy things. I want to fuck you every fucking day. You're intoxicating. But Asuna is warm and understanding and smart and beautiful in her own way. I love her, but I love you too. Is it so wrong to love two people at the same time? I can't control who I love."

Maja sat on the edge of the bed swinging her stubby legs and thought about what Tan-tan said.

"I mean, I love you, and I love Mei, and Alexander and Mama. I guess it's okay."

"No Maja...I mean I love you and Asuna like wives. Like, I would be happy married to either or both of you. I know you're a sweet loving person, but I'm talking about romantic love."

Once again Maja stared at the floor, processing what was said.

"Well I, I'll be your girlfriend if it makes you happy. Alexander will always come first though. I love him very deeply. But I can be here for you...ro-man-tic-ally."

"I would like that."

"But...why did you hide me from Asuna then? Are you ashamed of me?" said Maja, grabbing at Tan-tan's hand. Tan-tan squeezed it.

"No! Oh no! Baby green! You're the best thing that's ever happened to me. I just think

Asuna will feel hurt if she thinks I'm choosing you over her."

"So she's your number one?"

"Yeah...she is. She deserves it."

"Well, then Alexander is my number one, and Asuna is your number one, and we still have each other. Everything has worked out, right?"

"Yeah, uh, just need to bring it up with her. And you need to get dressed and go downstairs to get my clothes from the treasure room."

"Treasure room?"

"You know...with the dicks in it?"

"Ohhhh! Okay!" Maja leapt off the bed and quickly dressed herself. Tan-tan helped her with the lacing of her corset and her garter straps.

"Right back!" said Maja as she scampered from the room. She was gone only a moment as Tan-tan waited naked and impatient on the bed until Maja's light footsteps came down the hall. She entered the room, handed Tan-tan her clothes, and stared at Tan-tan as she dressed.

"What?" said Tan-tan, looking behind her then back at Maja.

"Your body is so beautiful. I wish I was tall and thin like you."

"Aww, baby green! Don't say that. I love your cute chubby body. It gives me bad thoughts," said Tan-tan with a grin, not dressing herself just yet. Her sexual appetite quickly registered the fact Maja was fully clothed and she was completely naked in front of her. She was wet again. She wanted to bend over and have Maja scrutinize her entire body and put her on a leash like a hound, but thoughts of Asuna downstairs quickly brought her brains back. She was beyond relieved to find the guardian rune still in her satchel. After dressing, Tan-tan left the room with Maja in her arms.

"Asuna is a very nice, very intelligent person. I'm sure she'll love you. But could you not mention we had sex? It would really hurt her feelings."

"I-I don't understand...."

"Just please promise me." Tan-tan stopped at the stairs to look directly at Maja.

"I promise."

CHAPTER 12

At the bottom of the stairs, Tan-tan set Maja down and they followed the hallway to the bar. Asuna was seated at a table in the back, away from all the windows. She wore a long dust-colored cloak pulled around most of her body. Aside from her, there were only four people in the bar besides the barkeeper, all of whom were old humes enjoying breakfast that morning. Asuna waved to them from the corner, and they joined her at the booth.

"And who may I ask are you?" Asuna looked at Maja who had help from Tan-tan getting into the booth. Tan-tan scooted next to Asuna and kissed her cheek, making her grin.

"I'm Maja. Nice to meet you," said Maja with a smile. Asuna smiled back.

"Well you are truly beautiful, Maja. How... do you know Tantra? I assume you're staying at the bar too?"

Tan-tan stared wide eyed as Maja hesitated with the question.

"She's uh--actually the newest member of our guild!" Tan-tan cut in, trying to sound casual. "She joined yesterday, and Alexander put her up at the bar. He hasn't invited her yet. You know how he gets about that stuff. And...I guess he won't for awhile. He had to leave Trinity yesterday."

"I know," said Asuna indifferently.

"How do you already know?" Tan-tan grasped Asuna's cold ashen hand and rubbed the back of it with her thumb.

"Well...was trying to hold onto the secret as long as possible, but Alexander made me the new guild leader!" said Asuna as she turned to hug Tan-tan.

"Babe, that's wonderful."

"I hope everyone is okay with a female guild leader..."

"Fuuuuck them, you're smart, and beautiful and powerful. If they don't like it, they can fuck right off!"

"I'm glad you're here to support me, babe." Asuna squeezed Tan-tan's hand and kissed her cheek.

"Do you know why Alexander left?" said Tan-tan as she pulled Asuna in tighter.

"No, he didn't say, and Mort is all but useless with information."

"Well, the thing is, The Guard is after him."

Asuna's eyes widened as she stared at Tan-tan. Maja swung her legs back and forth restlessly on the edge of the booth.

"My lords! What did he do?"

"Here you ladies go!" The barkeeper startled them, setting down identical plates of food in front of Asuna and Tan-tan. "Toasted bread, eggs, bacon, and some butter. Ya'll set?"

Maja whimpered as the greasy, sizzling food was laid out before them.

"You can have some of mine. It's okay," said Tan-tan as she tousled Maja's hair.

"I'm sorry, sweetie. I didn't know you would be eating with us," said Asuna, "you order whatever you want, my purse."

"What kind of candy do you have?" Maja squirmed in her seat and grabbed at the table. The barkeeper touched the back of his head and forced a smile.

"Sorry, little girl, we don't really serve candy here. My woman makes some excellent preserves though."

"What are preserves?" Maja stood up in the booth then sat down without even realizing it.

"Well, it's like mashed up old fruit with sugar." The barkeeper looked at the other women for some clue to placate Maja.

"I like sugar..." Maja said to herself, looking at the table.

"Why don't I bring out some toasted bread and a few preserves to try?"

"That sounds wonderful, thank you," said Asuna. The barkeeper nodded and returned to the kitchen behind the bar.

"Ya' know, just because you're a goblin

doesn't mean you need to eat candy for every meal," said Tan-tan. Maja flinched and stared at Tan-tan as if she had just questioned the very fabric of reality.

"Well, I disagree."

"Here try this." Tan-tan held out a piece of glistening bacon near Maja's mouth. Maja eyed her suspiciously, then eyed the bacon even more suspiciously before carefully biting into it.

"Well?" said Tan-tan. Asuna and her both watched for a reaction.

"It will do...for now..." said Maja begrudgingly, taking the bacon in both hands and chomping on it. Asuna couldn't help but giggle as she hid her face in Tan-tan's neck.

"Isn't she the cutest thing ever?" Tan-tan cupped her girlfriend's face. Asuna looked up at her.

"Not as cute as you," said Asuna with a grin that made Tan-tan blush. "But wait, why did Alexander leave the city? You said The Guard was after him. What did he do?"

"Well...it's not so much what he did as what The Guard did," said Tan-tan as she watched Maja chomp down the last bite of bacon.

"I don't understand," said Asuna.

"Do you remember when Alexander said he wanted to investigate the rumors of forced sterilization in The Steps?"

"Of course."

"Well...he found some people doing it...to Maja. He killed them and saved her, and at least one of them was in The Guard."

Asuna's eyes glistened as she lunged across Tan-Tan to hug Maja against her body.

"You poor thing, are you okay?" She was in tears as she held Maja against her like a doll.

"Yeah! Alexander saved me. And Mei healed me!" Maja did not appear to mind being hugged.

"You poor creature. The horrible things humes do to other people. It's unforgivable." Asuna's irises changed from a dreamy violet to a flickering crimson.

"Babe, you're a hume," Tan-tan reminded her, "So am I, technically."

"Still...oh, you poor thing. If you need anything, ANYTHING, you just ask me okay? We're going to take care of you. Right, babe?"

"Right..."

"But why do you think The Guard is involved?" Asuna allowed Maja to climb over Tan-tan's lap and return to her seat.

"Have toasted bread and the preserve sampler plate!" The barkeeper barged in again, startling the three of them before he set down a plate of toasted bread and colorful jams.

"Thank you," said Maja.

"Such a polite girl. Can I get you ladies anything else?"

"No, but thank you," said Asuna. The barkeeper returned to his spot behind the bar. Tantan looked around, eyeing the senior citizens in the bar with suspicion. She carefully removed the guardian rune from her satchel and kept it under the table. Asuna's eyes lit up.

"I found this on one of the guys Alexander killed when we went back to investigate."

"He killed one!" said Asuna, drawing glances from the other patrons before lowering her voice to a whisper. "You didn't tell me he killed a Guard."

"I just did, babe."

"Yeah but...this is messed up. We have to do something about this. Tell someone."

"We already did. Me, Maja, and Alexander went to The Starlight yesterday and talked to an investigator. She believed us and supposedly interviewed Mei who healed Maja after the attack."

"It must have been horrible if you had to get Mei involved..." said Asuna who watched Maja stuff jam soaked, toasted bread in her face as fast as she could.

"Alex said it was pretty bad. Me and Maja were going to go to The Starlight and see what the investigator turned up. You can come if you want to."

"Of course I'll come!" said Asuna, smiling down at Maja who was sucking jam from her fingers.

"Not as good as candy, but it'll do," said

Maja, smiling up at Asuna. "Thank you for breakfast."

"Oh, of course, sweetie. Don't worry about it."

"And I wanted to take Maja to see a class interpreter after The Starlight. She's still a Novice and doesn't have a strong idea of what she wants to be."

"Hee, sounds like an Ultimate Novice." Asuna giggled.

"Come on, babe, I want her to have a real class, a sense of purpose, she wants to make real contributions. Right, Maja?" said Tan-tan.

"I don't want to be a burden to everyone. I want to help. I trust you to make the right decision for me."

"If it was up to me, I would make her be a Healer," said Asuna.

"Come on, babe! That's a horrible thing to say, especially for a female Novice."

Asuna took a heavy breath and stared across the bar as if gazing across a vast distance. She folded and laced her fingers as if kneading an invisible material.

"The only reason people don't become Healers is because of the horrible stigma. Female Healers were horribly abused throughout history, and men still think it's humiliating to be one. Mei doesn't care what others think of her. You know I would never let any guild members abuse Maja, you know that right?" said Asuna.

"I know, babe, it's just...it's such a disgusting history of abuse. I don't want Maja to be a part of that."

"I wouldn't let anything happen to her."

"Hey! Why don't we just talk to the interp-uh-ter first?" Maja spoke up.

"That's a wonderful idea," said Asuna.

CHAPTER 13

After the discussion, Tan-tan and Asuna quietly ate their breakfasts. Asuna paid the bill as Tan-tan wiped the jam from Maja's face with a cloth napkin. The three of them left the bar together and began their trek across Trinity. Asuna and Tan-tan walked together with Maja in Tan-tan's arms. Asuna's cloak covered her entire body and was pulled up over her mouth only revealing her mysterious purple eyes.

"Why do you carry her like that? You can keep up with us, right Maja?" said Asuna as they walked.

"Well...she's just so squishy and fun to squeeze. Bloop!" said Tan-tan as she gave Maja a squeeze which made her giggle. "Here you try it."

Tan-tan held Maja out like a giant newborn, and Asuna carefully handled her, wrapping her up in her arms.

"Isn't she just the squishiest?" Tan-tan poked Maja's tummy and made her giggle again.

"You have a very beautiful body," Asuna said politely.

"So do you," said Maja. Tan-tan knew her girlfriend was blushing underneath her cloak.

"And you keep me cool. Your body isn't warm like Tan-tan's."

"I'm sorry! Do you want Tan-tan to carry you? Or I can set you down."

"No, it's comfortable. Tan-tan gives off so much warmth, she makes me feel sweaty."

"You said you liked my body!" Tan-tan swallowed hard, fearful she had just revealed too much information in front of her girlfriend. Asuna did not appear to notice there was any kind of slip up. They made their way into the Administrative District and across The Square to The Starlight. The Starlight's guards met them at the receiving hall to disarm them.

"A Revenant," said one of the guards in her strange monotone.

"That's right," said Asuna with a smile.

"We simply ask that you do not annihilate us during your visit," the other guard said with no emotion in her voice.

"I...wasn't planning on it," said Asuna.

"This way, please." The other guard gestured towards the interior of The Starlight.

"What's a Revenant?" said Maja.

"Don't worry about it," whispered Tan-tan as she pressed her lips against Maja's head. The building was as empty as the day before with Amy working furiously at her desk. She scribbled notes on crisp parchment before she paused to consult another article and then returned to her furious note taking. She didn't even notice when the three women gathered around her desk.

"Ahem!" said Tan-tan.

"Oh, oh! It's you. Do you have any more details you want to share? The story goes out this afternoon."

It took a moment for the reality to register with Tan-tan, but when it did, she shouted in triumph and pumped her fist in the air. She snatched Maja out of Asuna's arms and twirled with her.

"This means you're printing our story, right? Right!" Tan-tan couldn't contain herself.

"Well, I kind of have to. This story is solid gold. We're going to sell a lot of pamphlets tonight. Mei was very cooperative. You two are very brave."

Tan-tan launched Maja in the air with another shout and caught her as she came down. Maja giggled and laughed the entire time. Asuna stepped forward and was snatched up too for an ecstatic embrace.

"I'm so proud of you two," said Asuna before she kissed Tan-tan.

"We have to celebrate after we go to the interpreter. And we have to get word to Alex somehow. He deserves to know this."

"I'll talk to Mort after we take Maja to the interpreter. I would bet any amount of gold Serana is with him, and she owns a com stone," said Asuna.

"I agree that Serana is stalking Alex, but why does she own a com stone? Those are really expensive."

"I couldn't tell you."

"Well, whatever. Important thing is we got Maja's story printed, and now we have to go celebrate. Let's get moving."

Tan-tan and Maja said goodbye to Amy and were seen out by the twin guards.

"This is just amazing. This is such good news. I can't believe things are working out," Tan-tan continued as they left The Starlight.

"You two are amazing." Asuna smiled at both of them.

"So what's the interp-uh-ter like?" said Maja.

"Well, he's pretty old. He's very wise. Really insightful. Talking with him, I dunno' it's like talking with your father if he wasn't an asshole," said Tan-tan.

"I don't even remember my dad..." said Maja as she looked at the cobblestone road.

"Awww, baby green, I'm sorry. I forgot you told me about him. I shouldn't have said that." Tan-tan rested her face against the back of Maja's head.

"Baby green?" Asuna gave Tan-tan a quizzical look.

"Yeeeeahha...it's a goblin candy. I guess I

started calling her that awhile back."

"My mama calls me baby green, too!"

Asuna smiled warmly as Maja shared her life.

"Did you use an interpreter?" said Tan-tan.

"Me? Noooo. I guess I always knew I wanted to be an Assassin."

"But you're a Revenant now. When did you start training? I know you're older than me, but most Revenants are REALLY old."

"I got pushed into training really young. After The Reckoning, my father wanted to be sure his children had some control in their destinies. I don't think he wanted this though."

"What's The Reckoning?" said Maja.

"The Reckoning," Tan-tan cut in before she offered a contrite look to her girlfriend for interrupting, "was when Lorena Charbelcher exposed the widespread abuse of guilds towards their female members and opened up every class to female Novices."

"It was actually Tantra Charbelcher who was the first to break the gender lock on the class structure," Asuna added.

"Well Tantra was Lorena's lover and bodyguard, and defeated countless men in combat, but Lorena did most of the work. Tantra was integral to their work, but Lorena broke the gender lock so that Tantra could show the world how capable female Warriors were."

"Tantra was a Fighter long before she met

Lorena, sweetie."

"Babe, I've probably read more on Tantra Charbelcher than anyone. She's the reason I started my career adventuring. I know what I'm talking about."

"Sure, babe," said Asuna with a smirk.

"Wait, hold up. This is the place." Tan-tan grabbed Asuna's arm and turned her. They stood outside a stone structure that did not look like it belonged in Trinity or even this world. The neighborhood they were in was right off the main cobblestone circuit of Trinity where the houses were in the classic hume-style of pointed roofs and glass windows. This building however appeared to have existed long before the neighboring houses, long before Trinity even. The entire structure was made of weather beaten stone with pores and dimpling along every surface from countless years of rain. There was an open doorway leading into darkness guarded by two statues so worn by the elements that it was impossible to tell what they were supposed to be. Above the open doorway was a large, golden seal depicting nine runes, one for each of the root classes and a ninth one in the center. One of the runes was scratched and defaced to the point it was unrecognizable.

"Is that Old Script?" said Asuna as she looked up at the seal.

"Yeah, I think it is. I've never seen it used outside a tome before."

“This place looks spooky,” said Maja.

“We’ll protect you, don’t worry.” Tan-tan gave Maja a reassuring squeeze before she led the way inside. At the doorway, a set of stone stairs descended into darkness. Two bronze braziers, one on each wall, lit the way. The building smelled very old, like soil, rain, and old books. Through the bottom entryway they found a room where a man sat cross-legged on a stone bench with two more braziers on stands lighting the room. The man was wearing a robe that was not for Mages or any class with which Tan-tan was familiar. His face was serene as he watched the women approach.

“Hello again, Tantra,” said the man as their eyes met. His smile was disarming but not menacing.

“You remember me? I haven’t been here in years!”

“You do have green skin which makes it easier to remember you. But we discovered you were suited to be a Rogue, and I see you’ve moved on to Stalker now.”

“Yeah, it really suits me. I’m really glad I came to see you.”

“Me too, Tantra. And a Revenant, oh my. You must have worked very hard. If I’m not mistaken, you’re the only female Revenant ever. That’s quite an accomplishment.”

“WHAT! How is that possible? No offense babe, you know I’m proud of you, but how can she be the only female Revenant? That's so...fucking pathetic. This fucking world..." Tantra set Maja down and grabbed Asuna by the arms. "You know I think you're wonderful. But lordsdam, babe, I thought we'd come further than this. Feel like the stunted gender. Things men accomplished hundreds of years ago, and we're taking pride in coming in last place. I'm sorry. This is a big accomplishment. You deserve to feel good about it. I always fuck things up. I'm sorry."

"No, it's okay. I know how passionate you are about female empowerment. I know it feels like a false victory, but it's a step in the right direction."

"I guess so...Maja, go and step up. Let him interpret you," said Tan-tan who sounded angry with Maja without intending to. Maja waddled over to the interpreter and looked back towards Tan-tan who gave her a reassuring nod.

"Let me have a look at you, young lady," said the man as he leaned forward and placed his hands around Maja's head without touching her. He studied her face, her big copper eyes and soft lips, the way her neon blue hair slightly hung in her face. He took in her aura, the way she simultaneously projected her innocence and sexuality. Maja stared back at him.

"A sweet, naive young woman. Loves her friends. Loves her Mama and candy. Extremely sexual and adventurous. Constantly fantasizes about the freedom of the wilds. Much smarter than she appears, no offense, child. Feels guilt and shame for...I see you now. Beautiful little creature. I see you Maja. I see who you are, and you are a beautiful bright soul. Take care of them Maja, remind them what they are fighting for."

"Well?" Asuna looked at Tan-tan then back at the man.

"Well what?" said the interpreter with a knowing smile.

"You didn't say what class she is."

"Oh she knows."

"I'm an, an, An...imist?"

Tan-tan smiled, walked up, and patted Maja on the head.

"Do you need help finding class training?" The man sat up right and took a deep breath.

"Just have to go out in the woods and find herself? We can come with her, right?"

"She must let her animal spirit connect with the natural world. Go far away from civilization and let yourself be. Find the animal within you. You know the sensation, Maja. When you lose your brains."

Maja blushed and held her cheeks.

"Thank you so much. We really appreciate the help," said Tan-tan before she led the way back out. After they topped the stairs, the three of them shielded their eyes as they stepped into the harsh sunlight of midday.

"He's the only enpaycee that doesn't creep

me out," said Tan-tan as she scanned the neighborhood. "Alright, let's take Maja out in the woods and have our way with her."

Asuna giggled, and Maja bounced up and down with excitement.

"You two! Stop right there!" a Trinity Guard shouted and ran up to them. Tan-tan lifted her leg and slowly pushed Maja down the first couple of stairs behind them. The Guard brandished his pike at them.

"Put that fucking thing away before you hurt yourself," said Tan-tan who didn't bother to hold her hands up in surrender.

"Tantra, don't agitate him." Asuna held her hands up to show she had no intention to resist.

"I'll come with you, but don't point that thing at my fucking girlfriend, asshole!" shouted Tan-tan, trying to instigate a fight.

"Stop..." whispered Asuna.

"I need to bring you two in for questioning. Don't make this difficult." The Guard seemed to lose his nerve at the woman who wouldn't be intimidated by his authority.

"And I said I would follow you, just stop pointing that damn spear at us!"

The Guard tucked his pike through his elbow to keep it pointed at Tan-tan as he reached into his coat pocket for something.

"I've alerted the other Guards of your detention. Don't try to escape."

"No one's trying to escape, asswipe."

In less than a minute, two more Guards ran to their location. They wore heavy white-grey coats with chain mail underneath painted with the Trinity three-point crest, and both carried pikes as well.

"What, you can't bring in two girls, Jameson?" One of the Guards laughed as they approached which elicited a chuckle from his fellow Guard.

"Tantra don't..." said Asuna as her girlfriend trembling with rage. Tan-tan melted into the air, disappearing from sight.

"Fuck! Where'd she go?" Jameson ran towards the doorway where he was leveled by an unseen force.

"Dumbass, use your rune!" His comrade shouted and removed his guardian rune from his coat. He swiped it with his thumb which sent out a rolling wave of light in all directions. The pulse revealed Tan-tan's silhouette in the doorway shining like stardust.

"Get on the ground, bitch!" The Guard swung the back of his pike which connected with Tan-tan's head. Her silhouette slumped to the ground, and she materialized.

"Tantraaaa!" Asuna screamed through tears.

"You too, bitch," said the Guard as he approached. Asuna lay on the ground and resisted the urge to slaughter all of them. Tan-tan's and

Asuna's hands were placed in shackles and they were led away from the scene.

The angry Guard quickly searched the area for the goblin girl who was suppose to be with the half-breed. He peered down the stairs of the temple but saw only darkness. Expressly forbidden from entering such buildings by his commanding officer, he left the scene.

Maja slowly climbed the steps after several minutes of silence from outside. Every second she lay in wait, she feared the Guards would come back and find here. She wanted to help her friends but was truly terrified of what the Guards would do to a little goblin. The wait was excruciating. Every minute she fought with the idea of helping her friends and getting caught. It seemed like Tan-tan wanted her to hide, but the tug towards helping them would not desist. For what could have been an hour or five minutes, Maja lay flat on the stone staircase of the temple, fearful that the Guards would steal her, but desperately wanting to help the people who had done so much for her.

The braziers on the walls re-lit themselves as Maja reached the top stair. No one was standing outside. There were a few drops of blood on the stairs from the fight. Tan-tan and Asuna were gone. Alexander was gone. She was alone again. She sat outside the temple and cried to herself. She had relied on everyone her entire life, and now they were all gone again. The ache of loss pulled and twisted her guts around inside her. The crushing loneliness of her life came roaring back like a pack of dogs. She stared out at the miserable city. The top of The Steps could still be seen from where she sat.

"Mama..." she said to herself and stepped out into the road. She moved through the alleys and tried to remain hidden as she made her way to The Steps. Once there, she was shocked to see Guards in her neighborhood for the first time ever. They seemed to scrutinize every goblin who passed them in the road. She carefully moved with other groups of goblins and tried not to look at any Guard who would certainly notice her looking at them. She reached the towering Steps and climbed up to find her familiar home empty.

"I'll just sit here and eat candy until Mama comes home," she said to herself as she pulled out a sack of candy from under the kitchen counter and sat on their makeshift couch. The misery was heavy on Maja, but it didn't stop her from mindlessly stuffing candy into her mouth. The misery and sugar rush had a twisting effect on her sexuality. She managed to push the candy aside then quickly undressed herself. With her new clothes off, she sat naked on the couch with her legs apart. She lifted her breasts and thought about Alexander's big hume hands touching her. She touched her tiny clit and thought about Tan-tan's smooth vulva. She pushed two fingers inside herself and spread her slit, imagining Asuna making her perform oral. She worked her clit in circles as she whined quietly. Fantasies of big hume men picking her up off her feet and fucking her like a doll seemed almost real in her mind. She thought about lycans surrounding her and taking sex from her. Her brains slowly disappeared as she dove deeper into her sexuality. She thought about Mama coming home and catching her touching herself. Her mama stripping down and making Maja lick her pussy. She thought about Mama putting her fingers in her and masturbating her. Maja squealed and broke into ugly tears as she orgasmed on the couch. She lay there naked and lost. Her mind was gone. She had no direction, no skill or ability. She couldn't help Tan-tan or Alexander. Everyone had helped her, and she failed everyone...

Mei! Mei said she could ask for anything! But where was Mei? Tan-tan said she lived in Gold Town? That shouldn't be hard to find. But what about the Guards? Surely they were in The Steps looking for her; that was the only thing that could explain their presence. She had to wait for Mama. Mama was very wise and would know what to do. Maja went into their shared bedroom which was also the only other room in the house. She took out a book, set it on the couch as she dressed, and sat down to read *The Legend of Tantra Charbelcher*.

CHAPTER 14

Alexander knelt down at the clear pond and splashed water in his face. Each splash of cool water was a welcome relief against the blistering heat of the Scoured Sands. He poured out his waterskin and submerged it in the pool, watching it bubble. He watched the large air bubbles escape until they stopped, and then chugged the entire skin before submerging it and chugging it again. He drank until it hurt, drank a little more until he thought he would puke, and filled the skin one last time. Then he poured out a fireproof potion on the ground, submerged the glass bottle in the pool, and corked it.

"I want you to drink as much water as you can tolerate before we go. The Scoured Sands are a brutal place. Fill up any containers you have with water as well. There isn't much in the way of monsters out there, but it's the heat that'll kill you. There's a reason no one becomes a Pyre Shaman." Serana was in her hume form as she tied the frayed edges of her robe into a cropped bustier. She smiled when she saw him accidentally catch a glimpse of her body. Alexander scowled and turned away as she flashed her bountiful breasts at him. She tied the edges of her tattered robe to support her chest then tore the rest of the clothing at the knee to create a ragged skirt.

"How do I look, Alex?" Serana posed for him.

"Same as always," he replied without looking, "would you please hurry up and gather some water."

"I don't have anything to carry it in."

"Of course you don't," said Alexander, unable to decide if he wanted to punch her in the face or himself. "Well, looks like you'll have to turn back. Let Asuna and them know I'm safe."

"You're silly," said Serana with a giggle. She reached in her purse and produced a crude necklace. On a thin leather strap were beads of polished stone and gold that led to a strange sapphire pendant with an etching in it. Serana secured the pendant around her neck then whispered a prayer in Old Script. Rain clouds rapidly invaded the once cloudless sky with a roar and a crash. A torrent of rain came down on them, and a small creature fell to Ur which nimbly landed on its paws with a light bounce. The creature was something between a fox, lizard, cat, and deer. It was mostly mammal, the size of a house cat, with tiny antlers and scaly hindquarters. The rain clouds cleared out as quickly as they had come and allowed the broiling sun to continue roasting them.

Serana bent down and extended her arm towards the strange creature. It scampered up her arm to perch on her shoulder. Her summon licked her cheek with its tiny purple tongue which made her giggle. It let out a long, high pitched call which generated a tiny rain cloud above Serana's head. A light rain fell from the miniature cloud, gently soaking Serana.

"Can we go, please!" Alexander nearly shouted.

"Sure," said Serana with a warm smile, "lead the way."

Alexander marched up a shallow dune and stopped at the top to take in the Scoured Sands. The desert was a hard deadpan of cracked dust that may have never seen rain since Ka Tuk was cast out of the Pantheon and collided with Ur, if one believed the legends. The pale, cracked soil rolled for miles into the liquid haze of the horizon. Even through the roiling air, the outline of the Blasted Mountains was visible as a long, low shadow in the infinite distance. The Scoured Sands felt like the edge of Ur: nothing but sky and baked earth. No plants, no fauna, no signs of life. The desert was a wonder and a horror all in one.

"You don't have to do this if you don't want to. I wouldn't blame you for turning back." Alexander looked over at his companion who smiled back at him.

"I would do anything for you, Alex. Anything." Serana tried to convey with her eyes the gravity of what she was saying. He pretended not to notice and conjured some coldfire for himself. The swirling flame was comfortably cool compared to the relentless heat of the Scoured Sands.

"Do you want me to let the guild know we've reached the Scoured Sands?" Serana slung her purse in front of her and pulled out her com stone. Alexander hesitated for a moment.

"Yeah…I guess it's okay now. If The Guard wants to come all the way out here to catch me, then let them. This is no place for people."

Serana flicked her thumb in several directions as she manipulated the runes inside her crystal.

"That's weird." Serana furrowed her brow.

"What's that?"

"Asuna hasn't checked in with Mort today."

"You know how she likes to sleep in."

"Yeah, I guess you're right. Okay, I left Mort a message letting him know we reached the Scoured Sands. Hey, you know I read this is where Lorena Charbelcher met her wife?"

"Right here?" said Alexander as he commenced their trek into the wasteland.

"No, not right here, but I mean the Scoured Sands. Was either at a lecture or in a tome, I forget, but apparently Lorena saved Tantra from some guildies and they fell in love instantly."

“How would a Healer save a Fighter from a guild? Sure Tantra didn’t save Lorena?”

“I don’t know. I’m just letting you know what I heard. Maybe it was the other way around. It would make a lot more sense.”

“You don’t have to agree with everything I say. You can have a discussion with me. Just wondering how a Healer saves a Fighter from a guild.”

“Well, they say Tantra was the best Fighter that ever lived. So if the guildies didn’t bring a Healer, maybe Lorena and Tantra just outlasted them?”

“If you were hunting Tantra Charbelcher, why wouldn’t you bring several Healers?”

“Look at our guild. We haven’t even had a Healer since Finn was killed, and Mei abandoned us.”

“Can we please not talk about him. It’s too depressing,” said Alexander as he tried to push that fateful day out of his mind.

“I’m sorry.”

“It’s okay...but look, back then EVERY guild had a Healer, multiple Healers. It was the only class women were allowed to be.”

“That’s so fucked. Can you imagine living in a time when men had that much power over women?”

“Serana...men still try to keep women out of a lot of the classes. I mean Mages, I would say…we’re pretty equal. But Acolytes, Fighters, any group that focuses on combat or is tightly knit, they actively keep women out. Don't you remember The Wrath? Were you even there for that?"

"I mean, I'm aware of it, but I wasn't there, no. Was still in the pack with my paw."

"It was madness. She killed so many Paladins, Acolytes and Guards. The city was a madhouse. Rioting, rape, murder. If it wasn't for the all guilds stepping up and taming the city, Trinity would have been destroyed."

"I never knew it was that bad. I just thought she killed a few Paladins. Didn't they rape her though? Isn't that what set everything off?"

"I've never heard anything like that, no."

The two guildies trudged on through the desert in silence. Nothing seemed to change except the sun which grew higher and hotter with every step. Alexander stopped to fold his coat and overshirt away in his rucksack before they continued again. Even with the coldfire and a miniature rainstorm, the unbearable heat of the desert sunk in and roasted them. Serana cupped the falling rain in her hand and threw it in Alexander's face who only muttered his thanks. As he walked, he began to hunch forward and drag his feet. The size of the mountains on the horizon didn't change at all. They trudged for hours, maybe days, it could have been years. The lifeless landscape never changed. Alexander looked over his shoulder to see it was identical to his forward horizon. The entire planet was yellow-brown, cracked earth, the color of an infected wound. The most enormous sky he had ever seen in his life brought on a mild sense of dizziness with its scope. The only reliable indication of direction was the low shadow of the Blasted Mountains on the horizon.

"Hey, hey Alex," came Serana's voice from miles away, "hey maybe we sh..."

Serana grabbed his arm, but he couldn't even lift his head to look at her face which made him inadvertently stare into her ample chest.

"My face is up here." Serana reached out and lifted his chin. Her face was a swirling mess. His entire vision blurred. He thought maybe he was too hard on Serana, and all she wanted was his approval. He thought about his purpose in life, why he was out in this lordsforsaken land. His thoughts fell through, melted, and blended. Then he snapped to attention. Water splashed in his face in a gentle stream. His vision focused. He was sitting on the ground, and Serana's strange creature was shooting a steady stream of water into his face from its mouth. His head swayed side to side, and he allowed the water to splash into his slacked jaw. His vision returned, and his brains were right behind it.

"I think you're dying of thirst." Serana held his glass bottle to his lips. "Slowly, go slowly. We're taking a rest."

Alexander sipped carefully from the bottle but still managed to dribble it down his chin. He took the bottle from Serana and drank deeply. His mind reformed. He knew where he was.

"I guess I pushed myself too hard," he said. The strange water creature stared up at him, its eyes like two polished turquoise.

"You're always pushing yourself too hard." Serana wiped his face with a pleasantly cool cloth. She stopped to stare in his eyes. Alexander stared back.

"I think we should eat, gather our strength." He made to stand up but was unable without the world threatening to flip upside down.

"No, sit down. It's okay. I got us." Serana reached in her purse and pulled out an unusually ordinary looking rock that was slightly bigger than her fist.

"I'm not eating that," said Alexander.

"No, just wait." Serana dug up the dry dusty earth, using the stone as a spade. After a suitable hole was dug, she buried the stone and gestured for her little blue friend to water it. The water-summon squirted water onto the stone, and after several seconds, a tortoise with a jagged shell broke through the earth and climbed out. Serana bent down and whispered to it. The tortoise shuffled its feet and stomped the moist soil from which it emerged.

A small tree about a stride tall exploded from the churned earth and made Alexander flinch. The little tree produced several apples which started as little more than buds but instantly grew into ripe fruit. The apples plopped onto the ground in a series of soft thumps. Serana wiped an apple on the breast of her robe then handed it to Alexander.

"I didn't really intend to eat out here. Just builds a greater thirst," said Alexander.

"I know, but they're juicy apples. Counts for something, right?" Serana encouraged him with a smile. He took the apple from her and bit into it. The flavor was an explosion across his tongue. The tart acidity mixed wondrously with the sugars. He devoured the first apple and calmly ate the second one, swigging water as he did. Serana ate one of the apples as she packed the remaining ones in her purse. After Alexander finished off his water, Serana had her summon refill the bottle and handed it back to him.

"I'm really glad I brought you," said Alexander as he gathered his things and stood. Serana's lower lip trembled and her dark eyes glistened.

"Calm down." Alexander held up his hands as Serana lunged at him and attempted to squeeze the life out of him.

"You shouldn't crave a man's approval so much. Especially not mine. I mean, I'm not even your guild leader anymore."

"You'll always be my guild leader, Alex." She kissed him on the mouth which forced him to pry her away and storm off into the desert. She touched her lips and smiled the biggest smile of her life. Alexander conjured another coldfire as he marched, and Serana protected herself with another magic rain cloud as her tiny companion napped on her shoulder.

The Scoured Sands would not relent as they trekked, but the guildies were infused with new vitality from their rest. Even after a half-day of journeying, the Blasted Mountains were nothing but a low shadow on the warbling horizon. The heat from the desert floor came up through their boots and slow-roasted the soles of their feet.

"Why do you want to be a Pyre Shaman so bad?" Serana, broke the silence. "I mean, I support your decision one-hundred percent. I'm just curious, ya' know?"

Alexander gave some thought to his words before he spoke.

"I don't know. I guess almost every class is about destroying things, and I want to bring something positive into the world? I don't know, it's like...it's a lot of small things that add up to make sense. I guess I kind of like being a class that no one goes for. I like the challenge. Well, I liked the challenge up until now. I guess I just really like the idea of helping others. And there's also the quiet spiritual dignity in it. The few who class change always go for Lavamancer, and it's a powerful class, just feels like no one is trying very hard anymore. Why did you become a Summoner?"

"Well, I think it's amazing you're even in the position to become a Pyre Shaman. I mean, most people that go Fire Mage stay there their whole lives. As for me, I guess it just felt right. I mean I love hunting and finding treasure--"

"The dirty rock."

"Yeah, heh, the dirty rock. Yeah, but it's like, really satisfying when you read about these ancient relics and you're actually able to hunt them down and commune with them, draw out their anima. Like, I wish I could give you some relics, but it wouldn't be the same, you wouldn't be able to summon the demons and spirits."

"You're saying 'like' a lot."

"Sorry."

"It's fine. I'm teasing."

"I guess what I'm meaning to say is, I love reading about history and hunting it down. I like this deep spiritual connection I've forged with the world. I like serving my guil--oh my Lords, Alex..." Serana stopped and stared out at the desert. Her mouth hung agape. Alexander squinted at the horizon to try and figure out what spooked her.

"What is it? What do you see?"

"I don't see anything, but there is something nearby more powerful than anyone or anything I've ever sensed. I've never felt anything like this. I'm scared, Alex. It's even more powerful than Asuna."

Even though the desert heat had not abated for a single second, Alexander felt a sickening chill roll up his body.

"Is it a Revenant?" Alexander lowered his voice.

"No, it's more powerful than that."

"A Harbinger..?" Alexander didn't even want to know if it was a Harbinger. If it was, they were already dead.

"No, more powerful than that..."

What in all the realms was more powerful than a Harbinger, and what was it doing out in this lordsforsaken place?

"What is it? Where is it?"

"I don't know. I wish I could tell you. It's hard to say where it is. It's anima is so powerful I can't feel how close it actually is. This isn't a person, Alex. It's too powerful to be a person. We have to turn back. I'm sorry, but I won't be able to stop this thing. WE won't be able to fight it. I know you wanted to be a Pyre Shaman so bad."

"What if we just...what if we swing wide, cut east or west until you can't sense it anymore?"

"We can try. But if this thing finds us..."

The two companions cut west away from their original path. The desert was no more forgiving than it had been earlier, and Alexander felt agitation build as they came no closer to the Blasted Mountains. The agitation was mixed with dread as he kept looking over his shoulder, expecting a shadowy figure to be pursuing them. This was not one of the tricks Serana would play to prolong their journeys together; this was real. The terror in her voice was real. Alexander could almost swear he too sensed the anima Serana tapped into.

"How about now?" said Alexander as he turned to look at the mountains on the horizon.

"No."

"How 'bout now?"

"No."

"Now?"

"Alex! You're silly!" Serana laughed, but Alexander could only force out an empty laugh to break the tension. It felt like a stupid time to make jokes, but the dread was making his sensibilities unreliable.

"Is it following us?" Alexander glanced in every direction.

"I don't know. I really don't. I wish I did." Serana's voice was strained.

"Maybe we should just start heading in again?"

"Okay."

The two guildies returned to their normal course that set the Blasted Mountains on their horizon. The sun finally started its descent across the sky.

"You'll let me know if you feel anything?" said Alexander.

Serana's face was sullen with worry. "Yeah. It's just...what if we can't escape? What if we die out here?"

"Well...then we die together. Like true guildies." He stopped and spread his arms for Serana who stepped in and hugged him lovingly. The vague menace of Serana's warning was nearly unbearable, especially with no clear sign or indication of the threat. The hug was desperately needed to sooth his nerves.

"I'm sorry I dragged you into this..."

"We both know you didn't drag me into this."

"I still feel guilty..."

"Alex...look..." Serana pointed behind him. He turned slowly and swallowed a dry, painful swallow. Behind him was a massive temple. The edifice towered several stories and was carved from cracked, black stone with menacing pointed spires and sharp arches that resembled claws. The whole structure pulsed with dim red light as the sun seemed to accelerate in its decline across the sky.

CHAPTER 15

"Now, how about you tell me where you were two nights ago?" asked the female Paladin who sat across from Tan-tan in the small, dimly lit room. The only light source was a flickering sconce hung from the ceiling.

"Was making passionate love to my girlfriend. Maybe you should try it some time." Tan-tan sneered and kicked her feet up on the table.

"You want me to make love to your girlfriend?" The Paladin feigned misunderstanding.

"You know what I meant."

"Listen, a Guard, *my Guard*, has been murdered, and we have reason to believe you know who did it, and unless you're culpable in his murder, I don't understand why you wouldn't want to help us. Now, either you're guilty, and that's why you won't talk, or you're heartless. Make a choice."

"You know what I think? I think you have no clue what happened, and I'm the only person who can tell you. Or! You know exactly what he was doing and are pretending it didn't happen."

"What do you think he was doing?" The

Paladin's platmail armor creaked as she leaned forward.

"Guessing your men found him in that basement, was a table there with restraints on it. Take a guess why he was there."

"You're correct, he was discovered in a cellar near a table, but there was no mention of restraints in the report. All this tells me is you were somehow involved with his murder. Now we have reason to believe that it wasn't you that murdered him, but we know a pale, hume male was directly involved in the incident. Please just tell us his name, and you can walk out of here the moment we capture him. Is this man really worth sacrificing your future for?"

"You said no restraints were found at the crime scene?"

"That is correct."

"Did you even go there yourself?"

"I am not allowed to investigate the murder of my own Guard. A special task force is put together for such horrible occurrences."

"...then why are you even talking to me?" Tan-tan suspected she might have acquired some leverage in the situation.

"You're the only person so far who might have any answers. I want to know why Wilson had to die, and you're the only one who can tell me. Please tell me." The Paladin quit her authoritarian countenance and sounded more like a widow as she spoke.

"Listen, bitch, my friend was tied up in his little fucking dungeon, and they tried to sterilize her! Either you know full well what I'm talking about, or your men are carrying out sadistic little operations under your nose, and judging by your reaction, this isn't the first time someone accused these fucks of being sadistic."

"Of course I don't want to believe my own men are breaking the law, but if you say there's a victim involved, I will listen to her story. Can you produce her?"

"Why, so you can silence her? Fuck you, bitch!" Tan-tan leaned her head back and hocked a large wad of spit in the Paladin's face. The Paladin produced an embroidered kerchief from her armor and calmly wiped it away.

"Bring in the other suspect," the Paladin called to the Guards outside the room. A heavy lock shifted in the door, and two Guards entered to remove Tan-tan. Tan-tan stood and lunged at her but was caught by the Guards. The Paladin was stoic as Tan-tan thrashed in their custody.

"You know what they're doing, bitch! You know they don't respect you! This is no place for a woman!" screamed Tan-tan as she was forcibly removed from the room and dragged down the hallway to her cell. The Guards returned moments later with Asuna in shackles and sat her in Tan-tan's chair.

"I'd like to thank you for cooperating with us," said the Paladin, folding her hands on the table.

"I haven't said anything yet," said Asuna with mild confusion.

"I know, but you're a Revenant. I know you could leave here any time you want and annihilate anyone who tried to stop you. I genuinely appreciate the restraint you have shown with my men."

"They could stand to be a little nicer."

"I agree their rapport leaves something to be desired, but it's very difficult work that doesn't pay nearly as much as it should. And they're risking their lives. It's not like the old days where the Mods would protect all of us. These men and women stepped up to protect everyone."

"In the old days, they would never let a woman be a Paladin," said Asuna.

"That's true, but ever since The Wrath visited Trinity, there aren't enough Paladins to discriminate anymore. And too many trainees pursue the dark path now. It's like they admire what she did..."

Asuna stared at the table as if she was seated before a well of memories. Painful visions of that night echoed in the back of her mind, and the smell of blood invaded her nose as if the room was painted in it. She looked up to see her interrogator staring off to the side in contemplation.

"I'm sorry my girlfriend said those things.

You're just doing your job, and I'm sure there are plenty of men who make that difficult enough." Asuna reached across the table and touched the Paladin's gauntleted hand.

"We need to get back to the business at hand." The Paladin sat up right and retracted her hands. "Your girlfriend is in a lot of trouble. She was spotted with a hume male suspected of murdering a Guard, and she had his rune on her person when she was apprehended. She might never leave this place if she doesn't cooperate."

"I know you're just trying to do your job, but I would never let Tantra rot in this place. Never."

The Paladin gripped the edges of the table as a menacing chill rolled through the core of her being. Asuna's eyes were now black pools filled with glistening ink. Nausea and fever washed over the Paladin's body like a warm river of refuse. She struggled to remain conscious as she held eye contact with Asuna who stared at her indifferently. Sweat dripped down her face in rivets, and a noxious burp escaped her mouth that threatened bile.

"You would kill innocent people just to keep your girlfriend from paying for the crimes she committed?" the Paladin gasped for air as beads of sweat hit the table. She wanted to cry out for back up but knew she would vomit if she tried. Her face flushed, and her eyes bulged like she was being strangled.

"I would do anything for Tantra, but I don't think she committed any crimes. She told me what happened, and she has no reason to lie to me. We have a friend who was gravely injured by your Guards, and the man you're looking for killed them to stop them from mutilating her. I completely trust his judgment and would trust him with my own life. He's not a murderer and neither is Tantra." Asuna's eye returned to their pleasant violet color. The Paladin gasped and held her weight up on the table as her breathing returned. A wave of relief washed over her body like a cool breeze. The bile that threatened to escape her stomach receded.

"I can't just let you two go. I'm sorry, but as you have said, I'm just doing my job. I'll die protecting this city." The Paladin used her kerchief to wipe the sweat from her face.

"Then why don't you investigate these accusations?"

"I want to. I want to talk to your people. If my men are hurting people, they have to be stopped. But I can't investigate this if I don't even have a victim. You must let me speak to her. You can come with me. I won't hurt her. I just want the truth. She would be a valuable witness to corroborate your story."

"I think we have a plan now," said Asuna. There was a knock at the door. The Paladin shot a hateful glance out the corner of her eyes. She stood up and cracked the door open only to spit a series of whispered cusses at the Guard outside. He replied with low mumbling and quick apologies. The Paladin slammed the door which shook the entire room and caused some dust to drift from the ceiling towards the floor. She took her seat and gave Asuna a serious look.

"Don't tell me Tantra escaped," said Asuna as she stood.

"Sit down. Some men came for your girlfriend. Not my men. Some higher-ups in the Trinity government. *Agents...*" the Paladin said the last word as if it was poisonous.

"I have to save her. I can't pretend to be your prisoner anymore." Asuna snapped the chains on her wrists like brittle twine then reached down and easily snapped the chains on her legs.

"Sit down!" the Paladin shouted, "She's not in trouble. She's been relieved from my custody. Do you even know who her father is?"

CHAPTER 16

Tan-tan was led from the Guard station freed from her shackles. Three of her father's men flanked her as they left the building. They all wore long black coats with dark vests, possessed inconspicuous short haircuts, and could have easily been mistaken for brothers. They made eye contact with no one as they marched out of the building with Tan-tan. The only way out of the dungeon was through the Guard station. Their path started and ended with a massive set of stairs which connected the dungeon to the exit as well as every area of the building. Guards and Paladins alike stepped off the stairs onto landings to make way for the Agents.

The instant they stepped out into the administrative square, a black carriage rolled up, and the four of them stepped in. The carriage departed before the door even closed.

"Couldn't even find a female Agent? Still an asshole..." Tan-tan said to anyone who would listen as she watched the city go by from the carriage window. If the Agents had heard her, they made no acknowledgment.

"Doesn't even realize I'm an adult now. I can handle myself."

The carriage made its way down the cobblestone road into Gold Town and came to a stop outside Diamond Heights. The wealthiest neighborhood in Trinity started at a long high wall made of ivory stone that blocked any view from the road. At the gate, the driver handed off a letter of permission to a Guard in ornate armor. The gate, which appeared to be made of gold pikes, silently slid into the ivory wall to allow the carriage to enter. Inside the Heights a cornucopia of flora burst forth. Well manicured trees and shrubs lined the clean brick road. Flowers of every species seemed to explode from random planters and nooks. All the people walking the road were well dressed and hume.

"Lords! Can't believe you archon turds brought me back home."

The carriage rolled up on a glorious white-gold mansion, not unlike the numerous mansions along the pink walkways. The carriage came to a stop in the crescent shaped carriage-way. One of the Agents opened the carriage door, and Tan-tan exited with the two others before the carriage pulled away. A familiar face ducked out of the massive glass window to the left of the gargantuan doorway. The front of the mansion was guarded by perfectly manicured hedges and another pair of Agents.

The colossal doors parted, and an old,

mottle-skinned goblin man stepped outside. His ears were clipped down to resemble hume ears, and his green skin had several white splotches. He hobbled over to his daughter who bent down to hug him.

"Tan-tan...I'm so glad to see you're safe. Come inside, daughter of mine," said Tan-tan's father as he reached above his head to hold her hand. He led the way up the steps into her childhood home. The interior still looked the same after the five years she had spent away: massive, dim, and devoid of warmth. Gaudy relics from extinct races sat on pedestals and ornate tables. Elven artifacts, which her father prized more than anything in the world, sat in the receiving hall so any guest would be forced to comment on them. He led her to the living room where a hume maid stood silently next to the sofa at attention. Her father took the ornate arm chair and gestured for his daughter to sit on the sofa. Instead, Tan-tan sat in the other arm chair next to his. The fabric was plush, bright crimson, and the wooden trim was painted gold. Her father looked beyond joyous to have her back home in his prison.

"Can I get you anything, anything at all?" Her father took her long slender hand in his small, fat hands. His voice was deep and thoughtful. If she didn't know him, she would have found his tone comforting.

"No thanks. I already ate this morning,

with my *girlfriend.*" Tan-tan threw the last word like a punch. Her father simply smiled and squeezed her powerful yet delicate hand.

"Come on now. You know I don't resent you seeing women. I mean, who could blame you? Women are gorgeous, and elegant, and mysterious. Please don't be purposefully difficult. Can't you pretend to be happy to see me?" Her father looked to be on the verge of tears.

"I can't pretend to be happy to see someone who resents me." Tan-tan withdrew her hand and crossed her arms, glaring at her father.

"Tan-tan..."

"Oh my Lords, is Tan-tan home?" Tan-tan's younger sister Makilja roared across the parlor and leapt into her sister's lap which sent her chair sliding backwards. Tan-tan's face finally softened. Her sister was one hundred percent goblin: small, green, with an enticing shape. Though she was tall by goblin standards, taller than her father, she was still shorter than the shortest adult humes. She wore a lavish princess dress which probably costed more than all the money Tan-tan had ever earned since leaving home.

"How are you, Ma-ma?" Tan-tan squeezed her younger sister and nuzzled their faces together.

"So happy now! Where have you been, Tan-tan? We missed you so much. Haven't we, papa?"

Their father closed his eyes and nodded in agreement.

"Makilja, your sister has had a little trouble in town, and she'll be staying with us until everything is sorted out."

Makilja squealed at the top of her lungs and hugged Tan-tan around the neck.

"Gahh, you're killing meh!" said Tan-tan half playfully before she pried her sister off.

"Tan-tan..?" came the tiniest voice from across the parlor. Tan-tan's heart plummeted a thousand feet, and she suddenly felt like she had entered a dream. She lifted Makilja off her lap and slowly walked to the tiny person standing across the parlor. She didn't even notice as her hip bumped into the table in the middle of the room. The journey across the parlor felt like lifetimes rolling by. Her father stood behind her with his arm around Makilja.

"She missed you so much when you left," said her father, "she asked about you every single day. We didn't know what to tell her. You just disappeared one night."

Tan-tan felt the tears flow freely down her face. She stopped and knelt in front of the tiny person she had left behind all those years ago. Her littlest sister, Alo, stood in front of the floor-to-ceiling window like a Fey in the sunlight. She was not a helpless toddler anymore but approaching seven years old now. Alo had her chubby goblin arms up, reaching for her big sister. Tan-tan pulled her in for a loving embrace.

"I'm so sorry, Alo. I'm so sorry I abandoned you." Tan-tan sobbed to drown all of Ur. Her heart ripped itself to pieces. She felt her shame and guilt rise in her throat as she struggled to breath.

"I missed you, Tan-tan," came Alo's soft, innocent voice. Tan-tan's vision was completely gone as were her sensibilities. She knelt in the cold parlor and squeezed her youngest sister as if it would be the last time she ever held her. The agony she felt the night she had left came roaring back and threatened to annihilate all the strength she had built up surviving on her own.

"I'm so sorry, I'm so fucking sorry!"

"It's okay. You're home now."

CHAPTER 17

Maja set her book down and fidgeted on the couch as she heard the familiar metallic clunks of her mama climbing up the hall. Her mama stepped through the sliding metal door of their home, and Maja leapt off the couch and into her sweaty embrace.

"Mama!" she cried out, squeezing her. Her mama squeezed her right back and kissed the top of her head before nibbling her daughter's ear.

"Baby green! I'm so happy to see you!" Her mama planted kisses all over Maja's head. Maja led her to the couch and sat next to her, so her mama could rest her head in her lap.

"You going out with your friends tonight?"

Maja looked at the floor and failed to stop the oncoming tears.

Her mama reached up and touched her face, wiping away a tear. "What's wrong? Did you and your friends have a fight?"

Maja sniffed and then broke out into full sobbing, unable to hold back her emotions. She chewed her lower lip and tried to avoid eye contact.

"They took 'em! They took my friends away!" Maja bawled and buried her face in her mama's breasts.

Her mama sat up to console her. "Who took them? What happened?"

Maja sniffled and tried to calm herself down as she clung to her mama. "The Guards...they took my friends, and they didn't do anything!"

"Oh, Maja, I'm so sorry. I know how much it meant for you to have friends. It's not fair. This world isn't fair, especially not for goblin women. Someday you'll learn to accept that. There's nothing you can do. I'm so sorry."

"There is...actually someone that can help them," said Maja as she tried to compose herself.

"Really?"

"Yeah, she lives in Gold Town. Mei. I told you about her. She's really nice and helpful. I think she can help me..."

"Well, you should go to her then if you really think she'll help you."

"I really think she will. She's a very kind person."

"I'm so proud of you. Being so loyal to your friends." Her mama started to tear up too.

"Mama! Don't cry! I hate seeing you cry. It hurts me."

"I'm not sad. I'm just so proud of the

woman you're becoming." Her mama kissed her forehead and squeezed her in tight. Maja squeezed her back.

"Go find her. Go help your friends." Her mama kissed her one last time then went into the kitchen and prepared a small candy sack for her. Maja hugged her mama and dashed from their home.

Dusk had settled on The Steps as Maja stepped into the roadway outside her home. The streets were less crowded after everyone had gone home from work, but there were still plenty of goblins up and about. Some outdoor torches were lit to illuminate the cramped, filthy roadways. A Guard stumbled through the cramped thoroughfare which was not intended for humes. The Guard caught her looking at him, and she froze. She held her breath without realizing it. Her tiny heart raced. She figured she could sprint back home if he came after her, but the Guard simply smiled at her, trying to alleviate the awkwardness of navigating her goblin-sized neighborhood. Her heart wouldn't stop pounding, but she forced a smile and continued towards the hume part of town.

After a little bit of wandering and a little bit of luck, Maja found that familiar cobblestone circuit that went through all of Trinity. She moved through The Steps as inconspicuously as she could, then much more quickly as she entered the nicer hume neighborhoods where she would certainly stick out. When the hume-style homes took on their familiar colorful exteriors, Maja sensed she was getting closer to Mei. She tried to stop a pair of well dressed humes to ask about the local Healer, but they seemed agitated and hurried past. Another hume she approached simply tossed her a piece of silver and forced an awkward smile. Confused, Maja picked up the silver and pocketed it. No one seemed to notice her, but at the same time avoided her as they moved to the edges of the sidewalk. She didn't notice as she stepped into the road, trying to get anyone's attention. Maja was knocked backwards onto the sidewalk as an unseen carriage clipped her.That's when she saw Mei in her plush white robe down the road, greeting a pair of humes. Maja dodged past plodding humes as fast as she could to get to her.

"Mei!" she shouted as she ran, "Meeeiiii!"

Mei turned and looked stunned to see Maja chasing after her.

"Maja, what are you doing here? Did you already spend all that money?" Mei hesitated as Maja ran up to her.

"No I...I think Alexander has the money. I...everyone's in trouble! The Guards took Tantan and Asuna! Alexander is gone! I don't know what to do!"

"Calm down, let's go to my home where we can talk."

As it turned out, they weren't more than

two blocks away from Mei's lavish, hume mansion. They entered her house, and Mei gestured towards the sofa before she went in the kitchen. Maja pulled herself onto the ornate sofa, fidgeting as she waited. Mei returned from the kitchen with a silver tray upon which sat a gorgeous ceramic tea pot, two tea cups, and a plate of cookies.

"It's awful! Everyone's in trouble, and it's all my fault."

Mei gave her a sympathetic look as she poured the tea and took a sip from her cup.

"Start from the beginning. What happened after you and Alexander left here?"

Maja recounted every detail she could remember, from the dress shopping, to meeting Tan-tan, the chase through the streets, the visit to The Starlight, reconnecting with her mama. Mei urged her to hurry up as she got into the sexual encounter with Tan-tan and grew somber as she described The Guard taking Tan-tan and Asuna away.

"That's awful. It must have been very scary for you. And you think The Guard is looking for you too?"

"Yeah, the mean guy that hurt Tan-tan, I think he was looking for me, and there were Guards in my neighborhood today, and there are never Guards in my neighborhood. I'm scared. I'm really scared. I didn't even tell Mama everything. I don't want to scare her too."

"It's a shitty situation. I don't know how they knew Tan-tan was involved, or why they took Asuna. Hrmm..." Mei paused to consider how the situation had unfolded.

"Let's assume The Guard knows Alexander is involved and...you and Tan-tan were spotted with Alexander at some point. I mean, a hume traveling with two goblin women isn't something anyone is going to forget immediately. I mean it's racist, but it's the world we live in. If The Guard really is involved with this ugly mess, that means they're either going to detain Tan-tan forever or kill her."

"Nooooo! Mei, noooo! I-I-I" Maja started to bawl. Mei set her tea down, picked up Maja, and cradled her in her arms like an infant.

"Shhh, it's okay. I don't think it will come to that. Asuna is with her. There's no way Asuna will let them be detained indefinitely. She's too powerful. She could leave that jail whenever she wanted. I think Tan-tan is safe. I...Lords, I have to talk to one of my clients in the Admin District. See what's going on with this. I'm going to have a carriage take you back to The Steps. You need to stay at home until Tan-tan comes to get you. It's not safe in the city for you."

"No." Maja crossed her arms and pushed her bottom lip out.

"*No,* no. It's dangerous. Those people... they don't care about goblins. It's not unreasonable to think they hate goblins. Your life is in danger."

"I'm sick of being useless. I want to help! I want to help my friends. It's my fault we're all in this mess. The interp-uh-ter said I'm an Animist. How do I do that? I don't want to be a useless goblin girl my entire life. I don't want to be helpless...please help me help them." Maja stood in Mei's lap and held her face with her tiny hands. Tears formed at the corners of Mei's eyes.

"Okay, sweetie. I'll help you become an Animist. I know what it's like to feel helpless, and I wouldn't wish it on anyone."

Maja squealed and hugged her around her neck. Mei hugged the tiny person back.

"How do I become an Animist?"

"If I remember what Serana told me, you have to get in touch with nature. But it's more complicated than that. It's not like elemental magic where you just break your back learning and practicing the spells. She said...she said it's here."

Mei clenched her fist in front of her stomach and Maja placed her hand over her fist.

"She said it's like a religious experience. That nature knows you, and you know nature. I wish I could help you more. The interpreter definitely said you're an Animist? It's not something just anyone can do."

Maja nodded.

"We need to get you out in nature as soon as possible. Tomorrow morning, at first wagon, we leave for the Northern Forest. If you haven't felt something by noon...well, I don't know. We'll go see my friend in the Admin District."

"Oh, oh, I remember something! The interp-uh-ter said...he said I have to find the animal in myself. That I have to lose my brains again."

"Lose your brains?"

"Hee, like when I have sex and stop thinking."

Mei blushed which made Maja giggle.

"Well, that's something to go on. Tomorrow morning at first wagon, we'll leave Trinity. You can sleep here tonight. You can have my bed. I'll sleep on the sofa."

"We can share the bed. I don't take up a lot of space."

"I...guess that's okay. First thing before dawn, Maja, no whining, no breakfast."

"I understand."

Mei set Maja on the couch and opened a closet near the front door. She dug inside and retrieved a large rucksack and a small purse then placed them on the armchair. As she walked back and forth through the house, Mei gathered supplies and placed into the rucksack and purse.

"We should go to bed early. Have an early day ahead of us."

After Mei finished packing, Maja held her arms up, and Mei carried her upstairs to bed. Mei's bedroom was beautiful with the most massive bed Maja had ever seen. It was as wide as her house! There were four towers, one at each corner, with curtains hanging between them. Mei stepped out of her robe, then out of her pants to reveal sensible underwear, and then helped Maja out of her corset. She lifted Maja onto the colossal bed and climbed in herself. She blew out the lamps around her bed and climbed under the blankets. She giggled as Maja squirmed and stirred under the sheets, trying to find the way out. Mei wrapped her arms around Maja and let out a long heavy sigh before setting some sort of spell above her end table. The spell looked like a star hanging in the darkness. Maja stared at it with fascination.

"It'll wake us in the morning. Ya' know, it's actually nice to have someone in my bed again."

Maja giggled and squirmed in Mei's arms.

"Not like that, you naughty girl!"

"No, I understand. Me and Mama have shared a bed my entire life. I don't think I've ever slept alone in a bed. It's nice. It doesn't have to be naughty."

Mei inhaled Maja's scent and held her tighter.

"You're a sweet girl, Maja. Don't ever stop being the sweet little person you are. You're the best of us."

"Do you think Alexander and Tan-tan and Asuna are going to be okay?"

"I don't know. Asuna can watch over Tan-tan. I have no idea what Alexander is up to, but he's a survivor. You shouldn't worry about him."

"Okay...I miss him a lot."

"I miss him too."

The two women fell asleep moments later.

CHAPTER 18

Maja awoke to a fully dressed Mei gently shaking her awake.

"Time to go, little girl. Today's your big day," said Mei in a motherly tone as she continued to shake Maja awake. Maja sat up in bed but failed to move further. Mei pulled her corset over her head and dressed her, smiling the entire time. She helped her with her skirt and leggings then carried her down the stairs.

"Okay, I know this is humiliating, but I'm going to need you to get in my rucksack."

"Wha..." Maja was still on the verge of sleep.

"If a Healer is leaving town with her supplies, no one's going to notice. I just want to go as unnoticed as possible. I want to help you, but I don't want my life ruined again."

"Again?" Maja yawned.

"Forget I said that. Please just do as I ask."

Maja had already fallen back asleep, so Mei lowered her into her rucksack and placed the purse in with her then carefully buttoned the sack closed. She hefted it over and across her shoulders and left her home.

"Wake up Maja, we're here," said Mei in a tender voice as she lifted her out of the bag. Maja stretched and let out a high pitch yawn which made Mei smile. They were in the woods which was dark in the shade of the trees and pre-dawn light. The sky was tinted a gorgeous pink like healed flesh, and the sun had not made an appearance yet.

"Where are we?" Maja asked.

"We're in the southern tip of The Great Northern Forest. We're only about a half mile outside Trinity. I hope this counts as nature. Don't really know the rules for this. Can literally see farms from here." Mei nodded behind Maja, and she turned to see a brown plow-archon tilling a field in the distance.

"So what do we do now?" said Maja as she scanned the woods for some indication.

"What did your interpreter say?"

"Uhhhhh, he said I had to find the animal in me. Something about my animal spirit and losing my brains. I mean, hee, I know how to lose my brains."

"Like when you have sex?"

"Heh, yeah."

"I'm not having sex with you, Maja...even though everyone else has," Mei muttered the last part under her breath.

"Perhaps I can help you," came a stranger's

voice. Mei jumped in front of Maja and launched an opaque ball of light like a tiny sun at the figure. The spell absorbed into the woman's body.

"Your spells don't work on me, child of Lorelei. Please calm down," said a beautiful green woman, but one that had no visible relations to goblins.

"You're a dryad," growled Mei as she reached behind her, urging Maja to flee.

"That I am. I want nothing from you, but I think your friend wants something from me." The dryad rested her long delicate fingers on her swollen belly and smiled serenely at her own body.

"Can you help me be an Animist?" shouted Maja who ducked under Mei's hand and stood in front of her.

"That I can, hun."

"Maja, no. Dryads are extremely dangerous. All they do is consume. Their boons are always tainted."

"Anyone who respects nature has nothing to fear from me, and I can sense your companion has a deep respect for my realm."

"I do! I've never gotten to explore the wilds, but I've read so much about it, about its dangers and blessings, and, and, how uncompromising it is. How humes bend to nature, nature never bends to humes."

The dryad smiled and held out her arms for Maja. Maja felt a cutting wave of sexual attraction spring from between her legs, and she waddled towards the dryad.

"Maja, don't...you don't know what you're doing." Mei stepped forward to grab Maja but tumbled face first in the dirt. A tree root was wrapped around her ankle. Maja snapped out of her trance and turned back to help Mei up. The dryad flinched as Maja turned around.

"Are you okay?" Maja lifted Mei's arm over her shoulder and helped her to her knees. A line of blood dripped down Mei's forehead. Her two fingers glowed white, and she slid them across her forehead, sealing the small cut.

"It's too dangerous. She's not going to let me be there to protect you. I don't know what she has planned for you."

Maja bunched her face together in deliberation. She pursed her lips together as if she could see the solution written on them.

"You have to promise not to hurt Mei, and we can leave together!" Maja shouted at the dryad, finding some resolve in the wake of her friend's injury.

"Whatever you say, hun." The dryad swirled her wrist to make the tree root retreat back into the earth. "But she cannot follow us. Humes have no business learning the secrets of nature after destroying so much of it. All you humes do is consume."

"I have to do this. I have to help the others. I'll be back. I promise." Maja held Mei's delicate, hume hand in her chubby green hands.

"Just be careful."

Maja nodded and scampered off with the dryad who smiled down at Maja as they walked deeper into the woods. The dryad's hands never left her swollen belly.

"Do you have a baby?" Maja pointed at the dryad's naked stomach.

"You could say that. I see you do too." The dryad smiled as she pointed down at Maja's tummy.

"How did you know!" Maja gasped and touched her tummy.

"I can sense anima, and you are giving anima to that baby, slowly but surely. And our babies have the same father as well. There's a spiritual connection."

Maja stopped, mouth agape as she stared up at the dryad.

"Al-Alexander was here!" Maja shouted and grabbed the dryad's hand.

"Alexander..." the dryad said to herself as she stroked her stomach. "The father of our children, yes. He was here the night before last. Filled with so much anger and guilt, followed by a lycan Summoner. He was handsome for a hume, and he gave to me, so I gave to him."

"Alexander is safe?" said Maja who was already in tears and unable to keep her composure.

"Yes, hun. He made his way safely through

my realm. I promise you."

Maja hugged one of her legs and continued sobbing. The dryad squatted down so they could hug properly.

"Thank you for keeping Alexander safe!" Maja howled. The dryad wrapped herself around Maja who could hear the song of the wind, and the running stream, and the roar of a volcano. The dryad's bountiful breasts hung in Maja's face. The overwhelmingly smell of fruit and flowers flooded her nostrils.

"Connect with me, young Animist. Don't fight it. You're feeling, not thinking. Keep feeling," said the dryad. Maja opened her eyes that were shut tight with tears and saw only darkness. She heard a heavy buzz, like a thrumming. It became a heartbeat, millions of heartbeats, all hearts beating together. It was a raging ocean of pumping blood that overwhelmed her. Maja screamed and the heartbeats stopped. Fingers placed bitter flowers in her mouth. She ate the bitters without thinking.

"Walk with me, Maja."

The meager forest of bare earth and dying trees exploded with color. Every sensation Maja experienced was amplified. She was naked now. She approached a pond where a pack of wolves drank while one stood guard. She heard their heartbeats and the splashing of water as they drank. They smelled like blood and musk. She bent down and drank from the pond. The water was cool and washed the bitter residue of the flowers from her mouth. She carefully approached the wolves who growled at her.

"Careful, nature is ugly AND beautiful." It was the dryad's voice, but she was nowhere to be seen. Maja swallowed and reached her hand out. The guard wolf approached and sniffed her outstretched hand. She tried to slow her heartbeat. In the back of her mind, she was living out her lycan fantasy. The wolf licked her hand then circled her to get a good sense of her smell. The pack surrounded her. Each creature rubbed its majestic, soft body against her as they circled and sniffed her. She felt each individual strand of fur as it caressed her body. She fell backwards into the pond.

She was in the ocean now, gliding through the water. The water was endless, touching all light near the surface and descending into the darkest dark below. Fish, real live fish, countless numbers swam through the blue depth. She had never seen a live fish before, and now there were more fish around her than the combined number of people she had ever seen in her life. The mass of fish swam and rippled like a sentient silver cloud. Maja inhaled the water, and it filled her lungs. There was so much blue. The blue of the boundless waters. The green of the endless forest. The gold of the infinite plains.

Maja was running across the plains with a pack of jackbeasts. She was hunting. The steady rhythm of paws tearing up the plains thrummed like war drums. She could hear their heartbeats as they pumped gallons of blood. She flanked a massive ridgeback lizard making it bellow in terror. She helped her pack kill that day. She tasted raw animal flesh. Tasted the primal anima of untamed animals. The metallic taste seemed to envelop her entire being. The blood carried memories of a time before humes when the world was less cruel and made much more sense.

Maja was back in the woods, a strange piece of fruit in her hands.

"Eat, Maja. Eat from me. I bless you with my Aspect." Maja bit into the green fruit which tasted clean and sweet, like water made of candy. It tasted of ancient sweetness, from a time before sugar ore was ever refined. She fell backwards onto the cold dirt of the forest floor. Her mind became overwhelmed as she sensed every single living organism in the area: every blade of grass, every insect burrowing, crawling, and flying, every bird, every small critter, Mei's soul shining bright nearby, the dryad cradling Maja. Their babies growing inside them.

"Try it. Try your magic," said the dryad as she set Maja on her feet. Maja held out her hand and tried to concentrate.

"No, hun, don't think so hard. Just feel. Feel the life all around you. It's not about bending nature to your will, but letting it flow through you."

Maja turned her hand palm up and took a deep breath. She thought about sex, and Alexander's fleshy hume cock, and Tan-tan's beautiful pussy lips. A strange, intensely pleasant energy roiled through Maja's body not entirely dissimilar to an orgasm. The sensation started at her feet, shot through her pelvis and out of her hand. Dozens of flowers sprouted instantly from the dirt in front of her with thick patches of long grass and several vines which quickly bore strange exotic fruit she had never seen before.

"Oh my..." said the dryad, "your anima is incredible, Maja. The anima of a mother is always strong."

Maja snapped back to reality as if awakening from the longest dream of her life. She was standing naked in the forest next to the dryad, her mossy pussy at eye level. Maja leaned in and kissed the dryad between her legs, bringing her right back to nature. The dryad gasped and shoved Maja's face in her mossy mound. Her swollen belly hung on Maja's head as she kissed between her legs again and buried her nose in the flowers and moss. The smell of ginger and flowers burned Maja's nostrils. The dryad sat back and sprawled on the forest floor. Flowers and blades of grass broke through the ground.

"You gave to me, and now I give to you," said Maja as she spread the lips of the dryad. Her pussy gushed nectar. Maja drank from her slit. It tasted of flowers and candy. She suckled the dryad's swollen, candy-green clitoris. The dryad cried out, and a small tree sapling burst through the soil near her. Maja inserted two chubby fingers in the dryad and played with her syrupy pussy. Her hand became coated with the thick nectar. She licked the dryad's juices from between her fingers then returned to suck the dryad's clit which was visibly throbbing and swelling. Maja sucked lovingly as she imagined her mama, and Mei, and Tan-tan, and Asuna, simultaneously pleasing all of her friends and family. Sucking their clits and giving them the orgasms they deserved. The dryad howled out, not unlike a wolf, and the entire forest rippled. The barren forest floor erupted outwards in a sea of grass and wildflowers. Leaves sprouted on every tip of every branch. The forest gushed with life.

"Oh, Maja, oh, she's coming. Nnnngghhhgh!" The dryad turned on her side and her pussy began to gape. Some object, like a giant seed or fruit, appeared between her labia and slowly slid out from inside her. She gasped and huffed as the the object stretched her wide. Maja stared in fascination as the dryad's mossy pussy stretched until a massive seed covered in nectar slid out.

"Bury it. Bury it so it can grow."

Maja lifted the massive seed and dropped it twice before deciding to hug it against her body. She waddled awkwardly to a grotto which she could sense nearby. The grotto was a high outcrop of stone where a short waterfall created a crystal clear pond. She set the seed down and dug up the dirty with her bare hands until she created a hole big enough to fit the seed. She buried it with only her hands available to move the soil, unsure if anything she was doing was correct. The hole was now a small mound with the seed inside. She leaned over the edge of the pond and cupped the water in her hands to take several sips. The water was cool, tasteless, and brought her fully back to reality. She made several trips back and forth to the seed, cupping the water with both hands and splashing it on the ground. After she sensed there was enough water, she scampered back to the dryad who looked far more like dead timber than a hume.

"Noooo! What happened!" Maja cried and rushed to her. She tried to lift her, but her limbs broke like dry tinder.

"Maja, are you okay!" Mei ran to her. "I heard you scream--oh my Lords, what happened here?"

"She died! She gave birth and she died!" Maja held the dryad husk and sobbed, breaking it into even smaller pieces.

"She didn't die." Mei squatted down beside her and pulled her in for a hug.

"But she's dead, look!"

"You said she gave birth, right? To a bulb?"

"A bulb? No, it was a seed."

"Same thing. That's her. Dryad's die and

are reborn for hundreds of years. Come on, where's this seed at?"

Maja led her by the hand to the grotto where a massive flower bud was already growing from the mound. The bud was mostly green fading to a white tip.

"That's it, isn't it?"

"Yeah, that's where I buried her seed." Maja slowly walked to the flower bud. "She's in there?"

"Yeah. She'll be fine, just needs time to grow."

"Okay."

"So where are your clothes at?" Mei looked at Maja's chubby naked body for the second time in her life. Maja didn't even realize she was naked and became aroused with Mei's eyes on her.

"At least tell me you're an Animist now."

Maja lifted her palm and thought about nursing on Mei's tiny breasts. Thorny vines shot from the ground around the massive flower bud and surrounded it.

"Wow, you're really good for just learning today. Would prefer if you put some clothes on, though."

Maja closed her eyes and exhaled. She thought about all her friends seeing her naked while they were clothed. She opened her eyes and found herself wearing a skirt made from layered leaves, decorated with big round gerbera flowers which faded from white centers to pink tips. Her breasts were concealed by two leathery leaves bound together behind her neck and back, giving her extra cleavage. Her tiny tummy and candy trail hung out over her skirt.

"Well done," said Mei, kissing the top of her head. "Now I need you to get back in the bag."

CHAPTER 19

"Where did THAT come from? Why didn't we see it earlier?" shouted Alexander, half at Serana and half at the strange temple.

"There's no way we wouldn't have seen it. It just appeared. Alex..."

"What?"

"That power I sensed, it's coming from that temple."

"Then we should get the fuck out of here, huh?" Alexander grabbed Serana's hand, and they hurried away from the temple. The sun had sunk suspiciously low, only half of it visible behind the Blasted Mountains which were suddenly much closer than they could have possibly been. Alexander whirled on his heel to take in everything surrounding him. Time and distance seemed to bend in and around his awareness. Mild vertigo tipped his mind side to side. The sterile mineral smell of the The Scoured Sands was replaced by nothing. The heat had dissipated too.

"What is happening? How is this real?" he said before he reached in his rucksack and removed his canteen. Everything was too vivid to be a fever dream but he drank anyway. His reality did not change.

"This is happening. But I don't know what IT is." Serana sounded just as worried as him.

"Well, we can't go in that temple. The Blasted Mountains are right there...I guess. Let's keep moving." Alexander marched on with Serana behind him. The sky was a rich purple tinged with crimson and long strands of yellow sunlight from behind the mountains. As they marched, the mountains did not come closer. The temple, thankfully, retreated with distance. The mountains seemed to slide back silently as they approached, never coming any closer no matter how many steps they took.

"Alex, I just realized something."

"What's that?"

"The sun's setting behind the mountains."

"Yeah?"

"Well, doesn't it set in the west?"

Alexander came to a halt. He turned back to see the haunting temple pulsating on the horizon behind him.

"Where are we..?" Alexander turned to Serana for answers. "This is like a nightmare."

"I think the answer is in there," said Serana, looking to the temple.

"Is this a dream? Is this really happening?"

"I'm here, Alex. As far as I know, this is really happening." Serana looked to her shoulder where her summon still napped comfortably. "I guess we have to go in there."

"Really?"

"I don't want to go in there either, but I think it's the only way to find out what's happening."

Alexander took a deep breath and marched towards the temple. "If I never tried to help Maja, I wouldn't be in this situation."

"Who's Maja?"

"That girl I saved. The reason I left Trinity. No good deed goes unpunished..."

"Well...I...I don't know."

"At least you're here, don't have to do this alone."

Serana ran up and grabbed Alexander's hand who squeezed it back and smiled. Hand in hand they drew closer to the menacing edifice. The red glow pulsated faster as if sensing their presence.

"I've never seen anything remotely like this in my entire life," said Alexander as he took in the bizarre, otherworldly architecture. The jagged monuments and gateways almost seemed to reach out for the guildies as they passed through the ebony arches and crossed the landings.

"I've been in a lot of strange places looking for artifacts. This beats them all, paws down. Do you think there's any chance we'll survive this?"

Alexander remained silent. He thought

about his life, his mother, his training at the mage's college, the secrets he hid there, starting his guild. He thought about his friends and his adventures. That girl sitting outside the bar stuffing her face with candy. All his memories seemed like they had happened to someone else.

They were at the threshold proper now. A wide flight of black steps ascended to the entrance of the temple. Serana and Alexander continued their march.

"If we don't survive this, I love you, Alexander Song."

Alexander squeezed her hand. Their steps were slow. No one was in a hurry to die. They reached the summit of the stairs. The inside of the temple was barely illuminated by red fire.

"It's like we're going down into the hells." Serana squatted down so her summon could scamper away.

"Then we go to the hells together." Alexander gave her hand another squeeze. Together they breached the temple entrance and entered a massive room with sconces on the walls that held red fire. The fire barely gave off any light and only hinted at the dimensions of the chamber.

"By the Devs, someone's here!" echoed a deep, sub-hume voice in the darkness. Two claps echoed through the chamber, and the room lit up brilliantly from unseen sources. In the middle of the room stood a being that was taller than the tallest hume and then some. His flesh was deep sanguine and rippled with horns and muscles. Between his legs hung an animal-like cock with enticing dermal bumps and bulbous ridges. Behind him were two female thralls who slept on the ground naked and wore oversized metal collars. Their pale skin and black markings indicated they might have been something less than hume. The collars had long black chains attached to them which led to a massive black throne with skulls carved into it.

"Who enters Ka Tuk's domain?" shouted the creature before he broke into a coughing fit. His monstrous hacks echoed through the chamber. He swallowed and approached his throne then yanked his chains to awaken his thralls. They stumbled forward and knelt beside the throne. Their irises were yellow-gold, and their eyes were smokey and half dead.

"We are simple travelers on our way to the Blasted Mountains. We didn't mean to intrude on your domain. We just can't seem to leave it," said Alexander, "Wait, did you say you were Ka Tuk?"

"Aye, mortal, you lay your eyes on the Lord of Flame." Ka Tuk raised his powerful arms in the air and the walls erupted with fire. "And you challenge me!"

"No! Noooo. This is all a misunderstanding. We're on a pilgrimage, you see. I'm going to train to be a Pyre Shaman and--"

"A Pyre Shaman?" Ka Tuk approached

Alexander. The ground shuddered with each step. His thralls crawled with him as their chains were pulled, theirs breasts swaying as they moved. Alexander shot a glance at Serana then back at the being who towered over him. The flames died down.

"Yeah, huh, uh, a Pyre Shaman." Alexander was drenched in sweat though the temple was pleasantly cool. He wanted badly to urinate.

"That is a dignified profession, mortal. It was I, Ka Tuk, who first gave fire to the humes, and I gave them the Pyre so that they could repel the monsters of the night and begin their civilizations. Not Alexandria, but I!"

"I-I-I've heard the legends. Humes owe everything they have to you...my Dev. Especially Fire Mages such as myself who tap into your power."

Ka Tuk grinned and rubbed his chin.

"You are a mortal who understands his place. This pleases Ka Tuk." Ka Tuk stepped back to sit on his throne. His thralls crawled to his sides and began to kiss and massage his demon cock. Alexander looked over at Serana who partially covered her eyes but grinned at the spectacle. Something itched in the back of his mind though. Some nagging sensation that something was forgotten, something crucial, like he had left a door unlocked or forgotten to bring gold somewhere.

"Well, as I said earlier, my companion and

I were on our way to The Blasted Mountains, and we seem to have become trapped here. If there was anyway you could show us out, or help us get there, we would be eternally grateful." Alexander felt himself talking too fast. Ka Tuk's cock rose as Alexander spoke. That sensation of forgetting something at home continued to tickle his mind.

"You would leave without an offering?" Ka Tuk growled.

"Off--offering? What did you want from us?" Alexander fumbled his words.

"You." Ka Tuk stabbed a finger in his direction.

"Me?"

"There's no need to become a Pyre Shaman. I can give you unimaginable power if you would give yourself to me."

"Wait," said Alexander, finally claiming that nagging sensation, "you destroyed Greenlan, didn't you? You're supposed to be destroying it right now."

"Greenlan? The realm of the goblins? Ka Tuk has no business with the green folk. Why do you accuse me of such?" Ka Tuk pet his thralls who continued to fellate him. Alexander looked over at Serana who silently mouthed, "What the fuck?"

Mechanisms and realizations reeled through Alexander's mind like a broken clock coming to life. He stood there stunned. Serana shook his hand to get his attention as Ka Tuk looked on expectantly.

"So, you didn't destroy Greenlan? The goblins didn't disturb you from your slumber under the surface of Ur?"

"You heard what I said."

Rage and realizations mixed inside Alexander's mind. For fifteen years it was widely considered fact that Ka Tuk had destroyed Greenlan which had forced the goblins to flee to Patriam. But if Trinity was really responsible for sterilizing the goblins, was it also possible they were responsible for what had happened in Greenlan? He wanted answers and the only place to start was back in Trinity.

"I accept your pact. I will give myself to you," said Alexander. A flush of feminity surged through his body like when he would pretend at the Mage's College. Ka Tuk grinned and stood. His thralls scampered to their corners.

"Alex, what are you doing!" screamed Serana as she tried to pull him towards the exit.

"Trust me. I know what I'm doing." Alexander squeezed her hand. Ka Tuk's footsteps shook the temple. Each footfall was a small explosion. Alexander stood stalwart and kept his eyes on the demon who had once been an almighty Dev. Ka Tuk grinned as his pointed erection dripped pre-cum which sizzled as it hit the floor.

"Very well." His cavernous voice rang out

through the chamber. Ka Tuk raised his hand, and Alexander was consumed by black flames.

"Nooooooo!" Serana's voice cracked in horror, and her sense of self shattered in that instant. The flames raged and rippled, resembling furious smoke. There was no sound from inside.

"Your companion is fine. He...I should say SHE, is more powerful than she could ever imagine."

The flames disappeared. Standing in Alexander's spot was a naked woman who looked remarkably similar to him. She was as tall as him, with the same frame, dark messy hair, and the same pained look in her face. Her body was elegant and pale, with hanging breasts and comfortable thighs. A whispy patch of black pubic hair was nestled between her thighs. She stared at herself, lifting her arms like a marionette. Her mouth hung open as if she had never learned to speak. Ka Tuk pulled Alex in by the small of her back and pressed her against his dripping erection. His pre-cum stung her skin and made her wince.

"Please leave, Serana..." said Alex, her voice breaking. Serana found no words, so she followed Alex's request. The demon began to dry hump Alex's stomach. His sticky hot precum smeared across her stomach and tinged her skin pink from irritation. He grabbed the back of her head with his massive claw and pushed her to her knees then used her face to massage his cock. Alex focused on her wish.

"You always wanted this, didn't you? You have always wanted to protect women. You wanted to save them. You wanted to be a comfort to them. You wanted to know what they went through. And you failed each and every one of them so miserably. Now you'll know how they felt."

Ka Tuk pressed his sanguine cockhead past Alex's lips and into her mouth. His precum sizzled on her tongue like over-seasoned gingered ale. She sucked his cockhead though, sucked like it mattered, how she would want to be sucked. She thought about all the women that did this for her in her lifetime and what they must have felt with her dick in their mouths. She felt small on her knees as this demon towered over her, his hand on her head, urging her to swallow more of his cock. She felt so vulnerable, so weak as his dick slid back and fourth over her tongue, tasting like bitter stone. She also felt... feminine? Not for the first time in her life, she understood that sensation, but in this moment it was amplified greater than she ever thought possible. It was like a blossoming inside her. She sucked more of his cock now and looked up at him. He grinned and urged her to throat him. She felt the dermal ridges against her tongue and his cock pulsating in her overstuffed mouth. She...was wet? She reached between her legs and felt the slickness on her fingers. The absence of her own cock was like a small burst of shock and feminine energy popping inside her body. She was wet for him, this man, this thing. Her body was ready to receive him. It was true that she had wanted to know and understand what women went through. At certain points in her life she had wanted to know it more than anything. She gagged on his cock and pushed herself away to swallow and catch her breath. Ka Tuk chuckled with his coarse cavernous voice as he watched her struggle.

"Good girl," he said. Alex remembered Maja in that moment. Ka Tuk easily pulled her head back in and punched at the back of her throat with his cock, using her head to masturbate. His hand was powerful and impossible to resist. His cock was thick and threatened to suffocate her. Alex felt helpless as he fucked her mouth, using her as a toy. She found herself crying, and Ka Tuk only seemed to fuck her mouth harder. She tried to pull away but couldn't. She was helpless to be fucked until he was done with her. In the back of her mind she felt desire stir. His strength and lack of compassion formed a paradoxical desire for him. She wanted him inside her, spreading her, making a woman out of her. His animal callousness awakened a primal need inside her to be mounted. Her thoughts swirled not unlike when she saw Maja gag on her own cock.

Without warning, her mouth was flooded

with cum as hot as fresh tea. Ka Tuk held her head in place and emptied his balls into her mouth as he sighed with ecstasy. The cum burned her tongue and the roof of her mouth, and she pounded on his stony thighs until he released her, coughing up cum on herself. She didn't even react as he splashed her face with a few remaining tendrils that stuck to her hair and cheek. She was forced to swallow about half the load and coughed up the rest on her chest. She felt used and...whorish. She felt like a piece of meat and a trash can. Her clit ached.

"Such a good girl," said Ka Tuk as he pulled Alex onto him. He reclined on the floor and lifted her on top of him with one fluid motion. His body stretched out like a mountain range with his muscles as hills and valleys. He was sadistic, but his brutishness inspired shameful sexual need inside her. She never felt she could do this with a guy before. But now that she was a girl, everything felt different. He lifted her body with ease and guided her onto his erection which refused to cease. She bit into her lip as she stretched around the demon's cock.

Ka Tuk grumbled and pulled her down forcefully. His raging cock spread every inch of her insides, and she felt like a sword had impaled her. He was inside her now. She was helpless, staked to the ground like a martyr. Her body opened up for him, welcomed the abusive cock. His claws dug into the pale flesh of her thighs and he thrust his hips up into her, lifting their combined weight. Her breasts bounced and fell. She was being fucked, really fucked, for the first time in her life. He threw his dick up her again and again, starting a rhythm. The entire experience shattered her former self as she balanced on the edge of consciousness. Her pussy drooled on his cock. It was so warm and thick inside her. Simultaneously, she hated herself and felt more complete than she ever had in her entire life. The cock continued to hammer her, drilling away at who she was before. She gasped and sobbed as the demon fucked her and transformed her mind and identity. She was elevated. The pain washed to the back of her mind as a current of steady pleasure and heightened awareness took over. She could feel everything, not just his thickness or the motion, but herself: her female self being impaled and fucked. She felt so feminine and wild, like an animal sprinting across the plains. Her breasts bounced chaotically as Ka Tuk penetrated her. She was in the storm. She felt savage animal lust and erotic wonder. She had completed a circle of human experience that was impossible to complete.

She spasmed and gasped as the longest and most intense orgasm of her life flooded every nerve ending. She moaned with double edged pleasure as the orgasmic waves rippled through her body, tingeing the tips of her toes and erasing the dark parts of her mind for only a moment. Ka Tuk continued to pound her as he raced to catch the orgasm he had thrust upon her. He growled like an animal and sprayed his stinging cum inside her. She felt it, all of it. She felt the orgasmic waves sloshing back and forth through her frame as the tickle of cum coated her insides and warmed them. She fought to catch her breath. The room was all color, an explosion of colors painted on her retinas. She collapsed on her demon lover. His claws found her soft ass and cradled her, gently playing at her vulnerable asshole. Her head was on his broad chest, but she felt no heart beating. He was still inside her, finishing with her hole.

"What happens now?" she asked, unable to even look up at him. She felt terrifyingly vulnerable. She felt lost, and scared, and as if at any moment someone could kill her. She felt guilty for enjoying sex with this thing, felt ashamed that his carelessness with her body excited her sexually. She felt horrible that she wanted it again, wanted meaner things. His wrapped his arm around her and her mind became tranquil. She kissed his body and clung to him.

"You have a much greater tap of my power, little ember. I have blessed you with the Dark Fire. Beware that it does not consume your soul." Ka Tuk almost sounded tender as he stroked her pale hume cheek.

"That's it, you fucker, this show is over!" shouted Serana from somewhere out of sight.

Ka Tuk turned over to see Serana by his throne, holding an ebony skull in her hand.

"Put that down!" screamed Ka Tuk before he threw Alex off of him and charged at her. Alex could only watch in stunned afterglow as her lover made to attack her friend. Serana did not flee or even flinch away, but instead she swirled one hand over the skull and stared down the charging demon.

"Ka Tuk abdu! Ka Tuk abdu. Ho-mei abdu Ka Tuk!" Serana chanted the strange words and the walls erupted with blinding fire, forcing the two mortals to shield their eyes. Then there was only the fading light from outside the temple. The sound of Ka Tuk's crashing footsteps had ceased, leaving only echos behind. The temple rumbled and the sky revealed itself as portions of the ceiling collapsed in with a deafening crash. The planet shook violently as Alex stumbled to her feet and ran for the entrance. The collapsing temple was a violent din as portions of the walls and ceiling fell and collided with each other.

"Serana!" screamed Alex after sprinting halfway down the stairs. She moved to run back inside but saw Serana in her lycan form bounding through the collapsing entrance with the skull tucked into her cleavage. She sprinted through the crumbling ruins and snatched up Alex without missing a step. With Alex under her, she loped down the steps as the menacing spires toppled all around and threatened to crush them. Once they were a safe distance away, Serana set Alex down on her feet, and they turned to watch the temple collapse and disappear into nothing. The countless tons of wreckage and debris disappeared into the desert itself. They stood there silently as the once magnificent and horrifying structure became nothing more than empty desert floor, vanishing into the desert's surface without a trace.

CHAPTER 20

"What now, Alex?" said Serana who was unable to make eye contact with her friend. Alex just stood there, naked, confused, feeling empty and alone. She held her stomach and stared at the desert floor where the temple once stood.

"Alex?" Serana raised her voice. Alex just looked at her, that same pained expression she carried her entire life.

"What's wrong?"

Alex fell to her knees and stared at the ground. "Everything's wrong."

"I'm sorry."

"I...what the fuck...why did you do that? What the fuck did you even do in there?"

"I thought he was hurting you. I noticed the arm of his throne was a summoning artifact. It was the only way to stop him. He WAS hurting you, right?" Serana looked over at Alex who grabbed at the dust and let it fall through her hand.

"No...he wasn't. It was something I wanted for a very long time. Now that I have this, I feel more confused than ever. About Ka Tuk. About

Greenlan. About this body. I don't have answers anymore. I don't know what to do."

"Whatever you decide, I'll support you. No matter what." Serana knelt beside Alex and squeezed her large lupine paw around Alex's small hume hand. The pads of Serana's paw were rough on the soft hume skin of Alex's hand.

"I don't even fucking know if I'm Alex anymore! Who the fuck am I!" Alex was in tears, looking at her friend for answers.

"You'll always be Alex to me. You'll always be MY leader, my friend, until we both die."

Alex leaned in and hugged her friend who returned a tight hug."I can feel your dick pressed against me."

"I'm not sorry."

Alex let go of Serana who tried to catch her gaze, leaning her head to the side.

"What's the plan, boss man--err, lady? I'm sorry, how do you...want me to refer to you now?"

"Just Alex, for now. I need time to think about that. Time I don't have. If Ka Tuk isn't destroying Greenlan, we have to do something. We have to find answers. I don't know if Trinity knows about Ka Tuk here. Either way, we have to find out what they do know. But I can't go into Trinity anymore..."

"Well...why not?"

"I'm wanted in Trinity."

"Nooo, there's a hume guy named Alexander Song wanted in Trinity. Not some demon lady."

"Demon lady?"

Serana looked up at Alex's hair, then at her pleasantly shaped breasts, and finally at her face. Alex reached up to touch her scalp and flinched when she found something new there. She grabbed at it but pulled her head around instead.

"What's on my head!" shouted Alex as she stood up.

"Whoa, they're just horns. They're kind of sexy, actually." Serana reached out to touch one, and Alex flinched away from her, slapping Serana with her new tail.

"What the fuck is that!" shouted Alex, spinning to find it. Serana giggled as Alex tried to see her tail. Protruding from the base of Alex's spine was an ebony tail. It started as thick as her arm and tapered to an arrow tip, a little longer than her reach. It flicked and wavered, seeming to have a mind of its own.

"I didn't even notice that earlier!" Serana grabbed it and rubbed the smooth flesh, "You are SO sexy right now."

Alex's face flushed and her knees pressed together when Serana grabbed her tail.

"What's wrong, does this hurt?" Serana released her tail.

"No...it aroused me," said Alex. Serana's face was one huge grin.

"I need some clothes. And we have to get out of this desert. It's at least a day's walk back to that cave we came through. I guess if we walk all night..."

Serana broke eye contact with Alex at those words.

"What is it?"

"You have to promise not to get mad."

"Serana." Alex dragged her name out like a parent chastising their child.

"I just wanted to spend more time with you."

"What did you do?"

Serana slung her purse against her hip and dug out a loop of golden rope that sparkled in the dying light of the desert. She whistled loudly and let the lead dangle from her hand. Large flapping wings approached them. A massive shadow moved across the ground in the moonlight. An elegant archon flew low over the desert floor and landed in front of them. The creature was pure, crisp white, with long, angelic wings twice as long as its body. Serana tied the golden lead to a luxurious collar around the archon's neck. Her summon bristled and shook its head then nuzzled against Serana who pretended to wrestle with its horns.

Alex stood there dumbfounded. She slowly shook her head side to side as she tried to disagree with the reality in front of her. She backed away, then turned and marched off into the desert.

"Alex, wait!" called Serana as she led the archon. "Alex, I'm sorry! I should have told you. It was selfish of me."

Alex continued her march. Nothing in her movement acknowledged Serana was speaking.

"You're going to die out there. Let me take you home. Please! Alex!" Serana was in tears now, her voice cracking as she shouted. "Please let me help you."

Alex stopped and turned to look at her, her face streaked with tears. She stood in front of Serana, balled fists trembling. Every duplicitous, stupid, selfish thing Serana had ever done while questing replayed in her mind. Alex had given her so many chances, and every time Serana proved she could not be trusted: putting up fake quests on the board just to make them quest together, lying about the time she was dying, lying about needing money and forcing them to quest together, purposefully forgetting adventure supplies to make them sleep in the same tent, risking their safety at the gates of Trinity, stealing her demon lover from her, possibly forever, and now finding out the deadly Scoured Sands could have been avoided...

"You're fucking manipulative. You caused this...I could have FUCKING DIED out here, you stupid fucking cunt!" Alex conjured a dark, swirling ball of fire in her hand and threw it as hard as she could at Serana. The fireball collided with Serana's chest and exploded. The archon wailed and fled into the desert. Serana launched backwards and crashed into the dust. A column of smoke rose from her body. A blackness crept up Alex's hand to her elbow. The dark unnatural rage left Alex as soon as the realization of what she had done crashed into her heart. She ran up to Serana's still body and knelt over her. An ugly black crater was the only thing left of her chest. The bottom half of her face was burnt off and revealed glimpses of the skull underneath. She stank horribly of burnt hair and sulfur.

Alex sobbed uncontrollably onto her dead friend. She cradled Serana against her and screamed until it caught in her throat and screamed more, almost forcing herself to vomit. She screamed for her friend, and her world, and all the people she had failed. She screamed until the tendons of her throat ripped and continued screaming. She screamed forever, screamed over the new worst thing she had ever done in her life.

"What did I do? What did I do to you?"

Once the hellish agony receded from its apex, and a portion of Alex's faculties returned, she began frantically digging in Serana's purse.

"I know she has it. She fucking told me she had one. Please fucking, Lords, demon, Devs, Mods, whatever the fuck is up there, please tell me this is the one thing she didn't lie about."

Alex dumped the purse on the desert floor. Inside were several random items including the dirty stone, a life sized golden spider, the black skull from the temple, and that special bottle Serana had told her about among other strange artifacts. Alex picked up the bottle and examined it. Inside the corked bottle was a tiny glowing person with wings like a dragonfly. She gasped. The relief of the discovery seemed to squeeze the air out of her lungs.

"She finally told the truth about something, this one thing," Alex said to herself. She pulled the cork out, and the miniature person lifted herself out of the bottle and floated to the ground. The tiny person gave Alex a mean look then climbed onto Serana's corpse. She crossed through the remnants of the black crater and then curled into a ball to sleep inside Serana's wound. Serana's whole body pulsated with benevolent white light. Her corpse levitated off the ground and rotated until she stood upright. Her arms moved into a prayer position. Alex stared speechless at the miracle. The light faded and Serana stood in front of Alex, whole once again. Alex hid her face in Serana's skirt, sobbing uncontrollably. Serana stared down at her crying friend.

"You are awful, Alexander Song."

Alex stood up and hugged her friend, sobbing the entire time. Serana let her have her hug but did not return it.

"And what if I didn't have a Fey, Alex? What if I was dead forever?"

“I would have killed myself. I couldn’t live with myself knowing I did this to you. I’m so sorry, Serana.”

“I forgive you, even though you don’t deserve it. You’re not allowed to yell at me ever again.”

“I’ll never yell at you again. I promise.”

Serana hugged Alex back.

“I’m a fucking horrible person,” said Alex.

“We should go home now.” Serana let Alex cry it out before she jogged after her archon and grabbed its lead, guiding it back. The archon resisted as it was pulled towards the demon girl. Serana helped Alex onto the archon, then leapt onto her mount with ease. Alex stirred uncomfortably as her bare pussy rubbed against the fine silky fur of the creature. She wrapped her arms around Serana who snapped the lead and made the archon gallop off into the sky. Serana kept her body low as the Archon took flight. Alex clung to her even tighter, sweating even though the night air was mild. They were high above the desert now. The edge of the The Great Northern Forest was visible on their horizon.

“I’m sorry,” shouted Alex through the rushing winds.

“I know,” Serana called back to her.

“No, I mean about everything. For the way I treat you. For yelling at you. For earlier...I know your father was a bastard, and you just want someone who cares about you. And I care about you Serana, even if I don't show it ever. I love you."

"I love you too."

"You can get another one, right? Another Fey?"

"No. Some Summoners go their entire lives and never capture a Fey. I don't think I'll ever see another one again."

Alex opened her mouth to respond, to make some offering for her, but couldn't think of anything that could realistically replace a Fey. Tears streamed sideways across Serana's cheeks, soaking into her fur. The desert floor sailed by under them, nothing more than a painful memory. The cracked earth was now a blank canvas painted with moonlight as their shadow slipped across the surface. They rode in silence and were pleasantly surprised to see the forest approaching them so soon.

Serana patrolled the edge of the desert where low dunes met the trees until she saw that familiar oasis and guided the archon down. After landing, Serana leapt from her mount and helped Alex down who was barely awake at that point. She removed the lead from the archon who pushed his big head in her chest for a hug then galloped away into the night. Serana led Alex to the low cave by the pond, helped her drink some water, then took some for herself. She situated herself to spoon Alex from behind and stretched out her legs, feeling the muscles in her feet start to relax. Soft rhythmic breathing came from Alex as she slept.

"I'm sorry," Alex whispered in her sleep. Serana reached her hand up and gently cupped Alex's breast and pressed her erection against her butt. She finally had Alex just where she wanted her. She reached down and touched Alex's soft stomach and deeper down to her dark pubic hair. Alex's tail flicked back and forth in her sleep, nudging Serana's dick at random intervals, making her cum in her robe. She wanted to mount Alex and knot her to become one with her boyfriend/girlfriend. She wanted to slam her canine cock into Alex until she cried in pleasure. She wanted to make Alex feel beautiful. She wanted to see Alex kiss her cock and drool on it, accepting and craving the person she really was. She felt Alex stir in her sleep and decided to stop molesting her, still unable to quell her erection.

CHAPTER 21

"Her father is in the sugar cartel. At least, that's what she told me," said Asuna, looking off to the side.

"It would seem her father is a big deal in Trinity, has amassed the kind of fortune that bends laws to his will," said the Paladin.

"Must be nice."

"I'm assuming you have no more business with us. The only suspect we had is out of our hands, and there's nothing we can do to compel information from you."

"Can talk to my friend, the one that was attacked. You can still do some good in this situation."

The Paladin remained silent as her eyes flicked back and forth across the table.

"You would have made a good Paladin. You have a strong sense of right and wrong. You have an instinct for good work, and your abilities would let us make headway into many of our fruitless campaigns. It's not too late, you know. A woman of your abilities would receive special entry into our guild. You would only report to the highest of the higher-ups."

"My brief interactions with The Guard were not exactly pleasant. It doesn't seem like the kind of guild I want to be associated with. Have things really changed that much since The Wrath?"

"You're smart, so I'm not going to lie to you. Things are better than before The Wrath. It's a sickening thing to admit, but for all the evil she did, it changed the attitudes of male Paladins and opened up the profession to female Acolytes. Personally, things could be a lot better, but if you join us, YOU could make things a lot better. I don't seriously believe any Guard or Paladin would try to give you a hard time. You could show them how powerful a woman is."

"Heh. Tantra would love that sentiment. I'll give it some thought. Would help if I ever actually had a positive experience with The Guard."

"Then let's find your friend. I'll prove to you being in The Guard isn't about knocking skulls and hassling the poor. We're here to protect people. It is our solemn oath." The Paladin gave Asuna a stoic look to show the gravity of her convictions.

"I guess we have a little goblin girl to find. Her name is Maja. She's small, voluptuous, with bright blue hair. She might be training to become an Animist. She has ties to the Healer, Mei Windsor in Gold Town, and the only people allowed to talk to her are us. This doesn't leave this room. You don't know who is involved and who is also looking for Maja."

The Paladin's mouth hung open as her head slowly swung back and forth. "You're a natural at this. You were never a Paladin before? You never multi-classed?"

"No, I...had a good friend that was a Paladin once. She was brilliant and principled. I learned a lot about humes from her."

The Paladin made an awkward smile at Asuna's word choice.

"Well then, let us find your friend. My name's Lindlithsong, my friends just call me Lin." Lin held out her hand for Asuna who shook it. Lin's grip was strong but no match for Asuna's power.

"Asuna, but I guess you already knew that."

"It's my job to know. Now let's go find Maja." Lin crossed the room and produced a key to remove the broken shackles from Asuna's wrists and ankles. Asuna rubbed her joints then followed Lin from the room and out of the dungeons. The interrogation room was right at the main stairway that connected all the parts of the Guard station. The stairway was several stories high and led directly to ground level. At each story a landing intersected the stairs, leading to other areas of the Guard station.As they followed the stairs out of the lower reaches of the Guard station, Lin turned off at the first landing to a small barracks that contained four sets of bunk beds.

"This is where some of the Paladins sleep during longer shifts," said Lin as she methodically removed her heavy plate armor piece by piece. Her teeth held leather straps as she loosened other sections of her armor until her invulnerable exoskeleton was slowly shed away.

"Do you need help?" said Asuna as she watched Lin fight the bindings of her pauldrons.

"No, but thank you," Lin managed to say with a leather strap clenched between her teeth. "Been doing it like this for years."

Asuna turned sideways and shielded her eyes as Lin stepped out of her cuirass and greaves to reveal a powerful brown body. Asuna snuck just a peak and felt her face go warm when she saw Lin's considerable abominable muscles contract. Lin hung her armor neatly on a peg rack then dug in one of the wooden footlockers for clothing.

"You can look if you want. I have to suit up and armor down all the time in front of men. Can't really feel self conscious at this point."

"No, no! You deserve some privacy," Asuna was able to stammer out. Lin smiled at her and missed Asuna sneak a peek of her bending over to dress. Asuna felt the pull in her groin as Lin's powerful hips squeeze into her pants.

"You're, you're very beautiful." Asuna

squeezed her eyes shut and covered them with both hands.

"Thank you," said Lin, fully dressed now, "okay, civilian, stop hiding your face."

Asuna turned to see Lin standing in a tight men's tunic and basic slacks. Her biceps shifted like small animals under her skin with every movement of her arms. Asuna dry swallowed and nodded.

"Have to stop by the armory to collect some gear. Did you need anything?" said Lin as she guided Asuna back to the stairs and to a higher level of the Guard station.

"No I, I don't really need weapons at this point."

"That's amazing. Not having to rely on anything but your own ability. I admire that," said Lin as they passed a pair of Guards down the stone hallway. Lin led them to a massive underground room the size of a city block with a stone counter secured into a wall of iron bars as thick as columns. A Guard stood at the counter and waved to Lin as she entered.

"Hey, aren't you on duty?" The Guard asked before he leaned across the counter to give Lin a hug. The Guard was an older hume male with a friendly face.

"Just taking a little break," said Lin as she braced her elbow on the counter.

"And who is this cool mug of ale?" said the Guard. Asuna bashfully pulled her arm across her chest.

"This is Asuna. Was a witness to a murder in The Steps. Just making sure she gets home safe. Asuna, this is my friend, Marv."

Asuna reached out her hand and Marv gave it a vigorous shake.

"So, *Asuna,* I guess you're going home to your husband?" Marv leaned on his elbow and tried to make sexy eyes at her. Asuna giggled and shook her head, covering her mouth.

"Aye, that's good to hear. Your laugh is adorable, by the way."

"You don't waste any time, do you?" Lin laughed and punched his arm, making him lose his balance against the counter. "She has a girlfriend."

"Of course she does, a beauty like that. Was silly of me. Now what do you need? I ain't got all day." Marv feigned serious business by looking past the two women as if there was a huge line forming. Asuna laughed again.

"Gimme' the claymore. The runic one."

"Dawnbringer? You got the clearance for that?" Marv's voice suddenly took on a serious tone. Lin's mouth began to open for an argument, but Marv playfully slapped her arm and chuckled, making her smile with anger.

"Every time! Every time I get you. You are TOO much."

"Just get the lordsdam claymore!" Lin tried to shout but couldn't stop chuckling.

"Sure thing, babe." Marv tapped her hand then disappeared into a forest of weaponry behind the counter. Countless racks of every conceivable weapon and armor were stuffed in nooks and hung on pegs. The armory seemed to go back for miles, impossibly deep underneath the city. The pet name Marv used made Asuna think about Tan-tan and what she was going through seeing her family again after five years.

"Sure you don't want anything?" said Lin as she drummed her fingers on the thick stone counter.

"I'm quite certain. Thank you though."

A metallic scraping sound rang out in the maze of weaponry. Marv appeared in the lane directly behind the counter, dragging something encased in leather.

"This lordsdam thing weighs a ton!" Marv gasped as he dragged the massive package. His face was a tableau of the indomitable hume spirit and its capacity to do mundane work. His skin was glazed with sweat and turning pink as he dragged the sword to the counter. With one big huff he lifted the handle onto the counter and let it fall with a massive thud. He dipped behind the counter and came up with a slate and a small stack of papers, leaning on the counter to catch his breath before he made a note in it.

"Just going to put a little star next to Dawnbringer and pretend it's still here. Have to shuffle some inventory around on paper. Go ahead and grab it," said Marv as he busied himself with the papers. Lin reached for the claymore and pulled it over the counter. A glassy, translucent barrier rippled across the armory bars as the sword broke the threshold. As the sword lay across the counter, Lin undid the leather bindings to reveal a brilliant white claymore as big and as wide as an adult hume. Inside the blade, near the hilt, was a blazing runic emblem, remarkably similar to an actual sun. Asuna approached the counter to gaze upon the claymore. As she neared the blade, she felt searing pain in her face and flinched away.

"What is that thing?" said Asuna, rubbing the stinging sensation out of her skin.

"This is Dawnbringer, my favorite blade. I don't get to use it much. It's not government sanctioned for Paladins, but I'm not technically on duty right now." Lin drew the blade across the counter and took it with both hands. She braced herself in a combat pose and stepped forward as she took several disciplined swings: cut, thrust, parry, roundhouse. She swung the titanic claymore with the ease of a standard issued blade, her muscles flexing as she practiced. Asuna felt the solar energy radiating from the blade and pulled her cloak around herself.

"As much as I want to try this in combat, I hope I never need it, but I'd rather have it and not need it, than need it and not have it." Lin set the claymore back in its binding and sealed it up, then used the loose straps to bind the sword to her back. Her considerable size prevented the gargantuan blade from dragging on the ground.

"Do me one last favor," said Lin, "please don't tell anyone we were here. As far as you know, I dropped my sword off for the interrogation and that's the last you saw of me today."

"Sure, Lin, but what are you up to? Where you going with that sword?"

"It's better if you don't know. Take care of yourself." Lin pounded the counter once before she left the armory with Asuna. The Guard station was almost empty midday with most of the Guards out on patrol. Asuna bundled herself up in her cloak as they stepped out into the afternoon light.

"So where is Maja?" said Lin.

"Tantra said she was staying at the bar our guild is based out of. It's in the The Steps, in the hume part of town. That's probably the best place to start."

"Lead the way then," said Lin, sweeping her hand in front of her. Asuna led them out of the Administrative District, passing The Starlight as they left. She wondered what would happen when Lin discovered the story. This was the kind of action they wanted though, someone investigating the abuse.

"Can I ask you something?" said Asuna as they left the Administrative District.

"Sure."

"Why did you remove your armor, and why the sword?"

"I don't want the Guards in The Steps to know I'm investigating this. I can't kick this through the proper channels because we don't how far up this abuse goes, if there actually is abuse. Some reason I trust you. Even with that ugliness you showed back in the interrogation, I don't think you've said a disingenuous thing to me this entire time. When you've been in this class long enough, you start relying on your instincts to get anything done. When you told me what happened to Maja, and after what your girlfriend said, my instincts are screaming right now. But I have to investigate this personally, and I don't need any Guards knowing that I am. If they see us, it just looks like two women on a quest, nothing more.

"And as far as the sword goes, I don't want any Guards challenging me. I've heard the stories about The Wrath, about the rapes. It's not that I don't trust my men, we rely on each other to survive out here. It's just...when someone's caught doing something like this, they'll do anything not to be caught. Walk softly and carry a big sword, no one wants to fight a Paladin carrying a claymore."

"Wow, you really thought everything through. I guess I'm just used to Tantra leaping into a fight and asking if it was a good idea afterwards. So how did a Paladin get trained with a claymore? Not even Fighters receive that training."

"I multi-classed. I trained all the way up to Warrior then hopped over to Paladin. It's served me well. I was first in line for promotion, and I got to hear a lot of men bitch about it. Now let me ask you something, how did you become a Revenant at your age? I've never even encountered a Revenant before you, thank the Devs. They're supposed to be ancient men, not beautiful young women."

Asuna turned away from Lin as she blushed.

"Just lucky, I guess."

"Come on, now. I just said how much trust I put in you."

"I'm sorry, I'm...much older than I look. I've trained a very long time, and I never wanted to feel terrified in combat again. I wanted it very badly."

"I can respect that. I hope you seriously consider joining The Guard. Like I said, a woman of your ability would receive special entry. Hells, I may even end up reporting to you. Not that I would mind. You seem like a good person. We need people like you."

Asuna covered her mouth as they walked and felt her cheeks go warm from the praise.

"Does it upset you when I compliment you?" said Lin. Asuna nodded, still covering her face.

"I'll stop if it bothers you."

"No...I know it's *normal* to give and receive compliments, just my father...he wasn't big on praise."

Lin grabbed Asuna by the shoulder then gave her a playful shake and a smile.

"I know EXACTLY where you're coming from. My dad was an archon's ass. Nothing was ever good enough. And his little girl becoming a Guard? He despised the idea. Women were Healers, that's where they belonged. But I wasn't going to spend my life supplementing men as they achieved glory. I wanted to prove everyone wrong about everything. After the Wrath came through Trinity, I knew what I needed to do. I class changed, and the rest was history."

"You were already a Warrior during The Wrath? How old were you?"

"Heh, was sixteen when The Wrath paid her visit to Trinity. I started training as a Fighter very young and just had a natural aptitude for combat. Wasn't going to let my old man push me into being a Healer."

"I actually have a lot of respect for women that become Healers. I've tried to learn the healing arts myself, but I have no aptitude for it." Asuna looked at her cold ashen hands with disappointment.

"Women only become Healers because they think they have no choice."

"I don't think that's true..."

The small disagreement brought silence to the new relationship. After passing through the working class hume neighborhoods, the two women found themselves at the bar. Asuna led the way up the steps and inside.

"What a shithole," said Lin as they entered the bar, watching the few daytime drunks who lounged in the main room.

"It certainly has character," Asuna said politely as she crossed the room to the bar where the keeper was wiping down glasses.

"What can I do you for?" the barkeeper asked with a smile as the women approached. His eyes fell on Lin's claymore.

"Hi, do you remember me from this morning?" said Asuna, rubbing her arm.

"Aye, miss. Sure do."

"Do you remember me eating with a little goblin woman with bright blue hair. She asked for candy for breakfast?"

The barkeeper chuckled, and Lin made a weird smile at the retelling of events.

"Aye, miss, would be hard to forget that one."

"Do you know what room you gave her upstairs?

"Nah, she doesn't have a room upstairs. I would certainly remember if that one was staying here, I would."

"Fuck..." whispered Asuna, "thank you anyway."

The bar keeper nodded and continued his chores. Asuna turned to Lin but was unable to look her in the face.

"I'm sorry. I really thought she was staying here. Tantra SAID she was staying here. I don't understand." Asuna crossed her arms over her chest and looked at the floor.

"I believe you. And I don't mean to start something, but do you think your girlfriend lied about her staying here?"

Asuna still wouldn't look up as doubt and suspicion slowly crept into her mind.

"Maybe Tantra was mistaken. Maybe Maja lied to her. I wouldn't be shocked if Maja was homeless the way she devoured breakfast. We should ask around The Steps."

"Look at that mind go, so deductive and rational. We could really use you, Asuna. Anytime you want to join."

"I appreciate the offer. Let's just find Maja first." Asuna led them out of the bar, across the cobblestone road, and into the hume part of The Steps.

"Would you mind waiting here a moment? I need to check in with my guild," said Asuna before she stopped a block away from Morty's cellar.

"Sure, go ahead."

Asuna left Lin on the corner and crossed through three alleys to Mort's cellar which was still missing a door.

“Hey Mort, it’s me. Do you have any news?” said Asuna as she descended into the cellar. The lamp came to life on the table and Mort appeared in the darkness.

“Two members have left the guild since yesterday,” said Mort with no inflection in his speech.

“Of course they have…” said Asuna with a sigh.

“Serana left you a message. Her and Alexander reached the Scoured Sands this morning.”

“That…was impossibly fast. Are you sure?”

”Yes, ma’am.”

”Any other messages?”

“No ma’am.”

“Here, get that door fixed.” Asuna produced a silver coin from her cloak and flicked it on the operating table. She climbed the cellar stairs and found Lin exactly where she had left her.

CHAPTER 22

"Everything okay in the guild?"

"Couple people left immediately after I took over," said Asuna as she stared at the ground. Lin gently punched her arm.

"Hey, don't give them the satisfaction. If they think a brilliant Revenant isn't an effective guild leader just because she's female, then they're idiots."

Asuna's face went warm, and she playfully punched Lin back.

"Let's just find Maja." Asuna led them into the goblin parts of The Steps as the sun began to set behind the colossal wall which protected Trinity. Crowds of people in the streets headed home from their fields and labors as they walked. In the goblin Steps, groups of male goblins huddled outside and played games around makeshift tables while stuffing candy in their faces. Lin eyed the filthy unkempt neighborhood with apprehension. Asuna silently examined the conditions the goblins lived in with stoic sympathy.

"How are we suppose to find one goblet in

this rat's nest?" Lin grimaced at every sight she took in.

"Should ask around." Asuna approached a group of goblin men gaming outside. "Excuse me, do you know a goblin woman named Maja? She's small and chubby with bright blue hair. Loves candy?"

The goblin men paid Asuna no more than a brief glance before they continued their game.

"Ahem!" Lin stepped up and made the collective group flinch. "The lady asked you a question."

"We-e-e don't know any goblet named Maja. Sorry, please don't hurt us," said one of the goblin men who trembled with his friends.

"Thank you," said Asuna who tried to sound as if she had no intention of hurting them. "Also, I hate to bring this up, but have you heard of any goblin women being sterilized in The Steps?"

The group of men all cast eyes at each other but spoke no words between them.

"Well?" said Lin, clenching her fist.

"We don't know anything about that, ma'am," said the goblin man, unable to make eye contact with Lin.

"You folks asking about the goblin women?" came a voice from across the roadway. Asuna and Lin turned to see a goblin woman hobbling over to them with a wooden spoon clenched in her hand.

"Have you heard something?" said Asuna, squatting down to her level. The goblin woman cast an angry inquisitive eye at the humes in her neighborhood.

"Bad make'ons in The Steps. Goblets get'on snatched off the street and have'on their precious gift stolen from them. Say Trinity is up to no good." The goblin woman held the wooden spoon in both hands as if she was ready to snap it.

"Shut your damn yap, Mulja! Don't need to be talk'on to humes about green business," hollered one of the men at the game table. Mulja darted across the roadway with a speed that contradicted her age. The speaker who had foolishly chastised her stood up from the table and fled for a nearby shack. Mulja was too quick though and tackled the goblin man before she gave him a sound beating with her oversized spoon. The man covered his head as the wooden spoon made loud vicious smacks against his bare skin. The rest of the men roared with laughter.

"Don't you point your tongue at me, Frahnco, unless you care to not have it! This is women's business, not men's business. Don't see the men do'on not'on about it," Mulja barked as she continued her beating. Lin effortlessly removed Mulja from the thrashing she was distributing. Frahnco fled into the shack and began to barricade the door with furniture. Lin set Mulja down after she stopped struggling.

"Tell us what's happening in The Steps," said Asuna as she squatted down again to talk at Mulja's level.

"Just told you humes, Trinity's go'on around snatch'on up young goblin women, steal'on the only bless'on the Lords gave them. Why you ask'on, anyway?"

"We're here to help. Do you know any women that have become victims? We really want to talk to them," said Asuna.

"I don't have any daughters, but I know folks that have. Sick humes only go after goblets just turn'on marry'on age. Sick business, I tell you. Will be hard to find a goblin will'on to talk to you two. Ya'll have Guards written all over you. Ya'll Guards, aren't you?" said Mulja whose words crashed together as she became more charged, shooting them a vicious squinting eye with her hands on her hips. Lin elbowed Asuna with a smile, but Asuna didn't feel like smiling.

"I am in The Guard, yes. This is Asuna. She brought this problem to my attention. We're here investigating. We just want to help." Lin squatted down to follow Asuna's lead. Mulja nodded as she looked around, smacking the wooden spoon in her hand as she gave the idea some thought.

"Okay. I don't like the idea of trust'on a pair of hume Guards, but I doubt we'll be get'on much in the way of help out in The Steps. Come on now, follow me. We'll see who's will'on to talk." Mulja tucked the wooden spoon into the waistband of her apron and led the two women through the maze of The Steps. They stopped at various, squat domiciles and gave Mulja space as she spoke with different goblin women. Each woman shook her head as Mulja gestured towards the two humes. At some homes a young goblin woman would peak out of the doorway and quickly hide back inside. Mulja shook her head each time they were refused.

"Like to hope these are just unfounded rumors," Lin said to Asuna as they followed Mulja.

"I don't think it is. Their faces...they're scared. Someone has been doing something horrible to these women. I'm not leaving until we get some information."

"I wasn't going to say anything, but there're a few too many Guards in The Steps. I started noticing them now that we're in deeper."

"How many is too many? Can't have too many Guards in place like this, right?"

"Asuna...we don't have a division for the goblin Steps. There shouldn't be any Guards in here."

"No Guards?"

"We don't have the resources for it. The higher-ups won't allocate men for it. I don't know exactly why, but we just don't. And we're sticking out like a sore tit. Hope they assume I'm just a Warrior."

Mulja hobbled up to them after another

unsuccessful conversation. "Ro-Rora lost her daughter a few months ago when some humes grabbed her and did some awful mess to her. Bled out right in her home. She don't want to talk to you folks."

Asuna looked at the goblin woman who Mulja had finished speaking with. The mother's face was pure rage and agony. The pain of the mother bled into Asuna and welled up the atrocities she had experienced in her long life. She could feel the darkness wanting to escape, darkness predicated on seeing the cycle of atrocity repeated over and over across generations.

"Come on. We have to keep going," said Lin as she shook her by the shoulder. Asuna pushed down the painful memories and followed Lin and Mulja deeper into the Steps.

CHAPTER 23

Mulja talked to another goblin woman inside the doorway of her home and this one nodded, gesturing for them to enter her tiny shack.

"I don't think I can fit in there," said Lin who failed to force a laugh.

"I'll go, don't worry." Asuna got on her hands and knees and crawled into the goblin shack. The inside would have been perfect for a child's playhouse. Against the wall was a couch made from scrap metal and covered in discarded fabrics. On a metal end table was a tiny metal statuette made from scrap. Asuna was able to sit upright against the wall while Mulja sat on the couch. The owner of the shack went in the other room and returned with a younger goblin woman who wouldn't look at Asuna. The goblin woman put her arm around her daughter.

"Go on, sugar, tell her what happened. She's here to help," said the mother. The daughter kept her eyes down as she recounted her ordeal. The story came out slow and trembling. Her mother rubbed her back and encouraged her at the painful parts.

"Several weeks ago, me and my boyfriend were walking home from the candy shop when a group of humes started chasing us. They beat Rolfo until he was unconscious and then took me away. They took me into the hume neighborhood into a basement...and then..."

The young goblin woman paused at this point to compose herself. Her mother held her hand and rubbed it. The young woman kept gasping for air as tears fell into her lap.

"Take your time, child," said Mulja before she passed a grave look to Asuna.

"They tied me to a table and then, and then, they forced a metal spike inside me. I screamed and begged them to stop, but they wouldn't. After they were done, they dumped me back in The Steps. It was very late, and I had to crawl on the ground because it was too painful to walk. The chirurgeon said...the chirurgeon, he said..." The daughter broke down completely and latched onto her mother, screaming into her dress. The mother rubbed her back and told her it was enough now. The mother finished the story.

"The chirurgeon told her she would never be able to have babies. Once she told that good for nothing Rolfo, he abandoned her. And then he told the whole neighborhood she couldn't have babies. If I ever see him again, I'll cut out his tongue myself, I will. I took it upon myself to tell a Guard what happened, but they didn't believe me. Nor did they seem to care."

The mother was in tears too, angry tears. Mulja and the mother embraced the daughter as she continued to bawl. Asuna's heart ached and twisted as tears rolled down her stunned face. She kept squeezing her fist, and her breath caught in her throat as if she was choking. The sadness turned over to rage. These men stealing her womanhood from her, stealing her value, her identity. For what? Why? Because she was a goblin? Tremors overtook Asuna. She couldn't keep her hands from shaking. Her tears wouldn't stop coming. The room was too small.

"You were so brave, little one," said the mother as she held her daughter's hands and bit her ear.

"I'm going to stop them," Asuna said abruptly as the hatred and outrage constricted her chest. "I'm going to stop them. Nothing on Ur or in Ur Tra will be able to stop me from getting to them. Nothing. They have crossed the wrong FUCKING path."

The words of anger were clenched in Asuna's teeth as she crawled from the home. Her hands still trembled even as she crawled. Lin stood outside with her arms crossed, trying to seem casual. She turned to Asuna as she stood up.

"Lords, are you okay?" Lin rested her arm on Asuna's shoulder who knocked it away with ferocious power. Lin's eyes went wide.

"You tell me now, right fucking now, that you had nothing to do with this. That you didn't know this was happening. Every fucking word that little person said in there...It's your people that are doing it. It's nearly the same lordsdam story Maja told me, and they were in the fucking Guard. I won't fucking let this stand. I can't. The Guard never learns its fucking lesson." Asuna clenched her teeth and fists and stared contained annihilation at Lin.

"How do you know it's the Guard?" said Lin, stunned at Asuna's power and at her eyes which had turned to swirling black pools.

"One of them had a fucking guardian rune on him! Now answer me, lordsdamit! Answer me! Tell me the truth!" screamed Asuna.

"I swear to you, I had nothing to do with this. I want to help as much as you do. Asuna, please calm down."

"I can't calm down. I can't! What they did to that girl in there is unforgiveable. I can't help you catch these guys. If I find them, I'm going to fucking kill them, and it's not going to be fast...it's going to take forever, and I'm going to enjoy every hour of it."

"Asuna, please. I know you're upset. Please be reasonable. We don't need another Wrath. Especially not a Revenant one." Lin had one hand up in defense as she reached over her shoulder for her claymore. "We'll get these guys. We'll expose them publicly. Their names will be a matter of record, forever. That's real punishment."

Asuna finally caught her breath and unclenched her fists. Lin stepped forward slowly then embraced her. Asuna sobbed on her shoulders.

"I can't do it. I can't deal with this suffering. I'm sick of seeing the atrocities humes carry out. It eats at me. It kills my soul. Humes deserve what they get."

"I know, I know. Coming up as a Guard, finding murders, rapes, abuse, then investigating them as a Paladin. I've seen the worst in people. It hurts me too. Just have to push through."

"How do you do it? What makes you want to keep helping people?"

Lin was silent.

"What? Please say something," Asuna begged as she shook with grief. She felt the void fill her. The realization came once again that atrocity came natural to people, that no matter where she went, she couldn't escape it.

"If I don't do it, no one else will. Maybe it's the only thing keeping civilization from ripping itself apart. Good people take it upon themselves to fight back," said Lin.

"It hurts me. I want to help these people, Lords and demons, you don't know how much I want to help these people, but the suffering...I'm reaching my limit of how much suffering I can bear witness to. It's devouring me."

"Then help me find these guys. Help me

make sure not another woman has to suffer them."

Asuna pulled away to compose herself, unable to look at Lin.

"You two make a cute couple," said Mulja as she hobbled from the shack. Asuna managed a smile and knelt down to hug her, half for herself and half for the goblin woman.

"I promise you, we'll find these guys. I'm never going to stop. I swear it to you," said Asuna as she watched the mother and daughter in the doorway.

"Aye, I believe you, pale one. You got the look in your eyes. I know these men are as good as dead," said Mulja as she stepped away.

"We can't kill them," said Lin.

"If they resist, I will not hold back. It will be the last mistake they ever make," said Asuna. Mulja gave her an approving nod.

"Come on. You know who we have to talk to next," said Lin.

"Who?" said Asuna. Her mind was still clouded with misery and thoughts of vengeance.

"The Guards, of course. Someone has to know what's going on here. Even second or thirdhand. Let's start interrogating."

Asuna took a deep breath and followed after Lin. "Where was the Guard stationed? The one that was killed."

"The Administrative District. It's the soft path. Every Guard wants to be stationed there.

Pays more, less crime, make connections with the right people."

"Then why was he in The Steps?"

"Not entirely sure. No one to corroborate his whereabouts before he was murdered. He lived in The Steps, most Guards do, but he wasn't anywhere near his home. The house they found him in was abandoned."

"Do you believe me now? About why he was murdered?"

"Hard not to believe you after that. Whatever that little goblet told you in there obviously set you off. I know something heinous is happening here, but I can't just assume it was him, that it was The Guard. It's my duty to remain objective until all evidence is collected. Hey you!" Lin shouted at a Guard as they rounded a corner. The Guard gave her a "what the fuck?" look then plodded towards Lin.

"What are you doing here?" said Lin.

"What do you mean what am I doing here?"

"Why are you in this goblin neighborhood? There's no patrols out here."

"And how would you know that?" said the Guard as he tightened his grip on his halberd. Lin reached in her pocket and produced a gold medallion with the Paladin class symbol on it. The Guard whispered "fuck..." under his breath and tried to maintain eye contact with Lin.

"Now answer the question, what are you

doing here?"

"Madam Paladin, you need to leave now." The Guard broke into a sweat.

"You are not one to give such orders to me. Now answer my question, or I will have you reprimanded." Lin's posture and tone made the Guard shrink away from her.

"Madam Paladin, these orders come from Lord Tychus. I cannot speak of the impending operation."

"What operation?" Lin reached for her claymore. Asuna stared on in fascination as Lin dominated this man with only her words.

"Madam Paladin, if you are on a duty, you are prohibited from being in the vicinity by Lord Tychus. If you do not vacate the vicinity, I will be forced to remove you." The Guard reached for his pocket but Lin's arm shot out like a snake. She snatched his wrist and slammed his body against a stacked dwelling behind them. All the goblins in the area stopped to watch the Guard about to be thrashed.

"You were going to call reinforcements against me, you little shit?" Lin growled with her face inches from his. She grabbed him by the throat and slammed him against the home again with a hollow clang. Her free hand reached in his pocket and removed his guardian rune. She whipped it at the ground where the crystal shattered into a fine sparkling dust.

"You're all alone now, rookie. You think

these people are going to speak a word if I snapped your lordsdam neck? Hells, I bet they'd help me hide your body. Now you answer me, what the fuck is happening in The Steps?"

"We're, we're moving the goblins out of The Steps, all of them. I'm just here to make sure things are ready. My commanding Paladin said to just to keep an eye on The Steps before the operation began tonight. That's all I know. I swear! Please don't kill me. Please!"

"What!" barked Lin, visibly confused about the revelation, "what about the sterilizations? You know Wilson was killed, right? What was he doing here in The Steps?"

"I swear to you, I don't know. I never heard anything about sterilizations. I swear!"

"Get the fuck out of here. Go cry to your Paladin. Let him have more sympathy than I did." Lin released the Guard who stumbled as he fled through the cramped roadways. The audience in attendance cheered and hooted at Lin for removing the hume Guard from their neighborhood. Lin was not amused by their adulation.

"Things just got way more complicated. I have to talk to my Tank," said Lin as she moved to leave the neighborhood.

"Wait, what about the girls? We have to bring them justice," Asuna called after Lin as she chased her.

"You think this is a coincidence? Assuming what you said is true--"

"It is true."

"Then that means someone higher up knows what Wilson was doing when he was killed. It can't be a coincidence that Guards are in The Steps now, getting ready to remove the goblins."

"You think the Trinity government would remove thousands of goblins just to cover it up?"

"No. Lords, no. I don't know how they're connected, but they are. When deduction fails, you have to go with your instinct, and my instincts are screaming right now. These two things are connected, and if we can make the connection, I bet we can find out who ordered the sterilizations."

"I thought you didn't trust anyone in The Guard with this investigation?"

"I don't, but if I had to trust someone, it would be my commanding Tank. If he knew this was happening, then I don't even want to be a Paladin anymore."

"Attention! Attention, everyone! Butchery in The Steps! Young goblin women mutilated by Trinity as part of an ongoing campaign to throttle the goblin population," proclaimed a voice surrounded by dozens of humes and goblins on the roadside. Each person leaving the crowd held a large pamphlet.

"What the fuck is this!" shouted Lin as she shoved her way through. At the center of the crowd was a goblin boy with a fat stack of pamphlets under his arm. He handed them out and collected coppers as fast as he could.

"Butchery in The Steps!" he shouted, taking no notice of Lin until she lunged at the bundle of pamphlets under his arm and lifted the him up with it. The gathering of people shouted and booed, trying to pry Lin away.

"Lin, no!" Asuna ran to the mob slowly forming, caught Lin under her arm, and pulled her away. "Let him go. What are you doing?"

Despite Lin's impressive strength, the crowd managed to force themselves between her and the goblin boy, booing and finding loose cobblestones and garbage along the roadside to throw at her. Asuna had leverage on Lin's body and managed to pull her away from the mob of people.

"What the hells was that?" said Asuna. Lin stood with her hands on her knees, breathing heavily.

"You didn't tell me you brought these accusations to the Starlight!" Lin glared at her.

"I didn't. My girlfriend and guild leader did. I had nothing to do with it. Tantra didn't even tell me until after it happened. Why are you so angry? This is what we wanted, right?"

"You realize now that whoever was sterilizing those girls now knows that we know? We'll never catch him!"

"Is that why you're really mad?"

"Yes," said Lin, unable to sound honest.

Asuna stared at her for a real answer.

"When stories like that come out, it just builds distrust and resentment towards The Guard. It makes our jobs more difficult and more dangerous."

"If The Guard behaved decently, then maybe these kinds of stories wouldn't be printed in the first place."

"You don't understand. We have all these men and women risking their lives and just a handful of scumbags makes us all look like scumbags."

"I guess that's true. Let's catch these guys then. Get ahead of the story. Your Tank, let's talk to him."

Lin nodded and set off at a jog for the Administrative District. As they moved through the various neighborhoods of Trinity, it seemed as if everyone returning home from their labors was reading a pamphlet, or at least discussing it. Asuna felt Lin's shame as they swiftly made their way through the post-work crowds and into the Guard station. The station buzzed with Guards ending and starting the evening shift. Several of them had pamphlets in their hands and loudly argued about the content. Lin deftly navigated the crowd of Guards and entered a bright tiled hallway before she turned off into a beautifully appointed office. At a desk sat a large, over-armored man examining some paperwork. His hair and beard were silver and his neck looked closer to a tree stump than an actual neck.

"Tank Ursa." Lin stood at attention at the threshold of the office.

"Enter, Paladin Lin," the man said, not looking up. Lin entered the office and sat in one of the leather easy chairs, nodding for Asuna to do the same.

"Sir, I have need of information. Information only you can give me." Lin sat upright like an arrow stuck in the ground.

"I'll see what I can do, madam Paladin." Once again, Tank Ursa did not look up from his paperwork.

"There appears to be a covert operation happening in The Steps, and I believe it is related to a crime carried out by Guard Wilson in the same area, sir."

"That is quite the imagination you have." There was no inflection or emotion in Tank Ursa's voice; he spoke as if stating a simple observation.

"Sir, please, you're the only one I trust to bring this to. What was Wilson doing in The Steps? The Starlight has the story now, there's no point in hiding it." At those words, Lin noticed a Starlight pamphlet sticking out from under Tank Ursa's paperwork. He finally looked up which forced a pleading smile from her.

"You're one of the good ones, Lin, the best of us even. You understand the nature of these things. Nothing will be confirmed or denied unless it's forced out. From the scant information I received, Guard Wilson was committing a crime in The Steps when he was killed, though what crime he was committing has not been shared. I do not know who ordered it, or if it was even ordered. It is not wise to poke your nose into such matters. As far as the Vanguards are concerned, you are disposable. Do not get involved."

"I won't accept that, any of that. I will find out who Wilson was working with, even if I have to do it as a civilian."

Tank Ursa let out a deep sigh and set his work aside.

"Why is this so important to you?" Tank Ursa looked at Asuna as if she might be the answer.

"Because it's one thing if we don't have the resources to help those people in The Steps, but to go after them like that, and no repercussions for it. I can't be part of a guild that operates like that. It's the same heartlessness that brought The Wrath down upon us. I can't let it happen again. I'm going down to The Steps, and you tell them I'm coming, and I'm bringing a Revenant with me." Lin stood up to leave when a chain made of light shot out from Tank Ursa's torso and melded into Lin's flesh.

"Did you just pull me?" shouted Lin in disbelief.

"It's for your own good," said Tank Ursa as he raised his hand. An invisible force shot from his palm that sent Lin's claymore magically from her body and into the stone hallway with a loud crash. Asuna let out a nightmarish half shriek, half hiss and turned into a hume-shaped haze with blazing crimson eyes.

"If you kill me, Revenant, your friend dies too. I have her soulbound now. Anything you do to me is done to her," said Tank Ursa in a booming voice as he stood. Asuna returned to her physical form. Her eyes darted between the two of them.

"Go help them. I can't do anything anymore, but you can do anything you want."

Asuna stood and made for the door.

"If you go there, a Harbinger will be waiting for you!" said Tank Ursa. Asuna froze in the doorway. The blood in her veins sent shivers through her every limb. Her heart pounded furiously in her chest. It had been several decades since anything had scared her.

"He's lying. We don't have any Harbingers," said Lin who attempted to stand, but her feet were planted to the floor as if bolted down.

"Not in The Guard, no," said Tank Ursa, "but ever since The Wrath visited us, we have kept a Harbinger under mercenary retainership, only to be used in emergencies, such as a Revenant interfering with a Guard campaign."

Asuna looked to Lin who slowly shook her head and shrugged.

"You have to help those people," Lin managed to say, her voice bereft of its natural confidence.

"I can't...I can't die. I'm sorry." Asuna lowered her head and fled from the Guard station in tears. She fled through the streets, bumping into people occasionally with her eyes on the ground. The mighty sensation of fear from a literal lifetime ago had come roaring back, making her legs move as if she could somehow escape it. She couldn't even remember the last time she was afraid of something.

"Assassins do not fear, they are fear," her teacher had said those many lifetimes ago. But today she was in fear. This day she remembered what fear was.

"Revenants are unstoppable. Everyone knows that," she had said one drunken night with her guild. She remembered Tantra making eyes at her from across the candlelit table.

"They're not actually," said Mei who had been nearly wasted on a half mug of ale, using the table as a pillow for her face. "A Harbinger could stop a Revenant, even in their shade form."

Everyone had turned to Asuna who had no argument.

Asuna sprinted through The Steps and to the bar. She pushed past idling drunks, down the hallway, up the stairs, and locked herself in her room. She threw herself into the corner, curled into a ball, and cried into her knees. The fear was real. She had never once contemplated the idea of dying, at least not since becoming a Revenant. Even the idea of encountering a Harbinger seemed as likely as being struck by lightning. No one had actually ever met a Harbinger, but the stories seemed all too real.

Harbingers were impossible to hit. They always seemed to be just out of range, to move without moving, as they slowly drew closer. You would exhaust yourself out of fear of their touch. Their right hand, black and decrepit, reached out for you. Just the one touch to kill anything or anyone. Tanks erupted in boils and fell dead in their impervious armor. Assassins were snatched from their cloak and vomited blood. Summoners fell over cast in solid gold. Just one touch to snuff out even the most powerful soul.

Asuna sobbed into her knees and gasped for air. She dreaded the sense that he was coming, that he somehow knew where she was at this very moment and was slowly drawing closer, ever more closer. She crawled across the small expanse of floor and cracked open her door. There was no one outside. She stood up and walked down the hallway, wiping away the tears from her face as she carefully descended the stairs, ready to bolt if she saw anyone suspicious. She made her way to the bar room and took a seat against the far wall, so she could watch the entrance in case anyone strange appeared. After ordering a mug of ale so she wouldn't be bothered, she never took her eyes of the entryway.

All the things she had wanted to accomplish in The Steps had gone out the window. All she could do now was focus on the fear of dying. The goblin girl sobbing on the couch, the complete injustice brought down on her, and Asuna could do nothing. Her mind would not let her go into the goblin Steps. She beat herself up viciously in her own mind, trying not to cry in public but wanting to torture herself for her cowardice. What was her life weighed against theirs? It made sense moralistically to give her life for them, but she had been alive too long to even fathom it ending.

CHAPTER 24

"Can you ever forgive me?" said Tan-tan. Her shame suffocated her as she tried to speak.

"I forgive you," said Alo, still hugging her big sister.

"Lords, I'm such a fuck up. Are you okay? Are you happy?" Tan-tan held Alo's precious tiny face and stared into her big copper eyes for answers. Alo nodded and reached up for Tan-tan's face, kissing her tears away.

"You'll never understand how much I missed you. I thought about you every single day. I wanted to take you with me, but you were so young and fragile. I'm sorry...I'm so sorry."

"Why did you leave, Tan-tan?"

"I can't tell you. When you're older, I promise I'll tell you, but I won't put that burden on you when you're this young."

"I want you to be able to spend every day with your sisters," said their father, "but first we must talk about this little trouble in town. Makilja, please take Alo to the dining room and wait for us. Lunch will be ready soon."

Makilja hugged Tan-tan from behind and

gently bit her ear before she took Alo by the hand and led her away to the dining room. Alo and Tan-tan never broke eye contact as she was led away to the dining room.

"Come, Tan-tan, I want to speak you to in my study." Tan-tan's father reached up to hold his daughter's hand and led her across the room. A massive door led to her father's brightly lit study. Two walls of paned windows looked out on the luscious garden in the backyard. An Agent standing against the wall closed the door behind him as he exited the study. Tan-tan's father released her hand and walked around his beautifully appointed desk to sit in a specially made, hume-sized chair which allowed him to see over the desk.

"Would you care to explain yourself?" Her father gestured towards her.

"Care to explain YOURself?" Tantra crossed her arms and stared him down.

"Tan-tan, you're wanted for the murder of a Guard. How...how does this happen? What have you gotten yourself into? I won't always be here to bail you out."

"I'm not wanted for murder, daaaaad. I wasn't even there when it happened." Tan-tan felt herself regress in age as she made the same lame excuses of her teenage years.

"That's not what it says in my report. It says here they found his guardian rune in your purse." Her father's eyes fell on a small stack of papers on his desk then returned to her.

"Sometimes your Agents don't get all the facts no matter how much you pay them. The Paladin in charge even said they're looking for Alex--" Tan-tan quickly shut her mouth.

"Who is this Alex person? Is he in your guild?" Her father leaned forward in his chair.

"That's none of your damn business."

Her father hopped out of his chair and moved across the room to open the door.

"There's a man named Alex involved with my daughter. Find him immediately," her father said to the Agent standing outside.

"Lordsdamit! Alex saved my friend from being sterilized. A young goblin woman not that much older than Makilja. He had to do it to save her."

"Regardless, I want to talk to this Alex on my terms," said her father as moved back to his desk.

"Don't you fucking hurt him!"

"Don't you dare raise your voice to me, daughter of mine! You may be an adult now, but you are still my daughter, and you will respect your father." Tan-tan's father pointed an accusatory finger up at her which made her shrink away from him. His raised voice made her heart tense up and her steely nerves turn to liquid.

"Now, why don't you tell me why you left us all those years ago," said her father as he climbed his special chair and took a seat.

"This place was slowly killing me. I had to escape. You don't understand what it's like to live in YOUR house."

"Is there anything more pathetic than a child complaining about living a life that affords her the security and comfort very few will ever know?"

"There's more to life than money."

"Someday you'll realize that nothing brings you more peace of mind than financial security."

"Is that how you felt about mom? Cared more about your money than her health? Do you even care about us?" said Tan-tan as she found her nerve again.

"What kind of daughter would ask such heartless things? I loved your mother more than life itself. I would pay any amount of money to spend even one more day with her."

"Loved her as long as she promised to give you a son..." Tan-tan slipped the accusation into the conversation like poison into a drink.

"What did you say?" Her father's naturally confident voice finally cracked as he stood in his chair.

"I said, you only loved her because you expected her to give you a son! That's all you fucking wanted, wasn't it? And her last fucking words to you were an apology. She gave you three healthy daughters, but she died begging your forgiveness. You're the heartless one in this household!" Tan-tan screamed the accusations, imagining they were daggers being slung at her father. He looked as if all the air had been pulled from his body. Three Agents burst into the room and surrounded Tan-tan, daggers ready in an underhand grip.

"Don't you dare hurt her!" her father managed to choke out as he swallowed air. "But don't let her leave the house."

Tan-tan stormed out of the study, slamming the door as hard as she could. The crash of the door echoed through the cold and empty house. She marched across the parlor and down an elegant hallway until she arrived at the dining room. Her sisters burst into smiles like two flowers blooming as they watched her enter. Tan-tan did her best to smile for them. She took a seat between them at a table set for a dozen guests. A floor to ceiling vanity window on the far wall looked out on the garden. Towering family portraits faced each other from across the table. Tan-tan looked up at the oil painting of the entire family together: her hume mother sitting in a chair with Alo swaddled on her lap, her father standing beside her on one arm, and Makilja on the other. In the painting Tan-tan stood behind them, her hand resting on her mother's shoulder. She had forgotten what her mother's face looked like after five years. In Tan-tan's memories there was only her warm countenance. Tears welled up, and Tan-tan covered her face to hide them.

Makilja clung to her arm."What's wrong?"

"It's nothing. I just missed you girls so much." Tan-tan planted a kiss on each of her sisters' heads. Makilja returned the kiss.

"Is papa gonna eat with us?" said Makilja before her hand snuck between Tan-tans thighs.

"We can't do that anymore." Tan-tan removed her sister's hand from her body. Their father entered without a word and took a seat across from his daughters. Not one second after he took his chair, several maids and servants poured in carrying enough food for an entire dinner party. Roasted meats and cheeses and fruit platters covered the table. Breads from all over Patriam. No pastries or desserts, never any candy. There was a large pan of scrapple still in the skillet which had been their mother's favorite when she was younger. Crispy flat breads covered in melted cheeses, oil-fried hunks of chicken. Tan-tan built a small plate of food for Alo and touched her head as she set it in front of her. Then she went to build a plate for Makilja and shook her head when she realized Makilja was old enough to do it herself now.

"Sorry," muttered Tan-tan as she almost reached for her sister's plate. Makilja laughed and kissed her sister's cheek, squeezing her thigh under the table. If their early conversation had upset her father, he showed no signs of it as he made a plate of food and ate quietly.

"What have you been doing for the past five years?" her sister asked as she rubbed her thigh. Tan-tan brushed her hand away and started in on some bacon and tiny cheese wedges.

"Well, I joined a guild and became a Rogue. Our leader is a great guy...was a great guy. I met a sweet girl named Asuna. She's older, but she's very kind and intelligent."

Makilja's face darkened when Tan-tan mentioned Asuna.

"After awhile I was able to job change into a Stalker which I'm very proud of, and lately we've been helping the goblins living in The Steps who are having a hard time of things, to say the least."

"Ewww, The Steps. I hope I never have to see it." Makilja grimaced and set her fork down.

"No, they're good people down there. Just handed the wrong end of the dagger. Don't be so hard on them, Ma-ma. They lost everything they had in the Passage."

"If you were a Rogue, you could have become an Agent. There's a lot of money in that. I would have hired you myself to give you work experience."

"I didn't know you hired women," Tan-tan said with a smirk. Her father was unfazed by her instigating, so Tan-tan stared at him for a retort.

"We don't fight at the dinner table, Tan-tan. Your mother raised you better than that."

“I’m happy you’re home,” Alo chimed in as she gently chewed on a piece of fruit. Tan-tan leaned over and kissed the top of her head, trying not to cry again.

”Me too,” said Makilja.

“I have some business to attend to today. Please look after your sisters while I’m gone.” Their father excused himself from the table and left the dining room. As soon as he left, Makilja snuck her hand between Tan-tan’s thighs again, and Tan-tan snatched it away, giving her sister a reproachful look. Alo put her food down and clung to Tan-tan’s arm. Makilja mimicked her little sister and clung to her other arm. Tan-tan carried them outside into the backyard as the servants cleared the table.

Their backyard was a perfect slice of manicured nature. A plush even lawn rolled under a massive oak tree and up to an artificial stream which flowed through the edge of their lawn and on through other backyards. Towering hedges lined with overflowing flowerbeds blocked their property from the view of neighbors. Their backyard was one of the only places on the property which Tan-tan didn’t despise. She sat on the lawn and took off her fingerless gloves to feel the pillow-soft grass under her calloused hands. Alo grabbed one of her hands and examined the calluses, touching them with her miniature chubby fingers.

“What happened to your hands, Tan-tan?”

said Alo as she traced her fingertips over each individual callous. Seeing her sister take such an interest in Tan-tan's hands, Makilja also examined them.

"Well...I got them through a lot of training."

"What were you training for?" said Makilja.

"I was training to protect my friends."

"Aww, that's nice. When will we get to meet your friends?" Makilja rubbed Tan-tan's calluses against her face.

"I don't know, someday hopefully. Would really love for you two to meet Asuna."

"And what's so great about Asuna?" Makilja crossed her arms and pouted her lips.

"Everything. She's gorgeous and caring and smart. She's powerful and thoughtful. She's not quick to anger. She always thinks things through. She makes me want to be a better person. And she's not my only friend, would love you to meet Maja, too. She's a goblin just like you. Lords, she must be so worried at this point. I have to let her know me and Asuna are okay."

"You're leaving again?" Makilja held Tan-tan's hand to stop her from leaving. Alo pulled on her other hand.

"Just for a little bit. I'm not abandoning you...again. I promise I'll never abandon either of you ever again. I just need to tell my friend I'm safe."

"Then I'll come with you!" Makilja shook Tan-tan's arm with excitement.

"No, you're staying here. It's a dangerous city out there. You have no idea what it's like."

"Well, you did it. Why can't I?"

"I didn't have a choice, and I almost died plenty of times. If something happened to you..."

Alo climbed into Tan-tan's lap and hugged her around the neck, crying quietly.

"Oh, baby green! I'm sorry. I didn't mean to scare you." Tan-tan was in tears but kept her composure as she hugged Alo.

"She missed you a lot. First mom, then you, it was hard."

"I know. I didn't want to leave, but I couldn't stay here. I'll never be able to forgive myself for leaving you two here with dad, but I wasn't going to survive if I didn't leave."

"What's so bad about living here? I don't get it. Why did you leave? Was it us?"

"No! Dad didn't want me here. That's all I can tell you."

"He seems to want you here now. I don't think I've seen him smile since you left."

Tan-tan didn't know what to say to her sister, so instead she held her baby sister down and blew raspberries on her tummy making her squirm and giggle. Alo's laughter felt like someone had dipped her heart in a warm bath.

Tan-tan and her sisters spent the entire afternoon in the backyard chasing each other, wrestling, riding Tan-tan around archon-back style, and forgetting the problems that lay outside the walls of their home. There was not one moment when at least two Agents weren't watching them. Agents watched them from the yard or peered down on them from the many windows of the back of their mansion. Tan-tan couldn't remember a time when Agents didn't skulk around the house. Even when she would lay day to sleep, sometimes she could catch a glimpse of them before they patrolled to another room. Over time the family just forgot they were there, and they continued their normal routines, but her training as a Stalker forced her to constantly notice the eyes around her that took too much interest in what she was doing. She knew she was safe at her father's mansion, but the constant scrutiny of her and her sisters kept her on edge the entire time, as if waiting for an ambush.

Dinner that night was eaten in silence with their father noticeably absent. In the evening the three sisters sat on the patio under crystal torches infused with anima which gave off brilliant white light. They listened to the tamer tales of Tan-tan's adventures as a Rogue. Alo sat in her lap and Makilja clung to her arm as Tan-tan tried to recall her earlier, more mundane quests before Alexander and the guild. After a couple hours, Alo was halfway asleep and Makilja let out a big yawn. Tan-tan carried them upstairs, Makilja on her back and Alo in her arms, and tucked each of them into their separate beds. She gave each of them a kiss on the forehead before retiring to her old bedroom which had not changed an iota since she left.

Instead of any pleasant reminiscing, Tan-tan only felt a heavy sense of regression as she entered her room. It was as if everything she had accomplished since she left home had been for nothing, essentially forced to stay in the same room she had occupied as a child. The stupid expensive toys lining the shelves made her feel mildly upset, as if her father still expected her to play with them. The bed was comfortable though: more comfortable than any bed she had slept in since she left. Not everything was so awful about coming home.

Tan-tan closed her eyes and pretended to sleep as she waited for the next Agent to check in on her before she made her escape. She heard her door move and let her eyes open imperceptibly, sensing a silhouette move through her room. It was uncommon, but not unprecedented, for an Agent to move through their bedrooms at night, especially if her father had reason for alarm. The silhouette moved to her bed, climbed in, and grabbed her crotch through her pants.

"Lordsdamit, I said we can't do this anymore," Tan-tan hissed in a loud whisper and grabbed her sister's wrist.

"Why not?" said Makilja as she stretched

touch her once again. Makilja's pussy was hairy like Maja's, just like the last time she had masturbated her. Makilja reached in the front of Tan-tan's underwear and spread her labia open before slipping a finger inside her big sister.

"Where did all your hair go?" said Makilja as they mutually masturbated each other. Tan-tan pressed her pussy into her sister's hand as they fucked each other.

"I waxed it," she whispered, trying to look into her sister's eyes in the dark.

"It feels amazing. I'll see if papa will let me wax mine."

Tan-tan imagined her sister with a smooth waxed cunt and felt that primal sexual pull behind her pussy. Makilja lowered herself in the bed, pulled Tan-tan's pants down, and kissed her sister's dripping pussy. She was as caring and as adventurous as always, spreading her big sister open with two fingers and fucking her with her tongue. Tan-tan covered her mouth to muffle a moan as her little sister devoured her. Years of "playing" had given Makilja the intimate knowledge of all of Tan-tan's weak spots. She sucked Tan-tan's clit, the slurping sound alarmingly loud in the otherwise silent bedroom. Tan-tan bucked her hips as she was overwhelmed by the acute pleasure of having her clit sucked. Makilja continued, and rubbed her clit vigorously with her thumb, until Tan-tan was forced to bury her face in a pillow for a screaming orgasm.

"My turn," said Makilja as she lay back in the bed. Tan-tan collected herself and stuffed some pillows under her sister's chubby hips to help her own neck. She buried her face between her sister's thighs and inhaled the smell she missed so much. Her sister's cunt was a wonderful mix of musk and expensive soap. Makilja giggled as her big sister inhaled her. Tan-tan spread her sister's lips open and slowly dragged her tongue up her slit until the tip of her tongue flicked off her clithood. She pushed her lips back back and kissed her sister's tiny clit, making her flinch. She gently suckled her clit as she slipped two fingers inside her and fucked her.

"It hasn't been the same since you left. I can't make myself feel the way you make me feel."

Tan-tan pushed her sister's hips up and pressed her tongue up inside her sister's asshole, wriggling it inside her. Short interrupted yelps came from her sister as Tan-tan tongued out her asshole while massaging her clit. The calluses worked magic to bring her sister her first orgasm, but Tan-tan wasn't done. She flipped her sister over and shoved three powerful finger inside her, furiously fucking her. Makilja squealed into the pillow as her big sister fucked her brains away. Her sister's juices began to coat her hand as she fucked her.

"We need to go now! Put some clothes

on, both of you!" An Agent burst in her room and barked orders. Tan-tan's heart tried to jettison itself from her chest the second they were caught. The Agent obviously knew they were in there together but didn't seem remotely perturbed at what they were doing.

"Move now, both of you," ordered the Agent before exchanging words with another Agent in the hall. Tan-tan quickly dressed her sister and carried her into the hall where a half dozen Agents stormed about and exchanged quick words with each other. Tan-tan felt herself slowly die from embarrassment and shame. The two sisters stank of sex, and Makilja's juices were dripping down her arm.

"We have to get you out of the house, now," the original Agent said with authority, grabbing Tan-tan by the arm. She was too embarrassed to stop the man from grabbing her.

"What's happening? Where the fuck is Alo?"

"Your sister will already be in the carriage. We're taking you to a safe house at an undisclosed location," said the Agent as he led her down the stairs.

"What in the hells is happening? Are we being attacked?"

"No, ma'am. The Trinity government is forcibly migrating goblins to an as-of-yet unknown location. Your family isn't safe inside the city."

The Agent didn't relinquish her arm until she was at the carriage where another Agent opened the door and guided her in. Inside the carriage were two Agents and little Alo half asleep. Tan-tan set Makilja down and pulled Alo into her lap. Once the door was closed, the carriage began moving. Tan-tan didn't bother to ask about her father.

CHAPTER 25

"Aww, why do I have to go in the bag?" Maja whined and pushed her lower lip out. "I don't think The Guards can tell goblins apart."

Mei sighed but kept a straight face. "I am sure you're correct, but a hume traveling with a goblin draws too much attention. I'm sure The Starlight printed your story by now if that investigator is to be believed. I know it's degrading, but I only do it for your safety. Come on, I want to check on Tan-tan and Asuna."

Overwhelmed with Mei's logic and consideration, Maja moved to climb into the bag. Without warning, Mei grabbed her, covered her mouth, and dragged her behind a fallen tree.

"Shhh, don't say anything. There's two people coming our way." Mei peered over the tree to get a look. Her instincts were right; the motion she had noticed was two people moving through the woods in the distance.

"So?" whispered Maja.

"They could just be hunters out for game, or they could be highwaymen this close to the road. It's not even dawn yet. There shouldn't be anyone out here. We'll just stay put until they pass. I don't want to deal with them."

"Come on, we can take them. I'm an Animist now."

"No. Maja, no. I don't fight anymore. There's no reason to be in a fight when you don't have to. But if we can't avoid them seeing us, can you snare them with a root tangle?"

"I'm sure I could." Maja gently waved her hand in the air, and a tree root emerged from the ground and circled itself. "Yeah, this is easy."

"We're not going to trap them just because we can. Not everything is a fight. The sooner you learn that, the further you'll go in life."

"How do you know they're bad?"

"I don't, but I don't want to find out." Mei watched the two figures meander through the woods towards their hiding spot, hopefully by pure coincidence. She studied them for signs of their class. As they approached, she realized one of them was completely naked and the other was a lycan. The realization of a lycan approaching made her drip sweat. Lycans were ferocious and unpredictable, more animal than hume.

"What's happening?"

"One of them's a lycan. We have to make for the road. Hopefully a patrol will be out there. Be ready to snare them, the lycan first. They're fast, so you have to be faster. I can protect us, but we won't win in a fight."

Mei turned back to watch the two figures.

They were much closer now, still moving towards the fallen tree where Mei and Maja hid. If they moved now, surely they would be spotted, but if a Guard was on the road, they would certainly be safe. But if the Guard seized Maja or started questioning them...

Mei's heart was out of control. She felt her body seize up. She couldn't make a decision. Incoherent thoughts surged through her mind, and she became coated in sweat. All she could do was watch the two strangers approach. The lycan turned back to his or her hume form. The other was still naked and looked strikingly like Alexander from a distance. Flashbacks of the last fight she was ever in swarmed through her head and made her grind her teeth.

"Mei, Mei!" Maja whispered loudly, tugging on her sleeve. Mei was soaked in sweat. She clutched her chest. Maja picked up her hand and squeezed it.

"What's wrong?"

Maja climbed on Mei and stood on her shoulders to see over the log. Two humes were approaching. They seemed harmless. The naked one caught Maja's eye, not just because she was naked though. She studied the naked hume with her soft thin body and wispy pubic hair.

"Alexander?" said Maja as she scrambled over the log. Mei sat against the log still frozen in fear. Maja sprinted to the two figures but stopped halfway when she realized that the Alexander person had horns and a flicking tail.

"Maja?" said the woman as she approached. Maja stared at the strangely familiar hume. The horned woman fell to her knees and pulled her in. Maja hugged her back.

"Is that, is that you?" said Maja.

"Yes, baby green," she answered in Alexander's voice. Maja squealed and squeezed her tight upon hearing that reassuring pet name.

"What happened!" Maja pulled back to hold Alex's face. Alex stared at the ground as if looking at a friend's grave before she looked at her. Her eyes were heavy and dark. She had seen horrible things which she couldn't forget.

"It's a very long story," said Alex as she tousled Maja's bright blue hair.

"Well, I still love you." Maja stood on her toes to kiss Alex's cheek.

"Who is this?" The other woman approached with a purse slung over her back.

"This is that little goblin girl I told you about. The one I left Trinity over. Maja, this is my friend, Serana."

Serana studied Maja in her little flora outfit.

"Hi." Maja reached up for a hug.

Serana ignored the offer. "So, you're the one who tried to steal my boyfriend."

"Boyfriend?" said Maja.

"Please don't start with that." Alex turned

to address Serana before facing Maja again. "What are you doing out here? You're suppose to be in The Steps. Where's Tan-tan?"

Maja's lip quivered and she was in tears again as she remembered that nightmarish afternoon. She pouted and threw her arms around Alex, remembering how she couldn't protect her friends.

"What happened?"

"They took her! They took Tan-tan and Asuna. Me and Mei came out here so I could be an Animist then we were going to go rescue Tan-tan and Asuna."

"Who took them, was it The Guard? Mei's here? Where is she?"

Maja nodded then pointed to the fallen tree. The three of them approached together and walked around the tree to find Mei on her side trembling.

"What happened to her? Mei, are you okay?" said Alex as she approached. Mei turned her head to see them and stopped shaking. She sat upright against the tree but couldn't make eye contact with them.

"Mei, it's me, Alexander. You remember Serana, right?"

"Would be hard to forget Serana," said Mei with a single empty laugh to herself.

"Why were you hiding here?" said Alex as Maja waddled over to give her a hug. Mei looked like she really needed a hug.

“Why all this?” Mei said defensively as she gestured at Alex’s body.

“Please don’t. Let’s just go to the bar and we’ll fill each other in, okay?” Alex held out her hand to help Mei up, but she ignored it and used the dead tree to lift herself up.

“Lead on, oh great leader,” said Mei. The party moved towards the road in silence. The once dying forest was now vibrant with plant life. A network of tension bound and repelled each member of the group.

”The forest looks so different from the last time we were here.” Alex, looked towards Serana who gave her an affirming nod.

“It was the dryad,” said Maja.

“You met the dryad?” Alex’s eyes flicked around the forest as if she expected the dryad to surprise her again.

“Uh huh, she helped me become an Animist.”

“You’re an Animist now? I guess that explains the clothes.”

“I was an Animist and never wore anything like that,” said Serana as if hinting at some lie.

“You look fucking ridiculous. Here.” Mei pulled her plush, white Healer’s robe over her head and handed it out to Alex. Mei stood in an old, stained undershirt and a pair of slacks that had seen better days. Alex forced a smile and climbed into the luxurious robe. Her tail made the robe billow randomly at weird angles in the back. The tension and unspoken words between the party became constricting as they moved through the forest.

"This is insanely comfortable," said Alex to break the tension.

"It's yours now, demon girl."

"Mei..."

"Demon girl?" said Maja. Serana shot her arm out to stop the group and squatted down. Everyone followed suit. No one but Serana had even noticed the procession on the road several paces ahead of them. A score of goblins led by two small teams of Trinity Guards marched away from the city. Everyone watched silently as a village worth of goblins were aggressively herded down the road. The goblins were loud and indignant but didn't fight the prodding polearms of the Guards. One goblin woman shouted for her son and asked the Guards for help. None of the Guards took notice of her.

"What is that? What's happening?" Maja whispered loudly, panic cracking her voice.

"Maybe they're criminals," said Serana which drew glares from the other three.

"This can't be happening," said Alex.

"We have to do something. Please! I don't want to be helpless anymore." Maja cried and tugged on Alex's sleeve.

"We can't let them get away with this." Alex conjured a swirling inky fireball in her hand.

"One second, boss lady." Serana dug in her purse and removed the ebony skull.

"No, we don't kill them. This is a liberation quest. No one dies today. We incapacitate the Guards and lead the goblins back to The Steps. Mei, are you with us? Your blinding spell would go a long way."

Serana placed the skull back in her purse and pulled out a life-sized golden spider. Alex looked to Mei for her answer.

"I, I, I don't know if I can do this. I'm sorry."

"If we don't do something, they could very well be killing all those goblins. We HAVE to do this. We're the only ones that can do anything. Are you with us?"

Mei took a deep breath and nodded. Her eyes focused with resolve.

"Mei, you're so experienced that your blind spell should override their armor enchantments. I'll take the front row. Mei and Serana, I want you to take the back row. Maja, I need you to stay here until I say it's safe."

"No, I can help now. I'm an Animist, watch." Maja reached her hand up and imagined an orgy with her and the three people surrounding her. Several fibrous tendrils burst forth from the ground and swirled before laying flat.

"Okay then…I guess you and Mei will subdue the front Guards. Serana and I will subdue the rear Guards. I count twelve total. Non-lethal only. We fight conservatively. We fight to disable them. We all make it out alive. Let's move."

Alex ran across the forest floor with Serana on her heels who stuffed the gold spider in her mouth as they flanked to the right to attack the rear Guards. Mei scooped up Maja and ran for the front Guards. Alex led with a twin pair of fireballs that exploded on contact with the Guards and knocked them off their feet. Each fireball collided with their armored center mass to prevent killing them. A chorus of screams came from the goblins who scattered in every direction. Serana spat out the artifact and whispered two lines of Old Script as Alex launched her fireballs. The artifact rapidly transmuted into a massive spider demon that was as large as an archon. The slimy, hairy monster charged into the procession to coat three Guards in a thick mucous web. The remaining rear Guard fled for the city.

While this happened, Mei whipped three blinding spells at the front Guards which flew through the air like sparkling stars. The Guards scrambled in the commotion of fleeing goblins which made her spells miss. Maja imagined a hume hand across her chubby butt, and a nearby tree bent down to knock over four Guards with a crushing branch that was too high to catch a single goblin. The other two Guards tried to flee but Alex stopped them with two fireballs that thundered as they collided with their chests.

The goblins who had not fled cowered in fear and covered their heads. Serana's spider was busy wrapping up the Guards in its sticky webbing while Maja conjured tree roots to bind the other Guards to the ground.

"It's okay, you're safe now!" Alex called out, trying to reassure the remaining goblins. "We're here to free you. Go back home now. We want nothing from you."

"It's okay. She's one of the good humes," Maja shouted to the group and caught their attention.

"We're not the only ones," a female hostage spoke up, "they were taking goblins out of The Steps in droves all night."

"All night?" Mei whispered to herself.

"What's happening in The Steps?" said Alex as she knelt down to speak to the goblin woman.

"We don't know. They came in the night, started grabbing us up. The Steps were a madhouse."

"Where were they taking you?"

"We don't know..."

Alex took a deep breath and looked at the ground.

"Where do we go now?" said the goblin woman as she tugged on Alex's robe.

"You'll have to go somewhere else then. I don't know what to tell you. I'm sorry." Alex stood up and turned to walk back to Trinity.

"But my son..."

"You're all dead! You hear me? You're all dead!" shouted a Guard writhing on the ground, securely bound in a thick layer of spider silk. "You think this will go unnoticed? You cunts stepped in it big time!"

Alex leapt to the screaming Guard and began to viciously stomp his head. Her horns grew longer and curled as she stomped on his helmeted head.

"Alex, no!" shouted Serana as she grabbed her and wrestled her away from the attempted murder. The Guard bled from his nose and mouth and had ceased moving or talking. Mei ran to him, her hands glowing white as she tended his injuries.

"No! Don't fucking heal him! We should kill these fuckers! Trinity knew this shit was happening. They fucking orchestrated it. They need to suffer for what they did." Alex moved to attack the Guard again, but Serana grabbed her and restrained her. The goblins who had not gotten away cowered.

"We can't just kill them," said Serana as she held onto Alex.

"Then what do we do! What do we fucking do! Every fucking time I try to give back, every single good thing I try to do gets thrown in my fucking face. I tried to be a good person and do good things but I can't fucking do this! Nothing I do fucking matters!"

"Oh, shut the fuck up!" Mei walked up to her and slapped her across the face with a loud crack. The audience of people all stared. Alex froze in disbelief. Mei's face scrunched in fury as she let loose another vicious smack across Alex's face, hesitated, then slapped her one more time for good measure.

"You don't think there's people out there suffering a lot worse than you! Look at these people. Forced from their homes and you DARE complain in front of them? You fucking little brat, you should be spanked for the way you act out."

Alex heaved and clenched her jaw, staring with fury at Mei who stared right back with defiance. A dark fireball swirled in her blackened hand.

"Try it, watch what happens," said Mei as she balled her tiny fist. They stared each other down as some of the goblins fled down the road.

"Come on, guys, don't fight." Maja stepped forward. She closed her eyes and imagined cuddling naked with her friends. A large flower bud shot out of the ground between Alex and Mei and bloomed into a massive pink flower with protruding orange stamens. The flower emitted a cloud of sparkling pink pollen. Their shoulders relaxed, and they blinked in confusion before looking at Maja.

"What was THAT?" said Serana.

"I, I don't know. I just imagined something

peaceful and sexy and that happened. Can't all Animists do that?"

"No Animists can do that," said Serana. Mei and Alex were both in a daze, looking around lazily, eyes out of focus. Mei shook her head and snapped back to reality.

"We have to help the other goblins. At least get them out of Trinity safely," said Mei as she marched towards the city before anyone could respond. Alex followed after Mei at a safe distance. Serana ran to catch up to Alex. The remaining goblins joined Maja as they hurried after the humes.

CHAPTER 26

The party marched silently past the edges of Great Northern Forest and into Outer Trinity which was mostly farms and vineyards with space for archons to roam. The sun had breached the horizon, but the air was still cool from the night. Mei led their group with Alex and Serana giving her plenty of distance. Behind them, Maja marched with the goblins they had saved. In the distance, a welcome party was forming at the colossal gate of Trinity. A dozen Guards were accompanied by two Paladins and an unidentified participant in strange armor.

"Everyone hold up," called Alex which made everyone stop, including Mei. "We can't fight our way through that."

"But we did before," said Maja, catching up.

"Last time we completely ambushed them. They were not expecting any resistance that time. They have two Paladins and looks like a guildie with them. We have to surrender. Serana, leave a message for Asuna that we're going to be imprisoned. I'm not crazy about breaking out of jail, but The Steps need us. We do not fight this group. We will lose if we do."

"How do they know we even did anything?" said Maja.

"That Guard there on the flank was in the party we attacked...couldn't even get back to Trinity without getting into trouble again," said Alex. Serana pulled the sleeve of Alex's robe, dug in her purse, and pulled out the ebony skull.

"We're not using that. We're not here to kill people, even if they do deserve it."

"But what about us? What will happen to us?" said one of the remaining goblins.

"The same lordsdam thing we were trying to avoid. I'm sorry. I tried," said Alex as she turned away from them. The goblin's mouth hung open but no words came out.

"We'll come for you guys. Our friend is a Revenant which is a big deal, I guess. I promise we'll help you," said Maja. Serana pulled out her com stone and flicked her thumb across the surface.

"Do we all understand what is happening? There is no fight. We lost. Serana, you ready?" said Alex as she looked over everyone. Serana nodded and put her com stone back in her purse. The goblins who had followed Maja ran off once they realized the humes wouldn't be helping them. The party approached the gate with their hands up in surrender.

"So you think you can surrender, huh?"

said the man whose class Alex couldn't identify, smiling in the way a demented person might smile at logic. His body looked like a living weapon made from long wiry muscles. His severe posture made him appear as if he was ready to explode with his pelvis forward and shoulders back.

"That's the idea," said Alex as she stepped forward. "We surrender."

"It's too late for that. You ambushed a government campaign and nearly killed a Guard. The orders are to kill you and your group." The man lunged forward and planted his fist in Alex's chest, launching her down the road. His fist crackled with electricity.

"Spread out." Alex wheezed from behind them. Mei fled in an arc away from the man then gestured with her hands which caused a column of light to shine on Alex. Serana bolted straight backwards and removed the golden lead from her purse as she fled. Maja ran as fast as she could along the Trinity wall in Mei's direction. The Guards lunged forward in formation and brandished their halberds.

"No need, men, I can take them all myself," said the man as he sprinted after Mei. His boots crackled with sparks and flames as he sprinted faster than any hume.

"Mei!" screamed Maja as the man sprinted past her. Mei turned to the man who had closed the distance with terrifying speed. She gestured her hand up and summoned a translucent barrier in front of her. The man's fist collided with the barrier and rang out like a massive bell. He punched the barrier two more times and shattered it like broken glass. Mei toppled backwards and clutched her chest over her heart. Her eyes went wide with fear as the man lunged at her. Two inky fireballs sailed past the man and a third collided with his platemail mantle which sent him tumbling sideways.

"He's a Spellfist, Mei! RUN!" Alex screamed and held her chest as she got to her feet. Mei froze in terror and could not move. The Spellfist ducked under another dark fireball and leapt at her, fist cocked. A grapevine shot out of the ground and caught the Spellfist in air around his torso, cinching his exposed abdomen. He gagged on his own breath as the vine constricted him. Grabbing the vine with both hands, it exploded with flames and sent him toppling to the ground. Another dark fireball flew at the Spellfist who caught it in his gauntlets and flung it back at Alex as if it were a stone. Alex braced her palms forward to catch it but was knocked off her feet again. The Spellfist tackled Mei and rained down punches on her as insane laughter escaped his mouth. Her body went limp as he bloodied her face.

"Nooooo!" screamed Alex, unable to find her footing. A grapevine burst from the ground and caught the Spellfist's hand but was quickly burned away. He cocked back for another vicious punch when Serana's archon collided into him with a sickening thud. The archon turned to the sky with the Spellfist plastered against its broad chest.

"Higher, higher!" barked Serana as the Archon soared into the sky and over the towering walls of Trinity. The view would have been glorious in any other situation. Serana hooked her leg in the lead and tried to pry the Spellfist's hands from the archon.

"You cunt!" snarled the Spellfist. His gauntlets burst with flames and scorched the archon which bellowed with pain and descended, its wings flapping erratically.

"What the fuck are you!" shouted Serana as the wind whipped through her hair. She dug in her purse and removed the ebony skull. With her leg securely in the lead, she used both hands to bring the ebony skull down on the Spellfist's face, knocking him free of the archon. His body plummeted back to Ur and crashed in a freshly plowed field. Serana guided her archon down as fast and as safely as she could near the wall of Trinity.

Alex hunched over Mei whose face was a sickening mess of blood and bruises. Awkward angles under her skin signified skull fractures. She wasn't moving or breathing. Alex sobbed loudly, choking on her own breath over and over.

"Not again! Not you, Mei. It can't be fucking you!" Alex screeched as she held Mei against her. Maja scampered up to them and stopped when she saw Mei bloody and lifeless. She fell to her knees and planted her hands on the ground. She thought about the way Mei had nurtured her, about the dryad giving life, the secret grotto, the baby inside her, and the animal energy of the world. A spring of water spurted out of the road and burst forth into a fountain. The paved stones of the road anchored up and formed a basin around the three of them that quickly filled with ground water. Maja envisioned her own life energy and saw it glowing brightly. She saw Alex's life energy shining furiously inside her body. Mei's anima was dim and flickered like a cloud of dying night flies. Maja enveloped them with the cool waters of Ur and watched as the glowing particles of their anima slowly shifted between their bodily vessels, willing her's and Alex's anima into Mei. After Mei's anima was sustained and bright, Maja exhaled, the drain of her own anima made her knees weak and her body cold.

"What did you do?" said Alex, unable to stop her tears.

"I don't know, but I think she will be okay. I don't know how this works."

As Maja performed her miracle, they didn't notice the Guards and Paladins had surrounded them. Their halberds were out and ready for a fight.

"We surrender, lordsdamit! You heard us surrender! What kind of Paladin would consider this a fight?" Alex cried at them, holding Mei in her arms. The Trinity Guards all exchanged looks before they turned to their Paladins for orders.

"We accept your surrender," said one of the Paladins as he reached out his arm. Alex held out Mei for him.

"Please save her. I don't care what happens to me, just please save her."

"Take her to the nearest Healer." The Paladin handed off Mei to a Guard who departed with an ally.

"We need to talk about what you saw on the road this morning," said the Paladin.

CHAPTER 27

"We're willing to be reasonable here," said the Paladin to Alex who sat across the table, "the reality is, your guild attacked us, and we're willing to show some leniency if you just cooperate."

"What were they doing?" Alex crossed her arms over her new chest.

"It was a standard military exercise. If for some reason Trinity needed to be evacuated, The Guard would be responsible for removing the citizens in a safe and timely manner." The Paladin tried a smile on Alex as if trying to convince her this was all just a silly misunderstanding.

"No one believes that. Not even you." Alex narrowed her eyes at him. Two thunderous knocks erupted from the door. The Paladin removed himself from his chair and stood at attention as an elderly yet powerful Tank entered the room. He was a fortress of a man wearing a full suit of thick, battle worn, plate mail.

"You're the one forcing goblins from their homes?" said Alex.

"Shut up." The Tank folded his massive gauntleted hands on the stone table. "We would like to make a deal with you."

The Paladin exited the room and closed the thick wooden door.

"Why would I ever make a deal with you bastards?"

"Because if you don't, you can expect to spend the next few years laboring under Trinity."

Alex had nothing to say and broke eye contact.

"We will grant your guild corporal probation in exchange for your silence. If you never have another interaction with The Guard, and do not go within one hundred spans of The Starlight, you will be free to continue your operations."

"Is Mei okay?" Alex felt ashamed for letting her wellbeing slip her mind even for a moment.

"Mei?"

"Our Healer, is she okay?"

"Your Healer is recovering just fine and will be sent home with you if you accept the terms of our deal."

Alex felt a massive weight removed from her chest. She felt herself smiling for the first time in a long time.

"What's to stop us from just sending a letter to The Starlight? Or just sending someone with our story?"

"That would be the last mistake your guild ever makes."

Alex shivered at the uncut truth laid upon her.

"You understand your relationship with The Starlight is over? No more stories, no more investigations. If anything comes out about this military operation, you and your guild will be hunted down and captured." The Tank stamped his finger on the table to reinforce his point. Alex smiled as she imagined how easy this was going to be with Asuna.

"I'm guessing our little story about The Steps got printed then?"

"Yes, and we genuinely appreciate you and them bringing this to our attention, though the choice of channels you used could have been better."

"Oh, I bet."

"This is over. The men responsible for the sterilizations have been routed and are awaiting judgment. A completely idiotic and poorly thought out operation by the worst The Guard has to offer. The depravity sickens me as much as the stupidity."

"So, I'm just supposed to take your word that anyone will be punished for the sick fucking things you did to my friend?"

"No. There will be a tribunal. These men will be shamed for their insidious behavior and punished accordingly."

"How do I know you got everyone? How do I know you're not sparing the person who orchestrated this entire thing? How do I know the people investigating these fucks weren't involved in the first place?" Alex could not escape the sensation that pieces were moving in a way to obfuscate the truth from her and the people of Trinity. It was too neat, too swift. It felt like a partial victory, a winning battle in a war she lost. It was like something an Illusionist orchestrated.

"We have a special contingent that investigates corruption in our ranks. These men were not hard to find. I can speak no more of this to a civilian."

She wanted to feel pride in a successful quest, but the circumstances nagged at her like a ghost screaming about some critical mistake she had made. The revelation in the Scoured Sands regarding Ka Tuk was like an ache. She wanted answers about it, but thought if she brought it up with this man that no one would ever see her again.

"So, they're going to be executed?" Alex leaned forward.

"Most likely. A mix of relief and regret to say the least. Men like that have no business serving our guild."

"And what about this 'military exercise'? Assume no one will ever hear about that?"

"There's nothing to report. Any planned future exercises have been canceled because of civilian scrutiny. You got the result you wanted. It remains to be seen if you can live with the means you used to achieve it."

The way the Tank spoke, the way he always had an answer for everything, it felt like she was talking to a Rogue or an Agent, as if he had pre-planned answers for her inevitable questions.

"I have to ask, tempting the Devs or whoever is watching over us, why don't you just lock us up? I'm guessing that Spellfist must have lived, or you'd be executing us too."

"Let it be known, I have no love for mercenary hitmen. I would have rewarded you personally for killing that carrion feeder who carries no sense of principles. As far as your punishment goes..." the Tank looked over his shoulder than back at Alex, "it was that lordsdam com stone your Summoner carried. We have no way of knowing what kind of information she disseminated before you surrendered or to who. You should thank her personally for your freedom when you see her, but if she revealed anything that will break our agreed upon confidence, your guild will disappear in every sense of the word. We are giving you a chance to quash any information she has released. That is the ONLY reason you are still alive."

Alex felt a new chill roll through her body.

His tone plainly conveyed that this was no empty threat.

"I understand," said Alex and reached out her hand. The Tank took her delicate hand and gave it a vicious grip but shook it professionally.

"One final thing," said the Tank, not relinquishing the handshake. "If you are seen with Alexander Song, you will all be brought up on conspiracy charges. If he opens contact with your guild, you are to report it to The Guard immediately."

The Tank stared her down, and Alex swore to herself that he was trying to determine if she was actually him.

"I understand," said Alex as bravely as she could. The Tank gave her a nod, and

Alex followed him from the room. She continued to follow him down a cell-lined hallway until they arrived at a cell containing Maja and Serana. Serana sat at an angle with her arms crossed away from Maja. Once Alex came into view, Maja and Serana leapt from the bench chained to the wall. Serana pushed Maja out of the way and tried to hug Alex through the bars. Alex just smiled at her.

"Your new guild leader seems to have quite a bit more sense than Alexander Song," said the Tank as he opened their cell with his massive key ring. Serana leapt through the doorway and tried to squeeze the life out of Alex. Maja scampered over and hugged her leg.

"Where's Mei?" Maja looked up at Alex, not breaking her hug. Alex looked to the Tank who said nothing as he turned back the way they came. The guild followed him to a pair of Paladins outside the interrogation room. The Tank spoke to a Paladin at the door and instructed him to take the group to the infirmary and collect the Healer there. The Paladin seemed put out as he led their group up the long stone stairway and down one of the many offshoots. He stopped at a brightly lit room with dozens of beds along each wall. In some of the beds were Guards. In one of the beds was the Spellfist from earlier who lay unconscious. Near the door was Mei. The guild gathered around her bed.

"She's so sexy when she's sleeping." Maja climbed into bed next to her. Alex felt her soul swell with joy seeing Mei safe and breathing. The idea of losing her too was too much to bear.

"Mei...Mei wake up. We're here to take you home," whispered Maja in her ear, gently shaking her.

"Ma-Maja?" Mei's eyes fluttered open, but she did not react to the goblin woman laying in bed next to her. Maja smiled. Alex wiped tears from her eyes seeing Mei open her eyes. Mei sat up and touched her head, wincing in discomfort.

"You took a beating. I'm sorry I put you in that situation," said Alex, moving closer to her.

"You're always sorry...I don't even remember what happened after my barrier broke." Mei rubbed her temples with the tips of her fingers.

"That fucker over there almost killed you." Alex nodded towards the unconscious Spellfist in one of the beds. "Maja saved you. I don't know what she did out there, but it saved you."

"I don't know what she did either." Serana gave Maja an accusatory look. Mei looked into Maja's big shining eyes, and Maja smiled bashfully. Mei gave her a quick kiss on the mouth, and Maja held her cheeks and squealed, kicking her legs gleefully.

"I really think we should get you home before that piece of shit over there wakes up and wants a rematch with us," said Alex. Mei lifted herself from the bed, and Alex moved to steady her, but Mei would not allow it. The Paladin led them up the stairs and to a new hallway where they entered the armory to claim Serana's artifacts. The Guard at the counter was helpful and personable as he asked Serana about her travels, her life as a Summoner, and if she was seeing anyone. Serana's com stone was missing. The Paladin casually mentioned it was confiscated as part of an ongoing investigation. The group was seen out of the Guard station and began their journey to Mei's home. On the way, Alex was able to retrieve a copy of the Starlight hung up on a building and read the story to the group as they walked.

Investigator Amy wrote about the bubbly,

sweet goblin girl who was attacked in The Steps two nights before the pamphlet was published. She wrote of the dashing Fire Mage and compassionate Healer who saved her life that night. She wrote about the subsequent investigation with the heroic Fire Mage and the competent Stalker who discovered the guardian rune.

"Tan-tan's going to love that," said Alex with a short laugh which made everyone smile.

She continued to read the pamphlet about the presentation of the guardian rune to the Starlight investigator and the heroic Fire Mage's decision to flee Trinity. Serana clung to Alex's arm at that part of the story, and Maja watched them with a confused look on her face. In Gold Town, the group stood at the roadside while Alex said goodbye to Mei outside her home. Mei pursed her lips quizzically while Alex shuffled her feet on the stoop.

"So I guess this is it?" said Alex with her hand on the back of her head and her eyes on the ground.

"I guess so," said Mei, looking past Alex to the group. Maja gave her a big excited wave and Mei smiled, returning a small wave.

"So where are we?" said Alex.

"Gold Town."

"No, I mean...us. Do you want me to stay out of your life forever...again?"

Mei's mouth was a thin line as she gave the idea some thought. "No...you and Maja and

Serana can stop by anytime after work. Well not anytime, within reason. No more fighting though, I'm not a guildie anymore."

"Sure aren't," said Alex, trying to make Mei smile. Mei gave a slight nod which made Alex feel bad about the timing of the joke.

"As terrifying as always." Mei extended her hand for a shake. Alex stepped in and embraced her, making Mei flinch.

"Fuck this, I want a hug too." Maja climbed the steps and ran up to Mei to hug her leg.

"Awww, I'm going to miss you," said Mei with a big smile as she bent down and lifted Maja up in a tight hug. Maja hugged Mei around the neck and nuzzled her face in, gently biting Mei's ear.

"You stop by anytime, little one," said Mei as she set her down. She nodded at Alex and entered her home.

CHAPTER 28

"We have a lot to talk about, huh?" said Alex as she looked down at Maja who held up her arms. Alex lifted her up and carried her down the stairs and then in the direction of the bar. Serana stared at them the entire journey, periodically shaking her head as if disagreeing with an unheard voice. They strolled down the cobblestone circuit of Trinity until they arrived at the bar.

Inside, Alex stopped at the main room. "Think we could use some new clothes, yeah? Let's all meet back here in five minutes."

The guildies took the stairs and went to their separate rooms with Maja in Alex's arms. After securing the door and setting Maja on the bed, Alex pulled Mei's robe over her head and stood in the tiny room naked. Her horns were only nubs at this point, and her tail lazily flicked back and forth. Maja stared in fascination.

"What happened to you?" Maja's mouth hung open in erotic eagerness. Alex felt a stirring between her legs as Maja stared at her.

"I made a pact with a demon. I didn't

know this was going to happen though. Never really get what you expect when you make a pact like that I guess..."

"How do you feel?" Maja swung her legs back and forth over the edge of the bed.

"To be honest, I feel amazing. There's all these new feelings. I had sex with him as part of the pact, and it left me feeling very confused."

"You had sex with a demon?"

"Yeah..."

"That's really sexy," said Maja with a grin. Alex smiled back.

"It *was* really sexy, and really intense. I've never even been with a guy...though there were times I came close. I really liked it. I want to explore it."

"Explore what?"

"Men..."

"Hee. I love men. Well, I love dicks at least." Maja giggled and covered her mouth.

"Think I might like men too...and women."

"Well, I still love you, and I'll support you no matter what you choose. But..."

"But what?"

"You put a baby in me." Maja placed her hand on her chubby belly.

"Wha-What?" Alex struggled for breath. The revelation was like a pillowy punch in the stomach that pushed the air out of her lungs.

"I'm pregnant. You made me pregnant."

"Fuck...oh fuck..." Alex fell to her knees and pressed her face against Maja's fuzzy tummy. Warm happy tears flowed freely down her face. There was so much joy in her heart it was painful. The joy suffocated her and made her tremble. The joyful pain felt like small knifes that left tiny lacerations against her heart.

"There's a baby growing in there." Maja ran her fingers through Alex's hair. Alex turned her head and kissed Maja's belly.

"Our baby..." Alex whispered and stared at Maja's torso as if she could see the baby inside. Alex scooped her up and laid her on the bed then pressed their lips together. Maja kissed Alex back, holding her face. Her big copper eyes blinked away tears of joy.

"You are so fucking beautiful right now. No matter what happens next, I want you in my life. I'm sorry I was so cruel to you," said Alex as she cupped Maja's tiny face.

"What about that girl Serana?"

Alex took a deep breath.

"I love her too, but not the way I love you. She's not my girlfriend. She just imagines it. Be your sweet self around her, and she'll soften to you. She needs a lot of positive reinforcement. She's had a very, very hard life."

"Tan-tan says she loves me too..." said Maja.

"Did you and Tan-tan..?"

Maja nodded.

"That's really sexy." Alex smiled. Maja smiled back and kissed her.

"I don't think we're going to function as a monogamous couple," said Alex as she lay alongside her girlfriend.

"Monogamous?"

"It means we only have sex with each other. I mean, I didn't consider us anything before. I pushed you away because I felt so bad about what happened to you. But now we have a baby and...and everything's different."

"Everything's different," said Maja, lacing her four fingers through Alex's five.

"Yeah, but...I love you, and you love me, and these things are complicated."

"What's complicated about that?"

"Because when you love someone, you're only supposed to have sex with them."

"I guess..." said Maja.

"But we're already way past that, so no more guilt. We can have sex with whoever we want, but we'll always be together." Alex played with Maja's bright blue hair. Maja kissed her and clung to her. Alex's tail flicked back and forth through the air.

"That tail is really sexy. Can you control it?" Maja watched it swing mindlessly.

"I haven't tried." Alex concentrated, and her tail stopped swinging. She thought about her minute muscle control, willing the new muscles in the base of her spine. She curled the tail towards them and Maja grabbed it. Alex cooed and shivered.

"Does that feel good?" said Maja as she massaged it. She rubbed the tail down to the flared tip and played with it. Alex's nipples went hard and she gripped the bed sheets, biting her lip. Maja grinned and kept masturbating her tail. She put the tip in her mouth and played her tongue over the fleshy folds. Alex's body spasmed, and she cried out in orgasm which made her tail slam against the wall.

"That was HOT," said Maja before she kissed Alex.

"Please don't grab my tail in public," said Alex as she caught her breath.

"No promises." Maja smiled. They were startled by a pounding at the door.

"Going downstairs," came Serana's voice from the hallway. Alex and Maja giggled after the tension was broken.

"I need to get dressed." Alex climbed over Maja and dug in her footlocker. She removed a pair of stiff wool pants and tried to slip them on but winced as the waist rubbed against her sensitive tail. She reached under her pillow, pulled out a small knife, and cut a hole in the back of the pants. Once she fished out a belt from the footlocker and secured her bottoms, she snaked her tail through the hole she made. The outfit was completed with a sleeveless black tunic. With Maja in her arms, she opened her bedroom door and made to go down stairs.

"Fuck, need money." Alex cradled Maja in her arm as she dug in the stand by her bed. "Fuck!"

"What's wrong?" Maja's head swiveled back and forth to try and see Alex's hands.

"I took the guild fund, and Ka Tuk destroyed all my damn money!"

"Ka Tuk!" Maja shouted back, squirming. "That was the demon!"

"Yeeeah, but he didn't destroy Greenlan. He was in the Scoured Sands which is on the opposite side of the Green Strait, and I think Trinity might know that he isn't in Greenlan."

"I don't understand. How can he be destroying Greenlan if he's in the Scoured Sands?"

"My theory is that he was never actually in Greenlan. I want to talk to him again as soon as possible, but I don't really want to ask Serana for any favors at the moment." The agony Alex felt when she thought she had killed Serana constricted her heart. It wasn't just the pain of losing her, a darkness had inserted itself in her that had made her want to do it.

"But there was so much destruction! So many people died. We lost everything. What could have done that except for a demon? Ka Tuk killed my daddy! How could you make a deal with him?" shouted Maja as she bounced in Alex's arms and gripped her tunic.

"Not everything is as it seems. With the

Guards lying to my face about what they were doing with those goblins, I don't trust Trinity. Those two things can't be a coincidence. I need you to trust me," Alex lifted Maja's chin with her finger.

"But, but...but, he took everything from us...He took my family..."

"And we're going to find out why. I promise you. It's going to be a lot of work, and it's going to take a long time, but I promise this to you. We will find out why this all happened."

"Okay...we have to find Mama too. I hope they didn't take her last night. Lords, I hope they didn't take her..." Maja's lower lip trembled, and she wiped the new tears from her eyes.

"We'll look for her first thing after breakfast. We're going to find her. I won't stop until we do. I want you to know you can rely on me." Alex pressed her face against Maja who nodded and kissed her.

"Now what do we do?" Maja hugged Alex around the neck and tried to finish her tears.

"One crisis at a time, baby green. We go downstairs and get some breakfast in us. Then we make a plan. But first, I got to see if Asuna has any money. She should be here. She likes to sleep in."

Alex crossed the hall and pounded on Asuna's door. "Asuna, wake up, it's Alex. I need to borrow some money."

Alex continued pounding "Oh fuck, forgot

she was in trouble. Maybe she's still at the Guard station. Why didn't I think--"

"Alexander?" came Asuna's voice from behind the door.

"Yeah, you want to eat breakfast with us? I got Maja with me."

"Come on, Asuna, let's have breakfast together again," said Maja.

"I can't," said Asuna, her tone hard to read through the door.

"What do you mean you can't? Come on," said Alex.

"How are you even back in Trinity?"

"Long story, and I would love to tell it to you downstairs."

"I can't. I'm sorry. Please go away."

"Please," said Maja as she touched the door. Asuna's door opened slightly, and her eye peered through the gap. Upon seeing Alex's face, she slammed the door shut and latched it. Alex and Maja exchanged looks.

"Thought you said I was sexy," Alex whispered to Maja.

"You are. Asuna, what's wrong? Aren't you happy to see me?" Maja placed her hand on the closed door again.

"Who IS that! That's not Alexander," Asuna shouted through the door.

"It is. She's just a little different now. Are you okay? Why are you hiding?"

"I'm going to go downstairs. See if you can

talk to her." Alex set Maja down and left for the stairs. Before she left, she knocked on Tan-tan's door which opened on an empty room.

"Ask her where Tan-tan is," Alex called to Maja as she went down the stairs.

"Can I come in? It's just me now." Maja heard the latch move, and the door opened an inch. She entered the room to find Asuna who sat on the floor against the bed and cried quietly into her knees.

"What's wrong?" Maja waddled over to her. Asuna leapt to her feet and slammed the door behind Maja, latching it. Her face looked as if she hadn't slept in days. She sat back on the floor and pulled Maja in to cry on her.

"Is there anything I can do?" Maja felt Asuna shake her head.

"Can you tell me what's wrong?"

"Someone's coming to kill me," said Asuna, choking the words out.

"What? Why?"

"I pissed off the wrong people."

"Well...Serana and Alex are downstairs, and I became an Animist. We'll protect you."

"That's sweet, but no one can protect me from this."

"Well, we'll try. If they're so dangerous, I don't understand how you're safer here. Come have breakfast with us."

Asuna set Maja on the bed and pulled her

dust colored cloak around her. She picked Maja up and delicately opened the door as if expecting a surprise attack. Once the door was open just wide enough, she dipped her head in the hallway. Seeing no one was around, Asuna made for the stairs. At the bottom of the stairs she peered around the corner to survey the hallway which was empty before midday. In the main room, Alex and Serana sat at one of the tables near the windows. Asuna pulled her cloak around herself and took a seat next to Serana.

CHAPTER 29

"You look like shit," said Alex, breaking the silence. Asuna turned to her. Her face was paler than normal, and dark purple bags hung under her eyes. She didn't make eye contact with anyone. Here eyes kept darting to the doorway.

"Late night?" Serana asked as she clung to Alex's arm. The daytime barkeeper approached the table.

"What can I get you ladies?"

"Preserves!" shouted Maja who pounded the table and kicked her legs which made the barkeeper smile.

"Would love a lot of bacon and a lot of sausage," said Alex before turning to Asuna. "Oh by the way, I need to borrow some money."

"Any fruit you have would be nice, and some water," said Serana.

"I am dying for some water, me too please," said Maja. Asuna waved the barkeeper away then propped her elbows on the table and put her head in her hands.

"How come Tan-tan's not with you?" Alex

looked to Asuna then Maja for an answer.

"Who the fuck ARE you?" Asuna gestured at her.

"Asuna! That's Alexander," said Maja.

"That's new..." Asuna checked the doorway for the fifteenth time.

"Okaaay, then. Guess the first thing I have to ask is, what is your fucking problem?" Alex's horns seemed to grow longer as she scowled. Asuna's sleepy eyes blinked slowly as she stared at her.

"Well? This isn't like you. Where's the even tempered, intelligent woman I put in charge?"

"She ran away. You're stuck with this coward now."

"Lordsdamit, just tell us what happened."

Asuna recounted to the group what had happened after Alex left Trinity. She told them about the interpreter and the arrests, how Tantan was taken to her father, and the team up with the Paladin, Lin. She told them about the goblin girl she had spoken to in The Steps. Her hand stroked Maja's hair as she recounted the girl's ordeal. She told them what they had discovered in The Steps about the impending operation then broke down crying when she told them how cowardly she had been when the Tank had threatened her. Maja stood up in her lap at that point and hugged her. Alex's face finally softened.

"We'll protect you. We promise," said Maja before she kissed her cheek.

"You really think a Harbinger is looking for you?" said Alex.

"They want me dead. They're making a point."

"I think you're overreacting," said Alex, "since when are you afraid of anything?"

"I had nothing to fear for many, many years. Now I have to accept the idea I might die someday." Asuna rested her chin on Maja's head and looked at the table.

"We're all going to die someday, even Revenants. You're just going to let this Tank spook you with an empty threat?" said Alex. Asuna wouldn't make eye contact with her.

"Asuna." Maja sat on the edge of the table to face her. Asuna kept her eyes low as she stared through Maja who lifted Asuna's head up to look in her eyes.

"Can you help me find my mama? She was in The Steps last night, and I don't know if she's still there."

Asuna gave Maja a pensive look as if deciding whether or not she wanted to cry.

"Please, Asuna?" Maja's lower lip trembled as she tried to be brave in front of her guild. Asuna lowered Maja's head and kissed the top then pulled her in for a long cuddle.

"Sure, baby girl. We'll look for your mama."

Alex smiled and squeezed Serana's hand, nodding at Maja for the excellent plan. Breakfast was served and eaten as they recounted what had happened to Asuna.

"So that operation you and Lindlithsong discovered, that must have been what we encountered before dawn this morning," said Alex.

"What did you encounter? How come you're back in Trinity?" said Asuna.

"Maybe it's better if I just start from the beginning."Alex went on to relay the definitive tale of what happened to her in the desert, except for the part where she murdered Serana.

"Ka Tuk! Are you fucking serious? And with Maja here? How could you betray her like that?" said Asuna as she aggressively stroked Maja's hair.

"No, listen. Ka Tuk was never in Greenlan. It looked like he had been in that temple for a very long time. You weren't there. I know it sounds completely crazy, but I trust him."

"You trust the demon that tricked you into sex and changed your gender against your will? Alex..." said Asuna.

"I agreed to everything he did," said Alex defensively.

"That's not how sex works, and you of all men should know that. I thought you were better than this," said Asuna.

"You weren't there! Lords and demons, I'm a girl for one day and you're already judging all my choices."

"Whatever. It was your choice..."

Alex continued as she told Asuna about their serendipitous encounter with Mei and Maja and their violent return to Trinity.

"Mei's okay?"

"Yeah...she's a tough bitch, but Maja was the real hero. I've never seen anyone of any class do something like that."

"Me neither," Serana chimed in.

"I'm so proud of YOU," said Asuna as she squeezed Maja against her. Alex continued her story as she explained the deal she made with the Tank and Serana's role in saving everyone. Serana smiled and squeezed Alex's hand at the mention of her role in their freedom.

"You were like the most paranoid, suspicious person I've met in a long time, and Lords help you, you discovered what was happening in The Steps. But now you're making all these deals with demons and The Guard. What happened to you, Alex?" said Asuna.

Alex wiped her hands down her face and looked off across the bar before she spoke.

"You weren't there. Maja said you were captured, and I had no idea if I would ever be able to get in contact with you. I made a choice to save the people I cared about. When you're a guild leader, you have to make tough decisions."

"But your guild is totally addled now, and I doubt Trinity will allow you to start another one, or you can even afford to," said Asuna.

"I don't care. Serana and Maja and Mei are safe. That's what I care about."

"So...I'm just going to ask, and forgive me if I'm out of line, but what are you going to do about your gender? Can you change back? Do you want to change back?"

"I'll figure it out one day at a time. I'm very comfortable right now, all things considered."

"Should probably talk to Ka Tuk, huh?" said Asuna as she stole a piece of bacon off Alex's plate. Alex gave her a critical look, but Asuna placed a silver piece on the table to extinguish the silent reproach.

"Can't imagine a safe place inside this city to summon him without causing a panic," said Alex, looking to Serana for a suggestion who shrugged.

"Just use the cellar," said Asuna. Alex rolled her eyes at the painfully obvious location.

"Yeah...makes total sense. Once we finish breakfast, we have to find out where Maja's mother is, then I'll have a nice long discussion with Ka Tuk. Is that alright?" Alex looked to Serana for an answer who was visibly taken aback by Alex's consideration for her in the plan.

"Of course," said Serana as she gave Alex's hand another squeeze.

"I bet you will..." muttered Asuna with a grin. Maja giggled and snorted.

"Look at you, little piggy, got more jam on

you than in you." Asuna dabbed a cloth napkin in water and wiped the jam smears from Maja's face.

"Do you think Mama will be there?" Maja asked as Asuna cleaned her.

"We'll find her," said Asuna, giving Maja a confident look which comforted her.

"What should we do about Tan--" Alex was cut off as synchronized heavy footfalls came from the hallway. Two Paladins with two Guards marched into the room. Asuna held her breath. The entire table watched them. The Paladins took no notice of the guild and approached the bar where the barkeeper stood and smiled at them.

"What are they doing?" whispered Maja.

"Shh, just watch," said Asuna.

"We're looking for a woman," said one of the Paladins to the barkeeper. His plate-metal armor clinked as he slid a piece of parchment across the bar.

"She's about six foot tall, two hundred and twenty pounds, brown skin, dark cropped hair, may be carrying a claymore."

The bar keeper picked up the parchment and examined it.

"Oh, uh huh, I've seen her! Yeah, she was in the bar yesterday, looking for a goblin of all things. Why over there, she was with that woman in the tan cloak." The barkeeper pointed at Asuna. Alex looked at Asuna then at the

Guards and Paladins.

"Be cool. The Guard gave us a pass. They're as afraid of us as we are of them," whispered Alex as the Paladins approached.

"You know this woman?" said one of the Paladins as he slid the parchment on the table for everyone to see. On the paper was a sketch of a handsome, brown, hume woman with short dark hair and a strong jawline. Asuna barely nodded.

"Use your words, please. Do you know her?" The Paladin changed his tone from professional to interrogating.

"I know Lindlithsong." Asuna stared defiantly back at the Paladin.

"When was the last time you saw her?"

"The last time I saw her, a Tank was restraining her with a pull."

The Paladins looked to each other than back at Asuna, confusion visible on their faces.

"And when was this?"

"Yesterday afternoon in the Guard station. I haven't seen her since." Asuna slid the paper back towards the Paladin who narrowed his eyes at her.

"We know she's in the area. We need you to come to the Administrative District and answer some more questions."

Asuna shook her head and clicked her tongue as if the Paladin had just asked her for a spare copper. The Paladins continued to stare her down.

"If she's caught with you, any of you, you'll all be brought to the dungeon. Is that understood?" said the Paladin as he retrieved the wanted poster. Maja nodded. The rest of the guild had no reaction.

"She's wanted for treason against the city-state of Trinity. We will not tolerate conspirators," said the other Paladin before he made his leave. Once the entourage left, the guildies all exchanged looks.

"Every time I hear about this Lin, I like her more and more," said Alex, "come on, we have some work to do."

After breakfast, Maja led the guild to her home. As they moved through The Steps, the atmosphere steadily became overbearing. The homes closest to the hume part of town were ripped apart as if a giant monster had been looking for tiny snacks. Most of the goblins fled indoors upon seeing the group. Other goblins stood defiantly outside their shacks with make-shift weapons from scrap metal and kitchen utensils. No one moved towards the group, but Maja felt the hostility surrounding them. They moved deeper through The Steps where almost none of the houses were destroyed or ripped open. Goblins went about their morning routines but eyed the humes in their neighborhood with suspicion instead of menace. Maja guided them to the base of The Steps' namesake.

"I'm just going to go up and check. Even if Mama's not there, she might just be at work," said Maja, more to reassure herself than the group. Only after speaking it aloud did she realize what a poor plan it was.

"Take your time," said Alex. Maja climbed up the dark hallways of her apartment, lifting herself up level after level. At the top, she waddled down the final hall to her home. Her heart wouldn't stop racing. She didn't know what she was expecting when she slid the door open and found a group of goblins inside.

"Sorry, wrong house," she apologized quickly and slid the rusty sheet shut. Her heart was doing somersaults. Something caught her eye though. She slid the door open again and noticed the far wall was completely gone. She entered her home as the goblins watched her with minor interest.

"I don't mean to sound rude, but why are you people in my home?" said Maja as she moved to the kitchen space.

"Oh!" an older goblin woman spoke up and climbed off the couch. "You must be Kaja's daughter. It's so nice to finally meet you. I'm Ro-Rok. I work with your mother at the jewelry shop. Lords, she's go'on to be so happy to know you're okay."

Ro-Rok moved across the room and hugged Maja. The rest of the goblins preoccupied themselves with a card game.

"Mama's okay?" said Maja as happy tears slid down her cheeks. Her heart pulsated with a relieving happiness that washed over her entire body like a warm summer rain.

"Oh, she's fine. Fine enough to go into work, if you can believe it. Rather get snatched up by a Guard than anyone think she's lazy. Your mama put us up here dur'on the mess last night. Lords, it was terrify'on, I tell you. Guards snatch'on goblins from their homes, it was nasty, nasty business. Your mama has such a big heart hide'on us up here. We don't know why the Guard want us so bad. But they can't get us way up here, get stuck in the doorway!" Ro-Rok said with a chuckle and slapped her chubby thigh.

"So, Mama's safe?" Maja had to ask again.

"Yes, dear, she's at work. Don't know who is show'on up to work after last night though. Might not be around long enough to get paid. I told her, 'you tell the boss, I quit'." Ro-Rok pointed her finger up at an imaginary boss in the room. Maja exhaled a calming breath and smiled to herself. Mama was safe.

"Okay, well, my friends are outside waiting for me. Tell Mama I love her," said Maja as she left.

"I'll tell her, dear. You take care," said Ro-Rok as Maja closed the door. Maja burst down the hallways as fast as she could. The incredible news made her legs seem weightless. She bounded down the levels on her butt and sprinted out into the roadway. Once outside, she leapt into Alex's arms who caught her and spun her around.

CHAPTER 30

"Guess your mama is okay?" said Alex, giving Maja a kiss on the cheek. Happy tears streamed down her face. Asuna stepped towards them and placed her hand on Maja's head, breaking into a smile.

"She's fine. She's at work. She's hiding goblins in our home." Maja squealed with delight.

"That's really good to hear," said Alex. Maja leapt out of Alex's arms and led them to the hume part of The Steps where Alex scooped her up and guided them to Mort's cellar. Fiery afternoon sunlight splashed against the wall as they entered.

"Morty, you here?" Alex asked playfully as she led them down the steps.

"Of course," said Mort in the dark before the lamp came to life on the table.

"Let's see what Ka Tuk has to say." Alex gestured to the open cellar floor. Serana held her purse towards the lamp light and dug out the ebony skull.

"Abdu Ka Tuk." Serana rubbed her hand over the cranium of the skull. She let the skull fall from her hand, and the guild watched as it rolled across the floor on its own volition. The entire building shook, and a demonic, ebony throne emerged from the floor as if rising from a pool. The skull rose into the air on the end of an armrest. In a burst of smoke, Ka Tuk appeared on the throne. Alex swallowed and watched Ka Tuk stand. Asuna took a step back from the demon. Maja used all her willpower to not hump his leg even though anger still boiled inside her. Serana simply watched.

"Come here." Ka Tuk curled his massive clawed hand towards himself. Alex hesitated then embraced her terrifying and powerful lover.

"My perfect, little, hume girl," said the demon as his hands went down her back to squeeze her flat butt. His animal-like penis started its rise to attention. Her tail flicked back and forth excitedly. Ka Tuk squeezed the base of the tail which made Alex's knees bend.

"I missed you." Alex rested her head on his broad sanguine chest. Ka Tuk lifted her chin with one finger and kissed her on the mouth. Her tail shot out straight, pointed at the ceiling, then continued swaying upright.

"I have to ask you something, well a lot of things actually," said Alex as she looked up at her demon lover.

"What is it, my little ember?"

"Did you destroy Greenlan?"

"I told you that I did not. Why do you insist on repeating your question?" Ka Tuk reached his rippling arm out and held Alex's chin.

"Everyone was told that you did. Everyone believes it. How can we believe you?"

"I have no reason to lie to...mortals. If I destroyed an entire nation, it would have been for a very just reason, and the Acolytes would be singing my proclamation." Agitation rose in Ka Tuk's voice as he explained himself.

"Everyone was told that sugar miners had awoken you from your eternal slumber below Greenlan, and that's why you destroyed it."

"I have spent countless eons banished in the Scoured Sands. Forsaken there by *Alexandria* and the other Devs." Ka Tuk's brow became a thick ridge as he pushed the name of Alexandria out of his mouth.

"I do remember that legend from my fire classes..." said Alex. "Are you satisfied, baby green? The only thing I care about is how you feel about this whole situation. I don't want you to think I'm betraying you."

"Uh, ummm...I don't know. I'm sorry!" Maja shuffled her feet and looked to Asuna and then Serana for hints.

"He's telling the truth," said Serana, arms crossed over her chest. "I'm very sensitive to anima, and it fluctuates when someone is lying. He's telling the truth."

"Oh, okay...I guess that's okay then..." Maja fidgeted and stared at the ground.

"Also, am I going to be a girl--a woman, forever?"

Ka Tuk grinned and squeezed Alex's butt with both hands.

"Why do you ask? I think being female suits you." Ka Tuk lifted her breast with one hand and rubbed it with his thumb.

"I think it suits me too, it's just, there are people in my life I have to be a man for. Especially that little person over there." Alex nodded towards Maja.

"Heh, very well. You've had the power in you to change back and forth at will."

"Wha-what?"

"Have you even tried to change back?" Ka Tuk squeezed Alex between her legs as if checking to be sure. Maja knew exactly what Alex was going through with that big powerful man who could make you feel feminine like nothing else could. She would never want to take that away from anyone.

"You don't have to change for me," Serana blurted out.

"Me neither!" Maja felt foolish Serana had said her words first. Serana glared at her then looked back to Alex.

"Do whatever makes you happy. There isn't enough of that in the world," said Asuna.

"I want to be a father for my child. I don't

want my baby to grow up like I did, and I want to do this for me. It's not over between us," said Alex as she looked up at Ka Tuk. "But I need this. I need to know how I feel. Ultimately, this is for me."

"You remember when I changed you?" said Ka tuk.

"Will never forget that as long as I live."

"You can do that. You have my power, little ember."

"Asunaaaaa! Asuna!" came a voice from outside the cellar.

"Fuck, fuck hide him." Alex raised her arms as if Ka Tuk could hide behind her. The calls continued outside from some distance away. Serana removed the skull from the armrest, and the throne vanished into black dust along with Ka Tuk. The room smelled burnt out like there had been a fire.

"Is that Tan-tan?" said Maja who was unable to contain her excitement as she dashed for the door. Alex grabbed her before she could leave.

"No...Tan-tan knows to come down here. She wouldn't stand outside shouting for Asuna. You think it's that woman you teamed up with?" Alex looked to Asuna who was watching the doorway. "Asuna?"

"I don't want to see her," said Asuna, "she knows the kind of coward I am."

"Lords and demons, you couldn't find a

single person that wasn't afraid to fight a Harbinger. Get over yourself. This woman sounds like she can do a lot for the guild. Your guild. Start acting like a leader and go recruit her."

"No...you're the leader now. Mort, put Alex in charge of the guild again. I'm not fit to lead people."

"It is done ma' am," said Mort who had not shifted away from his table the entire time despite the presence of Ka Tuk.

"You go recruit her." Asuna sat on the floor in the dark with her knees brought to her chest. Alex shook her head and climbed the stairs with Serana right behind her. Maja chased after them.

"What was her name? Lin? Lin!! Over here!" shouted Alex from the stairway.

"Asuna?" Lin shouted back from at least one alley over.

"Lin, over here!" Alex shouted again in her gender neutral voice. A large brown hume turned the corner and froze upon seeing the guildies. She reached behind her back and drew a colossal sword which was even bigger than Alex.

"You're not Asuna," said the woman as she planted her foot forward in a battle pose. She wore thick armor around her torso with free hanging plates below her waist. Between her substantial muscles and massive claymore she looked unstoppable.

"Whoa, hey! We're friends of Asuna's. She's downstairs. Promise," said Alex with her hands up. "Asuna, for the sake of our lives, please come up here."

"No," came Asuna's voice from the cellar.

"Ha! She's just embarrassed you saw her flee. She never runs from anything, and she's a bit shaken up about the whole situation. Asuna, PLEASE come up here before your friend tries to kill us."

Asuna poked her cloaked head out of the basement to see Lin standing at the end of the alley, still brandishing her sword. Serana held the ebony skull in her hand.

"I don't trust her, Alex. Just give me the word." Serana ran her thumb over the skull. Alex turned to her and flinched when she saw the skull in her hand.

"Put that lordsdam thing away. This isn't a fight. We need her to protect the goblins," said Alex.

"You're protecting the goblins too?" Lin lowered her sword but kept it between her and Alex.

"Yeah. We saved this one and then saved about a hundred more outside Trinity who were being forced out by The Guard."

"That was you guys?" Lin finally allowed the tip of her sword to rest on the ground.

"Yes..? How did YOU hear about it?"

"Let's just say, I have a friend that speaks to every single Guard in Trinity." Lin returned her sword to its makeshift scabbard and secured a strap behind her back. Serana placed her skull back in her purse.

"And what are they saying at the Guard station?" said Alex, still maintaining their distance from Lin.

"That's why I sought your group out. I need to speak to Asuna," said Lin. Asuna ducked back into the cellar without a word. Alex hesitated then gestured for Lin to follow. The stairs groaned under each step Lin took. Everyone gave her a wide berth in the basement. Asuna wouldn't make eye contact with her.

"I'm sorry I ran away," said Asuna with her arms wrapped around herself. "I'm a fucking coward."

"What were you supposed to do in that situation? Sometimes a tactical retreat is the only move you have left," said Lin.

"She's even bigger than Tan-tan," Maja said quietly to Alex.

"Is this Maja?" Lin moved towards her. Alex stood between them with her palms up but forcing a smile.

"Are you still in The Guard?" said Alex. Serana had her hand in her purse again. Lin clenched her jaw then relaxed.

"No, I'm a Warrior now. I plotted against The Guard right in front of my commanding Tank, and now they're looking for me. Probably going to make me disappear if they find me. They seized me, but I escaped thanks to a massive sacrifice by a dear friend."

"I'm sorry I dragged you into this," said Asuna.

"You didn't drag me into anything. It's my job--was my job to investigate crime in Trinity. Stop beating yourself up. This guild needs a leader."

"I'm not the leader anymore," said Asuna.

"Why? Because you fled a battle you couldn't win?"

Asuna shook her head.

"I'm actually in charge agai--now," said Alex, fumbling her words. Lin gave her a critical eye.

"And what are you supposed to be?"

"I'm a Dark Fire Mage," said Alex with some confidence.

"Is that like a Dark Paladin?" Lin shifted her feet towards the exit.

"No, we're on the same side. Please trust me. We took it upon ourselves to protect the goblins. No one asked us to. We did it because we knew it was the right thing. That's why I'm here," said Alex as Maja clung to her leg.

Lin's face softened. "I can respect that. It's also why I came looking for Asuna. The Guard is planning something and soon. I'm not exactly sure what, but it's happening in The Steps."

"That really isn't much to go on," said Alex.

"No, I know. It's just the little bit of information my friend relayed to me. I think we should lay up in The Steps tonight. But you're the leader, it's ultimately up to you."

"I don't know. It's up to Asuna. Without her, I don't know how effective we can reasonably be. Are you with us?"

Lin and the guild all looked to Asuna. She shook her head slowly as she spoke.

"If there's a Harbinger, it doesn't matter what we do or who we bring," said Asuna.

"They only bring in mercenaries AFTER an attack has happened. If we use skirmish tactics, utilize you as a failsafe, have an active route of retreat...they don't want to bring in a Harbinger. I don't even know if we--if they have one, and they would be ridiculously expensive on top of that. You can't let the fear of what might happen stop you from doing anything. You have the capacity to make a difference. Let them know their actions won't be tolerated." Lin stepped towards Asuna and placed her powerful hands on her slender shoulders. "You can do anything you want."

Maja approached them and hugged Asuna's leg, looking up at her. The rest of the guild huddled around her in a group hug.

"Alright, geez! Everyone get off of me," said Asuna as she gently pushed everyone away.

"Perfect. Now, is there anyone else in your guild that can help us? Where is Alexander Song?" said Lin. Alex let out a quick laugh then covered her mouth.

Lin watched her. "You look A LOT like him, you know that? From what I've seen of the wanted posters at least. And a Fire Mage on top of that. What did you say your name was?"

"Al-Alex...Song. I'm his sister..."

Everyone watched Lin for a reaction.

"Bet you hear that all the time, huh? Guess your parents weren't very creative with names?" said Lin who forced out a laugh. Alex laughed nervously.

"But seriously, where is he? We need someone with that kind of passion."

"He uh, he's headed for the Blasted Mountains right now. Our guild porter relayed me the message yesterday. Guess he's training to be a Pyre Shaman," said Asuna.

"That's amazing, a Pyre Shaman? Too bad he can't be here for this. Who else is in your guild? Do you have a Healer? Anybody will do really," said Lin, facing Asuna as they spoke.

"Uh, I'm actually in charge here," Alex spoke up. Lin turned to Alex, one eyebrow raised, then forced a smile.

"I'm sorry. Who else is in your guild?"

"Well, we have a pair of highly trained Archers, Lou and Lila. And a Fighter, Mage pair that are basically Novices," said Alex.

"The Fighter and Mage quit after Alexander put me in charge," said Asuna. Lin shook her head.

"Can you get the Archers here? Send them a letter?" said Lin, turning to Asuna then back to Alex.

"Our mail privileges have been revoked. And our guild is too small to afford com stones for everyone. If they show up, they show up. They check in every few days," said Alex.

"So it's just us then," said Lin. Alex nodded.

"What is everyone's class? I know I'm controlling things, I'm just trying to think tactically in case we have to fight tonight," said Lin.

"No, it's okay. We could definitely use a tactician," said Alex, "well, you already know I'm a Dark Fire Mage. Asuna is a Revenant. Serana is a Summoner. And Maja just started training as an Animist."

Lin smiled at Maja who shuffled her feet and smiled back bashfully.

"She's not like any Animist I've ever seen," said Serana, crossing her arms.

"What does that mean?" Lin asked. Serana remained silent.

"We should find Tan-tan," said Maja.

"I'm sure she'll be excited to see me," said Lin, laughing silently to herself.

"You met Tan-tan?" said Alex.

"Unfortunately, yes. She doesn't care much for Guards, does she?"

"Not really...but where is she? Why wasn't she at the bar?" Alex asked, looking at Asuna.

"She‘s with her father I told y--"

"In Diamond Heights," Lin cut Asuna off, "and you're not getting in there unless they want you there. That place is locked down harder than the Guard station."

"Let her spend time with her family. I bet she really missed her sisters after five years. I can handle whatever they throw at us," said Asuna.

"So now we just wait for nightfall?" Lin looked to Asuna then back at Alex again.

"I could invite you into the guild. I need to initiate her anyway." Alex nodded towards Maja.

"Yeah, let's do it," said Lin, making a fist.

"Do you accept my invitation into our guild?" Alex looked down at Maja. Maja nodded furiously.

"You have to say yes or I do."

"I do."

"Do YOU accept my invitation into our guild?" said Alex, looking at Lin.

"Yes."

"Alright then, I guess we just wait for dark now."

CHAPTER 31

Night in The Steps was ushered in by screams. The guild stormed up the stairs and out of the cellar. Asuna led them into the goblin Steps towards the screams. As they entered, goblins poured out in the opposite direction.

"What's going on? What's happening up there?" Alex shouted at the goblins who ran past them. No one would stop to explain. The neighborhood seemed to glow in the dying light of the day as they moved deeper into The Steps. As they rounded a two story stack of houses, they found several homes ablaze. A squad of Guards was knocking panicked goblins down and herding them out of The Steps.

Lin nearly knocked over a home as she brandished her claymore, but Asuna was strides ahead of her. She transformed into a screeching haze as she dissipated into the shadows. The Guards abruptly stopped what they were doing as if a hound whistle had been sounded for them. The guild stopped and watched. Wailing and screams echoed in other neighborhoods, but a menacing tranquility fell over the immediate area.

One of the Guards fell to his knees, his halberd clanging on the ground beside him. He held his stomach as he moaned and then whimpered like a beaten child. He vomited onto the ground and fell to his side, curled into a fetal position. His breathing became choked as he wheezed for every breath. As he slowly died, another Guard screamed as if he had been stabbed and tumbled into one of the squat goblin shacks. The remaining Guards fled but stumbled on the filthy ground. All three of them spasmed with violent seizures like broken automatons.

"Lords, help us all..." whispered Lin as she watched Asuna work. A buzzing black smoke came from the Guards' mouths, and Asuna materialized from the haze with her fists clenched, standing over the Guards.

"This is what you GET," said Asuna through clenched teeth, "anyone that disturbs these people will feel my curse, MY WRATH. The goblins are under my protection now."

The sounds of panic continued elsewhere in The Steps.

"Serana, can you put out the fires?" said Alex. Serana said a prayer which made her sapphire necklace glow in the waning light. Thunder crackled overhead and a rainstorm began. The downpour did not last long, but it was enough to put out the fires in the immediate area.

"I can only do that a couple more times," said Serana. Maja tugged on the sleeve of her robe.

"Thank you." Maja scampered to join her guild who were already moving to another neighborhood. Serana scooped her up and howled as she turned to her lycan form, bounding with her guild to the next confrontation.

"A lycan?" muttered Lin under her breath as they ran. Past the swaying, rusty structures was a circuited roadway surrounded by small metal shacks. A half dozen Guards were knocking goblins down and organizing them into ranks. Other Guards used their halberd blades to pry the roofs off of houses and violently remove goblins from their homes as they found them.

"What's the plan?" said Lin as she squatted down behind a row of houses and moved closer. The guild followed her lead.

"We can't let any goblins get hurt," said Alex.

"Can you ward them?" said Asuna, looking to Lin. "The goblins?"

"Yeah, what are you going to do?"

"Going to put the fear into them." Asuna vaulted over a home with Lin right behind her. Lin slowly swung her sword, and the ranks of goblins were encased in translucent blue bubbles. Asuna let out a nightmarish scream like the sound of animals and children being slaughtered. The macabre wail sent sickening chills through the guild members and forced everyone but Lin to tears. The Guards fled, sobbing as they ran. Maja cried in Serana's arms. Lin stared with dreaded disbelief at Asuna.

"The wards," Alex managed to say as she held her chest with one hand. Lin waved her sword and the bubbles popped, sending the goblins scattering into the homes.

"Please don't ever do that again," said Lin as she leaned against a taller home to compose herself. "That felt so wrong."

"Not half as wrong as what they're doing," said Asuna with a shimmer of tears on her face.

"Please, we don't need another Wrath," said Lin.

"What they're doing is evil, and I can't tolerate it anymore! They need to be taught a lesson, and I'm the only one that has the power to do that. I'm going to fucking stop them," said Asuna, every sentence pushed out through her clenched jaw. Without another word, she sprinted off into the winding roadways of The Steps. Lin was quick to pursue, followed by Alex, and Serana carrying Maja.

"Serana, stop her!" shouted Alex. Serana tossed Maja into Alex's arms and bounded ahead on all fours.

"Asuna, please stop!" shouted Lin, unable to catch her. Serana ran past her guild and tackled Asuna to the ground, pinning her. With a single wave of her arm, Asuna launched Serana off of her and into a stack of goblin homes. Alex set Maja down and ran to check on her.

"They have to pay for this," Asuna hissed, her voice raspy and fear inducing. Her eyes were now glistening black orbs.

"You can't kill the Guards. We need them to protect the city." Lin approached her slowly. Asuna rose to her feet.

"No one is protecting these people but me," said Asuna, her fists trembling. "Fear is the only thing they'll understand."

"Asuna, please!" cried Maja, scampering up to her and hugging her legs. "Please stop hurting people!"

Maja hugged Asuna's legs and sobbed. Asuna's scowl softened, and she relaxed her fist, staring at the ground as if it had wronged her.

"I can't let them keep hurting these people. It's wrong. They're fucking monsters. I'm not the monster here. I can stop all of them. No one has to get hurt but them. Please understand, Maja, I do this because I care about you and your people, and we cannot just stand around and hope one day they see justice. You have to take justice, you have to force it down their throat. I'm sorry I scared you, but I'm not sorry for what I'm about to do." Asuna caught her breath and looked at Lin. "You weren't in that home. You didn't have to listen as that scared little girl told me how they mutilated her and ruined her life. YOU DIDN'T HAVE TO LIS-

TEN TO IT! You didn't have to sit there knowing you could stop it from ever happening again. I can still here her crying..." Asuna turned to haze and merged with the darkness.

"What the fuck have I done?" said Lin. Alex walked over with Serana's arm around her shoulder.

"This was a fucking mistake," said Alex, "how are we ever going to stop her..."

"With this," said Lin, brandishing her sword.

"Swords don't work on Revenants," said Alex. Lin closed her eyes and focused. The sword sparked with brilliant light which forced everyone to wince.

"This sword is blessed by Dev Allo. It's rune was used to repel the Wrath. I think it can damage her."

"Think?" said Alex.

"In the armory, she flinched away from the rune when it sparked. I think it hurt her."

The screams of slaughter echoed in the distance, making the guild cringe.

"Are we really going to kill Asuna?" said Alex.

"Nooo!" cried Maja, grabbing Lin's leg as if to stop her.

"We can't have another Wrath. I'm sorry, but it's the only way." Lin looked down at Maja. Alex bent down and pried Maja away who kicked and struggled the entire time.

"There has to be another way," cried Maja as she thrashed in Alex's arm.

"We tried to reason with her. If we don't stop her, she'll bring the whole city down," said Alex. Another echo of unholy screams rang out in the night which sent a wave of goblins fleeing in their direction.

"Where is it?" Lin shouted at them, "Where's the Revenant?"

Guards followed behind, not antagonizing the goblins, but running in fear for their own lives. Their faces were frozen in horror. Lin threw out her arm and clotheslined one of them as he made to pass then grabbed him by the collar of his chainmail.

"The Revenant, where is she?" said Lin, inches from his face. The Guard stammered out nonsense.

"Where!"

"The-the-the cobblestone circuit, it's-it's-it's heading for the in...terior. Let me go, lordsake," stammered the Guard. Lin let him fall to the ground, and he ran for his life.

"This neighborhood is a damn labyrinth," growled Lin who tried to gather her bearings as she examined her surroundings. Alex stepped away from Serana and looked into the sky.

"There. See that structure that leans against the rotunda? If we move directly away from it, it should lead us toward central Trinity, and we'll have to cross over the cobblestone," said Alex as she pointed at the towering goblin shacks.

"Lead the way," said Lin.

"Serana, are you okay to follow us?" asked Alex.

"Yeah, I can keep up with you humes," said Serana, trying to push out a smile. Alex grabbed Maja and took off at a brisk pace towards central Trinity with Lin and Serana behind her. Alex adjusted her path as they heard the unmistakable Revenant fear. Small goblin shacks gave way to the pointed roofs of hume homes, and a trio of convulsing Guards laid out in the roadway was new evidence that Asuna had been there. They finally crossed into the cobblestone road which was completely devoid of goblins or humes.

"I don't think I've ever seen the cobblestone empty," said Alex. None of the street lamps were lit. The dark empty roadway was like a nightmare version of itself. There was another hellish scream in the distance, closer than any of the previous ones.

The distinct sound of hooves on cobblestone approached them from the opposite direction. The guild turned around to see a row of grey archons pull war wagons up the cobblestone road. On one of the wagons stood a stone-faced elderly Tank behind a Guard holding the reigns. On the other wagon, a tall androgynous woman stood with another Guard holding the reigns.

"Is that fucking Tan-tan?" said Alex.

CHAPTER 32

The guild stepped to the sidewalk as the war wagons slowed to a stop in front of them. Each archon wore plate armor and the Guards had special armor to mark them as drivers.

"Is that Maja?" shouted Tan-tan before she leapt off the wagon. Maja jumped out of Alex's arms and into Tan-tan's.

"Oh my lords, I missed you so much," said Tan-tan who shared tears with Maja. "Who are these people?"

"No time for that, Stalker, we have to repel this Revenant before Trinity burns once again," said the Tank.

"But sir, there's a lycan, and that's, that's Paladin Lindlithsong!" said one of the drivers who removed his sword from the scabbard on his back.

"Dammit, Lindlithsong! I should have known you had something to do with this," said the Tank.

"Let me help you fix this!" pleaded Lin.

"I'll fix this," said Tan-tan, "I can stop her. I promise you."

"How would a Stalker ever defeat a Revenant?" said the Tank.

"She's my girlfriend. She'll listen to me."

"Very well then, if you can stop her from tearing Trinity apart, consider your father's proposal as good as sealed. Otherwise, I will have no choice but to deploy the Harbinger."

"Then let's hurry the FUCK up." Tan-tan planted her arm on the frame of the wagon and hopping over with Maja in her other arm. She set Maja down in the Tank's wagon and helped the others up.

"Go, dammit, go!" shouted Tan-tan as she smacked her driver on the back. The Guards cracked their reigns and the two squads of archons took off.

"This isn't over, Paladin Lin. Once we repel the Revenant, you and Guard Marvin will answer for your crimes," said the Tank.

"If we live to see tomorrow," said Lin.

"What the fuck is happening, Tan-tan? Why are you with The Guard?" said Alex.

"Alexander? Lords and demons! You're fucking hot."

"Nevermind that. What's happening? Why are you here? Why are you with The Guard?"

"It's a long story. It'll be a lot more interesting if we all survive this," said Tan-tan. The war wagons were forced to stop as a crowd of screaming goblins spilled into the street.

"Stay behind me," said the Tank as he led

them towards the source of the goblins' fear.

"How can you work with them?" snarled Alex under her breath as they moved back into a goblin neighborhood.

"Just trust me, please. There's a plan," said Tan-tan. Everyone in the group crouched as they crept forward.

"Everyone have their weapons ready?" said the Tank as they entered the roadway. A Guard screaming hysterically ran past them. Glowing light against the side of buildings suggested flames. There was the sensation of descending into the hells. Whatever was around that row of houses would be the most fearsome and nightmarish thing any of them had ever experienced. The silence was the most terrifying of all. There was no indication of what lay ahead as they crossed into the open.

"Let me lead. I can stop her," said Tan-tan as she stepped in front of the Tank.

"Do you really think you can reason with her? Let me ward you just in case," said the Tank.

"No. She needs to know I'm not afraid of her."

The group turned the corner, Tan-tan first, followed by the massive Tank, and then the guild. The drivers remained at the wagons ready for a tactical retreat at a moment's notice. The archons shifted restlessly under their reigns.

In a small neighborhood square, multiple Guards writhed on the ground. Goblins cowered in corners, and small fires blazed. The Revenant was nowhere to be seen.

"Asuna! Babe! I know you're here. I just want to talk," Tan-tan shouted to the empty air.

"Go away," came Asuna's disembodied voice, emanating from everywhere and nowhere at the same time.

"Have Dawnbringer ready," the Tank whispered to Lin.

"Aww, come on. I really want to see you."

"I don't want you to see me like this. I don't want you to see the monster."

"Babe, it's over. The goblins are safe now."

"The goblins are not safe!" Asuna's voice warbled and took on a demonic tone. The darkness around them seethed.

"No, just now, we brokered a deal with Trinity, me and my father. We found a home for the goblins. Trust me, babe."

"You hate your father! This is a trick!" The shadows in the square pulsated and grew, but Tan-tan stood stalwart.

"I still do, but you gotta' trust me, babe. I would never lie to you. I can see you care about the goblins as much as I do, and that's why I could tolerate my father long enough to work with him. And we're willing to make a deal, right?" said Tan-tan, looking towards the Tank who gave an almost imperceptible nod.

"You, me, we leave Trinity forever, and you can protect the goblins in their new home. I promise you, babe."

Shards of shadows split off and pulled together in front of Tan-tan. Asuna materialized from the darkness, her arms across her body, unwilling to make eye contact with Tan-tan.

"There's my ice queen," said Tan-tan as she stepped in to hug her. Everyone breathed a collective sigh of relief. A flood of warmth rushed through the group, knowing the scale of disaster they had just avoided.

"She did it," said the Tank.

"I'll be leaving too. With her," said Lin.

"We'll see about that."

CHAPTER 33

"So what happens now?" said Tan-tan as she leaned towards the desk.

"The Banshee, as she's being called by The Starlight, will face a military tribunal along with the wanted criminal Alexander Song. The results of the trial are already predetermined. They will face exile, along with the rest of your guild, as per our agreement. In exchange for your quelling of The Banshee, you will be given corporal rights to Niffelheim, as well as one hundred tons of scrap metal," said Lord Tychus who wore decorative service armor and was impeccably groomed. His office was like a miniature library, each wall lined with shelves of leather bound books. All the walls were bookshelves except the far wall which contained a large window above an end table.

"The trade agreement is in place?" said Tan-tan's father as he sifted through a pile of stiff documents.

"It...is being finalized. By the time you arrive in Niffelheim, all the signatures will be in place," said Lord Tychus. Tan-tan found him insanely attractive for a man.

"No," her father said flatly, "all signatures are required before we depart, not after. I have been doing this a very long time, you will not play these games."

"I assure you, we mean no disrespect towards your enterprise. We will have the papers signed before you leave." Lord Tychus signaled for a Paladin to collect the papers from Tan-tan's father.

"You will only receive your windfall after thirty-five hundred goblins have left the city limits of Trinity, not before. That is understood, correct?" said Lord Tychus, speaking only to Tan-tan's father.

"By my reports, we already have those numbers en route to the city. Your Agents can confirm that, preferably sooner rather than later. We have much work to do." Tan-tan's father slowly climbed out of the chair, waving Tan-tan away as she moved to help.

"All's well and good then." Lord Tychus reached across the desk and shook Tan-tan's hand. "And let's not forget the two percent tribute to Trinity."

"I have not forgotten. After six months you will begin to receive your tribute," said Tan-tan's father as he moved for the door.

"It has been changed to three months, you understand?" Lord Tychus smiled at him. Tan-tan's grip tightened in their shake. Her father simply stared at him and continued for the door. Tan-tan followed her father out into the hall.

"I've underestimated our business partner." Her father hobbled down the hallway as he held his daughter's hand. Two of their Agents stepped off the wall and fell in line as they exited the Lord's office.

"You thought because Tychus was a fresh Lord that he couldn't negotiate a contract?" said Tan-tan.

"Precisely. Never underestimate your opponent. Truthfully, it is how I got as far as I have in business."

"Never underestimating anyone?"

"No, everyone underestimating me."

"You still want me to act on your behalf in Niffelheim?" said Tan-tan, walking as they spoke. Her father stopped and pulled her hands until she squatted down to face him.

"I know you still bear a lot of anger towards me, and I do not blame you. But I always wanted you to take over my business when I retired. And your willingness to become an Agent proves just how serious you are. I trust you. Your sisters trust you. You will have all my resources at your disposal, and I will check in as often as I can." He pulled her in for a hug and gently bit her ear before stopping himself. Tan-tan pulled away and nodded. They continued towards the exit hand in hand. The hallways of the palace were composed of polished stone and decorated with elaborate embroidered tapestries that illustrated the most significant events in Trinity's history. Tan-tan wanted to explore the palace more in hopes of finding a tableau dedicated to Tantra Charbelcher, but she knew there was no longer a time or place for her whims. After they left the palace and descended the stairway, Tan-tan helped her father into his black carriage which awaited them outside. The two Agents following them climbed in after him. Tan-tan waved as the carriage left. She re-entered the palace and wandered down the winding hallways until she found the holding room for Asuna and Alexander. The room was comfortably appointed with polished furniture, decorative linens, a well stocked bookcase, fireplace, and a dry sink. It was a room designed for special circumstance criminals with two Paladins in service armor standing watch outside. At the table, Asuna and Alexander discussed the events of the past few days. Upon seeing Tan-tan enter, Asuna shot up from the table and into her arms with a smile and a kiss.

"What's the word, babe? What's happening to us?" Asuna planted a deep kiss so Tan-tan couldn't answer immediately.

"The deal has been finalized. The papers are being signed. You and Alexander will be facing a staged military trial where you'll be exiled. The city gets to look like it knows what it's doing, and everyone I care about is safe. I'm really hoping you'll come to Niffelheim. I need all the allies I can get." Tan-tan looked to Asuna then to Alexander to let him know he was being asked as well.

"Niffelheim..." muttered Asuna as she pulled away from Tan-tan. Her eyes darted back and forth and her mouth hung open.

"Yeah...you've heard of it?" Tan-tan approached her as she continued to back away.

"The City of Evil..." whispered Asuna, stumbling backwards as she found her seat at the table. Here face kept twitching and her mouth wouldn't close. She looked as if she had just been told her parents were dead.

"What did you say?" Tan-tan grabbed the chair between Asuna and Alexander and sat directly across from her.

"You can't bring the goblins there," said Asuna as she grabbed Tan-tan's hand. Asuna's hands were frigid and trembling. Alexander leaned in with Tan-tan.

"Niffelheim was Trinity's sister city. In the old days, Niffelheim was even bigger than Trinity. Then one day, everyone in the entire city disappeared. No bodies, no destruction, everyone was just gone. Can you imagine that? An entire city, tens of thousands of lives, just vanished. No one knows what happened. That city is cursed. You can't bring people there." Asuna's words were quiet and hollow. She shook her head as she spoke.

"Babe, that's just an old legend from time out of time. We researched it. We investigated it. The city is safe. There's thousands of houses in liveable condition. It's the perfect place for the goblins. It's not safe for them here. They need their own city. They need a place to call their home, and I can give it to them." Tan-tan squeezed Asuna's hands.

"Take them back to Greenlan then. This is a terrible idea. You can't go through with it. Please, Tantra..." Tears formed in the corners of Asuna's eyes.

"Babe, you know I love you, but this is happening. Greenlan is a clusterfuck to say the least, especially going on what Alex told me about Ka Tuk. We'll personally go into Niffelheim, you and me, and Alex if you haven't totally freaked him out at this point." Tan-tan turned to Alexander.

"Well, I gotta' see this city now." He forced a smile.

"We won't let anyone in until we personally see it's safe, okay? You trust me, babe? Trust me to help these people?" Tan-tan looked to Asuna for an answer who nodded and hugged her.

"I need you for this. It's going to be a lot of work and a lot of mess, and I need someone like you who the goblins trust. I'm counting on you, babe." Tan-tan kissed the corner of her girlfriend's mouth.

"I trust you," said Asuna. Tan-tan looked at the floor and then back to her girlfriend.

"I have to go check in with the guild. Just triple checking everything. Once your trials are over, we can all leave this lordsforsaken city. You going to be okay?" said Tan-tan, one arm on her girlfriend's shoulder. Asuna wiped the tears from her face and nodded. Tan-tan gave her one last kiss and left.

Outside the palace, Tan-tan gleefully made her way through the Administrative District and towards the bar where the rest of her guild waited. She felt like a happy cloud floating down the street in the final steps of putting Trinity behind her. The goblins would be safe, and she would be able to spend her days taking care of her sisters. The city no longer seemed as shitty as she remembered. The light seemed brighter. The people seemed happier. A mess didn't seem as massive when it wasn't yours, especially when it used to be yours. She stepped onto the cobblestone circuit and followed it to the bar, nodding and smiling at strangers as she walked. She climbed the few steps outside the bar and entered the main room to find the rest of her guildies at a table with empty plates in front of them. Maja was licking preserves from the plate in front of her.

"Don't do that." Serana watched Maja as if she was an animal feeding.

"Oh, let her be. Never seen anyone enjoy

food as much as her." Lin leaned back in her chair with one arm over the backrest. Upon seeing Tan-tan enter, Serana nearly climbed over the table to get to her with Maja right behind. They laid into her with questions about Alexander, their future, The Steps, and the guild, before reiterating their concerns for Alexander.

"Shaddup!" shouted Tan-tan, stepping past them to the table where Lin sat. She and Lin exchanged uneasy smiles.

"Not going to tell you girls the same lordsdam story three times, so just listen. Alexander is going to trial, and he's going to be exiled. Asuna too, thanks for asking...as far as I know, they're coming with the goblin convoy to Niffelheim, and we're going to be working out of there for the foreseeable future. I'm going to be in charge there with my father breathing down my neck the entire time."

"Wait, Alexander Song is in Trinity?" said Lin, sitting upright. The guild all looked at her.

"Yeah...as part of my arrangement with Trinity, Alexander and Asuna are facing a military tribunal. Going to really give the people the illusion that Trinity knows what it's doing. They don't want you though. Apparently you're a black eye for The Guard. But you absolutely have to leave," said Tan-tan.

"What happened with his sister? Alex?" said Lin.

"I guess after the Night of Screams, she

didn't want anything to do with us," said Tan-tan, "now Maja--"

"Whoa, wait. What's happening with Marv? You secured his release, right?"

"Uh, no...they're not going to release him...they want to send a message with him."

Lin clenched her jaw then pounded the table which startled Maja and Serana.

"Fuckers..." said Lin through clenched teeth, "we have to save him."

"No. I'm not going to foul up this deal, put thousands of lives in jeopardy, just to break your friend out of the dungeon. You can't have it every which way you want it. I mean, my girl-friend is going to stand in front of a military tri-bunal while a bunch of Paladins that have never seen combat scream at her for hours on end to make The Guard look tough. You think I want that for her?"

Lin stared at the table fuming.

"Now, Maja, I really want you to come with us. I need goblins I can trust to help me deal with the population. You lived in The Steps your entire life. I need your insights. As per your request--"

""Per my request?" Maja looked to her guildies for an explanation.

"Listen. I have commissioned a home for you and your mother. It'll be ready when we ar-rive in Niffelheim. Will you follow me there?"

"Of course I will. You're my friend."

"And Lin, your knowledge and skills as a Paladin will be invaluable for forming a new Guard in Niffelheim. Do you think you could train goblins to patrol and protect themselves?"

"You want me to train an all-goblin Guard?" Lin stared at the table.

"That's the plan, an all-goblin Guard protecting the goblins."

"That's a really smart idea. Yeah...I'll help you build a home for these people. Count me in." Lin thrusted her hand out. Tan-tan took the handshake and was shocked by the power of Lin's grip.

"Serana, I didn't ask you for anything because I know you're going to follow whatever decision Alexander makes."

"That's what you do when you're in love." Serana lifted her chin in a dignified way.

"Once the trial is over, I have transportation arranged for all us. Some nice luxurious carriages big enough to sleep in. It's two days trip by archon. Don't leave anything here," Tan-tan said with a laugh, "I have to go finalize everything with my father. I don't know when I'll be able to check in with you girls again. I'll be sure to come by when we leave. Take care of yourselves."

Tan-tan got up to leave, but Maja climbed over the table and stood on it to hug her.

"Awww, baby green. It's just a few days. I'll be back before you know it," said Tan-tan, kissing the top of her head. She gave them all one last wave before she left the bar and headed for Diamond Heights. The city seemed more pleasant than it ever had in the past, knowing now she didn't have a future in it. It was like vacationing in a foreign land. She watched the humes move along the sidewalks and through the roadways and imagined their complicated but simple lives. At the gates to Diamond Heights, Tan-tan handed over her letter of permission and entered. She was genuinely happy to put this facade of civility behind her. As she approached her father's mansion, her sisters rushed out the front door and into her arms.

"Missed you girls." Tan-tan knelt down for a hug then scooped them up and carried them inside. She planted little kisses on Alo's face as she walked.

"We missed you so much!" Makilja shouted in her ear.

"Is dad home?" said Tan-tan, taking a seat on the couch with her sisters in her lap.

"Yeah, he's in his office," said Makilja.

"Alright, I just need to have a little private time with him, then we can go and play in the backyard, okay?" said Tan-tan. Makilja grabbed Alo's hand and they ran for the back door. Tan-tan knocked as she entered her father's office. An Agent was plastered against the wall next to the door.

"Tan-tan, of course, come in," said her father, setting down the papers he was examining.

"Just wanted to double check, make sure everything is going as planned," said Tan-tan as she took the easy chair.

"It is fine. Your diligence will get you far in business. So far everything is in order. Once Trinity sends over the trade agreement, we'll be ready to set out. Our first shipment of sugar ore will be arriving in Niffelheim tonight. Word has spread fast through The Steps. Imagine, goblins want to be sugar processors."

"Yeah, I kind of figured they would. Did you...are you aware of Niffelheim's history?"

"What's that? Oh, you mean the disappearances. I am quite aware, yes." Her father lifted up a piece of parchment to scrutinize.

"It wasn't just disappearances though, the whole city vanished."

"Who have you been talking to? It is not wise to share the terms of our deal with anyone, especially when things haven't been finalized."

"Was just my girlfriend. She said one day all of Niffelheim just vanished."

"Daughter of mine, that's just a very old legend. Why, I have personally read that there was a great migration out of Niffelheim when the land turned and wouldn't yield crops. But seeing as goblins don't need crops for sustenance, that isn't much of an issue, now is it?"

"I just want them to be safe."

"Trinity has sent Scouts into Niffelheim,

and they have assured us it is quite safe. This is a business deal. One you helped construct. Never forget that. It is about silver and gold, nothing more."

"It's more than that to me. I have to help these people no matter the cost."

"No matter the cost?" Her father lowered the paper to look at her. "Your passion is admirable, but this is money. If this venture is not profitable, you will be cut off. Is that understood?"

Tan-tan nodded then waved to her sisters in the backyard who were waving at her through the glass wall. Her father spun in his desk chair to smile and wave at them before turning back to her.

"You can help the goblins and make money in the process. They do not have to be mutually exclusive."

"I understand."

"Good. Now, is there anything else you wanted to discuss?"

"Oh, I've hired a liason for the goblins, and a Paladin to help train up a militia."

"Already? That's good work."

"And...I might have some people ready for the privateering quests."

"Might?"

"Once they understand how important it is to the livelihood of the goblins, I'm certain they'll want the jobs."

"Okay, then. Everything should be finalized by the end of the week. I look forward to working with you." Her father broke into a smile. Tan-tan returned an uneasy smile then left for the garden to play with her sisters.

CHAPTER 34

Their last weeks in Trinity began with the military tribunals of Asuna and Alexander. Each one lasted only hours without the need to determine guilt. Both suspects faced a maelstrom of righteous screaming and indignation by stuffy old Paladins who had not seen combat in decades. Asuna was convicted of terroristic acts against the city-state and Alexander was convicted of murder under special circumstances for the killings of Guard Jason Wilson and a civilian whose name could not be released, pending further investigation. The convictions and exile of Asuna and Alexander assuaged the doubts of the citizens of Trinity in the ability of The Guard to protect the city, as reported by The Starlight.

Alexander's guild, as well as Tan-tan's family, departed at dawn for Niffelheim along with a convoy of 1,000 goblins. The convoy brought the total immigration count to 4,500: a number fiercely contested by Trinity and the Bloodwater Cartel. Alexander's guild and the Bloodwater family rode in luxury carriages. Tan-tan's father and sisters had their own carriage, as well as Asuna and Tan-tan. Maja, Serana, Alexander and Lin all shared a third carriage. The luxury carriages led a long trickling stream of goblins out of Trinity heading east.

Asuna looked across the carriage cabin and smiled at Tan-tan who smiled right back at her.

"Would you get your ass over here?" said Tan-tan, sweeping her hand towards herself with a grin. Asuna crawled like a predatory cat across the spacious, carpeted floor of their carriage. Tan-tan bit down on her plump bottom lip. Asuna knelt in front of Tan-tan and forced her knees apart with one powerful motion. Tan-tan felt a tight pulling sensation behind her groin.

"Take that top off. Let me see those little tits," said Asuna. With the help of Asuna, Tan-tan removed her Agent's jacket and top to reveal her slender wiry frame and tiny perky breasts which arched up slightly at the tip of her nipple.

"Look how little they are." Asuna reached up with her cold ashen hand to squeeze one, fondle it, and give it a jiggle. She climbed on the bench seat and overpowered Tan-tan, pulling her backwards. Her chest pressed against Tan-tan's powerful backside who let out a low coo in sheer animal arousal. Reaching under Tan-tan's arms, she fondled her girlfriend's breasts, kneaded them, bounced them on the pads of her fingers, then pulled her nipples. She licked and kissed Tan-tan's salt tinged neck, making Tan-tan gasp. Asuna continued to fondle her, working her small sensitive breasts, whispering insults in her ear until Tan-tan was so overcome she began to drool.

"Now eat my pussy, you dumb animal," whispered Asuna, callously pushing Tan-tan onto the floor. Asuna rolled her crimson singlet down her ash-colored body until her pussy was revealed. Tan-tan pulled the singlet off by the legs and dove into her girlfriend's mound, inhaling the mild mineral smell of the patch of charcoal pubic hair above her slit. Asuna's labia were stone grey and barely perceptible. Her clit stuck out like a little smooth pebble. Tan-tan spread her open with two calloused fingers and dragged her tongue up her opening, making her tremble. She sunk two fingers inside her and opened her while sucking her clit. Asuna rubbed her hand over Tan-tan's soft cropped hair, shoving her hips further into her face. Tan-tan continued sucking her clit as she fingered her, eliciting coos from Asuna. She turned Asuna over so she was kneeling over the bench seat and laid into her girlfriend with measured, vicious spanks. Each smack brought a coo from Asuna's lips and sent a ripple through her pleasantly round butt. After several spanks, Tan-tan thrust her long powerful fingers inside her girlfriend and fucked her as fast as she could before she pulled out to continue her spankings.

"I love the way you whimper when I spank you," said Tan-tan, laying into her girlfriend with another smack. Asuna looked over her shoulder and flinched, biting into the skin on top of her wrist. Tan-tan was vicious, smack after smack so strong that they lifted Asuna off her knees. Then Tan-tan fucked her girlfriend with three fingers as fast as she could until Asuna cried out and crumpled against the bench seat, gasping for breath.

"You are so fucking sexy when you cum. Look at that beautiful body." Tan-tan climbed on top of her girlfriend and kissed her. Asuna's eyes were unfocused, and she allowed Tan-tan to pin her down as she kissed her.

"You, you don't have to use three fingers. Just next time, you know..." said Asuna between kisses, aftershocks rolling through her naked body.

"Sure, babe." Tan-tan pawed at Asuna's breasts as she kissed her. Asuna smiled and shoved Tan-tan off of her with ease, pinning her down by the wrists then forcibly removing her pants. Tan-tan felt her mind tip away as her girlfriend overpowered her then stripped her. She snapped back to reality when Asuna gave her a firm smack between the legs, making her cross her hips to protect herself. Asuna turned her over and easily forced her knees apart, giving Tan-tan's pussy another hard smack. Tan-tan tried to cover her pussy with her hands, but Asuna once again restrained her, using just one hand to pin her wrists above her head as she smacked her again, making her tear up in pain.

"Are you my dumb animal?" said Asuna, smacking Tan-tan's pussy again. Tan-tan nodded as she struggled against Asuna's power.

"Say it."

"I'm your dumb animal," Tan-tan said through tears, looking up at her powerful naked girlfriend.

"Look at the way your lips hang out." Asuna leaned in and gently pulled Tan-tan's labia. She leaned in further and licked them. Her thumb pressed against Tan-tan's clit and rubbed it in circles.

"I know you hate them, the way they hang out of your slit. You think it makes you ugly."

"I am ugly!" Tan-tan shouted back at her, her face a mess of tears.

"You're my ugly little animal." Asuna pulled Tan-tan's head to her breast and kissed the top. Tan-tan nursed on Asuna's cold breast and cried as she masturbated. Asuna stroked Tan-tan's hair as her girlfriend nursed and cried the entire time.

"I can literally hear them fucking in the next carriage." Serana crossed her arms over her chest and scowled.

"Oh, let them have their fun. They've been

through a lot." Alexander patted her on the knee.

"If Lin wasn't here, I bet we could have a lot of fun." Maja giggled and looked at Lin then to Alexander. Lin gave her an awkward smile then looked out the carriage window. Everyone's body shifted side to side as the carriage rolled on.

"Please don't interpret this the wrong way, but why isn't your mother riding with us?" said Alexander who sat between Maja and Ser-ana.

"She didn't want the other goblins think-ing she was better than all of them, so she's in the convoy." Maja stood up then hung halfway out the window to see a line of hundreds of goblins stretched all the way back to the walls of Trin-ity. Near the front was her mother and a dozen or so goblins riding on a flat bed wagon with as much scrap metal as they were allowed to bring. She gave her mother an excited wave who smiled and waved back, blowing her a kiss.

"Ya' know, I still haven't met her yet," said Alexander, pulling Maja back into the carriage.

"Yeah but, the demon and everything..."

"I don't have horns or a tail in my male form. I can control it at will now. She doesn't need to know everything else. She probably wants to meet the father of her grandbaby. I have no problem meeting your mother." Alexander took her tiny chubby hands in his large hume hands.

"I...no, it's just..."

"It's because I'm hume, isn't it?"

"Yeah...I'm sorry. I love that you're hume. It's sexy! But I don't know how Mama will feel. I never want to do anything that disappoints her..."

"Are you saying I'm a disappointment?"

"No! No!" Maja stood on Alexander's lap and hugged him, tears in the corner of her eyes. "It's just what humes have done to goblins. What they did to her."

"I guess that makes sense, but we have to tell her though. We can't just ignore it. Once we stop for the night, we meet her together, and tell her, okay?"

Maja nodded and kissed Alexander's cheek. Serana reached over and squeezed his hand.

"You two really are a cute couple," said Lin who paused for a moment, "Ya' know, I think Asuna might have a crush on me."

"Well, I would be careful then, if Tan-tan thinks you're trying to steal Asuna away..." said Alexander.

"I'm not afraid of Tan-tan."

"That's because you don't know her very well. She's a good person but...she's filled with a lot of rage. I think she's only tolerating her father to help the goblins, and I think she might be barely hanging on."

"Listen. First off, I like dudes, okay? I have no attraction whatsoever to Asuna, especially after the Night of Screams. Second, I'm not afraid of a Stalker, or an Agent, or whatever the hells Tan-tan is now. Was just making a comment."

"I'm just giving you fair warning," said Alexander, "not implying you're not a very capable Warrior."

Lin continued to stare out the window.

"Are you excited for Niffelheim?" Serana smiled at Alexander.

"An entire city that disappeared one night? Can't say I'm not a little nervous, but I do really want to see it, so yeah, I'm excited. You think there's going to be artifacts there?"

"Oh, there's artifacts there. I've been reading up on Niffelheim ever since Tan-tan told us about it. Let's just hope the goblins there haven't already turned them into game pieces," said Serana, giving Maja a condescending smile.

"Don't be such a bitch," said Lin offhandedly, staring out the window with her arm on the sill.

"So what happens when we get there?" said Asuna, cuddling naked with her girlfriend on the floor of the carriage.

"Well, they're building a house on the outside of the city for me which I'm going to be forced to share with my dad and sisters. But after he decides everything is going smoothly, he's going to head back to Trinity with my sisters and leave me completely in charge."

"I still don't understand how you got your father to broker this deal with Trinity. What does he have to gain from helping the goblins? You said he doesn't care about goblins which after all this time doesn't baffle me anymore."

"I basically blackmailed him into doing it. You remember I told you what my mother said said when she died?"

"Of course."

"Well, we were being rushed to our summer house on Lake Elyria that first night when they were forcing goblins from their homes. We swapped carriages outside the city because he wasn't even with us when it happened. He acted like he was so happy to see us, but those last words my mother said to him, those fucking haunt me, babe. I knew we were still disappointments to him.

"Anyway, my sisters were asleep, and I fucking told him. I told him I would never forgive him for holding that over my mother. And he practically begged me, asked if there was anything he could do to earn my forgiveness. And I thought about Maja. Me and my sisters slip out of Trinity with ease, but what was she going through? Was she even alive? And I told him, if he could protect the goblins, then I would forgive him. And he's been negotiating with Trinity non-stop since that night. Left my sisters at the lake house and me and him rode right back into Trinity and we made a deal."

"Why are you still bitter towards him then?"

"His fucking nature, babe. He's looking at this like some money making enterprise. I just want them to have homes and protection. He wants to make a stack of gold off each one. He can fuck off and die for all I care," said Tan-tan as she stared at the upholstered ceiling of the carriage.

"You need to forgive him. You're only hurting yourself with this grudge."

"Even on his deathbed, I'm going to tell him he's not forgiven. He's going to die the way my mother died, begging forgiveness. And the goblins will finally be free."

"That's so cruel."

"Nothing is as cruel as what happened to my mother. I'm going to keep dangling my forgiveness in front of him until the goblins are free."

"You have to forgive him. This hatred, it's a burning ember in your hand, and you're just waiting to throw it at him, but the entire time it's damaging you. Don't do this."

"No, this is for the goblins. This is the only way that they'll be able to live in peace. Their own city, their own laws, their own Guards."

"I still think Niffelheim is dangerous, what did the Scouts come back with?"

"Lords fucking demons, would you please support me! Please! You are the only person I genuinely trust in the entire world. Please support me in this. Please stop fucking battling me! I need you at my side. I cannot do this alone. You are my sword, you are my shield, and you are my Pyre that keeps the darkness away. Please tell me you support me in this." Tan-tan turned and held her girlfriend's cheek, kissing her and staring into her eyes.

"I support you."

EPILOGUE

The Scouts moved quickly and quietly between the stone houses of Niffelheim, leapfrogging past each other like playful spirits in the night as they made their way through the vacant city. The center of the city was a massive well the size of The Square in Trinity's Administrative District. Wrought iron bars covered the well with enough space in between to lower buckets into the gargantuan pool several feet below. The water was perfectly still in the moonlight.

"Hard to tell if the water is drinkable," said the Scout leader as he leaned over the retaining wall that came up to his thighs.

"They're going to want to know in the report," said one of the Scouts, "what should we do?"

The Scout leader kicked a discarded bucket resting next to the well.

"Put a brick in it so it sinks." The leader nudged a brick on the ground from a small portion of the retaining wall which was damaged. The Scout rolled her eyes and set up the bucket before she carefully lowered it into the well. She watched as the bucket broke the surface of the pool and sent ripples out across the surface. It was like watching a mirror ripple. The bucket sank and filled with water. Hand over hand, the female Scout pulled the bucket back up and over the low wall.

"You have antidotes on you, right?" said the Scout before she drank from the water, "I know it's a dumb thing to ask."

"I do have antidotes, and it's never a dumb thing to ask. Scouts never assume, that's how we survive. Go ahead," said her leader. She dipped her hands in the bucket and sipped the water. Her squad watched silently for a reaction. She looked at each of them then back at the bucket.

"Drink a little more. We need to know," said her leader. She dipped her hands in two more times and drank deep. It was refreshing and tasty, the pleasant nothingness of fresh clean water.

"It's actually really good." She took a third drink then passed the bucket to her comrades.

"No one else drink it. We'll see what happens after a day passes. If you're still healthy after a day, then we'll allow the goblins to take from the well." The Scout leader looked up the western stairway of Niffelheim to see several green figures watching them from the top.

"Can't blame them for wanting water, sir," said the female Scout, watching them too.

"We're getting paid a lot of money to not

half-ass this. Otherwise, they could swim in the well for all I care."

The leader's comment elicited quiet laughter from the squad before he was launched into the air by an unseen force and brought down on the iron grating covering the well. He made to get up but was snapped in two with a sickening crunch and pulled down into the water.

"What the fuck was that?" screamed one of the Scouts who sprinted for the stairs. A long fleshy tendril shot out of the well, snatched his leg, and whipped him back onto the iron grating with a clang. He screamed in agony as his body was forced between the rows of iron bars and into the well. As their comrade was pulled into the water, the remaining two Scouts ducked silently into empty homes across the circuitous roadway of Niffelheim.

The female Scout sat near the doorway, listening for any cues from their assailant. There was a wet flopping sound outside the home, like wet clothes repeatedly tossed on the floor which inched closer and closer to her. She watched in silent horror as a tendril of glistening flesh entered the home, feeling around on the floor.

"It's fucking looking for me!" she thought to herself as it prodded around.

"Get the fuck away from me!" her comrade screamed from nearby. His shriek was followed by a metal clang, a wet crunching sound, and finally a large splash. Then there was only silence. The female Scout watched as the glistening tendril inspected the home. She moved away from the door as quietly as she could. Her eyes never left the thing as she moved through the barren home. It kept growing longer as it reached deeper inside.

She calmly and carefully stepped around the tendril and moved towards the door. Before she could clear the home, the tendril bumped against her ankle and she dove for the street. She somersaulted into a sprint and made for the stairs. The wet packing sound of the thing moving behind her made her reflexively dive off to her right where she watched the tendril miss her by inches. In an instant, she had her shortsword out and slashed the tendril in two. Dark inky blood sprayed from the stump. She vaulted over the wall of the lowest circle of Niffelheim and sprinted up the stairs faster than she had ever ran in her life. At the top, the goblins shouted and waved their arms. Adrenaline flooded her veins. Every sense was heightened.

She heard that familiar wet packing sound of raw meat being thrown on a counter over and over. She turned and slashed the air behind her. Black blood sprayed into her face as another hunk of tendril flopped harmlessly on the ground. She continued her run up the stairs, the goblins jumping up and down now. She was as fast and as athletic as any Scout her age, but

Niffelheim had a nine story staircase leading from its center to outer rim.

After clearing the fifth story of stairs, she ventured a look over her shoulder and saw absolutely nothing behind her. Not only were there no more tendrils lunging for her, but the ones she had severed were gone as well, leaving behind only stains on the stone stairs. She continued her mad sprint up the stairs, waving for the goblins to get away from the city.

"It's never over," she remembered her trainer saying once, explaining the philosophy of Scout combat. The simple Scout mantra meant that a crisis/battle/conflict was never officially over. This quiet wisdom was the backbone of Scout training.

Two more stories were left in front of her. She slipped and smacked her chin hard on the stairs, feeling her teeth break in her mouth. She hadn't just slipped; something had made her slip. She was being dragged. A tendril, hundreds of feet long and emanating from the well, was dragging her. With her free hand, she gripped the wall which separated the seventh and eighth levels of Niffelheim. She swung her sword at the monstrosity, but it was too short. If she leaned in closer, she would lose her grip on the wall. With primal survival instinct, she hacked at her knee with her shortsword, screaming in rage as the tendril ripping it from her body. Her blood spray coated the steps. She watched as the tendril dragged her bleeding limb down the stairs and into the well.

A small group of brave goblins descended the stairs and dragged her out of Niffelheim into the camp that the earliest settlers had setup to the west. Her last memory that night was of a small chubby hand cupping her face.

SPECIAL SNEAK PEEK

The City of Evil:
Book Two of the Goblin Girl Series.
Read the full book on
https://www.patreon.com/illyhymen
for as little as $1.

Promo Code: JBQED8RM
Message me on Patreon with your unique code for a chance at a $100 gift. Winners will be messaged on May 28th

Preliminary Report of Niffelheim

Attn: Lord Tychus

Scouts have confirmed the migration of X,XXX goblin migrants from Trinity to Niffelheim. Census officials estimate we may see upwards of 1,500 more goblin migrants leave Trinity by year's end, fulfilling the first provision of the Trinity-Bloodwater Pact.

The majority of the goblin migrants have made temporary settlement in the western fields of Niffelheim, with numbers slowly pouring into the western and central sections of the city proper. The Bloodwater family will have arrived in Niffelheim by the time of this missive.

The Bloodwater family departed Trinity, along with a convoy of X,XXX goblin migrants, four mornings before this missive. Fero Bloodwater has established a base of operations directly outside the city limits of Niffelheim. His daughter, Tan-tan Bloodwater (alias: Tantra Charbelcher), is helming the resettlement of Niffelheim. By all accounts she is beholden to her father for all aspects of the operation. Fero Bloodwater's other two daughters, Makilja Bloodwater and Alo Bloodwater, have also arrived in Niffelheim, but there is no evidence of their participation in the cartel operations. Per Lord Tychus's request, the agreed upon materials for the Bloodwater family have not yet been delivered. Trade agreements are in place, and the Artificer's Guild has been given proper notice of new opportunities in Niffelheim.

It is with great suspicion I report that the Scouts dispatched to Niffelheim have not filed a report or returned from their quest. Without any persons of their guild to question, we do not know the circumstances under which they have failed to perform their duties. We request two more Scouts be dispatched to Niffelheim. A report has been sent to Fero Bloodwater with the assurance of Niffelheim's safety.

By corroborated reports, we have confirmed that The Banshee (alias: Asuna) is working with the Bloodwater family, and any move against the cartel operation would be met with significant casualties. Reports also confirm that the exiles Lindlithsong and Alexander Song are working with the Bloodwater family.

Preliminary reports suggest that the Bloodwater family is investing a significant portion of its financial resources into structural engineering and weapons technology. The structural engineering endeavors have been attributed to the clandestine workings of sugar processing. The purpose of weapon engineering is still unknown.

Our scholary reports on the history of Niffelheim have led us to believe almost a century ago the city was a pinnacle of civilization to match Trinity, and the cities shared a wealth of trade and commerce. In an unrecorded year, all trade and communications ceased with Niffelheim. After a scouting mission, no origin for the disappearance could be ascertained. Other documents claim a terrible drought had seized Niffelheim and forced residents to migrate to Trinity and to other locations.

Further updates on the Bloodwater operations and the fracture of the Greenlan Sugar Cartel are pending.

CHAPTER 1

The Bloodwater knarr boat deftly skipped over the choppy waves in pursuit of the Greenlan Cartel cog ship. Maja and Alexander stood on the bow deck and watched as the distance between them and the cog ship shrank. The morning sun caught the water like glowing gems as it sprayed over the sides of their knarr. Maja held onto Alexander's pant leg for balance atop the rocking boat.

"I can't believe we're really doing this." Alexander scooped up Maja and kissed the side of her face.

"Tan-tan said we need that sugar to feed the goblins." Maja nuzzled her face into his.

"She's not telling us something. I know her father is in the sugar cartel. Why doesn't he have his own sugar?"

"Tan-tan said they cut off Trinity after The Night of Screams. She said they wouldn't sell sugar ore to a city that mistreated goblins like that. She said we're just getting the sugar that already belongs to her."

Alexander kissed Maja's forehead making

her smile. "You're so sweet and trusting, little girl. I just can't shake the feeling Tan is manipulating us for her father."

"Tan-tan wouldn't do that."

"She wants me to test this thing in the battle to take the ship." Alexander held his tiny lover in one arm as he pulled a malformed club of twisted metal and wood off his belt and held it up for her.

"A mace?" Maja reached out to hold it.

"She calls it a gonne. She said point this hollowed end at an enemy and insert a flame in this little notch. It's like she has no respect for the danger we're facing out here. I can't be testing her toys in battle. She's been off since we arrived in Niffelheim. I think her father is getting to her."

Maja turned the gonne over and looked inside the hollowed out section. She saw only darkness and handed it back to Alexander who secured it to his belt.

"You remember what we have to do?" he said, moving strands of hair out of Maja's face.

"Uhh..."

"We have to secure the ship. We can't sink it, and we'll probably have to kill some people. That's part of being in a guild. I know you think it's awful, but it's what we signed up for."

"I can feel the life in the boat and under it. I think I can use it," said Maja as she looked into Alexander's eyes. Alexander kissed her as Maja's tiny hands held his face.

"Get ready to board!" Alexander shouted to his crew. The cartel cog ship was close now. In moments they would be on top of it. Alexander set Maja on the deck and moved to the mechanism controlling the talon: a portable bridge that was stored upright at the bow of the boat. A large iron spike at the top could pierce the deck of an opposing ship when it fell. The knarr boat approached the cartel cog ship at a shallow angle to allow the use of the talon. Alexander watched as the two vessels closed their distance. The talon swayed upright in the air, ready to puncture the cog ship. Alexander's hand moved to the release mechanism. The timing had to be perfect to snag the cartel cog or the fight would be much more difficult given the high gunwales of their target. The entire crew continued to row as they watched Alexander time the drop of the talon.

He took a deep breath, pulled the locking pin from the pulley, and pressed down on the handle of the talon mechanism. The handle furiously spun around the mounted pulley that released a length of chain. The talon crashed into the stern of the cog and shattered a portion of the cog's gunwale, impaling the quarterdeck. The knarr lurched as it matched the speed of the cartel cog. Alexander led the crew as they charged across the talon bridge.

A squad of Archers assembled along the starboard gunwale of the cartel cog and released a volley of arrows at the invading Privateers. Each arrow found its mark, sending four Privateers into the water off of the talon bridge. Maja raised her palm and thought of Alexander tying her up and penetrating her. Long, green tendrils of kelp shot out of the water and seized the bows from the Archers, pulling one into the ocean with his weapon.

As Alexander led the charge, orange fireballs materialized in his hands. With a quick gesture he released each projectile that collided with the chests of three sailors before he allowed his Privateers to engage in melee combat, as was planned. The Privateers overwhelmed the enemy crew, not in numbers, but in tenacity. Swords clashed, and the main deck of the cartel cog was in all out melee. Both crews were a mash up of goblin and hume deckhands. The cartel cog seemed prepared for an invading force, each sailor armed with a sword and skilled enough to wield it. Alexander's crew had two female goblins, Samwa and Bol, who dashed across the maindeck of the cartel cog. They ignored fair fights with enemy goblins and slashed the ankles of hume sailors in their blind charge.

The fighting only lasted minutes as Alexander's and Tan-tan's strategy was executed to perfection. Six crewmen of the cartel cog surrendered to Alexander and his rag tag group of Privateers. After the cartel crewmen were safely bound in rope, Alexander gave the signal to Maja who scampered across the talon bridge, down the stairs to the maindeck, and leapt into his arms.

"We did it!" said Maja, kissing Alexander then turning to the crew, "You all did it! Tan-tan is going to be so happy."

Their crew, many covered in blood and shining with sweat, smiled at the tiny goblin girl they had grown to love on their mindnumbing voyage across the Green Strait. Maja leapt out of Alexander's arms and took the time to hug and congratulate each member individually.

"Do you have any idea whose ship this is?" said one of the humes bound to the base of the mast.

"Yeah, it's the Greenlan Sugar Cartel's. Why do you think we're here?" Alexander stepped over to the man and squatted down to face him.

"Then you know what kind of hells you just brought down upon yourself." The man stared with fury at the knarr crew but specifically Alexander.

"Why do you even care? How much do they pay you? Are you the captain?" Alexander's mouth opened for further inquiry, but his voice stopped. His heart sped up as he moved across the deck. His movements were frantic, as if looking for something he had lost.

"Where's the captain? Did any of you battle the captain?"

The crew exchanged looks, but all of them shook their heads. The door to the captain's quarters exploded into shrapnel, and the most massive hume Alexander had ever seen squeezed himself through the opening. He was a bulbous heap of greasy muscles and carried a warhammer the size of a lamp post. The ever vigilant goblins fled immediately, but the rest of Alexander's crew were caught off guard as the massive warhammer swung into them, toppling them in a spray of blood.

Maja cast her palm up to summon a half dozen tendrils of kelp that seized the captain's arm. The captain brought his rippling arm forward and tore away from the vegetation. Alexander fumbled with the gonne as he stumbled to get between the captain and Maja, taking his demon form without thought. The captain raised his warhammer above his head to crush Maja who was stunned by how easily he had broken through her bindings. Alex was at least two strides away from the captain and Maja. Her heart tried to rip itself free from her body in fear she was too late to save Maja. Time seemed to slow down as the captain's hammer began its descent.

A white blur collided with the captain that knocked him over the gunwale of the cartel cog and into the water. Serana guided her archon along the length of the cog ship, finishing a full sweep of both sides before she guided her summon back to the sky. High above the ships, she appeared as little more than a seagull drafting on the sea breeze.

"Oh, thank the Lords." Alex stumbled to her knees and pulled Maja into an embrace. "I thought I was going to lose you."

Alex tried to compose herself as she hugged the most important person in her life, not wanting to seem weak or frivolous in front of the enemy crew, let alone her own crew. The knarr crew was aware of her transformative abilities. They respected and feared the rumor Alex was actually a demon conjured by the Summoner, Serana.

"Rogues, please investigate the captain's quarters for any more holdouts. I'll give you cover." Alex wiped away her tears and kissed Maja deeply before she stood up and moved to the captain's quarters. Samwa and Bol returned from the far end of the deck and carefully entered the room. Alex gave her remaining crew a contrite look as they laid out the two men killed by the captain and his warhammer. The goblin Rogues crisscrossed through the darkness of the cabin like two dancers.

"No one in here, captain," said Samwa, the taller, more lithe one.

"Look at this!" said Bol who stood in a chair over a table as Alex entered the room. On the table near the door was a considerable stack of coins, some discolored sugar crystals, and a smoking alembic.

"Stupid! That could have been ours." Samwa smacked her smaller comrade over the back of the head, "that should be ours, right? I didn't see any hume risking his perfect pale skin to come in here."

"You're all being compensated very well for this quest. We will find a way to distribute this fairly among the crew, and I'll make sure Madam Bloodwater knows of your contributions."

"Well at least let us have the sugar," Bol took a crystal off the table, tossed it in her mouth and, chomped down on it.

"Don't eat it all, you greedy little goblet." Samwa grabbed a handful and stuffed it in her mouth. Alexander gave them a sympathetic look, unsure if they had just stuffed unrefined sugar ore in their mouth which she had been told was very bitter and caused horrible stomach problems.

"This is the best fucking sugar I've ever had!" said Samwa as she reached for more. Bol seized her wrist and dragged her to the floor.

"don't eat it all, it's mine!" screamed Bol before she bit her arm to get to the sugar in her hand. The two goblin Rogues tumbled across the cabin floor, biting and punching each other for the crystals.

"Little help in here!" said Alex to her crew. The two humes and two goblins who remained of the boarding party entered the cabin and managed to separate the two women.

"Are you two really fighting over candy?" said Rafranco, an old but experienced goblin deckhand Tan-tan had poached from the Greenlan Cartel. He wrestled the crystals from Samwa's hand, gave them a sniff, and flinched away.

"Fucking, rock candy." Rafranco snarled and handed the crystals up to Alex. Alex took the crystals and stepped out onto the main deck to examine them in the morning light. They looked exactly like raw sugar ore, but the reaction in the captain's quarters suggested something else. Maja approached her.

"Is that sugar? Can I have it?"

"No, sweet thing. It's something else, and I don't know if I should bring this to Tan-tan or not. I have a feeling whatever this is, it's too dangerous for Niffelheim. Have you ever heard of candy that makes goblins lose their minds?"

Maja shook her head. Alex looked up into the sky to see Serana circling overhead on her archon.

"Okay, everyone, we need to man this cog and set the knarr up to be towed. Let's get everything we don't need back on the boat, then set sail for Port of Niff. And would someone please help with the bodies."

The two goblin women darted out of the cabin like trained hounds. They managed to lift the body of one of their hume comrades and drag him up the stairs with incredible speed. In just seconds, they had the body across the talon bridge and were already moving their other loss onto the knarr. Alex gave the crystals another look before she watched Samwa and Bol start prepping the Cog to return home.

"What the fuck is this stuff?" she whispered to herself before pocketing it. Alex moved back to the cabin to collect the miniature alembic and found it, as well as the gold coins, missing. Alex took a deep breath.

"I don't care who took the gold as long as everyone got some, but I need that alembic," said Alex, pressing her palm to her face. Her crew exchanged looks but remained silent.

"Now, lordsdamit!" Alex conjured a dark fireball in her hand but no one responded. The crew poured out of the cabin to start preparations, as well as to avoid her wrath, only to find the goblin women had already cleared the main deck and quarter deck of bodies, carrying the final one across the talon bridge. Once all preparations had been made, the remaining crew of the Knarr stood on the deck at attention.

"What's next, captain?" Samwa saluted Alex and hopped in place, unable to stand still. Bol chewed the back of her wrist and looked around nervously.

"I think you two have done more than your fair share of the work. Why don't you relax while we make preparations?"

Samwa gave an awkward shudder and pulled Bol into the captain's quarters, dragging her on loping steps. The sound of riotous love-making issued forth from the cabin. The crew broke ranks and gathered around the doorway to watch. Alex tapped her foot and crossed her arms as everyone neglected their duties.

"Okay, I get it. Why don't we give them some privacy?" said Alex as she approached her crew.

"Let them watch," Samwa cried out. Maja pushed through the crowded doorway to see. On the floor, in the cabin, the two goblin Rogues laid completely naked, cuddling and kissing each other. Samwa's butt hung in the air to reveal her chubby cheeks and furry pussy. She had Bol pinned down and was kissing her. Maja held her face and let out a quiet squeal upon seeing the two women making love.

Bol, who was smaller and chubbier, pushed herself up and latched onto Samwa's hanging breast to suckle. Approving murmurs came from the men in attendance. Samwa reached between her friend's thighs and vigorously masturbated her as she bit down on her pointed ear. She pumped Bol with chubby fingers and sent errant juice drops onto the wooden floor. Bol gasped and thrusted her hips in the air. A long drawn out whine escaped her lips until she sprawled out on the floor.

Samwa mounted Bol's face and ground her furry pussy against her head. Bol's head lolled side to side as Samwa humped her face. A whine built up as Samwa grabbed her hair and slowly dragged her sopping pussy up and down it. Her protruding clit slid across Bol's lips, sending shivers through her body as it pressed against each angle and contour.

"What's going on in there?" said one of the crewmen of the cartel cog.

"Alex, you gotta' watch this. This is hot," said Maja from the front of the audience. Alex squeezed the crystal in her pocket.

CHAPTER 2

"Give me your report," said Tan-tan's father.

"I'd rather not..."

"I don't expect the world of you, especially so early in the operation, but I need your updates if we are going to design a business strategy moving forward."

Tan-tan shuffled some papers on the desk she shared with her father for business, pretending to search for a report.

"Tan-tan..."

She sighed and held her face in her palm. "The scrap metal never arrived from Trinity even though your--OUR Agents have assured me we have met our quota. I have already sent three missives to Trinity demanding the scrap metal."

"I assumed the metal was to be a point of contention. It is not your fault, daughter of mine, please continue."

"Sugar stores are running dangerously low. In the next three days our reserves will be empty." She gave another weighty sigh and stared at the door in front of her, wondering if her father would send Agents after her if she fled the city with Asuna.

"I see. So then the privateering quest was a failure?"

"I have no idea at this point. They're two days behind schedule. It's possible your information was wrong."

"Tan-tan..."

"Where is our sugar ore? You said when you left the cartel you would be able to retain control of your mines. Why aren't we getting shipments? For fuck's sake, people are getting desperate out there. They're fighting and robbing each other for pieces of candy."

"Calm down. This is a business meeting. Please carry yourself like an Agent. You must remain objective."

"Fuck that! I started training as an Agent to help the goblins. I didn't do it for money, and I sure as shit didn't do it for you." Tan-tan thrusted an accusatory finger at her father. The two Agents on the wall shifted their weight. Tan-tan knew they were preparing to intervene if the circumstance arose. Her father's body language betrayed no anxiety, and his face was nothing but calm. He was a rocky promontory, and she was the churning sea.

"I cannot disclose to you the status of my sugar ore mines."

"Why the fuck not?"

"How does our domestic security progress?"

"Fuck!" Tan-tan took a deep breath as she crumpled the mess of papers on their desk, speaking through clenched teeth. "Surprisingly well, considering that no goblins want to be Guards. The goblins love and respect Asuna and are well behaved in her presence, but she can't be everywhere at once. Lin is doing her best to keep order, but the goblins resent her, and again, she's only one person. I don't know how to get these goblins to take care of themselves."

"You didn't give away our sugar reserves, did you?"

"What was I supposed to do, sell them?"

Her father looked at her to answer her own question by tilting his head slightly forward.

"That's all the food we have left. I'm not going to charge them for it."

"This is why you have unrest. The moment you start providing for them, they start to rely on you to solve all their problems. Now they've come to expect you to be a nursemaid."

"I'm not going to charge them survive!"

"I want as many of them as alive as possible, but the path to the hells is fraught with heroic deeds. Now tell me, are refinery operations ready?"

"Supposedly, but we have no ore to refine, so we don't actually know if it's ready. We uh, we connected several of the homes and basements in the northwest districts and have a functioning refinery, in theory."

"Splendid. Are there any developments in your technology program?"

Tan-tan remained silent.

"Daughter of mine, please move the meeting along. You cannot stall every time there is unfortunate news."

"We've developed a weapon. It's compact, easily and affordably manufactured, lethal in theory, and takes minimal training to use. We call it a gonne, after the dev of death."

"I like everything you have said so far. How progresses your preliminary testing?" Her father leaned forward in his special chair which allowed him to be close to eye level with his daughter.

"Well, it's really hard to test the lethality of a weapon without, ya' know, killing someone. In all our early tests, the gonne operated dependably, above eighty-five percent reliability."

"Tan-tan, is it, or is it not, an effective weapon?"

"I don't know. I gave it to Alex to test on the privateering quest...which hasn't resolved."

"Very well. And finally, what information have you ascertained from our guest?"

"Guest?" Tan-tan's eyes bounced between the two Agents at the door then back to her father.

"Yes, the Scout you've been keeping in

our home, have you spoken to her?"

"I...don't know what you're referring to. I never contacted you about any Scouts."

Her father held his hand up. His palm faced Tan-tan as if ready to produce a spell.

"Do not play games with me. There is nothing in this city you can hide from me, let alone in this house where my daughters sleep. My Agents work for me first and foremost. Now tell me of this Scout."

"Some goblins found her in Niffelheim proper the night before we arrived. They kept her in the settlements for several days and tried to nurse her there. By our Agents' accounts, she's been unconscious since then, fighting an infection. Her leg was ripped off, and she suffered serious blood loss. I've sent for a proper Healer to tend to her. She's been put up in my bedroom, the Healer tending to her around the clock. I promise you, the Scout has not said anything. The Healer has strict orders to tell me anything she says."

"Very good. My Agents have discovered she was part of the scouting party Trinity sent to ascertain the livability and safety of Niffelheim."

A cold chill slid down Tan-tan's body. She scanned her desk as if looking for a clue as to what to say next. Asuna's trembling words at the palace echoed in the back of her mind.

"I...what does that mean? Where's the rest

of her party? Where did she get that injury, and why wasn't it in our report?"

"We do not know the answers, yet. Scouts are a peculiar bunch. They may have left her behind for their own self preservation. It is equally likely that Trinity altered or even completely falsified the report they sent us."

"Asuna said people were going to disappear. If her party disappeared--"

"Now don't start with that. The answers await us when she recovers. I'll have my Agents dig more thoroughly into this report though. You seem to have everything in hand. You're doing a good job, Tan-tan. I know it seems like everything is tearing at the seams, but you're making progress."

"Is that supposed to be some kind of cruel joke?" Tan-tan's heart pounded with agitation at the perceived slight.

"Of course not. You must understand that every budding enterprise has a tumultuous start. It is only by persevering through these setbacks that we become successful. Now, I'll be back in a week, and I expect operations to be fully underway. I trust you."

Tan-tan's father climbed out of his chair and walked to her. Tan-tan stood up from her chair then squatted down to give her father a polite hug as she turned her face away. He led her by the hand out of their office and down the stairs to the front door.

To the east of their small mansion was the city of Niffelheim: a sprawling, crater-shaped city with eight concentric levels of stonecut homes that descended to a massive well the size of a small lake. Over the well was a rusted metal grating to keep people and animals out. Lin was very strict about repelling goblins who were tempted to throw their garbage over the knee-wall into their only reliable source of drinking water.

The only homes occupied by goblins spilled into the city from the western stairway, spreading out north and south closest to the exit and hugging the stairway more closely as the levels approached the well. To the west of the Bloodwater mansion was a vast tent city containing the thousands of goblins who had migrated from Trinity after the Night of Screams. A little over one hundred goblins had settled into Niffelheim proper which left the rest to spread out on the barren plains that surrounded Niffelheim. The goblins lived in tents and poorly built lean-to's made from the scrap metal sheets they had transported with them. The tent city was restless as goblins lazed outside their homes with little work to be done. The surrounding area was flat barren land which had once been rich farmlands. The plains were totally devoid of life, including flora, and gave the anxiety inducing impression they lived in a barren wasteland.

"I don't understand why the goblins would rather live in tents then perfectly good homes already built in the city," said Tan-tan to her father as he led the way to his waiting carriage.

"Perhaps you should ask your adviser. Use all the information you can to make intelligent decisions. You grew up among humes, do not assume any of their traits transfer to the goblin population. They are truly a different animal."

Tan-tan stared at her father as if mentally willing him to realize he was in fact a goblin and no amount of cutting his ears or damaging his skin would change the fact.

"Tan-tan!" screamed Makilja as she leapt from the carriage and sprinted to her. Tan-tan released her father's hand and squatted down to brace for the impact of her little sister. Makilja launched herself into Tan-tan's open arms and knocked her into the dust. Makilja squeezed Tan-tan and gently bit her ear before kissing her cheek.

"I thought we weren't going to get to see you before we left." Makilja held Tan-tan's face and kissed her on the mouth.

"I wouldn't let you girls leave before saying goodbye. Where's Alo?"

Tan-tan sat up and saw one of the Agents help her tiny baby sister out of the carriage. She was still barely bigger than a hume doll and looked more like a toy than a person in her elegant princess dress. Tan-tan grunted as she pushed herself to her feet with Makilja in one arm. She walked to baby Alo who had her hands up to reach Tan-tan. She scooped up Alo and planted kisses on her face and neck which made her baby sister squirm and giggle. Alo's petite laughter removed the iron pins that had been in Tan-tan's heart since her father arrived the evening before last. Tan-tan blew raspberries on Alo's chest, making her squeal with delight.

"Okay you two, behave while you're gone, and come back to me really soon." Tan-tan placed her sisters one at a time in the carriage doorway then helped her father in before closing the door. She could not convey to her sisters how much she needed them to come back.

"Maybe someday you can leave them here with me, just for a week?" said Tan-tan to her father who sat in the window of the carriage.

"When things are safe and have settled down, I will consider it. The faster you accomplish these tasks, the more you'll be able to see your sisters," said her father. Tan-tan hid her clenched fist behind her back as it trembled with anger.

"Bye, Tan-tan, we love you." Makilja waved from the window as the carriage departed in a cloud of dust. Makilja held Alo up to the window so she could wave goodbye too. Tan-tan waved to them then held her face in her hand as she cried. She hurried back to the mansion before anyone in the tent city could see her being weak.

"You okay, babe?" said Asuna who approached from behind and placed her hands on Tan-tan's shoulders, staying out of sight until Tan-tan's father left. "I saw them leave. You already miss your sisters, don't you?"

"Every time I watch Alo leave...it fucks me up inside. I can't watch her leave another time. I feel like I'm abandoning her all over again." Tan-tan was barely able to compose herself as she relayed her words.

"Okay, okay, let's go inside so you can let it all out." Asuna guided her inside but was approached by a small group of goblins along the way.

"Mistress Asuna, there's a fight in the settlement. We need you to help stop it," said a goblin man at the front of the group. Asuna looked at the hopeful group of goblins, then back at Tan-tan hunched over in pain.

"Go help them. You're the only thing in this shithole that's actually functioning," said Tan-tan as she moved into the foyer.

"I will be there in a minute. There is urgent business I must attend to inside," said Asuna. The goblins exchanged confused looks and made for the outskirts of the settlement. Asuna led Tan-tan down the hall and to the northeast corner of the house where a comfortably appointed parlor sat away from prying eyes in the settlement. She guided Tan-tan to a luxurious sofa where Tan-tan threw her arms around her and sobbed.

"I'm not strong enough for this, babe! Every fucking thing is fucking up. The sugar's gone. Alexander and Maja are gone. The goblins are out of control. And to top it all off, I have to explain every fucking failure to my father in minute detail. All the goblins fucking resent me, and I just had to watch my baby sister leave again. I've fucking had it. Next fucking briefing, I'm telling him he's in charge. I'm fucking useless."

Asuna held Tan-tan close and kissed the top of her head. Her hands ran through the fuzz of Tan-tan's cropped purple hair. Tan-tan trembled between gasping and sobbing.

"There there, babe, you're trying your best. I promise you, there are plenty of goblins who have said good things about you. I know how much this means for you to save them. People don't always love the only person who is actually fighting for them. Trust me, I know."

"What? The goblins love you, babe. You're a goblin folk hero and you're not even a goblin. They literally light braziers at night in your honor."

"Yeah, but I had to do cruel things to attain that status. They like me for all the wrong reasons. They resent you, some of them do, for all the wrong reasons. People will resent whoever is in charge no matter how much they do for them. Trust me, babe. I've seen it hundreds of times over my life. You do it because it's the right thing to do, not because it's easy or makes you revered. After the Night of Screams, I have no real responsibilities to them. You have all the responsibility and I know you can do this."

"If Alo and Makilja were here, I know I could handle this. I'm just so fucking glad you're here, babe. You don't even know. I would be fucking lost without you. You're the only thing keeping me going."

Tan-tan looked up and held Asuna's face before she placed a kiss on her cold, charcoal colored lips. She slid down Asuna's crimson singlet to reveal two grey breasts with nipples that matched the color of her lips. Tan-tan leaned down and sucked her girlfriend's nipple. An occasional tear slid down her cheek. Asuna ran her hand over Tan-tan's short hair as she nursed at her cold breast.

"You're my hero, Tantra Charbelcher. You can do anything you put your mind to," said Asuna in a comforting tone as she stroked Tan-tan's head. Tan-tan pulled Asuna's nipple with her teeth to suck more of it and fondled Asuna's open breast. Asuna placed her arms around Tan-tan and rested her face on top of Tan-tan's head.

Tan-tan moved her hand to Asuna's pussy and felt warmth radiating from it. She pressed her long fingers against the material of Asuna's singlet until she found the nub of her clit and began masturbating her. Tan-tan moved her fingers in circles, making Asuna moan. She raised her head to kiss Asuna's neck and exhaled on it.

"I love you. I love you so much it hurts. Please don't ever leave me. I need you."

Asuna lay back on the sofa with Tan-tan on top of her as she opened up her body to her girlfriend.

"Madam Bloodwater!" Agent Marco stood at attention in the parlor doorway staring straight ahead. His eyes avoided the scene on the sofa. He was a pale hume with short dark hair who wore the dark jacket which indicated he worked for the Bloodwater family.

"What the lordsfuck do you want!" screamed Tan-tan, sitting up to face him. Her tear strewn stare seethed with hatred.

"Ma'am, the Privateers have returned from Port of Niff. You asked me to report to you the moment they were spotted."

Printed in Great Britain
by Amazon

62064567R00241